A
WHITEWASHED
TOMB

Cover art and book design by Rebecca Loomis Media

ISBN-13: 978-1978084926
ISBN-10: 1978084927

To the literary line of Loomi preceding me.

CONTENTS

A
WHITEWASHED
TOMB

BY REBECCA LOOMIS

CHAPTER ONE

ANNIVERSARY

THE AGE OF THE INTERNET HAD PASSED. Tabitha fidgeted with a hand-written letter, and for a moment wondered if the ancient concept of an email would be more efficient. As quickly as the thought came, however, she pushed it to the recesses of her mind. The Privileged were not permitted to wonder.

The automatic doors of the Axelle Provisionary parted and greeted Tabitha by name in a smooth, canned voice. The swarm of happy humans there to collect their rations engulfed her. Giant screens covered every wall up to the high ceiling, playing the usual feed of pointless, petty gossip, completely biased news highlights, a slew of new items their rations could buy, and an occasional message from the Provision elites.

Sometimes Lilith Damara herself would show her picture-perfect face to remind you how she'd brought about world peace.

Tabitha pushed through the crowd toward a less populated section of the room, where there stood a wall of small square postboxes. Above them was a sign that read *The New Order Delivery Service.* Approaching one labeled *Clay,* Tabitha hesitated.

A white finger scanner flickered at her in expectation.

She'd been here yesterday. And the day before. Today would be no different. He probably wouldn't even remember. To him, it was just another Thursday in October.

Tabitha tilted her chin up in defiant hope and moved her hand forward.

Deep breath. She slapped her thumb to the screen. The postbox opened.

Scooping out its contents, Tabitha flipped through each parcel like a machine, examining every envelope. Junk mail. Gossip. Propaganda. At the last piece, she lingered with an air of disappointment. Nothing. No sign of the man who'd left without a word.

Happy Anniversary. Tabitha tore her own letter in half and tossed it in a nearby trashcan.

Ignoring the stinging sensation that welled up behind her eyes, Tabitha strolled mechanically down a round-walled corridor that opened into an expansive store. The sound of commerce filled her ears, and she let it drown out her thoughts.

Tabitha glared up at the massive signs hanging from the Provisionary's high ceiling that marked each section of the store: *Electronic Entertainment, Home Goods, Clothing, Spirits,* and so on. Keeping her eyes on one labeled *Recreational & Pharmaceutical Drugs,* she followed it to a sterile, white counter.

"Clay, right?" the pharmacist's smooth yet innocent voice asked. He was young, handsome, and harmless—but he'd picked the wrong day.

"Correct," Tabitha replied curtly, avoiding eye contact. She pulled a small, crumpled piece of paper out of her dress pocket, on which was a short list.

"Thursdays, 9:00 a.m.," he declared.

Tabitha scowled, keeping her eyes on the list. "Also right."

"Couldn't help but notice. You're a regular!" A hesitant grin tickled the corners of his mouth.

Tabitha pasted a halfhearted smile on her mask, though she didn't find his joke at all funny. Of course she was a regular. Every Privileged Grexovian was a regular in the routine of being hand-fed by the Provision once a week.

"Do you have any of these?" Tabitha asked, handing him the paper. She wasn't about to attempt the pronunciation of *Rifampin, Isoniazid, Pyrazinamide* and *Ethambutol*.

The man pursed his lips. "Sorry, you're not going to find any of those in Axelle—or any Privileged sector for that matter. I'm pretty sure only the Provision have access to that sort of medication."

Figures.

"Maybe some Tylenol, for the pain?" the pharmacist suggested.

Tabitha gritted her teeth. She didn't want his pity, but she shrugged and replied, "Sure."

He turned the thumb scanner toward her and she placed her finger on it systematically. A moment later, the members of her household appeared on the screen: *Tabitha Clay, Mayra Mae Clay, Natalie Clay.*

The screen beeped and turned red.

"What's wrong?" Tabitha asked.

The pharmacist scrunched his brow. "Looks like you've used up your drugs ration for the month already. Got a sweet spot for the strong stuff, eh?"

Heat rose up in Tabitha's cheeks and an image of her slapping him across the face appeared in her mind. *He's not worth it*, a voice in her head whispered. It was right. He was just trying to be playful. He didn't know what the drugs were for.

"Thanks anyway," she said, and turned to walk away.

Then she spotted a man with a treacherously imbalanced armful of items, topped with Tylenol. An idea crept into her mind. Ideas were dangerous. That's what the Provision told them. They were probably right.

Tabitha moved past the man, then bumped suddenly into him, knocking the loot out of his hands.

"Oh, I am *so* sorry!" she cried, and bent down to help pick them up.

He was a heavier man, who seemed often deprived of sun, as well as exposure to the world of women. He watched her breathlessly as she picked up a box of frozen pizza. Her chin-length hair fell in rippling waves across her forehead, obscuring one eye. Her slender neck strained above chiseled collar bones as she turned her head and reached for a stray can. Her strong yet delicate hands moved with regal grace.

"It's okay," he replied, shyly, his eyes glued to her.

Tabitha looked up suddenly to meet his gaze, her pale green eyes glimmering under long, dark lashes. Her pastel lips parted ever so slightly as she inhaled, as if she had forgotten to breathe. Then they twitched into the tiniest of smiles.

He was mesmerized.

The Privileged makeup ban and standard-issue gray outfits were no hindrance to this temptress. Tucking her reddish-brown curls behind one ear, Tabitha looked bashfully away and continued to place his things back into his arms. Then, right under his nose and undetected by any bystanders, she slipped the Tylenol into her pocket. She stood as suddenly as she'd knocked into him, and left him gaping after her.

As she rounded the corner, Tabitha glanced back at the jealous pharmacist with a Cheshire grin and waved.

Her mission completed, Tabitha hurried through the compartmentalized sections assigned to the various necessities of Privileged everyday life. When she reached the checkout, she paused to scan the crowd.

Amid the mob, she spotted her spitting image: a tall, slender but shapely woman with a face full of freckles and almond-shaped eyes. The only ways Tabitha's twin differed from herself were that her wavy auburn hair rippled long past her shoulders, and in her eyes there was peace. She stood at the checkout with a large sleek trunk behind her and passed items to the cashier.

Mayra Mae smiled as Tabitha joined her and began to aid in transferring items from cart to weigh station.

"You're two pounds over," muttered the clerk, a bored-looking young woman with a massive wad of gum smacking between her teeth.

Tabitha huffed in exasperation. "Mae, what weighs about two pounds?" she demanded over her shoulder.

"The pineapple, I'd guess," her clone responded.

Tabitha snatched a cardboard box off the pile of groceries that read *Make Your Own Pineapple—Just Add Water!* and tossed it blindly behind her. Mayra Mae instinctively caught it, fumbling only a little, and left to return it to its place.

The bright red number above the scale turned green. Tabitha slapped her thumb onto the finger scanner and the clerk let out a reluctant, "Have a nice day."

Tabitha beamed a phony smile in response, then began to collect their rations.

As she did so, a few cans fell from the counter and delightedly embraced their freedom, rolling away as fast as they could. This day was turning out to be fantastic. Tabitha bent over to pick up the cans.

"May I help you?" offered a deep, male voice.

Again? Seriously? Tabitha did not look up as he crouched beside her, his musky scent reaching her nostrils—too close for comfort.

"No thank you, I can manage it myself." She used everything she knew about body language to imply his invisibility.

"Are you sure?" His hand went to help her. "It's really no trouble!"

"No, but *you* are!" she snapped back, looking him in the eyes for the first time.

They were blue eyes, gentle and presently wounded. He stared at her for a moment, his dark brows slowly contracting, hand suspended above a can of cheddar broccoli soup.

Tabitha regretted the statement immediately. It wasn't his

fault. *He* wasn't her father. He couldn't possibly know what she was going through. That's what Mayra Mae would have said, anyway.

Digging her fingers into her temples, Tabitha began, "I'm sorry, that was—"

But the damage was done. Putting his hands up in surrender, the young man backed off, replying, "It's fine, I'll leave."

He turned and walked straight past Mayra Mae, bumping her with his broad shoulders. Tabitha's eyes lingered on him until they caught Mayra Mae's. She looked from the man to Tabitha, and shook her head.

"Another one?" she accused when he was out of ear shot.

"Shut up," Tabitha retorted.

Mayra Mae giggled. She leaned down to help pack the groceries into their trunk and said, "God definitely has sense of humor. What a cruel joke, to make me the twin of a woman who would scare off every suitable man in Axelle."

Tabitha's attempt at holding back a smile gave way, and the two laughed. A loud accusatory pop from the clerk's gum silenced them, and they hurried on their way.

Outside the Provisionary, they waited in a line of people alongside a silver light rail track. Tabitha pulled the Tylenol out of her pocket, tossed it in the air and caught it with a rattle. Mayra Mae eyed the bottle.

"What is that?" she asked evenly. Tabitha shoved her prize into a corner of the trunk.

"It's not much, but it'll help with the pain."

"You didn't answer my question," her twin replied firmly.

"It's Tylenol, can't you read?" Tabitha replied, avoiding eye contact.

"We didn't pay for that."

Tabitha snorted. "I know you're good with numbers and all, but wow—that's impressive! That thing weighs like—what—a milligram, and you could tell it wasn't on the scale?"

"You stole it," Mayra Mae declared, half question, half accusation.

Tabitha's lightheartedness faded. "It's for a good cause," she muttered.

Mayra Mae looked in disapproval at her sister, but chose not to pick a fight.

As light rail pods arrived one after another, everyone outside the Provisionary piled into their own, each with a heavy trunk behind them. Tabitha placed her thumb on a finger scanner, spoke the word, "Home," and the curved metal door sliced closed with a sharp, airy suction. Outside their window, the Provisionary courtyard blurred into motion as they sped away.

"Mute," Mayra Mae commanded to silence the babbling voice of a rounded TV screen along the pod's wall. Tabitha pressed her face against the window and watched the pavement zoom beneath their five-person pod, sleek and fast as a bullet. The ground below them was a road, once. Cars still drove on the shoulder, sometimes—or so Tabitha was told. Only by the Provision, though. Why was that?

Tabitha shook her head to stop the thought. Questions created disorder.

The large and glamorous courtyard of the Axelle Center Square whizzed by and grew smaller as the pod took Tabitha and Mayra Mae into the web of Privileged neighborhoods. Out among the rolling Northeast hills, all the houses were the same: a decent size, gray, and surrounded by a fenced-in yard. Each was marked with something unique to the owners—porch furniture, a dog—but nothing too extreme; and underneath it all it was the same canvas: standard issue.

When they arrived at their own, Tabitha pushed roughly through the front door. Like every other Privileged home, no family photographs—nor decorations of any kind—adorned their walls, except for a few hand-drawn sketches. As they passed through the hallway, Mayra Mae glanced at a framed drawing of the four members of their family.

Flinging open their case in the middle of the floor, Tabitha sifted through its many contents and pulled out an electric foot massager. She tucked the mail under her arm, ascended a flight of stairs, and entered a small, sunlit bedroom.

"Hello, Mom," Tabitha said to the woman on the bed. Natalie Clay was frail, with pale skin and sullen eyes, bones that looked as though they'd break under the pressure of a hug, and wrinkles that lied of years not lived; yet her smile bore the joy of a child on Christmas day.

"Tabitha!" she exclaimed with her arms outstretched, as though seeing her daughter for the first time in weeks. Rather than receive the offered embrace, Tabitha kissed her on the forehead and simultaneously filled her mother's hands with the stack of mail. Then she propped the foot massager at her mother's feet, gently guiding Natalie's paralyzed legs into the cushioned machine.

"What's that?" Natalie asked.

"A foot massager. Everything we could want, right?"

Tabitha's voice dripped with sarcasm, but Natalie nodded in gratitude. To herself Tabitha added, *And nothing that we need.*

She sat at the edge of the bed sadly as Natalie sifted through the mail. The foot massager filled the silence with a dull, melodious hum.

"Did you meet any nice young men today?" Natalie asked.

Tabitha rolled her eyes with a light smile. Natalie may as well have been psychic, but there was one thing she couldn't seem to pick up on.

"You know I'm never getting married."

"Why not?" her mother asked with a tone of false ignorance.

Tabitha's smile faded. "You know why."

Natalie raised her eyebrows in sassy disapproval, but didn't pick a fight. "Draw me something?" she requested, changing the subject.

Tabitha sighed. "It's been too long since I was at the Provisionary, the only thing I'd remember is the front door."

"Perfect."

Tabitha sat silently for a moment, observing her sick, childlike mother. She supposed even the front door must be interesting to someone who had been bedridden for three years.

Three terrible years.

"All right," Tabitha surrendered, and reached into her purse to reveal a hefty, hand-crafted, and well-worn sketching journal. Flipping to a blank page, she closed her eyes for a moment to remember. Then she drew a perfectly accurate depiction of their front door, in every detail, down to the subtle scrapings that differentiated it from those on every other cookie-cutter house on their street.

It was only three minutes later when she finished and presented the piece to her mother.

Natalie beamed. "Who needs cameras?"

Soaking in her mother's appreciation, Tabitha felt a swelling in her chest as her heart grew slightly less cold.

"Just like your father," Natalie concluded, proudly.

Tabitha's softness retreated. Cold, sharp, and with all the venom of a snake, she spat, "I am *nothing* like my father," and left the room.

Mayra Mae was on her way up the stairs when Tabitha slammed the door.

"Tabitha," she began with gentle reprimand in her voice. Tabitha gave her a look that said *Don't*, and tried to evade her on the narrow stair. Mayra Mae followed.

"You can't keep doing this. It's time to let go."

"What, let Mom die?" she hissed back over her shoulder as she snatched a cleaning rag and began dusting a shelf to occupy her frustrated hands.

"That's not what I'm talking about, and you know it."

Tabitha had no answer, but kept her eyes averted and meticulously rubbed the glass of a picture frame she'd picked up off the shelf.

"It's been three years," Mayra Mae cautiously continued.

"I miss you. The old you. It hurts me to see you like this. And yes, I miss him too, but I need to know that if he never comes back, you still will."

Tabitha looked down at the frame. It was a sketch of their mother, standing, leaning in to kiss a man's cheek. A drop of water appeared on his almond-shaped eyes, and Tabitha was startled to realize it had come from her own.

"*Let it go,*" Mayra Mae whispered.

Tabitha reeled in her disobedient heart, angrily wiped the tear off, and replaced the frame on the shelf.

"Mayra," she said sternly and emotionlessly, facing her twin with a new composure, "you're right."

Mayra Mae's eyes softened with the hints of an oncoming hope.

"You're right: it *has* been three years—three years of waiting, in agonizing silence. Three years of wondering when those promised antibiotics were going to start showing up in our mailbox. Three years of vain hope that our oh-so-heroic father would walk through those doors triumphantly proclaiming, *Look at me, I've saved our family!* How could you possibly ask me to just, *let it go?*"

Tabitha's voice fumed with disgust, a fume that veiled the air with poison. Mayra Mae swallowed it. Her lips formed a hard line, but her eyes maintained pity.

"Maybe he had a reason," she tried gingerly. "Maybe something went wrong and he wasn't able to get the medicine after all."

Tabitha meticulously scrubbed a spot on the shelf that was

already as clean as fresh snow. "And what if his reason was he never intended to save her in the first place?" she muttered. "What if he was just running away from it all—from us?"

Mayra Mae shrugged. "Forgive him, I guess."

Tabitha's hand stopped scrubbing and her eyes glared with resolve. She shook her head. "Never."

Mayra Mae closed her eyes and breathed a soft sigh, then retreated to the living room sofa. On her face was a look Tabitha knew well: weary defeat.

Tabitha tried to walk away, as she'd done to the three men at the Provisionary that day. *She's wrong!* her demons cried in stubborn resolve. Her hot anger sat bubbling in the pit of her stomach, but the pang of guilt did not go away.

Mayra Mae was strong, but she was not unbreakable. She was not hard and fortified like her twin, and Tabitha knew she'd hurt her.

Damn. Tabitha stood in the foyer and racked her brain for something to say to ease the tension. A hundred phrases came to mind, a hundred things she ought to say daily but didn't, thanks to her rock-solid pride: *How do you put up with my stubbornness? Please forgive me. You're the best sister anyone could ask for—my dearest friend, my only friend.*

Tabitha opened her mouth to speak.

Suddenly, the massive screen of a wall in their living room turned itself on, startling them. There appeared a Provision elite in her standard, dark blue uniform, with a short blonde bob and commanding shoulders, contradicting a disarmingly broad grin.

"This is a public service announcement," she chimed.

The voice boomed through the living room, and Mayra Mae glanced up toward their mother's bed chamber. Tabitha noted her concern and found the TV's remote to lower the volume.

"Are you a passionate Privileged ready to make the world a better place? Are you *gifted?*" The elite said "gifted" like it was a secret. Tabitha glanced at her sketch journal on the coffee table.

"Well, now is your chance to give back! Located in the sparkling Provision sector of Tolliver, surrounded by gorgeous Southwestern landscapes as endless as your opportunity, Providence Institute for Higher Education provides nothing but the best for our best apprentices, who go on to give nothing but the best back to you, our dear Privileged.

"And guess what? That could be *you!* That's right, our recruitment team is coming to *your Privileged sector!* Pack your bags and bring your talent to the Axelle Center Square to audition. One of our specially-trained Providence Recruitment Officers will be there to assess your compatibility. Don't forget, chosen ones are given elite perks for the *whole family!* Don't miss out!"

The blonde elite was replaced by the familiar face of Lilith Damara, the Institute's founder. Her message was brief: "At Providence Institute for Higher Education, anything is possible."

The screen flashed to elegant portrayals of a sparkling white city perched in a crevasse of red canyon, followed by laughing apprentices and helpful Provision elites.

Mayra Mae averted her eyes from the screen in obvious pain. The civil war within Tabitha surfaced again, sending pinpricks up her spine. Her tongue felt thick and dry, her heart swelled within the cold hard chains she'd forged around it. *Today, of all—*

"Of all days," Mayra Mae said, finishing the statement in Tabitha's mind. Tabitha swallowed, regaining her composure and adding a few links to the chain.

"That's probably just how they schedule their recruitments," Tabitha stated unconcernedly. "Once they map out all the sectors to visit, they just put it on repeat. Same day, three years later, they've gone through the list and they're back here again."

She hoped it would comfort Mayra Mae, though it didn't bring any comfort to herself. Her father occupied her mind enough as it was. It was too much for Tabitha that a Providence Institute recruiter—the same kind that her father went running off with three years prior—would return on the anniversary of his abandonment.

Mayra Mae studied her sister. "Are you all right?" she asked.

"Of course I'm all right!" Tabitha responded, but the words contradicted her tone. *Keep it together,* she demanded.

Tabitha glanced back at the screen and raised the remote to click it off when something stopped her dead in her tracks.

The chipper elite babbled about the Institute's high security as the camera panned across a line of uniformed peacekeepers. In the next clip, one stern face flashed by so fast that Tabitha couldn't be sure she hadn't imagined it. The sight opened a hollow pit in her stomach, vast and terrible as the trenches of hell.

It was her father.

Tabitha clicked the TV off reflexively, as if doing so could remove the sight from her eyes. Had it really been him? Or had her grudge grown so much that it intruded now into her senses as well as her subconscious mind?

Tabitha glanced at Mayra Mae, seated on the couch. Her sister showed no signs of having noticed it, but looked off into nothingness, deep in thought.

Tabitha was imagining things. She must be.

But the wick was lit, and there was no stopping its rush toward the dynamite strapped to Tabitha's heels. She had to know for sure.

"No, really—I'm all right," Tabitha assured, as the statement became true with the thoughts that occurred to her. "Mae, this could be what we've been waiting for! Didn't you hear what she said? *Elite perks for the whole family.* Those perks might include medications. They might consider my drawing ability a 'gift,' I could go and earn perks for Mom!"

"Tabitha, are you crazy?" Mayra Mae breathed, aghast. She stood erect and faced her twin.

"What, you don't think I could manage it?" Tabitha countered.

Mayra Mae shook her head. "I have no doubt you'd be able to, but if anything could beat tuberculosis in the race to kill Mom, it's losing another one of us."

"Mayra Mae, we're running out of time. She needs those meds."

"We're already out of time! What she needs is to have her daughters here for her when she passes."

Tabitha swallowed hard. "Don't talk like that."

Mayra Mae took a deep breath that asserted her rights as the oldest by six minutes. "No. Tabitha, absolutely not. Out of the question."

Tabitha bit down the urge to lash out and searched for a convincing argument.

Tell her, some unknown side of her civil war whispered. *Tell her what you saw!* She ignored it.

"We have to do *something*," Tabitha said with sincerity. "We've done everything we can as Privileged; there's no way we're getting our hands on those medications unless one of us becomes Provision… can you think of any other option?"

Mayra Mae's eyes were downcast and worn as she managed to say, "Just accept the inevitable."

Tabitha's face contorted in horror at the statement. Mayra Mae did not take it back. She only looked with sad submission at her twin, wishing it wasn't true but convinced there was nothing more to be done.

"No," Tabitha decided, taking Mayra Mae's hands in hers. "I can't do that. You cover for me at the Grind, I'll go to the auditions. If nothing else, I can at least try to talk to a Provision elite and find out if there's any way for us to obtain elite perks as Privileged. All right?"

Mayra Mae did not agree, but her capacity for conflict was spent. She nodded.

CHAPTER TWO

STAGE FRIGHT

THE AIR WAS THICK WITH THE SMELL OF SAWDUST. The Axelle Center Square, kissed by the midday sun, echoed with the sounds of hammers against nails as Provision elites in their midnight blue uniforms pounded a stage into existence. Tabitha cautiously approached the scene, sketchbook in hand, in search of someone who looked important.

"Lookin' good, Chad, keep it up!" sounded the phony voice of a narrow-shouldered Provision elite. He had salt and pepper hair, tanned skin, and walked with slinky, cat-like movements. He patted "Chad" on the back and moved on to the next worker to deliver some other canned compliment. By the look he gave in response, his name wasn't Chad—but he nodded with respect. Tabitha had found her target.

The elite turned and began walking toward a nearby coffee shop. Tabitha slipped down an alleyway and entered the same shop, but through a back door. Then she stealthily eased into a dark corner booth and waited.

Salty came through the front entrance moments later with

the same grin pasted on his face. His masquerade wavered for a split second as he caught the eye of the barista: a busty woman with long, curled locks of gold. Tabitha stifled an indignant chuckle as she witnessed him puff out his chest and slick back his hair. *Subtle.*

"How does a dame like you end up working at a coffee shop like this?" he charmed as he propped his right elbow on the counter and stuffed his left hand into his pocket. Just before it disappeared, Tabitha spotted a glimmer of gold on his ring finger.

The barista played along. "Well," she replied, "I'll have you know that this is no ordinary coffee shop. You're standing in the best coffee shop in all of Axelle, and I'm its queen."

The elite let out a phony gasp. "My gravest apologies, your majesty!" he exclaimed as he stood erect, putting both hands stiffly behind his back in a militaristic manner. "Recruitment Officer Logan Malloy," he barked, whipping his right hand up from his back to his forehead in salute. The ring went with it. "At your service!"

"At ease, soldier," the barista muttered seductively.

Tabitha's jaw dropped. Just as smoothly as it came off his finger in the motion of his salute, the ring made its way into his back pocket and they continued their conversation, leaning ever closer over the counter toward one another.

Their voices got softer so that all Tabitha caught was a question of where they could go to be alone. At one point, he toyed with her curls with his ringless hand, and she gave him a wink just before leaving to fix his coffee. He mindlessly placed his thumb on the finger scanner, collected his purchase, and left with a smirk.

What Tabitha had hoped for was a professional connection. What she'd gotten was blackmail. It was all the same, she supposed.

Tabitha wasted no time. Flipping to a new page, she sketched the moment when Logan's ring-free hand caressed the barista's hair, her smug wink frozen forever on the page—in perfect detail. As Tabitha left out the back door, she saw Goldilocks flip the *Open* sign on the front door to *Closed*, lock the entrance, and ascend a set of stairs to what was presumably a storage loft above the shop.

Tabitha made her way around the back of the building, only to duck into an alleyway to avoid running into Recruitment Officer Logan Malloy himself. He looked over his shoulder before taking a chug of his coffee and tossing the rest of it in a nearby trashcan. Then he slipped in through the back door of the shop, locking it behind himself.

Mission accomplished, Tabitha thought.

• • •

Within the hour, a crowd had grown like a fungus on three sides of the stage. The back of it was blocked with a royal blue rope. Inside, a small group of young men and women—Tabitha among them—stood in a line to audition for the Institute. Elites with expensive video cameras covered every angle of the scene and projected their vision onto large screens above the stage. Along the side streets were food and beverage stands marked with the New Order seal, closed but ready. Logan mounted the platform with a skip in his step and grabbed a microphone that hung upside down from a beam above center stage.

"My fellow humanity!" Logan's coy voice sounded through the mic. "You are about to witness the rise of tomorrow's Provision leaders! Only the best of the best, to be trained by the even better best, are recruited in this rare moment of your little history. But first…" Logan signaled to the elites manning the stands, who opened their windows. "Who wants free booze?"

The crowd cheered and dispersed like cockroaches exposed to light, racing to the concession stands. Meanwhile, the contestants began their interview process. As each completed an individual questionnaire with Logan, they were either ushered onstage to perform a presentation of their skill, or rejected and sent back into the crowd.

Tabitha reached the table where Logan sat. "And what would your unique contribution to society be?" he asked her with his phony charm, pushing a finger scanner toward her. She placed her thumb down and began.

"I have a photographic memory," Tabitha stated confidently. "Everything I see, in every detail, is fused into my brain so concretely that if I close my eyes and remember, I can recall *everything*—down to the most minute detail. Some call it a curse." She paused, as if about to challenge the notion. "I don't disagree with them."

Logan half listened, nodding and *uh-huh*-ing, while reading Tabitha's profile, brought up from the finger scan.

Annoyed by his lack of attention, Tabitha straightened her shoulders and spoke a little louder. "The visuals of these memories last for about seven minutes before fading into the equivalent of an old memory—faded, blurry, dark. Useless, unless paired with an additional gift. Do you have access to a camera, Logan?"

Logan looked up. "Officer Malloy will do—how do you know my name?

You may not have a name tag, but you wear it on your sleeve... Tabitha resisted the urge to show him up and remained poised. "Word gets around when so fine a man is in town!" she flattered instead.

"Charmed... but of course I don't have access to a camera. Only elite photographers have that clearance."

"Exactly. What if you could have a drawing that was so perfectly accurate, it might as well be a photograph?"

There was a brief silence as he pondered the possibility. The crowd clapped in the background as one contestant completed their performance. Tabitha kept eye contact.

Finally, Logan scoffed. "What good would that do? Add some extra sentimental value around the house? Ha!" Tabitha began to open her mouth in protest, but he cut her off. "Besides," he went on, "our records indicate that you don't qualify for an audition."

Tabitha was on the edge of bursting in rage, but she collected herself. Suddenly, her voice softened like a damsel's in distress. "Not qualify? How can that be?" She did her best to bat her eyelashes and tear up a little.

"Does it matter? Next!" he shouted over her.

"Wait!" she cried, genuinely this time. "Please, it does matter. It's a matter of life and death! But everyone I've asked has shot me down and I'm at the end of my rope—I need to know! What do I have to do to qualify for family elite perks?"

"Josiah Clay is your father, yeah?"

This caught Tabitha off guard. "Regrettably. Why?"

"Then there's nothing you can do. It's against my protocol to recruit anyone with a family member on the list of wanted felons in any of the Provision sectors."

"A felon?"

"It's the hottest gossip in Providence at the moment. Josiah Clay is the bane of Lilith Damara's existence. He'd be behind bars if they only knew where he was. Now, if you'll excuse me, I have apprentices to recruit. Chad, will you show Miss Clay to the door?"

Tabitha's mind was racing. Her father was alive, and—a felon? Was that why they hadn't heard from him? What other crime had he committed on top of breaking his family's hearts?

But Tabitha had no time to process what she'd heard. "Chad" was already guiding her gently toward the rope that divided the crowds. He unlinked it to let her out when she suddenly turned toward him.

"Your name's not Chad, is it?" she said in a hushed voice. He didn't answer. She held out her hand for a shake. "My name is Tabitha."

He cautiously took it and replied, "Michael."

"Michael, I need to get to Providence. If you get me on that stage, I'll get Logan back for every time he's ever bossed you around by the name of Chad."

Michael's eyes lit up, but he refused himself a full smile. He turned, however, breaking her eye contact and said, "I'm sorry, I can't do that."

Tabitha ground her teeth in disappointment.

"But I won't stop you," he finished.

Tabitha grinned from ear to ear. Michael flashed her a wink and she bolted around the back of the platform. As another contestant finished his act, she cut past the next in line and claimed center stage.

Flying by the seat of her pants, she snagged the mic and blurted, "My name is Tabitha, and I'm an—" she stumbled, searching for the right word, "illustrator."

Logan's plastic grin shattered into an enraged scowl at the sound of her voice. He stood violently from his chair to face the stage.

"Not just any kind of illustrator, though… but before I blow your minds, I'll need a participant from the crowd!"

Logan was hastily making his way up the steps to drag her off stage.

Tabitha turned to him gleefully. "Ah, Logan, thank you for volunteering!" Her theatrical innocence matched her mother's.

Logan stopped at the applause of the crowd, forced a smile, and nodded.

"Everyone take a good hard look at that face—that expression, his posture and demeanor. Now, watch. Without looking at him, I'll draw him in perfect detail."

She turned, closed her eyes momentarily, and opened her sketch book, which had been tucked under her arm. Then, as fast as she possibly could, she drew him. It took about a minute and a half. Proudly, she held up the sketch toward the cameras so they could blow it up on the big screens.

The crowd applauded her. Logan joined in, saying, "Well done! Now, let's move on to—"

"Look at that face!" Tabitha interrupted. "You can't forget a face like that! I had the privilege of seeing it earlier today—at the coffee shop down on Seymour Street." She glared at Logan from the corner of her eye with a wily half-grin, and toyed with a corner of a page in her journal. "Would you like to see it?"

Her threat was registered. Logan eyed the cameras in a moment of panic. "That's all the time we have for now! We'll be back after a short break!" he erupted. As the screens began to flash mindless entertainment, he dragged her by the arm off-stage.

"What are you doing?" he demanded roughly when they were out of earshot.

"What does it look like?" Tabitha replied. "You help me get into Providence Institute, I don't jeopardize your job by making your little class-crossing affair go viral."

"Like I said, I'm not at liberty to do that. I don't make the rules, I just follow them."

"Do you, now? I'm pretty sure it's against the rules to cheat on your wife—much less with a *Privileged*."

"The drawing of an ignorant girl is hardly proof of an affair."

"Would you like to test that theory? We'll see what the peacekeepers think of it when they find your thumb print in the coffee shop finger scanner, or the security camera footage that caught you slipping through the back door after the sign was turned to *Closed*. You're right—hardly proof of anything."

Despite Logan's rough grasp on her arm and his status-bestowed power over her, Tabitha stood devoid of fear, with an air of ruthlessness that could not be shaken. A fire shone in her eyes that was both terrifying and enticing.

Logan's tone switched from defense to pleasure. "Oh, I like you."

"Don't give me a reason to change that."

Logan thought for a moment, studying her. "All right, fine," he concluded, "I'll get you in—but not with the name *Clay*. There's too much talk about what Josiah did for that to fly under the radar."

Tabitha extended her hand and concluded, "Hello, my name is Tabitha Beckett. It's a pleasure to meet you, Logan."

• • •

The Grind was not a real place. "The Grind" was what some ungrateful Privileged used to describe the factories at which they worked, on account of their easy, mindless tasks. The daily grind for every Privileged was grunt work—anything that anyone could do without much skill or know-how. People seen by the New Order to have unusual skills and particular potential beyond that were recruited for Providence Institute, where they were trained to be employed in Provision sectors throughout Grexovium. From there, they provided the Privileged with everything they needed, and were looked up to as heroes for making the world go 'round.

Most didn't mind. They put in their time and the Provision gave them every mundane pleasure they wanted, once a week on the dot. Mayra Mae didn't mind. She made the most of it, switching off with Tabitha at the bakery to put in their household's required quota and enjoying every minute they had together at home.

Tabitha, on the other hand, did mind. She was a firecracker itching to explode but deprived of an adequate sky. Unlike her mother and twin, she lacked a quiet spirit. Her distaste for passivity was too powerful for her level of power to do anything about it, and it drove her mad. Yet, even after three years of being powered by that zeal, searching for answers to the questions that plagued her daily, she wasn't any closer to finding them; until now.

"Dad's alive!" Tabitha said enthusiastically to a flour-covered Mayra Mae over the bakery counter. Tabitha cheerfully slapped her thumb on the finger scanner, made a selection and snatched a cookie from the display. She took a rather masculine bite out of it and continued, mouth full, "He's not living it up, either. He's a wanted felon. Isn't that great?"

Mayra Mae stood motionless, unsure how to respond to Tabitha's hysteria. "No," she said flatly. "That's not great. That's bad."

Tabitha wasn't phased. She waltzed around the counter and threw on an apron. "No, it means you were right," she said. "He did have a reason for not sending the medicine!"

"And now we know for sure that none is coming," Mayra Mae continued, watching Tabitha shove her hands into a bag of genetically engineered flour. "So again—how is this a good thing?"

Tabitha clapped her hands in a cloud of white and concluded, "I'm going to find him."

Spinning on her heel, Tabitha skipped into the back kitchen, passing under a bright screen that flashed the words, *Bread—Handmade Daily!* Mayra Mae followed her.

"What? How?"

"I'm going to the Providence Institute for Higher Education, where as Lilith Damara would say, *Anything is possible!*"

Tabitha scooped up a wad of pre-made dough from a vat and rolled it into a ball. Mayra Mae slapped it from Tabitha's hands onto the machine's conveyer belt.

"Tabitha, no! You can't leave me to do everything on my own! Someone needs to stay home with Mom. There's no way I could meet our quota by myself!"

"Your quota will go down when I'm out of the house; it'll be fine!"

"How could you say that? Look, I want to help Mom, same as you... but don't think you can fool me into believing this isn't one-hundred percent about Dad."

"Josiah is just a bonus," Tabitha shrugged. "I was going to go anyway to get perks."

"Would you stop calling him that?"

"Well, it *is* his name..."

"Tabitha, your obsession with getting Dad back is destroying our family."

"*I'm* destroying our family?" Tabitha dropped sarcastically. She hid the sting of the statement by kneading her frustration into another wad of dough.

"What is the point of finding him?" Mayra Mae asked, almost pleadingly.

"You said it yourself: to get him back," Tabitha replied. "I'm going to get him back for the last three years of misery." Tabitha smirked and would have laughed at her own play on words were it not for the look of horror that spread across Mayra Mae's face.

"You're doing this for revenge?" she growled.

The sound of it stilled Tabitha's hands and sent an odd sensation to her stomach, one she was little acquainted with: fear. Mayra Mae only used that voice when things were very, very bad.

"No," Tabitha denied in a less convincing tone. "Of course not..." She said it more to herself than to her sister. Then the civil war inside her turned and, catching herself, Tabitha spouted, "Why are you so mad? I'm going to save Mom!"

"Yeah, that's what Dad said when he got recruited," Mayra Mae jabbed.

"Well, I'm not him!" Tabitha yelled back.

Mayra Mae knew at this point the conversation was over. Throwing the dough down she looked Tabitha dead in the eyes and said, "Fine. Go. Leave us behind for your oh-so-noble cause. But when you find yourself on the other side a lonely, bitter woman with no one left but yourself, don't say I didn't warn you."

"As you wish," Tabitha snarked with a bow. Pulling off her apron, she walked away, leaving her teary-eyed twin staring hopelessly after her.

Tabitha maintained a blank expression as she climbed onto the light rail, but once in her seat, she pushed her forehead against the window and shut her eyes tight. She purposefully banged it a few times on the glass before looking out over the passing landscape.

The peaks of the rolling hills loomed high in the sky, rich with the vibrant hues of summer's death. They awakened something in Tabitha against her will: feeling. Her cold and aching heart melted at their majesty, and she longed to be free—of nothing in particular and everything all at once.

In her reflection Tabitha could see the glistening of tears streaming down her face, but no one was in the pod to see it, so she let them be.

• • •

From the living room of the Clay abode, Tabitha heard the faint ring of a bell. She quickly put down her sketch journal and ascended the stairway to her mother's bedside.

"What is it, Mom?" Tabitha asked, gently grasping her hand.

"My sweet Tabitha!" Natalie responded with fretful countenance. "I couldn't remember, I couldn't—oh, Josiah. Oh dear. Sweetheart, will you turn on the air conditioning?"

Tabitha nodded and adjusted the thermostat on the room's wall, then returned to the bed.

"Mom," she began with some difficulty, "I'm going away."

Natalie leaned up on her elbows and listened intently, but said nothing.

At her lack of response, Tabitha continued. "I've done everything I can here to make a case for your treatment, but as a Privileged of your age and condition, there's only so much we have access to... I'm going to the Institute. I auditioned this morning and got in. All I have to do is make the right connections, pull a few strings, and I'll be able to start sending you everything you need."

"Tabitha," Natalie interjected. Her voice was patient and gentle. She took Tabitha's forlorn face in her hands and, shaking her head, continued, "My time is coming. There's a reason they refused me treatment when I first got sick, why I tried to convince your father to stay. I doubt I'll last the winter. The only thing I want from you is to be by my side until the end. Please."

Tabitha pulled away and turned to hide her eyes, which had swelled with fresh tears. With shaky breath, she responded. "I can't. Mom, I can't live with myself knowing I could have done something about it. I want our family to be like it was: intact and alive. I can't endure this dull and hopeless existence."

Natalie looked at Tabitha with pity. "I know. But it is what it is. Let's just make the most of it."

Tabitha turned back to her and finished, "That's what I intend to do." She leaned down and kissed Natalie's forehead. "I love you, Mom," she said.

Then Tabitha stood and retreated to her room, grabbing her journal on the way. In solitude, she flipped to a fresh page and marked the corner with the date and time. After closing her eyes for a moment, she drew her mother's face as it looked when she held Tabitha's own in her hands. Then she packed it in a suitcase with everything else she cared to own in the new life she was about to embrace.

CHAPTER THREE

PROVIDENCE

Tabitha didn't say goodbye. She left before the sun had risen, her last word a small bouquet of wildflowers on the kitchen table. The early morning autumn air was crisp and the sky was bright with stars as she made her way to the light rail stop, but her steps felt heavy. Mayra Mae would be waking up soon.

A kind-looking old man greeted Tabitha at the long-distance travel station with an echoing, "Where to?"

"Tolliver," Tabitha announced.

"Ah, a new apprentice, are you?"

Tabitha nodded and attempted to look proud of herself.

"Good for you!" he beamed. "Now, you won't have to use travel allowance for this trip if you were recruited by the New Order—it should be included in your enrollment packet. If you'll just place your thumb on the scanner…"

Tabitha did as she was told and held her breath as the screen loaded her information. After a few seconds, the name *Tabitha Beckett* appeared at the top, followed by *Age: 20.*

Occupation: apprentice. Family/household: none. Logan had held his end of the bargain.

The man at the booth typed some things into the computer so she'd have clearance on the train, and sent her to the platform. Once settled in her own private room, Tabitha curled up and fell into a restless sleep.

• • •

Tabitha woke late to the mid-morning sun that pierced through the train car window. For a moment, she wondered if the happenings of the previous day were all a dream. Part of her hoped they were. A repetitive clanging sound reached her ears, each gong sending a shard of pain through her skull as her consciousness drew up from the darkness.

Wincing, she sat up and raised a hand to her forehead. The early stages of a headache pinched behind her eyes like an oncoming storm. She blinked her blurry vision into focus and saw the source of the sound: the handle of her luggage striking the metal bars of the storage rack as the train trembled.

So she *was* on a train, and it was not a dream.

Looking outside, she saw a vast body of water, shimmering under an open sky. Sea gulls danced along the edges of the shore, sandy and wet from the cold, crashing waves. It was beautiful.

But it wasn't home. And somewhere far behind her, Tabitha knew that her twin was disappointed and heartbroken.

Pulling her journal from her suitcase, Tabitha flipped through the pages, looking for a sketch of her sister. She found one from a year or so back, in which Mayra Mae peeked at

Tabitha from the corner of her eye with a playful mischievousness. Tabitha brushed her fingertips along the edge of the paper and held the book close to her aching heart.

Then suddenly she wrenched her journal from her chest and slapped it down on the train car bench. This wouldn't do. Tabitha had made her choice, and she would prove to Mayra Mae that it had been the right one.

Tabitha rose to explore the train, not bothering to slip on her shoes. She padded aimlessly down the corridor to the dining hall: spacious, dome-like, and comprised mostly of windows. She gazed upward and around at the scenery that whirred past.

Seating speckled the floor, and in the center of it all were three round serving buffets, adorned with a selection of breakfast, lunch, and dinner food. Determined to cheer herself up, Tabitha lifted the dish coverings, welcoming each scented waft. Everything smelled pretty much the same, of course—all Privileged food had an identical genetically engineered makeup—but Tabitha liked to pretend that the smell of bacon, eggs, and pancakes were blissfully unique. That would have been more interesting.

Just as she was heaping portions far too large for her lean figure onto a plate, Tabitha's solitude was broken. A woman near her age with chocolate brown skin peered around the corner. Her hair was a mess of thickly twisted locks that were tied up in twine and decorated with an occasional silver bead. She had a rather large, protruding upper lip, and her lower was adorned with a stud lip ring centered above her chin. Her fingers also glinted with silver, covered in a variety of rings. Though she carried herself with indifferent confidence, her eyes glistened with the same curiosity and fascination as Tabitha's. The two made eye contact.

"You headed to the Institute?" the young woman asked. Tabitha nodded with a grin, which was requited. "Me too."

She strode across the room on muscular legs that would put a body builder's to shame, and extended her ringed hand. "Ella Reeves," she introduced.

"Tabitha Beckett," Tabitha replied, welcoming the sturdy shake. As little as the lie was, the sound of her new name felt dirty on her tongue.

Ella lazily let a pack fall from her shoulders to the floor in order to more easily serve herself breakfast. It was made of wicker, like a picnic basket propped up sideways, and from beneath its lid crept a vine, green and slithery as a snake. Its living leaves were such a surprise that they seemed almost indecent, and Tabitha cocked her head at them, intrigued.

"So where are you from?" Ella asked.

Tabitha jerked her eyes back to her new travel companion. "Axelle," she replied. "You?"

"Right here in Felicity," she answered, jutting a thumb toward the city that was quickly disappearing out the window. "Best Privileged sector in Grexovium, if you want my totally biased opinion."

"You sad to leave, then?" Tabitha asked.

Ella shrugged. "Nah. I've learned everything there is to learn in that sweet ol' place, and I went and ran out of travel allowance." She sighed dramatically and paused for an uncomfortably long time, pondering her unfair situation.

Tabitha fidgeted.

Suddenly, Ella's shoulders rose and fell in a shrug and she declared, "So, I'm cheating the system! A whole new terrain means a whole lot of plants I ain't never seen, even heard of yet. Oh—I'm a botanist. Or at least, I think that's what I am. Plants are my thing."

"So I guessed!" Tabitha replied, gesturing toward the plant.

Ella leaned in close as if to whisper a secret. "You'd be surprised how much you can do with what looks to y'all like a common weed."

"Such as?" Tabitha inquired.

Ella smiled and shot Tabitha a devious wink. "I'll show you sometime."

Tabitha liked Ella.

The two chattered pleasantly about petty things that didn't matter, until Tabitha's shell began to soften. Ella wasn't Mayra Mae—nor could she ever be—but she was company, and there was no harm in a little company.

Ella convinced Tabitha to demonstrate her artistic talents, and gave her more praise for it than Tabitha thought she deserved. She then shared her botanical skills by removing Tabitha's headache with some plant-based concoction that she rubbed against Tabitha's temples. It was like a two-person show-and-tell, and just as easy as kindergarten. Their mutual interest and appreciation for one another was as soothing a balm to the sore of Tabitha's loneliness as the oil that took her migraine away.

For two more days they traveled thus, passing the time in each other's company and ignoring their fellow passengers, who mostly kept to their rooms, utilizing the free games and trinkets provided them. Hills rolled and mountains loomed, moving backwards in season. There were no more red leaves painting moss-covered hills. Instead, the red was found within the rocks. Pine trees turned into cacti, gray mountains into jagged shards of rusty stone—copper castles without kings.

The morning they were to arrive in Tolliver, they woke early to watch the sun rise in the domed windows of the dining car. They lay back upon the dining car booths and stared up at the wide open sky, painted pink.

"What do you think it'll be like in Providence?" Ella asked after some time.

Tabitha pondered the question and realized she hadn't thought much of Providence itself—only what she suspected her encounter with Josiah Clay would be like. "I don't know," she replied. "Don't really care, to be honest. I'm here by necessity."

Ella turned inquisitively toward her.

"My mom is really sick," Tabitha explained. "She's had extra-pulmonary tuberculosis in her spine for the last three years, and if she doesn't start getting treatment ASAP…" She trailed off.

Ella looked at her intently, with compassion in her big brown eyes.

"I've tried everything but I can't get what I need as Privileged," Tabitha went on, "so I decided to come here and try to become a Provision elite. I've heard that the Institute offers perks if you do well with your apprenticeship, so even as a student I might be able to start sending her the treatments she needs. That is, if I do well."

"I'm sure you will," Ella said after a moment. "I'm sorry about your mom. But you've got what it takes to make your way, I can tell."

Tabitha thanked her, but felt slightly unworthy of Ella's admiring gaze.

Just then, the train lurched to a stop. Tabitha and Ella rose to look outside. The landscape was pale brown and leeched of all moisture. The two gathered their things from the sleeper car and exited to the platform. Clouds of dirt kicked up from beneath their feet as they stepped off, and the air tasted dry and dusty. Ella, stretching lazily, didn't seem to mind the blazing heat which already threatened to leave Tabitha scarlet with sunburn.

Two passengers got off with Tabitha and Ella. Judging by their ages, suitcases, and dumb doe-eyed expressions, they were also recruits for the Institute. One was a massively muscular but harmless looking man-child, with a vacantness in his eyes and slouching troll-like shoulders. The other was quite the opposite: a dainty and poised woman, quiet and dignified with her pointed chin held high. She had long platinum blonde hair pulled tightly into a high pony tail by a blue ribbon, and her every movement was a dance.

The train pulled away, leaving them alone in the southwestern vastness. No one moved. Tabitha and Ella's new companions gawked timidly about.

Upon seeing their paralysis, Ella shook her head. "Y'all—everything is going to be fine," she insisted. "C'mon."

Ella strode confidently toward a silver light rail, which looked oddly mismatched among the ancient, abandoned feel of the place. Tabitha caught up to her stride, and the others followed. They entered the solitary pod that was parked at the station, and turned on its seldom-used console. It hummed to life and shot them down a long cracked road, which seemed to go on forever into nothingness.

They wound along a path up the steeps of red mountains, and eventually reached the rail's end. They stepped out. Vast canyon valleys surrounded their patch of flatland farther than their eyes could see, making them feel small and insignificant in comparison.

Tabitha found herself unable to resist the urge to trot to the edge of the cliff and look down. She strained her eyes in an attempt to see the heart of the canyon. Her vision was blurry, but she could somewhat make out the scene. The treacherous rocks crumbled into what looked like pebbles, shrunken far below. Among them were spidery red veins that must have been rivers once, fingering their way across the sand, pooled in craters like the surface of Mars.

Suddenly, their hair flew wildly and it became hard to breathe. Tabitha squinted her eyes to shield them against the dust that rose from the ground. Sheltering her face, she backed away from the ledge and returned to the group. A large helicopter descended from above them and landed a few paces away.

Excitement bubbled up in Tabitha's chest. From the vehicle

stepped forth the very same blonde from the audition advertisement, dressed in dark royal blue. On her shirt pocket was a gold name tag that read, *Cassady Reinhardt, Providence Recruitment & Welcome Committee.*

"Welcome!" she chimed with the same bright smile. "Ella, Tabitha, Toby, Maddie, we've been expecting you."

The four looked at one another, flattered to be known by name, and climbed aboard.

"When we arrive on the grounds, I'll be giving you a tour of the city and school facilities," Cassady continued once they were settled in their seats and in the air.

Tabitha was mesmerized by the copper terrain as it shrunk beneath them, but she resisted the urge to stare out the window and instead gave the woman her full attention.

"Here are your welcome packets," Cassady said. "In them you'll find a map of the grounds, information about your trainers, instructions on where to be for group sessions, rules, and so on."

The four opened the envelopes given to them. On the map were detailed notes concerning each area, except for a few marked in red.

"What are the red parts?" asked Maddie. She had a brightly toned, sweet voice.

"Restricted sections," the woman in blue responded cheerfully.

Tabitha glanced around at the other passengers. If anyone else found the statement questionable, they hid it well, and Tabitha decided to do the same.

Cassady went on. "Once you've adjusted to our way of life

in Providence, you'll move into your new apartments. There will be a welcome banquet for you with some of the elder apprentices, who will share a little bit about their experience at the Institute and answer any questions you may have.

"Following this, you'll hear a few words from our founder, whom you all know well. Lilith Damara does not appreciate tardiness, so don't be late!" Cassady rapped on the schedule sheet in Toby's welcome packet. "When she's finished her welcome, you'll have a chance to meet your fellow entry-level apprentices, as well as your hand-selected supervisors, who will do an evaluation to determine the nature of your apprenticeship."

The newcomers nodded silently, though none of them could fully comprehend the information dump that had just landed on them. The helicopter began its descent.

"Oh, and one more thing," Cassady added abruptly, "I'll need your thumb signature on this form." She pushed a multi-page packet of fine-printed papers at each of them and opened a pad of ink.

The four glanced around at one another. This time, their confusion and concern showed more plainly.

"Ink?" peeped Maddie.

"Yes. Go ahead."

"What's the form?" Toby asked with a hint of skepticism.

"It simply states that you agree to participate in the programs assigned to each of you, and that you'll comply to our rules and standards," Cassady said. She moved the ink pad closer to them.

Picking up on her hint, the four skimmed through as fast as they could and planted their thumb prints on the bottom.

Collecting the packets with a smile, Cassady exclaimed, "Welcome to Providence!"

The helicopter doors opened and they all stepped out. Before them was a great stone wall, nearly thirty feet thick and six miles long. It spanned to either side of a moon-shaped natural ridge that shot into the sky in jagged shards of crimson and orange.

There was about half a mile of flatland surrounding the wall, but little beyond that. Looking back, they could see there was no way to or from the grounds, save the helicopter or a steep cliff of loose stone—no doubt riddled with scorpions.

The whirling sound of the helicopter blades quickened as it departed into the sky behind them. The new apprentices followed their guide toward the front gate, and she pulled from her belt a string of large, unusual keys fastened to a thick wire.

"No thumb pad? Seem's a bit... primitive." Tabitha commented.

"When you're housing the most ingenious minds of the world all in one location, it's better to use a security system that cannot be hacked," Cassady responded. "We may have reverted to more traditional methods, Miss Beckett, but I think you'll find we are far from primitive."

Cassady began to push the keys into their prospective slots, one at a time. Tabitha studied them carefully. Each, when turned, revealed a wheel of pegs that could be cranked. Loud clangs and thuds echoed through the metal gate and reverberated through the stone as Cassady rotated the wheels.

"How intricate!" Maddie remarked after the third key. "What is it they're trying to keep out?"

The elite didn't answer.

Six keys later, the doors began to move, creaking anciently. The gate was nearly as thick as the wall itself, made of layer upon layer of twisted metal beams, presumably part of the locking system. When they opened to reveal the city of Providence in all its shining brilliance, the newcomers gasped.

From where they stood, the apprentices could see layers of buildings, each taller than the one in front of it. One pointed skyscraper towered over the rest of the city from where it stood against the mountain ridge. All monochromatic hues of diamond and pearl, Providence was as mismatched as the light rail among the desert sands. Tabitha had never seen architecture so beautiful. An unfamiliar sensation fluttered through her, which no manmade thing had ever instilled before: awe.

Four men dressed in the same royal blue appeared in a white car with blacked-out windows. They collected the bags of the new apprentices, and drove away without a word.

"Your luggage will be taken to your rooms. Now, if you'll follow me…" their guide began.

Tabitha stopped her. "If you don't mind, may I use the restroom before we continue with the tour? My stomach doesn't agree with… heights…" She stumbled over the last few words, gagging slightly.

"Right this way!" Cassady replied, eager to put Tabitha at a safe distance from herself.

They hurried to a nearby building. Above the entry doors was a sign that read *Providence Music Department.* The lobby was massive. Far above them, a chandelier glittered at the center of a dome, pierced by rays of sun, which shone through surrounding skylights. In a nearby corridor, Tabitha could faintly make out the sound of a cello playing, low and mellow. Again, she was overcome by that same dumbfounded feeling, and had to remind her feet to keep walking; though her eyes stayed glued to her marvelous surroundings.

Maddie followed Tabitha to the lavatory while the others waited outside. It was no less extravagant than the lobby. Each stall had its own thick, ornate door, and the room smelled freshly of lavender and mint. Neither had ever known such luxury in their lives. The two stood for a moment, open-mouthed.

"Wow," Maddie finally breathed, shaking off the shock.

"Yeah," Tabitha agreed.

She waited until Maddie had entered the first stall before silently creeping to another one farther down. Closing the door behind her, she sat on the porcelain throne and snatched her journal from her bag. As quickly as she could, Tabitha sketched each of Cassady's keys and took note of which ones went where and in what order to open the great gate. Tabitha didn't know what she'd do with the directions, but they were a weapon in her arsenal to be used against anyone who got in her way.

A flush echoed through the lavatory, followed by the sink and bathroom door. Tabitha stealthily left to return to her company. As she walked through the lobby once more, she heard the cello stop abruptly, followed by a banging like a chair falling over or something being thrown to the floor.

It was a moment before she realized her feet had ceased to move. A voice inside her commanded that she keep walking. She looked ridiculous, like Toby and Maddie, gawking at the hallway from which the sound came. But before she heeded the internal command, a young man stepped angrily out into the lobby.

Ripping his hands furiously through his dark hair, he stormed as if ready to strangle someone. Tabitha looked away, but a moment too late. He noticed her. His heavy steps slowed to a stop, and though Tabitha had begun her retreat toward the door, she could feel his eyes on her back.

Don't do it.

Tabitha glanced over her shoulder. The man was still staring. *Rude!* But upon looking closer, she thought she recognized him. He tilted his head and squinted his light blue eyes, as if he thought the same... but Tabitha couldn't put a finger on it fast enough to justify staring at him a moment longer. She turned her back to him and rejoined her party.

"Perfect timing!" exclaimed their guide as the party emerged from the building. "You'll get to see one of Providence's many marvelous features."

As Cassady spoke, a clattering noise filled the air. Looking up, they saw shimmering, translucent panels flutter like white wooden dominoes along wires above the buildings, starting from the tallest skyscraper and moving outward. Within seconds, they formed a vast canopy over the whole city.

The bright sun was dimmed as the umbrella blocked its heat, but was not blacked out completely. Each panel was slightly transparent, letting in just enough sun so it was comfortably warm and pleasantly bright. They could feel a sudden and soothing drop in temperature.

"Oh good," said Toby, wiping sweat from his upper lip.

"Like I said, Miss Beckett, far from primitive," Cassady sneered at Tabitha. "The panels are set to shelter Providence during the hottest hours of the day, and change depending on the time of year. It's especially handy in the summer months. It usually gets up to around 120 degrees in July and August. And in the winter, we have heating panels."

"Is that necessary?" Tabitha asked. "I mean, it's already October and it's got to be—what—eighty degrees? How much colder could it get?"

"Negative five," Cassady replied acidly. "Now if you don't mind, we'll continue with the tour. We're on a tight schedule." Her pearl teeth sparkled as bright as the panels, but her smile was sharp as a blade.

Tabitha bit her lip and exchanged a wary look with Ella.

Cassady talked as they walked, commenting on the beauty of the buildings they passed, always concluding with a remark about the New Order's generous nature. Tabitha listened and learned, stowing every snippet of information away as a potential resource.

The only inhabitants of Providence were Institute teachers and apprentices, Providence City Officials, a few members of the New Order Council and the Damara family. All graduates from the Institute were given a position in a Provision sector, and the very best apprentices got to work for the New Order Council in Grexovium's capitol, Forsythe. No Provision sectors were more luxurious than Providence and Forsythe.

Cassady pointed out the communal dining hall, various training facilities, a fitness center, and entertainment house. Tabitha mentally linked each location to those on the map Cassady had provided, and by deduction identified those places known as *restricted sections*.

All the while, her eyes were peeled for a familiar face.

The next tier of the city was the apprentice apartments. The outer ring housed entry-level apprentices. The apartment complex was long and C-shaped, broken into sections bridged by open balconies that cut through from one side to the other. Beyond them—past a large, secured iron gate—were the elders, upperclassmen at the Institute. That was as far as the four of them were permitted to go, Cassady explained.

Tabitha squinted through the gate at the sparkling city's heart. The center was a skyscraper with ornate reflective windows and flowery balconies. At the very top was the tip of the canopy, symbolic of the New Order's provision to them all. Tabitha wondered if Lilith Damara lived in its heights.

And where are you*, Josiah Clay?*

"That concludes our tour!" Cassady said with a clap of her hands. As if on cue, four smiling elites clad in white hospital uniforms approached from behind them. "Before any welcome ceremonies may commence, you'll be required to undergo a detoxification period, in order to acclimate you to our screen-, drug-, and alcohol-free campus. This will last six weeks. Should you need additional care, it may be provided on a case-by-case basis."

What? Tabitha thought despairingly. Six weeks was too long. If her father was really a felon, he could be caught by then. Her mother could die by then. Mayra Mae could hate her by then.

"You'll now be escorted to your temporary housing. Happy Detox!"

Cassady walked away without another word, and the medical elites surrounded them.

Tabitha resisted the urge to throw punches as two grinning mannequin-like nurses extended their hands toward her purse and tugged it from her shoulder. Toby seemed to be feeling the same temptation, and though he did not fight back, he did give one of them an "accidental" shove with his massive shoulder before they managed to remove his backpack.

"You best water that thing if you care to keep your teeth!" Ella called after the medic holding her precious vine.

Tabitha thought of her journal, containing all her memories, now in the hands of strangers. Strangers who were holding her hostage. What kind of school was this?

Sweet Maddie surrendered her purse willingly, determined to remain dignified.

"Right this way!" beckoned the only remaining nurse with empty hands. The four followed.

CHAPTER FOUR

DETOX

Tabitha understood now why she awoke each day with headaches. In Privileged sectors, every home, every shop, and every public space was lined with wall-sized screens. Recreational drugs were not only available, they were encouraged. Binge drinking was commonplace. While Tabitha never cared much for the petty distractions, they had influenced her nonetheless.

"What can you see?"

Tabitha stood stripped of her garments and draped in a scratchy, unbecoming hospital gown. Its starchy scent had grown all too familiar. A white-clad elite held a clipboard and watched Tabitha from the corner of her eye.

Tabitha squinted and tried desperately to identify the blurry blobs printed just twenty feet away from her. The strain was more frustrating than anything. She remembered experiencing the same annoyance when looking for the first time out at the Tolliver canyons. Had she really spent so much time with her eyes averted from horizons that they'd forgotten how to see them?

"I can't," Tabitha admitted begrudgingly. "I can't see anything."

The nurse nodded and ushered her forward to a new notch in the floor. They began again.

The laser surgery to correct her eyes came first. That was when her sense of time went out the window. Her isolation was acute. Toyed with and manipulated day in and day out, Tabitha felt out of sync with her body, which the nurses poked with countless acupuncture needles. Could there be another nerve they hadn't prodded yet?

Tabitha's only comfort was that Ella, Maddie, and Toby found themselves just as incompetent as she was throughout their detoxification process. Ella experienced massive withdrawals and was in denial that she'd had a drug addition. Maddie developed a nervous tremor and couldn't bear to be in silence for more than twelve seconds. Toby suffered muscle spasms and mild seizures.

None of them had realized how much media and substance use had controlled them. Being Provision required them to regain that control. The Provision were the order in the natural world of chaos. That meant no dependencies, whether physical or mental. It was a sacrifice they made to ensure that the Privileged could live in peace; or so Tabitha had been told. When had she been told that? Was it yesterday? Or three weeks ago?

Night followed day, and day followed night, until the line between reality and dreams became unclear. The white walls of the hospital all looked the same. Tabitha saw them when she opened her eyes upon waking, and when she closed them to sleep. No windows gave her a glimpse of the sun; it made no difference if it was four in the afternoon or one in the morning.

Eventually, it was too strange to imagine that normal life was just beyond the borders of the ward's doors. Why was she here again? How long was six weeks supposed to feel like?

Tabitha scratched an itch through the sticky, plastic-infused gown draped over her figure. Her muscles felt foreign to her touch. She was neither bigger nor smaller than when she'd arrived, but her body felt different. Stronger, easier to control.

The springs of her mattress dug distantly into her rear end. Tabitha leaned forward with her hands propped on the side of the bed, and wondered again why she was in her room instead of with her nurse. What time was it?

A knock sounded at her door.

"Come in," she invited, and the door opened. Mayra Mae stepped through.

Tabitha sprung to her feet. "Mae!" she cried. "How did you get here?"

The twins embraced each other, laughing.

"I've missed you so much!" Tabitha moaned into Mayra Mae's shoulder.

Mayra Mae pulled away. She looked at Tabitha with excitement in her eyes, then turned toward the open door.

"Look," she beckoned.

Natalie walked through the frame.

Tears streamed down Tabitha's face, and she ran into her mother's arms. "It worked! They saved you!" she cheered; though she couldn't remember who "they" were. It didn't matter. Her mother was healed, and they were together again.

Then a man set foot into Tabitha's room, and time stood still.

Tabitha wasn't sure where they went, but Natalie and Mayra Mae were no longer in her peripheral vision. She saw only him.

"Dad?" she asked.

"Hello, Tabitha."

Tabitha's hands trembled. Her heart pounded in her chest and she took a timid step closer to him. He opened his arms and a smile spread across his face.

All fear left her. Tabitha broke into a sprint. She ran toward him, willing to forget all her grudges. They were a family again! He'd come back!

But he wasn't drawing any closer. Tabitha ran with all her might, yet she stayed stationary. Suddenly, her legs felt like lead. Her feet became rubbery, glued to the sterile white floor. She was sinking. The tiles wrapped around her legs like scales, cutting into her bare skin as they latched onto her.

"Dad!" she screamed, reaching up for his hands, which seemed so far away now.

Josiah folded his arms. His almond-shaped eyes turned black from corner to corner—one massive pupil with no white. His smile remained, but it was a wicked, cruel smile, which emitted a hoarse, guttural laugh. Tabitha pleaded and wailed, but her father merely stood as she fell farther and father away into nothingness.

Tabitha sat up in her bed. Her breath came out in hollow bursts and sweat dripped down her face. She looked around for her family, but they were gone. The walls were the same white, but this time the floor tiles were planted firmly on the ground.

It had been a dream.

Was this a dream, too?

Tabitha got up and padded barefoot along the cold, hospital hallway.

"Hello?" she called, her voice echoing back at her. "Hello!"

Tabitha started to run. Adrenaline pumped through her veins. She was sure that the floor tiles would clatter to life again at any moment, ready to swallow her in the abyss.

She was stopped abruptly as a pair of firm, brown hands gripped her arms.

"Tabitha, you all right?"

Tabitha was so startled, she would have slapped Ella across the face had she not been so much weaker than her muscular counterpart.

"What's happening?" Tabitha asked, still disoriented.

Ella smiled and shook her head. "We did it—we're done."

Ella led Tabitha by the hand to a bright room where Toby, Maddie, and a circle of nurses stood waiting for them. The one who had first ushered Tabitha into the hospital ward stepped forward.

"You are ready, Tabitha," she said.

• • •

When the apprentices exited the building, the sun was blinding. Tabitha blinked, and the deja vu hit her like a ton of bricks. They were in Providence. Of course they were—they had been for the past month and a half.

Tabitha gasped at the stunning surroundings as if seeing them for the first time. The only difference was that the air had dropped in temperature as winter took the seasons' stage, but it seemed prettier than she remembered it; perhaps because her eyes were now able to clearly see the intricate details, even up to the city's central skyscraper.

As her eyes adjusted to the light, Tabitha's mind also adjusted to reality. It looked the same, but a lot could have changed since she stood there last. Was her father still a felon? Was he still here? Had he ever been here?

The nurses led Tabitha and her friends through the cobblestone streets toward the entry-level apprentice apartment complex. Tabitha looked desperately about herself for some signs of her father. Suddenly, six minutes seemed like too long a time to wait for answers, regardless of the six weeks she'd spent without them. Did Providence have wanted posters?

Before Tabitha realized they had reached the apartments, she found herself face-to-face with Cassady Reinhardt. She looked less than pleased to see Tabitha again, but maintained her plastered politeness. She revealed four glittering keys, each quite different from its siblings.

"Toby," Cassady began, holding up the first key. "You'll find your apartment on the ground floor, 1F. I think your fitness needs will be more than met."

The man-child looked at the key curiously and, taking it slowly, he turned and entered the hall.

"Maddie, you'll be in apartment 5G. We've prepared your room with full wall mirrors, removable floor padding, an aerial hoop, and fabric mounts. Should you require any other equipment, please speak with your supervisor."

Maddie's round eyes widened. With a sudden burst of excitement, she took her key and ran inside gracefully on her toes.

"Ella, you'll be on the top floor, since you'll need more sunlight for your greenhouse. Apartment 7A."

"Oh, hell yeah," Ella hummed. She received her key, tossed it in the air and caught it.

"Tabitha, you're also on the seventh floor, 7C. The equipment provided will be explained by your supervisor when you meet her after Lilith's address." She handed her the key coldly.

Tabitha took it, looked her in the eyes and said warmly, "Thank you, Cassady."

The unexpected appreciation caused Cassady's chill to waver, and she parted from them with a nod.

When she had gone, Tabitha and Ella exchanged an eager smile. They pushed through the doors. At the center of the entrance room was a beautiful white spiral staircase, and decorating the walls were large photographs of Providence, important and well-known Provision elites, and maps of the Institute grounds. There were no screens.

The women ascended the stairs and reached their apartments, which were side by side, facing outward over the city.

"Knock when you're ready to give me a tour," Ella said, and entered her room.

Tabitha looked at her little gold key excitedly, pushed it into its keyhole and turned.

Tabitha's breath caught in her throat. The whole outer wall was clear glass overlooking the diamond city. Through them, she could see a sliver of the red rocks beyond the great stone barricade. Facing the window was a cozy seating area with a coffee table and throw blanket. A huge desk, a book shelf, and a hefty set of drawers were stationed against the left wall. A few paces away from them stood a tall wooden easel with a matching stool. Tabitha caressed its beams lovingly, as that same strange stirring arose in her.

Tabitha almost cried out in joy as she spotted her journal on the desk. Scooping it up, she twirled around and kissed it, then eagerly ripped open the drawers of the desk like a child unwrapping presents. In them, she found endless art supplies, along with some strange objects she couldn't identify: thin but incredibly strong wire, binoculars with too many settings, a compact gas mask, and more.

To the right, the room was divided in half by a bedroom loft with an open balcony, accessible by a rope and wooden ladder. A kitchenette occupied the space underneath, and a granite countertop with three bar stools acted as a table.

Tabitha excitedly climbed the ladder to her room. A queen-sized bed was made up with cream and gold-colored accents, beside which were dark wooden bedside tables and dressers. Everything was openly exposed except for the bathroom, which had a lavish shower and tub. Opening the closet doors, she found an extensive assortment of clothing—in countless different colors! No one wore colored garments in the Privileged sections.

Tabitha threw herself on the bed and sighed. Axelle had nothing on this.

In the hours that followed, Tabitha refreshed herself and

made the apartment her new home. Sitting at her desk, she found a piece of paper in its drawers and flattened it to draft a letter.

Dear Mayra Mae,

I know… I should have said goodbye. I'm sorry. But you'll (hopefully) be happy to hear that I'm alive and well, and Providence is spectacular. Remember that hand-me-down diamond and pearl medallion Mom keeps in her sock drawer? Picture that, except buildings. Yeah. It's pretty amazing.

I've just finished six weeks of "Detox" to acclimate to my new life here (hence the tardiness of this letter). It's set me back, but I'm better prepared for what's to come now, I think.

How is Mom? Keep me updated… I'm not entirely sure how to get or send mail here, but I'll find a way; unlike Josiah. Yes, I know— but that's his name. If I see him here, I'll let you know how our reunion goes.

Love you always, write soon.
Tabitha

Tabitha folded the note and tucked it in her journal. As the sun set violently in bloody hues and the scale-like panels retreated up to the heart of Providence, Tabitha collected her welcome packet from her arrival at the Institute, and went to find her eccentric neighbor. Together, she and Ella walked to the dining hall, where their welcome banquet awaited.

• • •

Tabitha and Ella navigated through the dining hall until they found the private banquet room reserved for the October recruitment welcome dinner. It was dimly lit by a warm chandelier, under which stood a long table, laden with perfectly placed table settings, candles, and an appetizing assortment of food. Two men and two women sat on the side facing them. On the other were empty spaces with place cards on each plate.

"Welcome!" said the first, standing. He was tall and gaunt, roughly thirty years old and had a commanding air about him despite his sullen eyes. Tabitha guessed he was the ring leader. "Please, do sit," he purred, gesturing toward a chairs with his cold, white hands.

Approaching, Tabitha saw her name printed in pretty script on the place card before her. *Madeline Meyers* was to her left, *Toby Frankfort* to her right and *Ella Reeves* to his right. "Thank you," Ella responded, and the two sat down. Maddie and Toby joined them shortly after.

The thin one introduced each member of their party. His name was Mason Boone. A curly-haired brunette sitting next to him was Leena Kitsy. To her left was Naoko Araki, a small pale woman with a gentle smile. Lastly, Bryce Connor—a rough-looking kid with a square jaw and fair complexion—sat on the end.

"Tonight is all about you," Mason began. "We're here to

answer any questions you have, share fun stories, and give you our two cents on how to make the most of your first year as an apprentice. To start, how about a toast!" He raised his glass of champagne and the others followed suit, giddy that their presence warranted an exception to the alcohol-free rule. "To the future leaders of Provision, bringing order, peace, and comfort to every person, equally," he said.

The eight of them clinked their glasses and began their feast.

As the first bite of steak touched Tabitha's tongue, she suddenly wondered if she had ever eaten real food before in her life. It was nothing like the bland, artificial grub dished out to the Privileged.

The air was thick with merriment. Small portions multiplied into massive mounds on their plates as they collected samples of every entrée. Whenever their glasses got low, Leena would offer to top them off. Though the atmosphere was elegant, they were not restricted to poise, and instead followed Bryce's example of eating like a fat king.

It wasn't long into their delightful chatter that Maddie leaned over to Tabitha and mumbled, "This champagne stuff is just—the wonderful!" Her mannerisms were less graceful than usual, and she spoke with a slur. "My dad never let me drink, nope! Even though they don't do that drinking age thing anymore... I feel warm all over the places!"

Tabitha smiled, leaned over to Toby—who had overheard—and whispered, "She's the cutest lightweight I've ever seen!"

He nodded in agreement, blushing a little, and his eyes lingered on Maddie a bit longer than was socially acceptable.

"Ah, what a feast!" Mason said at last when the passing of platters had ceased and chewing had slowed. "But would you believe you can eat like this every day? You don't have to, but it's always here for you—as are we."

"Yes!" Noako piped in. "Anything you need! You can see us as your big brothers and sisters."

"The Institute is like a family," Leena agreed. "Your supervisors aren't just your instructors, they're like aunts and uncles. They learn about you and your life and get real personal. And the teachers are so friendly, helping you become your new self! Lilith is like a mom to everyone."

The four elders nodded in agreement.

"That's right," Bryce said, "don't mess with Mama!"

"That's interesting," Ella commented, "Lilith just seems so important, I wouldn't expect her to be that close with the apprentices."

"Thankfully, the Institute is very selective about its recruits, so we are few enough that she can get to know everyone personally," Mason responded. "It's one of the many beauties of Providence!"

"What exactly is it that the recruits look for when selecting new apprentices?" Tabitha asked. She wondered what it must be like for those of them who had actually earned their acceptance, not blackmailed their way in.

"Individuality. Awareness. Creativity. Drive. We look for the people who don't look at the screens," answered Mason, "You may have experienced some withdrawals in Detox, but here you are—six weeks later, completely functional. Anyone else in the Privileged sectors would go crazy in a distraction-free environment like this."

"You've heard it said that ideas are dangerous," Leena added. "We find the people with ideas and foster those thoughts into something good. Our recruits are the ones with superior gifts or intellect, who have something unique to contribute to society."

"How can there be superior people if everyone is equal?" asked Toby.

Naoko and Bryce looked at Mason and Leena, unable to answer.

"We've grown up being told that no one is better than anyone else," Toby continued. "Is that just a cover to pacify the Privileged?"

"Everyone is equal within their own playing field," Leena said, mildly defensive. "The Privileged could not exist without someone to provide for them. We are not greater than them, per se, but we have certain gifts that make us... different. So we come here, and become Provision."

"Yes," Mason went on, "if we lived among the Privileged, it may be cause for jealousy. By relocating to the Provision sectors, we not only increase Privileged satisfaction by our absence, we enhance it by what we go on to do for them."

"It's a noble sacrifice," Naoko remarked.

"Yeah," Bryce agreed, "but we're justly rewarded for it. Clearly!" He indicated the food before them.

"I guess that makes sense," Maddie commented, trying to ease the tension caused by Toby's question. "Though, it is strange—being on the other side."

"That's normal. You'll get used to it the more you're enlightened," chimed Naoko, kindly. "You'll be doing such a good thing for humanity! That's the best reward of all: to know you've helped bring order to a chaotic world."

The four of them nodded again, satisfied with their answer.

Toby didn't seem convinced. "Why are there gates between the entry-level apprentices and the elders? If the only two classes are Privileged and Provision, and we're all equal within our class, shouldn't we be able to go inside the inner gates?"

"You're still in a transitional period," answered Naoko. "Technically you are neither Privileged nor Provision at this point. Once you graduate your first stage, you'll be able to talk with the rest of the elders."

"Wait, you mean we can't even talk with them?" Ella asked suspiciously.

Naoko shifted in her seat. "Um, no, well—you see, there are some things you can't know—I mean, you can talk to us," she stumbled.

Mason cut her off. "Naoko, don't you have somewhere to be right now?"

She looked at him, open-mouthed. Sweat beaded on her forehead.

"Oh yes! Is it that time already?" Leena continued. "You really should get going. You'll be late!"

Naoko looked back and forth between them nervously.

Bryce stood, his massive shoulders casting a shadow over her face. "I'll walk you out," he said with a hand toward a back door.

Naoko reluctantly stood and, like a dog with its tail tucked between its legs, went through the door, Bryce close at her heels. The four apprentices watched the scene unfold, unsure of how to react.

Tabitha felt uncomfortable. Something was wrong.

It's not your problem, she told herself. If this frail little woman had made some slip up that put her against Mason's good favor, Tabitha wasn't about to vouch for her.

Mason beamed a broad smile. "Now, where were we?" he said, "Ah yes! Leena, won't you tell us that delightful story of when you earned your first elite perk?"

Leena laughed, "Oh my goodness, it was incredible! Everyone was so supportive…"

She babbled on about how wonderful it all was, about the funny things Carey Finn said and Josh Something-or-Other did. The tension died down, and Bryce slipped back into the room quietly. They laughed and spoke of agreeable things, and no one asked any more questions.

CHAPTER FIVE

A FAMILIAR FACE

THE GRAND AUDITORIUM WHERE LILITH'S ADDRESS was going to be was packed with people. It had a high ceiling and glamorous stage. The structure was rounded, and the seating was wider than it was deep, so that everyone could have a spot close to the stage. No one was higher than anyone else, except for the speaker at the podium.

Tabitha scanned the scene. Apprentices talked loudly from their seats and in groups around the doors. Cassady shuffled about on stage, preparing the podium for the headmistress. Ella, Maddie, and Toby sat together, quietly observing it all, and the elders from their welcome banquet—Mason, Leena, and Bryce—stood nearby. There was no sign of Naoko.

Tabitha continued her scan. The room was brightly lit, both with natural and man-made light. Like the entire city, everything was lightly colored, which made the auditorium feel larger than it really was. In truth, there were only about fifty people in the room, seven of whom Tabitha already knew—or was it… eight?

"Well, look who it is."

A familiar pair of blue eyes—wounded blue eyes—confronted her. It was the man from the Music Department, but he was no stranger.

I know you... Tabitha searched her memory. It took her a moment, but it clicked; and when it did, her poker face shattered. He was, in fact, the very same man she had blown off at the Provisionary grocery section, just months before.

She hadn't noticed then how tall he was, or how angular his jaw; perhaps because it hadn't been clenched before. He appeared more intimidating now, with his broad shoulders and big paws, callused and strong. But she recognized his eyes: those blue rimmed pupils—once an ocean of kindness, now ready to pick a fight under that worn and heavy brow.

"Thought you'd gotten rid of me, did ya? Sorry to disappoint," he commented coolly.

Tabitha shifted from one foot to the other. "How are you here?" she finally blurted, not meaning to be rude, but unable to find a less blunt way to cut to the chase.

"Ambrose Hurley."

"What?"

"My name is Ambrose Hurley; it's good to meet you too." He held out his hand and she took it slowly, still perplexed and a little bit frightened. Her cruel behavior toward men seldom came back to bite her.

But Ambrose didn't bite. He laughed suddenly, beaming a wide smile wrapped in laughter lines. Tabitha didn't join him. Surely it was a trap.

"Don't worry, Sweetheart, all is forgiven." His voice was deep and warm, and in his expression she saw again the selfless man who had reached out to catch a rebellious can of soup.

"Right," Tabitha finally replied, letting her guard down ever so slightly. "The name's Tabitha—not *Sweetheart*—Tabitha Beckett. What brings you to Providence? I didn't see you audition in Axelle."

"No, but I saw you," Ambrose replied. "You're quite the little artist!" He paused, smiled wryly and added, "Con artist, that is."

Guard back up.

"Excuse me?" Tabitha interjected.

Ambrose just laughed again. "Think I didn't pick up on the tension between you two? I've never seen Logan so nervous! But don't worry, I think it was overlooked by most."

"Oh, but *you* noticed?" she challenged.

"I'm very perceptive."

Apparently not, Tabitha thought, wondering when he'd pick up on her distaste for the conversation. The two stared each other down for a moment. Tabitha wasn't used to being on the defensive. She didn't like it.

"You still haven't told me why you're here," she diverted.

"A better question would be why I was there," Ambrose answered. "I was recruited three months ago. The recruitment team brought me with them to Axelle as part of my apprenticeship."

"What for?"

"Crowd control."

Tabitha sized him up and concluded that this was not far-fetched in the slightest.

"Wonderful," Ambrose finally said in conclusion. "Now I know you and you know me. Does that make us friends?"

"Not in the slightest," she jabbed.

"That's too bad. What will you do if your soup runs away again?"

"Live happily ever after." Tabitha turned to walk away.

Ambrose laughed in mockery. "I highly doubt that."

She whipped back around. "What do you mean?"

"Just look at you! I swear, there's a three-foot radius of negative energy around you. You may as well paint *piss off* across your forehead."

It was Tabitha's turn to clench her jaw. "I have good reason for that."

"Oh yeah? And what might that be?"

"None of your business!"

He studied her. "I'll figure you out soon enough, Sweetheart," he ventured.

"Like hell you will. And quit calling me *Sweetheart*, I don't appreciate your flirting."

"Flirting? Is that what you think that was?" he chuckled.

"Why else would you help a total stranger in a Provisionary?"

"Hun, that's called kindness."

"It's Tabitha."

"Right. If I had been flirting with you, that *piss off* would have melted off your forehead in an instant."

"And why's that?"

Ambrose grinned crookedly. "You're smart." He stepped uncomfortably close to her. "Figure it out."

Tabitha shook off the sudden wave of—what even was that? *Just walk away, Tabitha!*

"If you think for a moment that sheer charm could win me over, guess again. There's not a man in the world that can lure my heart to his."

Ambrose stepped suddenly back with an indifferent shrug. "Good thing that was never my intention!"

The nerve! Tabitha planted her feet down hard and shook a finger in his face, flustered. "See this, this right here, is why I don't trust your species."

"Wow Sweetheart, that's a low blow—"

"My name is Tabitha!" she shouted, louder than she'd meant to.

A handful of heads turned in their seats, and Tabitha strained to reel in her anger. She expected Ambrose to make that difficult—but to her surprise, he stopped pushing.

When she turned back toward him, he averted his eyes to the floor. A strange expression came over his face that Tabitha didn't understand. His cool, arrogant demeanor faded, and when he looked up at her again, his eyes were gentle once more.

"Tabitha," he said softly—so softly.

A sudden calm came over her. He took a strangely timid step closer, and she felt her heartbeat quicken, but her hands stayed clasped in tight fists at her side. Ambrose opened his mouth to speak, taking in a small breath as if to give himself a moment more to form the words.

"Mr. Hurley, if you don't mind?" Cassady's voice in the microphone caused Tabitha to startle.

Ambrose stepped abruptly away from her and nodded to Cassady in acknowledgement.

"Excuse me," he said politely, and retreated to the back of the room.

Tabitha's eyes followed the puppeteer, who had so easily played her at her own game.

She hated him.

Ambrose sat in a chair concealed in shadow, pulled a cello from a large case, and turned on a pedal loop station. Quietly, he began to play a very soft melody, hardly noticeable by the crowd. He recorded a loop, then played over it in haunting harmonies.

Tabitha felt a wave of goosebumps crawl down her arms and tension leave her shoulders as the music swept over her. There it was again—that strange clash of excitement and calm that she'd felt when she first witnessed Providence. Was it the effect of beauty? It then dawned on her that, with the exception of her mother's lullabies, the Privileged didn't really listen to music at all.

She couldn't fight its effect—and part of her didn't want to. Hiding an unintentional sigh, Tabitha looked around to find that she wasn't the only one. The whole room had begun to grow quiet. People relaxed in their chairs, and soon the noise level was next to nothing. As they hushed, his music got quieter and quieter, then stopped.

"Thank you for gathering here today!" Cassady began once there was silence.

Tabitha looked back at Ambrose in awe at what had just happened. He met her gaze with a smirk and a wave that was like looking into a mirror. She quickly broke eye contact. *Crowd control*, she repeated to herself. She did her best not to appear as impressed as she was.

Tabitha sat down by Ella, who'd been talking with a short man seated next to her who looked older than he probably was. He had a broad face speckled with stubble and shaggy black hair scattered in all directions. He slouched in his chair past the point where Tabitha thought could be comfortable.

"Tabitha, Milo. Milo, Tabitha," Ella introduced, nudging Milo so he'd look up from a notepad in his lap.

"Hi there," he said with a mild stutter, extending a hand for a sturdy shake.

"Hello," Tabitha said in return, though she was hoping to evade yet another difficult conversation.

To her surprise, he beamed a wide grin, but then quickly went back to jotting something down on the notepad. She let out a sigh of relief and looked back at Cassady. Just when Tabitha thought herself free of uncomfortable interactions, however, Ambrose eased his way into the seat next to Milo. They showed all the signs of being best bros. *Figures,* she thought.

"In just a moment, you will have the privilege of hearing from our very own founder, the revolutionary woman who brought our beloved Providence into being," Cassady announced. "Though we all know and love her as the mother of our day, she would claim she merely continued what was started long ago by the giants upon whose shoulders she stands."

The window curtains were lowered and the lights dimmed to accentuate a screen that appeared on stage. It was the first Tabitha had seen in Providence since arriving. As Cassady spoke, it began to flash images and video clips.

"A long time ago, there lived a woman named Alice," Cassady said. "Alice envisioned a unified society, a new age of peace and plenty. Amid a world of war and weapons, she imagined an existence where the strong demonstrated restraint toward the weak. This new group of world servers would lead in giving vision for the betterment of humanity. Now, centuries later, her dream has come true.

"But first there was war. There was devastation and ruin at every turn, and such a marvelous idea seemed difficult to imagine. Still, the wars that raged also gave society an opportunity to rebuild itself. Scarred by the impact of nuclear weapons, the country awoke and chose to abolish such violent tools of death. The believers of a better world attained a huge victory when guns were banned from the public and reserved for select elite peacekeepers only.

"We had not yet procured peace, however. This was only the beginning of many radical shifts for Grexovium. Next, under the leadership of Master Karl Thorne, the monetary system was replaced by provisions equally distributed to all, ensuring the eradication of poverty. A few years later, organized religion was removed—along with all other expressions of division—and gradually the New Order began to take shape."

Milo shifted noticeably in his seat.

"But the system was still unstable. Believe it or not, not

everybody believed in peace, and a rebel group known as *Exodus* rose up in an attempt to assassinate our beloved Master Karl Thorne, who had made so much progress for the population.

"Fortunately, they were unsuccessful. More than that, they were the very reason the New Order decided to reform the education system to prevent these false teachings that threatened the peace. Headmistress Lilith Damara took the burden upon her shoulders, creating this institute to replace all other methods of higher education. In so doing, she secured the sector system and solved the imbalance of power in Grexovium.

"This year, thanks to her, we celebrate thirty-five years of educating people of peace! She was only twenty-nine at the time, much like some of you. Now imagine what you can go on to do, standing upon her shoulders. You are the new face of Provision, bringing order to a once chaotic world.

"Please welcome: Lilith Damara!"

Lilith was beautiful. She didn't look like she was in her early sixties. Her skin was only lightly wrinkled and she stood with strength and composure. Her hair was short and silvery blonde, elegantly styled in large curls cropped at the base of her neck.

Tabitha used to poke fun at Lilith when she'd show up on TV, but now that she stood before her in the flesh, Tabitha felt a strange draw to her, like the calming enchantment of Ambrose's music. She understood now why everyone called her motherly, especially when her smooth voice began to speak.

"Welcome, new recruits," she said, warmly but abruptly.

Though akin to music, her speech was quick and to-the-point. "It once was said that peace comes at a price. We are that price. We, the elites and soon-to-be Provision, are the source of Privileged life, of peace and security.

"It is a noble thing you've done, leaving home and Privileged society to come here, and you have been specially chosen for this task. Each one of you is unique, unlike the Privileged. You are superior, in a way, and with superiority comes responsibility.

"Do not be surprised, then, if we expect high standards of you. You *will* prove yourselves worthy of the title *Provision.* You *will* follow the instructions of your trainers without question or exception. And rebellious behavior of any kind *will not* be tolerated."

The new recruits looked around at one another. Those who had witnessed the address before, with the exception of Ambrose, showed no signs of unease.

"But," Lilith continued, "that is no reason to be afraid. Providence is your home now, and should you require anything—anything at all, you need only ask. I will personally see to it that you receive everything necessary to become the elites you were born to be. Thank you."

The crowd applauded and Lilith dismounted the podium into the shadow of the stage's curtains, where she stood stoically. Tabitha could faintly see another woman beside her, roughly forty years old and similar in facial structure. Lilith's daughter, Tabitha presumed. The woman held her hands together over her stomach.

"Any questions?" asked Cassady, who had returned to the podium. A large, scruffy hand shot into the air a few seats from Tabitha.

"Yes, Toby?"

"How often do we get to visit home?"

Cassady hesitated, then concluded, "You don't. Next?"

An image of Mayra Mae flashed into Tabitha's mind.

Toby's hand rose once more. Cassady reluctantly indicated that he may speak again.

"What if we change our minds and want to leave the Institute?"

Tabitha glanced warily at her broad-shouldered friend. Cassady had her phony pleasant face on again, where she looked happy but you could tell she hated you.

"I don't think you'll have any reason to want that!" she chuckled. "You'll leave when you graduate and move into your Provision sector."

Cassady moved on, but he persisted, this time without raising a hand. "How do we decide what our job is going to be?"

"That's not for you to choose," she answered, growing more impatient. "That will be decided for you after your evaluation with your supervisor, who can answer any further questions you might have." Cassady clapped her hands together. "That's all the time we have for now! Feel free to meet and mingle with your fellow entry-level apprentices as you wait for your supervisor to come find you."

A wild hum erupted over the crowd as the apprentices began to talk. Tabitha started, unable to process the implications of the information, and disappointed that Toby had taken up all the Q&A time. She was surprised, too, that he'd had so many questions. For one with so dull a voice, he seemed to have a head on his shoulders. She'd seen his physical strength in Detox, but had underestimated his strength of will.

For a moment, she worried that her friendship with him might become a problem.

The apprentices began to "mix and mingle," most simply flocking to their pre-existing cliques; though a handful approached Toby and Maddie to introduce themselves. Tabitha found herself staring right back into those pestering blue eyes. Her budding friendship with Ella stopped her from seeking alternative company.

"I could recite that speech blindfolded!" Ambrose spouted with a stretch.

"What do you mean?" Tabitha asked.

"They give the same one every time a new group of recruits is brought in," Ambrose explained, "and all entry-level apprentices are required to attend. Same exact lines, every time: *Rebellious behavior of any kind will not be tolerated,*" he mimicked. He glanced momentarily at them from the corner of his eye as if to judge their reactions.

Suddenly, Ambrose sat up from his lazy, lounging position and leaned toward them. In a hushed voice, he asked, "Doesn't that seem odd to you?"

Tabitha glanced at Lilith, who was still in the shadow of the stage with her daughter. Why *would* she tolerate rebellion? It seemed more odd to rebel in the first place.

"Conspiracy theorist," Milo accused without making eye contact.

Tabitha and Ella looked at one another, but said nothing.

Ambrose shrugged, then changed the subject. "I haven't met you yet. My name's Ambrose," he said to Ella.

"Ella Reeves," she replied with a smile. "I don't think I've shaken so many hands in my life," she pointed out. "I like not having any screens on the walls; people actually look at each other."

She glanced at Milo, who had his face in his notes again, muttering to himself with an occasional scratch of his head.

"Well, *some* people," she added.

"But what if-if the arroyo was actually a p-prehistoric wall…" Milo suddenly said out loud.

Tabitha and Ella looked at him, confusedly.

"I'm sorry?" Tabitha asked.

Milo shook his head quickly, eyes clenched shut. "No. Could you please—just—don't interrupt me when I'm talking to myself!"

Ambrose smiled apologetically and said, "He does that."

"You need to put your dog on a leash," Ella told Ambrose, like a stern mother. "What is he muttering about, anyway?"

"Milo is an archaeologist, so probably… rocks."

"That's *geo*logy, not *archae*ology, Ambrose," Milo said, returning again to reality.

Ambrose grinned and shook his head.

Well this has been fun…

"It was nice to meet you both," Tabitha lied, "but I need to go introduce myself to someone."

She stood and turned her head in search of Lilith. If Cassady wouldn't answer Tabitha's questions, maybe Lilith would. She would certainly know if the "hottest gossip in Providence," Josiah Clay, was still at large.

Tabitha started to leave, but Ambrose stood suddenly and reached for her arm, beckoning her to wait. Tabitha whipped herself away from his grasp and looked fiercely into his eyes.

"Tabitha, listen—" he started, glancing at the others uncomfortably. "I'm sorry about earlier; that was uncalled for."

Tabitha narrowed her eyes but was saved the necessity of giving a response. Just then, a quiet-looking man approached Ambrose and touched him lightly on the elbow. Ambrose turned and, seeing him, bid his companions goodbye, and was gone.

Tabitha huffed.

"What happened earlier?" Ella asked.

"It was nothing," Tabitha diverted.

Ella raised her eyebrows just as Tabitha's mother would have done. Ella could see right through her bull.

"He played me like a puppet," admitted Tabitha, "twisting my words and turning them back on me. It wasn't a big deal, but faking an apology just to get the last word in? Mature, real mature."

"Fake?" Milo looked up for the first time.

There was a pause.

"What, you expect me to believe that was serious?" Tabitha provoked.

Milo shook his head. "Nah, nah, you see, Ambrose, he

just says what's on his mind, you know? I mean, it's not always a good thing, a lot of times it's inappropriate—or, not inappropriate, exactly; I guess it's what you might call, in*opportune*—which, granted, can rub the wrong way—"

"What's your point, little man?" Ella interrupted.

Milo shot her a perturbed glare. "My p-point is he's not a liar. Everything that comes out of Ambrose's mouth is as true as he knows it to be. If he said he's sorry, he's sorry."

"Well, I'm sure he hates me regardless," Tabitha dropped.

"Trust me: if he hated you, you would know."

Tabitha resigned and searched the room again for her target. In the few minutes that Ambrose had interrupted her, Lilith had retreated behind the curtains of the stage. She wasn't sure when she'd get another opportunity to butter up the headmistress, but she was determined to get on her good side. She needed allies in power if she was ever going to find her father and get those medications.

Just then, a sleek woman with straight, black hair down to her waist approached Tabitha and gently tapped her on the shoulder.

"Tabitha," she said with confident grace, "my name is Rebecca Moore, your supervisor. Please follow me."

CHAPTER SIX

APPRENTICE

REBECCA LED TABITHA TO A LARGE white room with no windows and thick sound-proof walls. It reminded Tabitha uncomfortably of the hospital ward. A simple white table sat in the middle of the room with a chair standing at attention on either side, and on it was a thick folder bound with a string. She shuddered as she heard the door close securely behind her.

Rebecca had a long face, oval shaped with a very straight nose, and in her eyes was wisdom. She put a long-fingered hand to one of the chairs and pulled it out, offering the seat to Tabitha. Taking the other, she sat and looked at her new apprentice for a while without speaking.

"Don't be afraid," Rebecca said at last.

"I'm not afraid," Tabitha responded.

Rebecca nodded her head gently. "I believe you."

She gathered the folder and sifted through its contents, then spoke. "Your name is not Tabitha Beckett; it's Tabitha Clay—daughter of Josiah Clay. You lived with your mother Natalie and twin sister Mayra Mae in the Privileged sector of Axelle, working at the bakery on Elm Street. You carry a sketch book with you wherever you go and you check your mail at the Provisionary every day, yet you never send the letters you bring there. Your mother lies on the verge of death from extra-pulmonary tuberculosis in the spine, deprived of much-needed medicine which you are here to acquire. Do you deny it?"

Tabitha lost her composure completely. Collecting herself, she replied feebly, "No."

"Good," Rebecca went on, in her calm, gentle voice. "Because Tabitha—there are no secrets that will not come to light. Lilith knows everything about you. Remember that."

So much for being in control.

"We would like, however," Rebecca went on, "if Lilith and I remain the only people who know your true identity."

You and me both, Tabitha thought. "Why?" she asked.

"Are you aware of the situation regarding your father?"

Tabitha swallowed hard. This was it. This was where she got to ask questions, and get answers. Yet, now that the moment had come, the tone in Rebecca's voice and the pit that hollowed out Tabitha's stomach made her wonder if she really wanted to know.

"Only that he's a felon," she managed.

Rebecca carefully removed a photograph from her packet and slipped it on the table before her. Tabitha froze, afraid that if she budged, the kind and familiar face in the portrait would come to life and turn on her like the foe in her dream.

It was no mugshot. Josiah stood proudly in a freshly-ironed

midnight blue uniform. A peacekeeper's symbol adorned his lapel.

"He was a peacekeeper?" Tabitha asked hesitantly.

"More than that," Rebecca corrected. "*Chief* Clay was Head of Security: the best of the best."

Tabitha felt something strange in the area of her heart. Whether it was awe, pride, or relief, she wasn't sure; but it felt good. It felt like hope.

A hope that was short-lived.

"That's why it was such a shock when he went rogue," Rebecca commented. "The higher the value, the greater the loss. And Lilith valued him highest of all."

Tabitha's heart sank. "What happened?" she asked. Her voice sounded dry and foreign.

Rebecca folded her long fingers. "Josiah Clay came to the Institute three years ago, roughly around this time—as I'm sure you remember. After two years, he had completed both his entry-level and elder apprenticeships, and landed an elite job here in Providence. On top of that, he went from Junior Peacekeeper to Head of Security almost overnight. No one has ever managed a feat like that, especially at his age.

"It's only speculation, but rumor spread that Josiah's leap to success could be attributed to his connection with the Damara family, specifically Lilith's only daughter, Athaliah."

Tabitha remembered the woman in shadow beside Lilith at her opening address, how close they seemed as they whispered beyond ear's reach.

"The Damaras are very private when it comes to personal

affairs, so I can't say I know the full nature of Athaliah and Josiah's friendship," Rebecca went on, "but the two were publicly amicable—until five months ago, when she accused him of rape."

Tabitha clenched the armrests of her chair, digging her nails into them until her hands were white and pinpricked with pain. Taking a deep breath, she released them and wiped the sweat of her palms on her jeans, desperately fighting the stinging sensation behind her eyes.

"Tabitha," Rebecca said, her tone more sensitive this time, "I understand that, Josiah being your father, this is probably very difficult for you; if at any point you want me to stop, just say the word—"

"No," Tabitha cut her off, shaking her head. "No. I need to know. Besides—I didn't expect much better from him."

Rebecca looked mournfully at Tabitha, but nodded in agreement.

"Is that," Tabitha asked, "why you don't want anyone to know I'm his daughter, so they won't associate me with a rapist?"

Rebecca pursed her lips. "Not exactly."

Tabitha listened.

Rebecca began again slowly. "Lilith doesn't get shaken up easily, but she was beside herself with fury over this. Naturally. At any rate, word got around that Josiah had managed yet another impossible feat: shaking Lilith up—and there are a handful of radical individuals who see him as an inspiration for it."

"An inspiration?" Tabitha gasped. "For raping someone?"

"It's not so much what he did that inspires them, but who he did it to… it's difficult to explain. Lilith has been running this Institute without opposition for 35 years. Josiah was a first—the first person to challenge her, and by extension, challenge the peace."

"But who would want to do that?" Tabitha asked, disgusted. Suddenly, a pair of light blue eyes came to mind. Ambrose.

"Rebels," Rebecca replied. "They are few, but they exist. They're the ones we need to protect you from, Tabitha. People like that, if they discovered your relationship to Josiah, might try to use you as bait."

"Bait for who—Josiah? He's still out there?"

"Yes. And the radicals are probably as desperate to find him as we are. That's why knowledge of your true identity must be contained, in order to keep you out of harm's way. Do you understand?"

Tabitha nodded. "How did he escape in the first place?"

"After Athaliah accused him, we began an investigation to justify an arrest. You don't just turn Security against its head without solid evidence, and we didn't have much to go off of. But before we could prove him guilty or otherwise, he disappeared. We took that as a confession. The hunt has been on ever since."

"How has he evaded you for so long?" Tabitha asked.

Rebecca raised her eyebrows in exasperation. "Josiah was Head of Security for a reason. Despite the rumors about the Damara family's good favor, he earned that position. I worked under him, and can attest to his skill set. He was exceptional.

Always had a knack for spotting inconsistencies or cracks in the system, and improvising under pressure—a trait he passed down to you, I believe.

"Obviously, there aren't many places for him to go. The city is rather small and well-secured, and no one could survive outside the walls for very long. Somehow, he's managed to hide within Providence, or break out and brave the Tolliver wilderness."

"And those are the only leads you have, from deduction?" Tabitha inquired. "No thumb scans, no security camera footage?"

"As you've surely noticed," Rebecca answered, "Providence has hardly any modern tech. Computer systems can fail, but we have physics on our side. No thumb scanners to get in and out, no phone lines to be tapped, no security cameras to be tampered with. We're impenetrable.

"Josiah's case is a perfect example as to why Providence is set up this way. Our few Security members who do have photography clearance offered some evidence to use in his investigation, but someone managed to break into the system and delete all files pertaining to him—most likely Josiah himself. All we have left are hard-copy notes, eye-witness accounts, and old-school spy clues."

Tabitha fixed her gaze on a groove in the desk and stared at it without words to say. The case seemed beyond hope.

When Rebecca spoke again, however, her voice was filled with an unexpected fiery confidence. "That's all Josiah ever needed, though. He could find a devil in Heaven using just his wits and a sketchbook." Rebecca leaned in across the table. "Another trait, I believe, he passed down to *you*."

Tabitha tilted her head inquisitively. Rebecca stared intently into her eyes.

"We need your help, Tabitha."

"Me?"

"The day you were recruited, I understand you blackmailed Officer Logan Malloy, is that correct?"

Tabitha blushed slightly, but did not deny it.

"We've kept his secret quiet, seeing as it could lose him his job—but it may surprise you to learn that it wasn't your blackmail that convinced him to give you clearance."

Tabitha listened.

Rebecca spoke on with excitement. "You went completely unnoticed in attaining information about his affair. You learned about your target and interacted with him according to how you predicted he would respond. You reacted quickly to the curve balls thrown at you and found a solution to them, flying by the seat of your pants. You fearlessly carried out an audacious plan that gave him no way out, and *that*, Tabitha, is the kind of unwavering nerve it takes to take on a case like this."

Tabitha hesitated. "You want me to hunt down my own father?"

There was a pause.

"*Regrettably…*" Rebecca said at last.

Tabitha looked up, confused.

"That's what you said to Logan: that Josiah was *regrettably* your father. Did you mean it?"

Tabitha swallowed hard. She hadn't meant it then… but now? She nodded.

"Then yes. That's exactly what I'm asking you to do."

Tabitha shifted in her seat.

"And if you manage it," Rebecca went on, "you get this."

Rebecca pulled a dark glass jar from a drawer and set it on the table. The label read, *Rifampin*.

The pills inside the bottle rattled as Tabitha lifted it cautiously. She'd done it. The medication she'd spent the last three years of her life trying to acquire were in her hands.

Tabitha looked up at her supervisor, who concluded, "You catch your father, your mother lives."

CHAPTER SEVEN

FAVORITISM

When Tabitha woke up the next morning, her angels and demons waged war loudly in her mind. Scampering down her loft ladder, she made herself some coffee as the sun rose to greet her through her massive window pane, and she peered out over the city with the pair of high-tech binoculars she'd found in her drawers.

Was she really doing this? For three years, Tabitha's life had revolved around two ambitions: solving the problem of her mom and the puzzle of her dad. Now, doing the latter would earn her the first—two birds with one stone, right? Yet, she never dreamt that repairing her family would involve putting one of its members behind bars. Could she manage it?

Maybe not before, but after what he did…

Yes, Tabitha decided. She could do it. Innocent, guilty, or otherwise, working with Rebecca on the Clay case would earn her perks for her mother and bring her closer to meeting her father again. At the very least, she'd find some answers.

Rebecca had explained that typically, an entry-level

apprentice like herself would wait to start their practicum until they'd completed their first set of core classes. Since Josiah's case was time-sensitive, she'd taken the liberty of making an exception.

Tabitha would be taking *People & The Mind, A History of The New Order, Elite Excellence* and *Survival of the Fittest* with the rest of the new recruits, along with some specialized classes Rebecca had selected for her: *Introduction to Criminal Justice* and *Disguises for Stealth & Stage.* At the same time, the two of them would jump right into the Clay case.

Tabitha fidgeted with the bottle of *Rifampin* that Rebecca had given her the day before. The weight of the information she'd received and the burden of her new purpose made every inch of her feel heavy. A very tiny part of her was starting to miss Detox.

A knock sounded at the door.

Tabitha quickly hid the binoculars and jar of medicine in her drawer of strange gadgets, which she now realized were intended for her use in the Clay case. She opened the door just a crack and peeked through it suspiciously. It was Maddie.

"Hi Tabitha!" she peeped, "Can I come in?"

Tabitha let her in with some hesitation, wondering what would call for such a meeting. She quickly learned that spontaneous girl talk before class was a normal and acceptable thing.

"I wasn't sure who to talk to," Maddie started, "but I simply had to tell someone!"

"And you thought of me?" Tabitha asked.

"Of course! You're the only one I feel like I know at all;

well, you and Ella, and Toby…" She trailed off with the last name. "But I trust you the most. You're so confident and wise! If there's anyone I should ask for guidance, I figured it's you."

"Wow—thanks, Maddie," Tabitha responded, surprised and touched by Maddie's trust.

Tabitha caught the sudden unexpected warmth with caution. She hadn't come to Providence to make friends.

But having a confidante was rapidly growing in appeal. With everything she'd learned about her father the day before, and with no Mayra Mae there to open her heart to, Tabitha wondered if maybe—maybe she could tell Maddie… just a little bit…

"What is it you need to talk about?" Tabitha asked.

Maddie smiled, then took a deep breath. "Okay," she said with some hesitation. "Now, you have to promise not to tell anyone—"

"Hold up. Are y'all having girl talk without me?" asked Ella, who had just let herself in. She waltzed sassily across the floor, shaking her head in disapproval.

"I can tell you, too," Maddie said in earnest, distressed at her own carelessness in leaving Ella out.

She started to speak, but Ella held up a hand in protest. "Nope!" She looked at her watch. "It'll have to wait—we're gonna be late for our first class!"

Ella turned around just in time to see Milo poke his head around the corner.

"'Sup, nerd?" Milo addressed her.

"Speak for yourself," Ella replied haughtily.

Tabitha wasn't sure how she felt about the assumed open-door policy. Suddenly, she felt a knot in her stomach as she remembered that Milo and Ambrose were a package deal. Sure enough, Ambrose peeked his head through the door moments after, followed by Toby.

"Good morning!" Toby greeted cheerfully.

Maddie blushed and looked bashfully away.

"I guess my *do not disturb* sign fell off the door, huh?" Tabitha dropped.

Ambrose merely grinned. "Come on," he beckoned. "Dr. Buckley's got something special planned for you guys."

They arrived with the other entry-level apprentices at a spacious classroom similar to the auditorium, and sat at a span of long tables. When the room had filled and the clock struck the hour, their teacher took the floor.

"Good morning and welcome to *People & The Mind!*" he began, raising his pudgy hands in the air. He was a stocky fellow, heavy in the gut and jolly in the face. He peered at them through thick, round, frameless glasses. "For those of you I haven't had the privilege of meeting yet, my name is Dr. Hugh Buckley, and I'll be teaching you the art of understanding people—through psychology and sociology."

Dr. Buckley had a way of pausing sporadically as he spoke and jutting his head out every time he over-emphasized a word—which happened multiple times per sentence, on average. His voice was raspy, but simultaneously cheery and warm.

"Today we'll be learning about the effects of an environment—that being the sensory elements present at any given time—on one's mood and therefore their perception and opinion of a concept. To start, I'd like to walk you through a social experiment. Mr. Hurley—as we agreed?"

Ambrose nodded and left his seat.

"If you would please, break into groups of five, and I'll give you a topic to discuss. Please designate one member of your group to take notes. This member will remain silent, and merely observe. Begin."

Tabitha, Ella, Maddie, Milo and Toby turned to face one another, as the rest of the room followed suit and Ambrose set up in the front.

It was decided that Tabitha should be the note-taker. Donning her new role, she immediately began to survey the environment. The apprentices were still talking happily, and it was only then that she noticed that Ambrose was playing his cello. The song was rather happy, with bright tones and quick notes. Dr. Buckley stood by a panel of light switches near the door.

"Now," he announced, "if you would, please discuss your thoughts on pets. Begin."

The apprentices turned to one another, rather unsure.

"Pets?" Maddie started. "I'm not sure what I think about them… but I had a rabbit when I was little."

Toby smiled at her, and she timidly smiled back.

"All I know is that cats are disgusting," Milo pouted.

"Oh, get over yourself," Ella said.

"I guess I'm just more of a dog person," Milo clarified. "I have a little black pug. Good ol' Spikenard."

"You named him Spikenard?" Ella judged.

"Correction: I named *her* Spikenard. And yes." Ella raised an eyebrow. "What? It's biblical!"

"Isn't reading the Bible frowned upon in Grexovium?" Ella asked.

"Not if you're an archaeologist. It's kind of a major historical artifact."

They continued to jokingly bicker in this way for some time, when Tabitha noticed a change in Ambrose's playing. It suddenly became sad—no, not quite sad, more like bittersweet. Dr. Buckley gradually dimmed the lights and opened the window curtains. Little by little, the conversation began to change its flavor. Dr. Buckley walked throughout the class and placed a kitten on each table, to their surprise.

"Aw!" Maddie gasped, and reached out for a pet. "I miss Biggles," she commented, looking off nostalgically.

They all reached out and interacted with the animal in their own way.

"I had a ferret once," Ella mentioned, smiling slightly to herself. She chuckled at her own thought. "We had about fifteen different names for him… none of which should be spoken in civilized company."

"I have to admit… my love for animals trumps my hatred for cats," Milo said as he tenderly stroked the kitten.

Tabitha watched in amazement as all of their demeanors aligned, overwhelmed by nostalgia. She took notes.

Suddenly, Dr. Buckley took the kittens away and bellowed, "Next topic: parents. Go."

Tabitha swallowed hard, grateful that she didn't have to speak. Maddie was again the first to answer.

"My parents were lovely!" she chimed. "My dad used to kiss me goodnight every night before bed and call me his Little Sweetums. And my mom, well... my mom..."

The curtains closed, and the lights remained dim. Ambrose's music went from long, soothing strokes of his bow to sudden, jagged movements in uncomfortable tones that put them on edge. He plucked and scratched the strings in fretful countenance, and Tabitha's blood pumped thickly through her veins. She thought of her father. She thought of her hate.

Focus, Tabitha!

Maddie started to shudder. The others too, appeared to be avoiding eye contact with one another, pushing down the dark memories that threatened to resurface. All the pleasant nostalgia that might have carried over into their depictions of their parents was clouded by the wounds, tragedies, or grudges buried deep within. Tabitha tried to take notes, but she was overwhelmed by the burden that weighed on her own heart.

Maddie started to cry. At first it was just a tear, which she wiped away with one swift, graceful motion; but before long, it became a sob that echoed through the whole classroom, increasing everyone's sense of dread. Tabitha looked regretfully at her, and wished she could do something to help. It was painful to hear. Too painful.

Ambrose stopped abruptly.

"Dr. Buckley, is this really necessary?" he yelled, standing and turning on the lights against the professor's direction.

"Dear boy, this is all merely educational!" Dr. Buckley stuttered.

"Look at her!" Ambrose pointed at Maddie. "She's hysterical! It's not right. I won't do it."

"Please, Mr. Hurley—"

Ambrose started to put away his cello. Tabitha gazed curiously at the enraged man, so indifferent to the many eyes on him and the reputation his temper would merit. He didn't care what they thought, or how his actions might affect his grade, progress, or perks. In that moment, all that mattered to him was that Maddie would be soothed.

Tabitha scolded herself for hating him a little less.

Suddenly, the door burst open, and Lilith Damara entered. A hush went over the crowd, and Ambrose froze.

"Is everything in order, Dr. Buckley?" she asked. Cool. Confident. In control.

"Ah, yes—quite—yes, Headmistress," the professor stumbled.

Lilith turned her attention to the apprentice hunched over his instrument on the floor. "Ambrose, I trust you are… cooperating."

"Yes," he replied rigidly, his anger fizzled out like a smoldering wick.

"Good. Continue, Dr. Buckley."

Lilith left as swiftly as she'd come, and Ambrose spoke no more.

Collecting himself, Dr. Buckley instructed the class to

return to their original seats for the lecture, in which he explained to them what had been happening during the experiment. Tabitha tried to listen, but found it hard to shake the shock of what had just happened.

Rebellious behavior of any kind will not be tolerated.

It may have been kind. It was certainly bold. But Tabitha could not form any alliance with Ambrose if she was to earn Lilith's trust.

The class period ended. All the apprentices rose and eagerly shuffled out the door toward the dining hall for lunch. On Tabitha's way out, Dr. Buckley stopped her.

"My dear, you must be Tabitha Beckett!" he beamed, like the sweet old uncle she never had. "I'm so very glad to have you in my class. I've heard so much praise of you from the other staff members."

"Really?"

"Oh yes! Bright, charming—I can see why they said so. If I may—though, I'm not really supposed to have favorites—don't tell the other apprentices, but I feel as though you're... special... *Providence's pride and joy*, they called you." He struggled to express his admiration properly. "At any rate, I'm very happy to have you in my class, yes, very happy."

Tabitha conveyed her thanks and left with a smile. *Providence's pride and joy* had a nice ring to it.

• • •

Tabitha was surprised to find her professor sitting atop his desk when she entered the room where her *Disguises for Stealth & Stage* class was to be. Though Dr. Buckley was far from rigid, there was a formality to his class which she quickly discovered was lacking in Professor Andy Popovic's.

"Good afternoon, Professor Popovic," Tabitha said politely, unable to go unnoticed as they were the only two there. It was a remarkably small classroom.

"You can skip the Professor part," he replied curtly.

Dressed entirely in black, he swung his legs as he sat staring at her from his perch. Popovic didn't smile. His hooked-nosed, black-bearded face was hard-set, as if determined never to laugh a day in his life; yet he didn't strike Tabitha as angry—just indifferent and carefree. He had a monotone way of speaking, and dark eyes that darted under half-closed lids.

Maddie was next to walk through the door. Popovic tilted his chin up in a half nod, jumped off the table, and shut the door. Tabitha looked about herself, confused. This couldn't possibly be the whole class.

"All right then," Popovic began nonchalantly. "Welcome to *Disguises for Stealth & Stage*. You seem to know each other already so we can skip the introductions. I'm told that I'm supposed to puff you up, tell you you're gorgeous or something, but I'm not going to do that. Neither of you are anything remotely special."

Maddie looked as though she'd seen a ghost, and exchanged a glance with Tabitha. He went on.

"Now, the nature of this class is going to be, frankly, weird. Tabitha being here for stealth, Maddie here for stage, you'll just have to deal with learning about both worlds. I'm too lazy to be creative and find a better solution. Besides, they're probably going to fire me midway through the term anyway, so it doesn't really matter."

The two apprentices sat quietly. Tabitha wasn't sure if he was being funny or serious, but it made her want to laugh.

"Today we're going to go over some simple ways to use common objects and spaces to go unnoticed, which, again, goes completely against why Maddie is here—but you'll live. Before I get into that, however, I want you to answer this question: what do you want to get out of this class?"

Tabitha pondered the question with true consideration. Rebecca had chosen this class for Tabitha intentionally. Whatever she learned here, she could apply to the Clay case.

"I can start," Maddie said. "I'm sure I'll learn a lot about performing, costumes, and all that, but I'm really more interested in the stealth aspect—though, I don't think my supervisor would want me to be... I'm also quite terrible at acting, when I have to talk. I speak more through dance—so I'm excited to get better at that."

Popovic accepted her answer without comment, then turned to Tabitha. She straightened her shoulders and spoke slowly, saying each word with care.

"I want to have complete control of my exterior and, consequently, of how others perceive me. I want to be able to draw or detract attention at will, with limited resources, so as to fulfill my duties at the highest level of performance, even when under extreme pressure."

Tabitha inhaled as she finished, pleased with her own answer. Maddie was on the verge of applauding, but her hands fell limp in her lap at the sight of their instructor's stern look.

Popovic showed no signs of being impressed, but looked down his hooked nose at them and said, "And so you shall."

Jumping suddenly from his desk, Popovic walked past the apprentices and across the room. From the ceiling, he pulled a silk screen depicting the cobblestone streets of Providence. Below it was a wooden trunk full of clothes.

"Go through the box and pick an outfit that would blend in best with this backdrop," Popovic stated.

Maddie and Tabitha smiled at one another. They were literally about to play dress up—for school.

Popovic guided them to use color and context to their advantage when selecting the outfits so that they could blend in with the backdrop, which he would change out periodically. He also taught them breathing exercises to keep their heart rate down when their fear might give them away to their "enemies," whoever those might be. By the end of the lesson, Maddie was still terrified of Popovic—but both she and Tabitha were giddy with excitement to learn more.

"That's all, kiddos," Popovic concluded when their session was up. "Same time next week." He ushered them out the door.

Once it had closed behind them, Tabitha and Maddie grinned from ear to ear at one another. Then Tabitha flattened herself against the wall and began sneaking down the hallway as if on a secret mission. Maddie dropped to the floor, crawling after her. They peeked around the corner.

"Coast is clear," Maddie said in her best peacekeeper voice.

They were about to bound to the next corner when Popovic's

door reopened. His head poked out, one eyebrow arched.

Maddie sprung to her feet.

"We've been spotted!" Tabitha cried, and they sprinted down the hall, bursting with laughter. Popovic shook his head at them, but Tabitha was sure that just before he turned away, she saw the hint of a smile appear at the corner of his mouth.

CHAPTER EIGHT

WILY WINTER'S WAR

As Tabitha and Maddie burst through the doors of the building, they buckled over to catch their breaths, still laughing.

"He's scary," Maddie panted.

"Yeah…" Tabitha replied, "but I like him."

Popovic's class had not only been enjoyable, it had given Tabitha another weapon in her arsenal to use in the Clay case. If her father was as good a peacekeeper as Rebecca said he was, she was going to need all the help she could get to catch him.

Just then, Tabitha spotted her supervisor approaching down one of the narrow streets between the sparkling buildings of Providence.

"Tabitha," Rebecca greeted, "I was just looking for you."

Tabitha said goodbye to Maddie and went to Rebecca's side.

"Do you have some extra time today?" Rebecca asked. "I wanted to walk you through a bit of a test-run before I throw you full force into the fire of your practicum."

Tabitha agreed, and Rebecca led her to a small coffee shop on the outskirts of Providence.

The café was white on the outside, like everything in Providence, but contrastingly dark inside. Rich brown panels of wood coated its walls, against which were deep maroon booths. A decorative fireplace tickled the room with warm light, and everything smelled thickly of cigar smoke and coffee beans.

"This café is the last place Josiah was seen, and the furthest we got when tracking him down," Rebecca explained. "We pulled his finger prints off the bar, right here, and haven't found any others since."

Rebecca revealed a paper copy of the finger prints and placed them on the bar. Tabitha studied them. All ten fingers were visible, spread out and smudged as if his hands had been pressed intensely on the marble slab. In fear, perhaps? Or anger?

Tabitha began to copy them into her sketchbook for future reference, along with the coffee shop in all its detail.

"The prints were left the day before Athaliah made her accusation," Rebecca continued. "Any ideas what might have happened here?"

Tabitha thought hard. She knew this was a test, and was determined to pass it—and not just pass, but impress. Rebecca already knew the answers; Tabitha had to surprise her, to give her something that only she could give. She had to become invaluable to the case. She had to make it personal.

A vague memory surfaced in Tabitha's mind. In it, a twelve-year-old girl sat perched on a grown man's knee, his arm wrapped protectively around her waist lest she fall. In his opposite hand, he held a mug that emitted a fragrant steam. The little girl leaned over it curiously, and the man allowed it to moisten her lip with the smell of honey and lemon.

"Josiah doesn't like coffee," Tabitha said at last. "Or smoking… he wouldn't be a regular at a place like this. So he wasn't coming here for a cup of joe; more likely, he was meeting someone."

Rebecca smiled.

"Very good! As a matter of fact, he was," Rebecca revealed. "Josiah was meeting Athaliah."

"Lilith's daughter?" Tabitha asked.

"Precisely. Now, why would he do that, and why here?"

"You said they were known by the community as friends, before—well, you know. Maybe he met publicly in an attempt to keep up appearances," Tabitha suggested. She picked up the picture of his fingerprints, and imagined his hands in their place. "But then she threatens to expose him. He gets scared and begs her not to, the next day she makes up her mind and he's gone."

"That's Athaliah's version of the story," Rebecca stated quietly.

"So I'm right?" Tabitha proudly asked.

Rebecca nodded, but did not smile. "Now, the real question is: how did he escape without leaving a trace? Where did he go from here?"

This was good. Tabitha was on a roll. Next stop: elite perks for the whole family.

"Well," Tabitha replied confidently, "if his fingerprints

haven't appeared anywhere else, he could be living outside the walls; but he'd probably starve out there. So, if he's hiding somewhere in the city to siphon off provisions, maybe he's wearing gloves."

Rebecca nodded knowingly. "But?" she encouraged.

"That would be easy enough to get away with now that it's winter, but it would have been pretty obvious when he first disappeared: a guy running around with gloves on in the summer heat; especially with everyone warned to be on the lookout," Tabitha brainstormed.

"Exactly," Rebecca said conclusively, but Tabitha wasn't finished.

"So he must have worn a whole outfit that would make it seem normal, where he could blend in better with a crowd. No one questions a uniform."

Rebecca dropped her teacher's air, genuinely impressed. "Tabitha," she said excitedly, "that's brilliant! We thought maybe he burned his fingerprints off with acid or quicklime— questioned every chemist in Providence. This is so simple… how did we miss that?"

Rebecca began sifting through her notes and writing something down. "I'll compile a list of all the places in Providence where the staff wears gloved uniforms, and you can start interviewing each of them after our next meeting."

Tabitha smiled. Then she remembered a question that had arisen in her mind the night before, and a letter that was still stowed in her bag when it should be in the hands of Mayra Mae.

"Rebecca, how am I supposed to send my mother the

medication you gave me? Is there a delivery service here?"

Rebecca's mouth formed a hard line, as if she'd seen this coming. "That's the other reason I wanted to talk to you. I've hit a bit of a road block."

"What do you mean?" Tabitha asked nervously. "Didn't you say that if I did well on this case I'd get family perks?"

"Yes, but—your situation is unique. So long as you're going by the name *Beckett*, your mother isn't listed as a relative and can't get your family perks; and if you go by the name *Clay*, you'll be refused elite perks on account of your relationship to a felon."

A lump formed in Tabitha's throat.

"Can't I just… send the medicine myself?"

"Lilith is very careful about what goes in and out of Providence, especially to Privileged sectors; so the only way to do so is if you get shipment clearance."

"And what do I have to do to get that?" Tabitha asked.

Rebecca shook her head. "It's an incredibly long process; background checks and all that. From what I understand, your mother's condition requires immediacy."

"Do *you* have shipment clearance?" Tabitha tried. Maybe Rebecca could send them for her.

"No—not yet," Rebecca replied.

Tabitha let her sense of defeat show on her face. She'd left her twin. She'd endured six weeks of Detox. She'd been willing to put everything on the line, and for what? A chance to fail in the same way her father had?

"Tabitha," Rebecca said softly, placing her hand on Tabitha's shoulder, "I promise you that by our meeting next week, I will have found a solution to this."

Tabitha nodded. But next week was too far.

When Tabitha emerged from the coffee shop, she spotted her new colleagues sitting around a stone table in the open courtyard.

She ducked her head, trying to remember Popovic's lesson on blending into her environment. She was not sure she could handle social interaction right now. Before turning away, however, Tabitha hesitated. Maybe being around other people would distract her from the weighty sense of helplessness she felt.

Ella looked up from the plant she was trimming in her lap and spotted Tabitha. She smiled and jerked her head to beckon her over. It was too late now to slip away. Tabitha heeded the summons.

Milo had brought out his legendary pug, Spikenard, who played happily at his feet. Maddie sat cross-legged on the ground, watching Toby, who occupied his hands by tossing a football up in the air and catching it. When they saw Tabitha coming, they each acknowledged her in their own ways.

Ambrose, on the other hand, moodily ignored everyone from a few paces away where he was playing a melancholic song on his cello.

Drama queen.

As she came within earshot, she heard Milo agitatedly ranting, "As if! Your darn p-plants are the cause of so much floralturbation, always dislocating ancient walls with their roots and pulling artifacts up from their stratigraphic context with them when they fall."

Ambrose suddenly appeared less dramatic in comparison.

"Says the one who would chop down an entire forest if it benefitted an archaeological excavation," Ella retaliated coolly. "What's in the ground belongs in the ground; let it lie."

"Don't be ridiculous."

"How am I the ridiculous one?"

"I'm just saying, your precious trees might be 4,000 years old, but we're talking specimens from millions of years ago! You botanists—you need to put things in perspective. You insult me."

Tabitha shook her head at their bickering and bent down to give Spikenard a scratch behind the ear. The little black pug's tongue panted crookedly out one side, and Tabitha couldn't help but smile.

"Okay then, tell me this," Ella said to Milo with an air of superiority, still unfazed, "if my company is so very insulting, why do you continually choose to sit next to me?"

Milo's eyes bulged in dispute as he shrunk into a denying shrug. "I'm not sitting next to *you*, I'm sitting next to… Tabitha! Isn't that right, Tabitha? Tab-Tab, Tabby-Cat, Tabarooni. Yeah, we're tight."

Tabitha neither confirmed nor denied the notion. "What's eating Ambrose?" she asked, changing the subject.

"He had to meet with his supervisor after Dr. Buckley's class because of what happened," Milo responded nonchalantly.

Tabitha wondered for a moment if this should be cause for

her to worry. What was done to the rebels whose behavior wasn't tolerated?

"Where were you?" Milo asked.

"I had my disguises class," Tabitha replied.

"The one Maddie's in?" inquired Ella.

Tabitha nodded, and Milo looked confused. "Why are you taking a class for—"

Just then, a teacher they didn't know approached them and put a hand on Tabitha's shoulder.

"Congratulations on a great first day, Tabitha!" she applauded. "At this rate, there won't be any crime left in Providence for the rest of Security to manage!" The woman smiled and left.

Thanks, Tabitha thought sarcastically, and searched for a way to evade the questioning looks on her companions' faces. The less they knew about her apprenticeship, the easier it would be to keep her identity a secret. Ambrose's music shifted in mood, but he showed no other signs of eaves dropping.

"I'm helping with some surveillance stuff," Tabitha explained. "My artistic abilities come in handy for Security since there aren't many people with photography clearance."

Ella grinned and turned back to Milo. "She's taking a disguises class so she can spy on criminals. They probably have her working on at least—six cases already."

Tabitha started to interject, but Milo cut her off. "What, you think your best friend is better than mine or something?"

"Precisely."

Tabitha felt her spirits lifted as she realized that Ella had just called her her best friend.

"Well," Milo began, "Ambrose can solve a 250-piece puzzle in ten minutes flat."

"That's pretty useless. Tabitha could solve a crime just as fast."

"Oh yeah, well, Ambrose was personally asked by Lilith herself to accompany the recruitment team and travel all over Grexovium in just his second month. You can't deny that the compliment of some random teacher pales in comparison—no offense, Tab-Tab."

"Well, *Tabitha* can—"

"Okay guys, this is getting weird," Tabitha interrupted with an uneasy laugh, and the two surrendered, returning to highly intellectual debates over botanical and archaeological things that Tabitha couldn't understand.

She didn't mind their banter, but it seemed such petty nonsense in comparison to the weighty secret she bore, the secret of her name and her mission. Without Mayra Mae to bounce things off of, they simmered inside her, ready to explode at any moment. Tabitha wished she could tell someone, that she could confide in these people who had called her their friend, their best friend. Best friends could trust each other with their secrets.

If the rebels discovered your relationship to Josiah, they might try to use you as bait, Rebecca's warning echoed in Tabitha's mind. The bottle of Rifampin pressed against her side from within her purse. If Tabitha's true name was revealed, she would no longer be eligible for those perks. She could not trust her friends with that secret. They were not worth that risk.

But could she trust Rebecca to find a way to send the medicine to Natalie? A week could be too long…

It was too much to think about. Tabitha stood and wandered over to Toby, signaling for him to throw her the football. He smiled and obliged. Neither spoke, and Tabitha let the systematic lull of the pigskin's round trips between them take her mind off the many cares that burdened her.

Catch.

Throw.

Catch.

Throw.

Somehow it settled the overwhelming mess of homesickness, confusion, anger, and impatience that cluttered her mind.

Just then, Tabitha recognized the song that Ambrose was playing. The soothing tones from his cello strings washed over her like a waterfall of peace. It was an old lullaby her mother used to sing to her.

Tabitha relished a memory of her and Mayra Mae singing it in harmony while they worked at the Grind, timing their tune with the conveyer belt's rhythmic hum and drumming against the counter with wooden spoons.

Without realizing it, Tabitha began to sing the song quietly to herself in company with Ambrose's playing.

"Wily winter snowflakes dance
Upon the wind they rise
Whispering of how they brought
About Autumn's demise…"

Ambrose stopped.

"You know this song?" he asked her, his mood brightening noticeably. He flashed a smile of perfectly white teeth.

Tabitha glanced at him in acknowledgment, then continued to throw the football with her back turned. "Yeah," she replied over her shoulder. "My mother used to sing it to us—I mean, me."

In response, Ambrose started to play the song again, this time singing the verses.

"But suddenly, the Sun awakes
And stretches out its beams!
The ice retreats into the ground
Joining the running streams."

Tabitha didn't turn around to face him, but neither did she resist the draw to sing along, as she used to do with Mayra Mae. How she missed Mayra Mae. Matching his pitch with a perfect harmony, Tabitha let the words fall off her lips, pouring her loneliness into each syllable.

Toby continued to catch and throw the football, but he could not wipe the enchantment off his face. Ambrose and Tabitha's voices together were captivating, haunting, angelic.

"The king of lights then summons forth
The flowers that he saved
To tell the story of just how
Harsh Winter's hands he braved.

"But pride engulfs the haughty king,
He fails to look around
And notice when the trees rise up
To take away his crown!

"*The shade shall rule!* they shout with glee
While blocking out the Sun,
Who, saddened and ashamed retreats
Into the horizon.

"The night descends, and with it, Cold
Upon the sleeping trees
Slowly, with their siren's songs
They creep in like disease.

"They never knew until they fell
That they had lost the war.
The children of the trees lie crumpled
On the stiffened floor.

"Autumn also noticed naught
When stillness gripped its water
And Winter rose again to reign
After her silent slaughter."

For the last two lines, Tabitha turned to face Ambrose for the first time since they'd begun to sing. In the moment their eyes flickered in meeting, a tiny piece of their souls touched timidly. As the final note came to a close, Ambrose looked at Tabitha with a mixture of admiration and gratitude, and she found it difficult to keep hating him.

Just as Tabitha began to question the discomforting squirm rising up in her stomach, a brown blur flew past her head, causing her to break eye contact with Ambrose.

"Sorry!" Toby called, and Tabitha turned to see the football bouncing merrily away.

Away into a provisions warehouse, which Tabitha distinctly remembered from her first day in Providence. It hadn't been marked on their map, only highlighted in red. *What are the red parts?* Tabitha remembered Maddie asking Cassady in the helicopter.

The ball rolled in between two massive storage crates and out of sight. With it, an idea rolled into the territory of Tabitha's consciousness.

Ideas were dangerous.

"I'll get it!" she announced, and followed the football straight into the restricted section.

EXTRA CREDIT

THE AIR SMELLED LIKE ALUMINUM. Large machinery loomed overhead, filling Tabitha's ears with a loud hum and an occasional clang as it moved the heavy metal crates. Tabitha slipped silently out of sight behind one. It took her less than two minutes to locate Toby's football and tuck it safely under her arm—but that was not why she was there.

As far as she could tell, this was where Providence got its food supply. If things were coming in through here, things could go out through here. If Rebecca was unable to find a way to send medicine and letters back to Tabitha's family, Tabitha would find a way herself.

Tabitha retrieved her sketch journal from her purse and began to survey her surroundings. She took in every detail, like the scanners that investigated the crevasses of her thumb print at the Axelle Provisionary. The crates were tall and gray with red and blue markings along their rippled sides, and heavy sliding doors that closed at their bases. They were arranged in long, parallel rows, perfectly aligned, save for one that was just a hair crooked, as if the employees in charge the day of its arrival had simply stopped caring. She drew them all.

Tabitha glanced around to make sure no one was watching, then grabbed hold of the handle of one of the crates. Watching a crane out of the corner of her eye, she waited for it to release another crate from its claw, which would drown out the sound of her opening the door. It turned at a sloth-like pace, aimed, and began to lower. Three, two, one—

The crate dropped with a crash and Tabitha heaved with all her might, but the door didn't budge. It was locked.

Tabitha continued to creep between them, adding new details to her drawings as she went. What was in them? Were they all provisions? Tabitha pictured a crate completely full of the cupcakes from the cafeteria, and chuckled at the thought.

Carefully climbing up the side of a crate to peer across the span of the warehouse, Tabitha noticed that it opened to the outside of Providence's wall. It made sense now why the warehouse was a restricted section. How hard could it be to slip out of a hole that big?

At the far end of the corridor, Tabitha could make out the warehouse workers, clad in uniforms and sturdy gloves. Her father could be among them, if her uniform theory was correct. Maybe he was stealing rations straight from the crates.

Suddenly, one of the workers holding a clipboard turned from the rest of the staff and began in Tabitha's direction. His regal footsteps echoed off the vast ceiling, pounding fear into her with every blow. Stifling a gasp, Tabitha slipped down the side of the crate to escape his line of vision, scraping her arm badly on its metal edge on her way down. She gripped the cut, wincing, and crouched low in shadow.

If you get caught… Tabitha warned herself. She knew. "Rebellious behavior" would not be tolerated.

Dodging through the labyrinth of crates, Tabitha distanced herself as far from the footsteps as possible. She curled up in a dark corner against the odd crate that was just slightly off from the rest of its row. There she sat and examined her drawings, looking for inconsistencies.

It was a moment or two later that she realized the footsteps had ceased to sound.

Tabitha felt pinpricks on the back of her neck and the overwhelming sensation of being watched. Rising swiftly to her feet and whirling around to look for an escape route, she saw the warehouse manager standing in the light of the entryway.

"Hey, what are you doing in here?" he cried out. "This is a restricted section!"

Sweat beaded on Tabitha's forehead and she took a step back, reaching behind her. Her arm bumped against the crate and she felt the cut's sting once more. Glancing at the blood that dripped down to her wrist, she got an idea.

"Please, can you help me?" she called, holding her scarlet arm out in front of her.

"What?" the man replied, his voice dripping with disdain.

"I went to get this football for my friend outside near the warehouse and got a cut when trying to reach it. So I came in here looking for someone to help me," she whimpered in her best damsel-in-distress voice.

"What the devil would you do that for?" he shouted, studying her. He was young, probably just shy of thirty—but his eyes showed signs of age beyond his years. They darted to their surroundings, looking for clues of what she may have been doing there.

Tabitha felt panic spread through her. Her ploy wasn't working. She started crying, using her fake sobs to hide the fact that she had nothing logical to come back with.

"I just—it hurts, and—I just thought maybe someone could—could—"

A picture of Popovic slapping a palm to his forehead entered Tabitha's mind. She was a better actress than this.

The warehouse manager was eye-to-eye with her now. He grabbed her bad arm and examined the wound. "This is barely a scratch," he growled. "You're coming with me." Keeping a firm grip on her wrist, he dragged her out of the warehouse.

Ambrose stood when he saw them emerge. The rest of her friends gawked at her, bewildered and worried. Tabitha glanced in their direction, but gave them no sign. When she passed Toby, she tossed the football over her shoulder without looking back to see if anyone caught it.

The uniformed man led Tabitha up the streets toward the inner gate. Her heart pounded. If he searched her bag, he'd see her sketches of the warehouse and know she was lying. What was worse, that would lead him to search the whole book and discover her true identity as Tabitha Clay.

To Tabitha's surprise, the warehouse manager unlocked the iron gate that led to the center of the city and lugged her through it.

Tabitha was entering the inner zone where no entry-level apprentice before her had ever walked! She surveyed her surroundings excitedly, forgetting for a moment that she was probably being led to some sort of interrogation. As they walked, heads turned and elders stared, and when she met their eyes, they turned away. That wasn't a good sign.

They climbed all the way to the sparkling tower at the highest point in the city and through its gargantuan doors. Inside, they entered a lift that shot them to the highest floor. Beyond the glass windows, Tabitha could see the surrounding buildings shrinking as they zipped off into the sky. The elevator doors opened and they approached a set of solid white doors, upon which the man knocked.

They opened, and Lilith Damara stood before them.

"What is this about, Dominic?" Lilith asked the uniformed man steadily.

"This girl was lurking around a restricted section, in the warehouse, Headmistress," he replied hotly, throwing Tabitha forward.

Lilith looked her up and down, and Tabitha looked back, no longer hiding behind her pitiful facade.

"I would appreciate," Lilith said at length, "if you would handle our guests with more gentleness, Dominic."

A mixture of disbelief, fear, and anger overtook Dominic's expression in the face of Lilith's betrayal, but he said nothing.

"Tabitha is working on the Clay case," she vouched, "I'm sure she had a good reason for being wherever she was." Dominic went to speak, but Lilith cut him off: "You may leave now."

He promptly shut his gaping mouth, bowed low, and turned. Tabitha timidly started to follow him through the thick white doors.

"Not you, Tabitha. I'd like a word."

Dominic did not look back. He walked straight to the elevator, leaving Tabitha behind. She turned to face Lilith, unsure if she should be grateful or afraid—but Lilith's hard and authoritative air dropped as soon as the doors were closed.

She smiled kindly, and placed a hand on Tabitha's shoulder. "Right this way," she instructed, guiding Tabitha softly into a small room with no windows.

Lilith invited Tabitha to sit at a chair before her desk, then disappeared momentarily through another door on the opposite side of the room. The office looked similar to the one Tabitha had met Rebecca in: plain white with a solid block of a table in the middle, a chair on either side. On the desk was a box of tissues.

The silence was so thick that Tabitha felt the need to hold her breath lest she break it in Lilith's absence. When the headmistress returned, she was holding a basin of hot water and a small bottle in her hands, a towel draped over her arm. She placed the supplies on her desk, pulled her chair up to Tabitha's, and sat down.

"You have very good timing, Tabitha. I was just going to send for you when Dominic brought you up," she addressed, while at the same time taking Tabitha's bleeding arm in her hands with care.

"You were?" The voice Tabitha expected to hear come from her own mouth was a foreign and faint squeak. She cleared her throat.

"Yes. Rebecca tells me you've been doing quite well with your apprenticeship," Lilith replied, beginning to clean the wound with the hot water. "We're very pleased with your contribution to our security efforts."

"Thank you." Tabitha still sounded stiff and afraid despite her efforts to regain herself. Lilith turned her eyes from the cut to Tabitha's face, leaned forward, and placed a hand on hers.

"Tabitha, it's okay. You don't have to be afraid of me. I'm on your side."

Tabitha looked up, pondering Lilith's use of the word *side*, but forgot what she was thinking when she met Lilith's eyes. Lilith gazed at her so tenderly, with so much understanding and consolation that Tabitha's tenseness melted away.

"Rebecca also told me that your mother is very ill," Lilith continued. Her gentle handling of Tabitha's wound made her feel vulnerable and close to the headmistress. Lilith's words were warm and comforting. "This is tragic, and were it not against my moral compass to have favorites, I would gladly give you all the elite perks you needed to return your mother to good health. Your success in the Clay case, however—which is of particular interest to me personally—should be able to secure those for you."

Tabitha nodded solemnly.

"Headmistress," she started, minding Popovic's lesson in calming her heart rate, "my supervisor told me that my unique situation hinders me from sending the perks that I earn to my family."

"Yes," Lilith replied. "She mentioned that to me as well, which is why I'd like to offer a solution. How would you like a little extra-curricular opportunity?"

Tabitha's heart floated back up. "Yes," she exclaimed, "anything I can do!"

Lilith smiled. "Good. If you succeed in the task I have in mind for you, I'll make sure Rebecca is given immediate shipment clearance to send medications to your mother on your behalf."

"Thank you!" Tabitha cried, moving to stand.

Lilith stopped her, indicating the half-bandaged wound. Tabitha sat back down, smiling silently from ear to ear, and let the headmistress finish her doctoring.

"What would you have me do?" Tabitha asked.

"I want you to plant something compromising in a certain individual's possessions. Some drugs would do the trick, which I believe your friend Ella Reeves has access to. Oh, don't worry, I'll see to it that you don't get caught. Consider it practice for your apprenticeship."

Tabitha listened, trying to hide her surprise. "But who—" she began to inquire.

"Don't ask questions," Lilith interrupted. "Just know that it's for a good cause."

After some hesitation, Tabitha nodded.

Presently, someone burst through the door without knocking.

"Mother, I—" started Athaliah. She halted when she noticed Tabitha.

Athaliah had a similar facial structure to Lilith, but a darker complexion. Unlike her mother, her wavy black hair fell sporadically out of its attempt at an up-do, and—though composed—she had a wildness to her narrowed eyes.

Tabitha wasn't sure why, but the woman frightened her. Maybe Athaliah was still coping after the traumatic experience Tabitha's father had put her through. Anyone might look that disheveled following such an ordeal. The reminder turned Tabitha's fear into disgust. Then, to her shock and horror, she realized something about Athaliah's appearance that had evaded her notice before.

Athaliah was showing.

Athaliah was *pregnant.*

"I'll come back later," Athaliah decided, and disappeared.

Lilith patted the bandage around Tabitha's arm. "There," she said. "All better."

Tabitha looked at the headmistress with admiration, and sorrow for Athaliah's injustice. A man whom Lilith had trusted had turned on her family, yet here she was, nursing the wounds of that man's daughter.

"I suppose we're family now," Tabitha ventured.

Lilith pondered her student's statement, but didn't understand.

Tabitha looked at her with an ironic smile. "Your grandchild is my half-sibling."

Lilith looked back toward where Athaliah had stood in the doorway, and put two and two together. She smiled back at Tabitha and replied, "I suppose we are!"

With that, Tabitha's suspicion was confirmed, and any hope she had of being wrong melted away.

At her mournful expression, Lilith took Tabitha's hands kindly. "I lost my father at a young age as well. He was a horrible man, and it left me scarred and angry at the world… but that didn't stop me from changing my name and forging a new future for myself. And it's not going to stop you, either."

Tabitha looked intently at this new motherly figure before her, and the fire in her soul was doused with gasoline. She'd wanted answers—she'd got them: her father was a bastard and he needed to be caught.

"I'm going to find him," Tabitha declared.

Lilith smiled. "I know you will."

CHAPTER TEN

SABOTAGE

TABITHA'S FIRST WEEK OF CLASSES FLEW by, and she met her second practicum with Rebecca eagerly. Her supervisor would be proud of her ingenuity, Tabitha thought as she waited outside Rebecca's office door. Her letter to Mayra Mae and bottle of Rifampin were in her hands.

The door opened. Rebecca did not smile, but ushered her apprentice in. As Tabitha passed, Rebecca took the bottle and letter from her.

"I hear you got yourself some extra credit," Rebecca declared evenly.

Tabitha hesitated. Was Rebecca mad at her?

"Yes," Tabitha stated. "You have shipment clearance now; you can send those to my family, right?" Tabitha pointed at the bottle and letter.

Rebecca nodded, her eyes fixed on the surface of her desk. Tabitha waited.

"What is it, Rebecca?" Tabitha finally asked cautiously.

Rebecca bit the inside of her cheek. "Just—don't forget,

the Clay case should take priority over your extra-curricular activities," she answered at last. "Try not to get distracted, okay?"

Tabitha nodded, attempting to be grateful for Rebecca's careful supervision rather than focusing on her lack of enthusiasm.

Rebecca then revealed a slip of paper with a list of names on it. "Here are the people I'd like you to interview for the case, as well as some sample questions. Feel free to add your own if you think it necessary. Have your findings ready for me by our next meeting."

Tabitha skimmed the list, and a knot formed in her stomach. Popovic's name was on it. *But he doesn't wear a uniform,* Tabitha considered, wondering what would warrant her teacher's listing as a suspect.

"I will," Tabitha assured, and began to leave. Just before walking through the door, she turned and asked, "Rebecca, do you know if I've gotten any letters from my sister?"

Rebecca hesitated before responding. "No. I'm sorry."

Tabitha wondered anxiously if Mayra Mae was still bitter about her leaving. It was a legitimate thing to be upset over, but it was unlike Mayra Mae to hold a grudge. That was one of the many ways the twins were different.

• • •

Tabitha went straight to work after her meeting with Rebecca. Her legs swung freely below her as she sat on a table in the Greenhouse, keeping Ella company as she worked, and waiting for an opportunity to smuggle out some compromising drugs. Maddie sat beside her, admiring a flower that grew in a nearby pot.

"So," Ella pressed, "what is it you were going to tell us last week before the boys interrupted our girl talk?"

Maddie went bright red, and Tabitha felt a sort of giddiness spring up in her, like when she and Mayra Mae would giggle over some stupid thing that didn't matter.

"Oh, it's nothing, really," Maddie evaded.

"I can make a truth serum, you know," Ella threatened.

That's all the pressure it took for Maddie to cave. "Oh, all right… but please don't tell anyone!"

"Cross my heart, hope I don't die," Ella promised.

"Okay," Maddie agreed, then took several preparatory deep breaths. Tabitha and Ella exchanged a grin.

"*I like Toby!*" she finally blurted without spaces between the words, followed by a gasp as if the thing literally came off her chest.

"I *knew* it!" Ella cried in triumph. Tabitha laughed outright.

"Is it that hopeless?" Maddie asked pitifully.

"No, not at all!" Tabitha replied, "It's just—I thought you were going to say something serious."

"It *is* serious!" Maddie cried back, defensively.

Ella and Tabitha continued to chuckle, but attempted to be more sensitive about it.

"Oh Tabitha," Maddie went on, "he's just so kind and gentle—but strong, too. And smart! Whenever he looks at me, I feel like we've always known each other, like he's got my back. You know?"

Nope, Tabitha thought, but she nodded dishonestly.

"Girl," Ella addressed, "Say hello to Cupid's daughter. What's the plan? Love potion? Because I can make one of those, too."

Tabitha laughed, but Maddie shook her head so violently that the blue ribbon holding her hair up threatened to fall out.

"Drug-free campus, Ella," Tabitha warned playfully.

"Not for me! Get this—after all that detoxification and those nurses saying I need to steer clear of drugs, what does my supervisor tell me? She wants me to go and make some more."

"No way!" Tabitha responded, though she'd figured as much from Lilith's instructions.

"Yes way!" Ella went on. "Technically I'm not allowed to test them, which is completely unscientific, if you want my biased opinion… but that's okay! They want me to create new genetically-modified species of plants, which is hella cool, so I won't complain. I've been given access to any of the plants in Providence's greenhouse supply, and I get to experiment on them. Here, check this out—"

Maddie and Tabitha were enjoying Ella's geek-out moment, and followed her across the greenhouse to a strange-looking fern.

"This is Giant Hogweed," Ella enthusiastically claimed. "It oozes a nasty sap that reacts with the sun, causing a chemical reaction that would burn up your skin in an *instant*."

Tabitha and Maddie's interested expressions turned to horror—more at Ella's happy demeanor than at the plant itself. They backed away slightly.

"And this one," she went on, leading them across the garden,

"Toxicoscordion venenosum, or death camas. They're one of the most poisonous plants in existence. One bite, and boom! Rapid, painful death by organ failure.

"Oh, and Angel Trumpet—this one's insane. Not so bad by itself, but if you extract certain toxins from it, you can make a powder that will literally *zombify* people. When they come in contact with the chemical, they lose all awareness, but remain fully conscious; so they'll basically do whatever you want them to do without knowing a thing. Crazy, right?"

Maddie stood speechless.

"Yes," Tabitha said with eyes wide, "yes, you are."

Ella rolled her eyes and Maddie allowed herself a tiny giggle.

"And what's that?" Tabitha asked, pointing to a bed of star-shaped leaves.

Ella snorted. "You're joking, right?" Then she pulled a small bag of crushed greens from her jacket pocket and tossed it to Tabitha with a wink. "I won't tell if you don't."

That was easy.

Tabitha pocketed the weed and put a check mark on her mental to-do list.

Suddenly, Maddie froze and looked up. Tabitha followed her gaze to see Toby outside the glass windows making his way to the gym. Maddie melted as his muscular frame disappeared through the doors. Ella and Tabitha exchanged a look.

"So I hear the gym has every kind of equipment imaginable," Ella mentioned nonchalantly. "I presume that includes stuff for—I don't know, aerial acrobatics?"

Maddie lit up. "Oh yes!" she confirmed. "I practice there for my apprenticeship sometimes. My favorite is silk; you know, standard climbs, wraps, and drops. I use 72-inch, typically. Though I'm trying to learn how to use a double tab hoop. My supervisor says—"

"Hun," Ella interrupted, "you realize we're not understanding a word of this."

Maddie thought for a moment, unsure how to translate the language that came so naturally to her.

"Why don't you just show us?" Tabitha offered.

"Yeah!" Ella added. "Let's go. Field trip to the gym. Come along!"

Maddie looked horrified. "But—Toby—he's in there!"

Ella smiled wryly. "Exactly."

Grabbing Maddie by the arm, Ella pulled her toward the greenhouse exit. Tabitha followed happily.

Maddie fought them all the way to the gym's doors, but once through, her posture transformed. She held her chin high and walked elegantly across the floor. Ella and Tabitha trailed behind her. In a nearby section of the expansive gym, Toby was lifting more weight than Tabitha thought possible. She noticed him flinch ever so slightly as they entered his line of vision.

Maddie approached a corner where the floor was cut out and blocked off by a railing. Different colored silks of about twenty-five feet in length hung from the ceiling. They trickled down through the hole in the floor all the way to the level below. Looking over the rail, Tabitha and Ella saw protective padding at the bottom.

"Wait here," Maddie instructed, and descended a flight of stairs to the level below.

The ghostly sound of an electric violin mixed with a touch of dubstep echoed up from the basement, and shortly after—to their amazement—Maddie hoisted herself up to eye-level, hanging delicately from two of the silk strips. For a moment, she stayed still as stone. Ella and Tabitha held their breaths.

The beat picked up. With it, Maddie began to twist and twirl, suspended in midair yet moving as though on the ground. Upside down, curled around herself like a spider in a web, she whipped around the silks with impeccable grace.

Tabitha and Ella leaned over the edge, totally transfixed. Maddie swung in circles violently fast, wrapping herself tightly around the waist. Then she unexpectedly let go, spiraling toward the ground. Tabitha caught her breath, sure that Maddie would cascade to an untimely end; just to watch her grip the silk once more and flip into a new pose.

As the music came to an abrupt halt, Maddie ended her performance with a stance where her back was so arched that her toes grazed the top of her forehead. It was mystical.

A loud clang startled the audience from their trance and Tabitha swung around to see Toby, gaping with his weight at his feet. It took him a moment to realize he had dropped it. Maddie blushed, and Tabitha and Ella exchanged a triumphant smile.

• • •

When Maddie and Ella had parted ways to do their homework, Tabitha attended to her own. Lilith had provided Tabitha with a house number to leave the drugs at, but nothing more. She supposed she didn't need to know who or why. Her job was to come up with how.

Heeding Popovic's lesson on blending in with her environment, Tabitha dressed in light, neutral colors like the white walls of Providence, and carried herself as though she belonged in the lineup of elders passing through the inner gates.

Tabitha turned her face away from the peacekeeper who stood guard, and to avoid the appearance of cowering, looked into her bag as if searching for something.

The door drew near. Each apprentice walked past with ease, and the peacekeeper did not ask for any identification whatsoever. This would be a piece of cake, Tabitha thought.

With one foot through the gate and her mind already in celebration over her victory, Tabitha felt a firm hand wrap around her arm and whip her back through the entrance.

"Nice try," the peacekeeper grunted, maintaining his grip on her.

Tabitha instantly sought for an escape, and had plan A, B, and half of C worked out when—

"She's with me," a smooth, feminine voice called from behind. Rebecca approached the peacekeeper with a gentle yet commandeering smile, and the man on guard let go. Tabitha thanked her supervisor with her eyes.

"I guess I still need more practice," Tabitha said in a hushed voice once they'd walked through.

Rebecca smiled. "It *was* a nice try," she said.

Tabitha pulled out her map of Providence to locate the

apartment where Lilith wanted her to leave the drugs. As they came to a crossroads, Rebecca bid her farewell by quietly directing, "Do what you have to do."

Tabitha watched her stoic supervisor glide away before turning on her heel and padding down a nearby breezeway. The setting sun cast a red glow on the white arches that adorned the narrow path and reflected off the architecture's glistening glass details. The streets were quiet and the air tranquil—but Tabitha kept her guard.

Her heart pounded faster as she approached her destination. There were multiple apartment complexes within central Providence. The elders she'd come in with shuffled into a tall, C-shaped building similar to her own home. Her target, however, lived in a spiraling structure like a vertical neighborhood. As a mountain road might wind around the rock to the top, this man-made road wound about itself, and little houses were perched on every side, guarded by individual railings made of white, flowery iron.

Tabitha quickly deduced that this neighborhood housed teachers and staff. She wondered for a moment which individual's life she was about to ruin. Did she know them? Would she hesitate, if she knew whom she was framing?

It's for a good cause.

Or perhaps they were dangerous. Perhaps, if they knew who had soiled their reputation, they would seek revenge. Who knew what kind of powerful elites lived in this place, and what they were capable of?

Tabitha suppressed her fears and focused on what her

senses could register. She smelled food wafting from the dining hall, far away as it was. A handful of the neighborhood's houses went dark as their lights were put out. The quiet echo of her own footsteps on the winding path became acute. When she strained hard enough, she could also make out the sound of a dog barking, the jingling of keys, and another pair of footsteps nearby.

Someone was coming from up ahead. The neighborhood's layout was spacious with no nooks or alleyways to hide in. Tabitha knew there would be no avoiding the passerby.

The footsteps drew closer, and Tabitha did everything in her power to ignore her anxiety. She stood tall and told herself again and again that she belonged there, that she had the authority and right to be within the inner gates, until she believed it and played the part.

Her target, house number thirteen, was so close. Maybe she could slip inside before the stranger crossed her path. It was just around the corner—

"My dear Tabitha Beckett! What brings you to my side of the inner gates?"

Jolly old Dr. Buckley came into view and beamed a great big smile at his student. Tabitha felt a mixture of relief and increased worry. At least a stranger might not have known she wasn't an elder… but maybe his favoritism would save her.

"Dr. Buckley!" Tabitha replied, "It's so good to see you! I'm here to meet with one of my teachers about some extra credit." Before he could ask what for, she added, "I'm looking forward to your class tomorrow! What will we be learning about this time?"

His facial features flickered as if switching gears took physical effort, but once latched onto the new subject, he grinned again. "We shall be discussing the functions of the cerebral cortex—memory, to be specific. One of my favorite topics, in fact!"

Tabitha was not acting when she responded with excitement. Her own fickle memory—unnaturally vivid yet lasting so short a time—had always perplexed her. "I can't wait!" she exclaimed.

Suddenly, Dr. Buckley's stomach growled. Tabitha couldn't help but laugh a little.

"And neither can I wait any longer to fill this empty belly of mine!" he joked, and patted his bulbous girth. "As always, it was very good to see you. Should you ever wish to stop by my house and chat after class, you can find me right up the road here. House thirteen!"

Tabitha's heart dropped into her stomach.

"I'll be sure to pay you a visit sometime," she said through her mask.

With that, Dr. Buckley walked away, and Tabitha stood disgusted at herself for what she was about to do.

It'll be fine, he won't know it was you, a voice inside her said. But Tabitha was no longer concerned with what would happen to her if she were caught. What would happen to Dr. Buckley? When they found the drugs she was about to hide in his house, would he lose his job? Would they send him away? Would his friends and family believe his innocence?

It's for a good cause.

Lilith's words echoed again in her mind and she did her best to believe them. When Dr. Buckley was far out of sight and ear-shot, Tabitha climbed the fence around his yard, crept to the back door, and found it unlocked. She slipped inside, did what she'd come to do, and walked away.

CHAPTER ELEVEN

PUZZLES

WHEN TABITHA AND HER FRIENDS ARRIVED at the door of Dr. Buckley's classroom the next day, they found it closed with a note posted on the window. A group of bewildered apprentices surrounded it, straining to read the writing. Tabitha stood up on her toes, trying to get a glimpse.

Toby pushed his massive, drooping shoulders through the crowd, and they parted like the Red Sea to make way for him. After reading the note, he returned to Tabitha and their friends, a worried expression on his dull face.

"What's going on?" Ella asked when he'd returned.

"Dr. Buckley's been put on probation," he answered. "Doesn't say why; just that his classes are cancelled until further notice."

Memories of Dr. Buckley's beaming smile popped into Tabitha's mind, and she pushed back the sick feeling they evoked. This was all her fault...

"This is all my fault," Ambrose muttered.

Tabitha and her friends looked up at him. Guilt bit at

Tabitha's insides and a part of her craved confession, but the other side of her inner war kept her lips sealed.

"Hun, this is not your fault—" Ella soothed, placing a friendly hand on his arm.

"Yes, it is," he argued. "If I hadn't disrupted Dr. Buckley's class last week, Lilith wouldn't have gone after him."

"Lilith?" Maddie asked quietly.

"Of course," Ambrose replied. "I made Buckley look incapable of maintaining control over his classroom; and if there's anything Lilith can't stand, it's not being in control."

"You really don't like her, do you?" Milo asked.

"That's an understatement," Ambrose mumbled.

Tabitha scolded the shame, regret, and general existence of feelings that sprung up inside her. There was something admirable in Ambrose's humility, taking the blame for Dr. Buckley's fate, but she couldn't relate to his loathing of the headmistress. Lilith had been so helpful and motherly when Tabitha met her. Lilith—not Ambrose—would help Tabitha find her father and save her mother. If she had to choose a side, it wouldn't be with the rebel musician. Her colleagues were disposable, just like Dr. Buckley; means to a worthy end.

"On a happier note," Tabitha said to break the tension and change the subject, "we have the morning free! I'm going to get a head start on my homework. I'll see you all later."

They bid her farewell, and Tabitha left for her apartment. On the way there, she opened her journal and studied her drawings of locations where elites wore gloved uniforms. There were the peacekeepers, the private dining hall servers and chefs, medical staff, construction workers, waste disposal managers, and the employees at the restricted warehouse she'd snuck into a few days before.

Tabitha added Dominic—the man who'd taken her to see Lilith—to the list of elites to interview about her father. On the bottom of the list, she again noticed Popovic's name. His was the only one that did not correspond with one of her locations.

That's not your puzzle to solve, Tabitha told herself. Buttering her teachers up was only meant to fuel their favoritism of her, not hers of them. If Popovic suffered Dr. Buckley's fate on her behalf, so be it. It *was* for a good cause. Because no results meant no perks, and no perks meant…

She didn't want to think about it.

It took Tabitha a few moments to realize that she'd already reached her apartment complex. She looked around. The elegant lobby was brightly lit by the midday sun. She had forgotten how very lovely it was.

Milo's sudden voice made her jump. "See ya, Tabby-Cat," he said as he passed. Had he been walking with her the whole time?

Tabitha half-acknowledged him as he climbed up the spiral staircase, his heavy footsteps leaving chaos in their wake. The rail trembled and a picture frame on the wall even slid out of place.

Tabitha shook her head and chuckled to herself. Going to straighten the frame, she appreciated the photography inside it. Some of the images had to have been taken from a helicopter, depicting the entire span of Providence nestled within its rustic surroundings. She had grown fond of her new, sparkling home.

Tabitha continued around the room from picture to picture, and presently came upon one of the same warehouse she'd drawn. Smiling in recognition, she opened her journal to compare the two.

Not half bad, she thought. They were nearly identical, save for one detail. Tabitha moved in closer, confused. She counted the large metal storage crates in her drawing, then in the photograph. She backed up, and counted again, then shook her head. There was a crate missing in the photograph—the one that had been crooked in the lineup.

Tabitha looked at the date engraved on a plaque at the bottom of the frame. It had been taken in the spring of that same year.

It was probably nothing. They brought new crates in all the time. Why they would go through the trouble of bringing this one so far into the warehouse instead of placing it closer to the outer wall was irrelevant.

Or was it?

After sketching a replica of the photograph, Tabitha turned back in the direction she'd come. This was a puzzle worth solving.

As Tabitha walked through Providence to the outskirts, she passed by Ambrose. He sat with his feet propped up on one of the little round tables outside the dining hall, a Rubik's Cube in his hands, enjoying the open air.

Ambrose perked up when he noticed Tabitha, but she ignored him and continued her pursuit. Unwilling to break into the restricted section again just yet, Tabitha found a spot she could view the warehouse from a distance. She angled herself to match the photograph as best as she could, and peered through her binoculars.

"What are you doing?" Ambrose asked from behind, startling her.

"Not now, I think I'm on to something," she mumbled shortly.

"Is it a puzzle? I'm good at those!"

He was acting a little too chipper for Tabitha's taste. "Please, Ambrose, this is important. I need to concentrate."

To Tabitha's surprise, Ambrose obediently went quiet, and she looked back at her sketches. Carefully comparing, she confirmed that there was, in fact, an extra crate at the front entrance of the warehouse.

"It still might be nothing…" she accidentally said aloud to herself.

"What might be nothing?" he asked.

"It doesn't matter—just a clue, I think."

"So it is a puzzle!"

Tabitha looked for a way to change the subject. "You've almost finished it," she said, pointing to the Rubik's Cube.

"This thing? This is easy; I just use it to keep my hands occupied."

Tabitha rolled her eyes. Showoff.

"No, really!" Ambrose sat down next to her and began twisting the cube's colored squares. "Because, think about it: once you have the system figured out, you've already won. Then it's just grunt work and time. It's the same pattern over and over again, depending on where the square is on the cube." He continued to flip it around. To Tabitha, it seemed random and sporadic. "A turn here, a turn there, and voila!"

Suddenly the cube was done, all colors in their prospective places. Tabitha did a double take, and hid it as soon as the expression had betrayed her. Ambrose smiled.

"Music is the same. But I'm sure you know that."

"How do you mean?" Tabitha asked in earnest.

"Your singing the other day was a perfect example of it," he explained. "There are certain notes that, by themselves, are nothing special; but then all together they make something that's just naturally beautiful to the human ear, whether you understand them or not."

Tabitha thought for a moment, forgetting that she'd initiated the conversation merely to distract him. "I've never understood them," she admitted. "The harmonies; I just hear them."

"You mean you did all that by ear?"

Tabitha nodded. Ambrose looked at her in admiration, and she found the need to look at her feet.

"That's amazing."

"Thank you," she said, cursing the warmth that rushed to her cheeks.

Ambrose went on. "Well, what you're hearing—it's all one big equation. Before you understand how it works, the possibilities seem endless and overwhelming. But once you fully grasp the concept, it's just like the Rubik's Cube: one, two, three, and poof! You have total control over the entirety of music, as well as its impact on everyone who hears it."

"Seems like a lot of power for one man to have," Tabitha said, remembering Dr. Buckley's experiment.

Ambrose surveyed the streets around them in thought. His eyes glazed over as if remembering something. "It is," he agreed solemnly. "Too much…" He took a deep breath, shaking off whatever it was he'd brought to mind. "That's why I'm so suspicious of Lilith," he said, lowering his voice slightly. He turned to her with some urgency. "Tabitha, she has so much power over us… over everyone!"

Tabitha looked around, suddenly wary that someone would hear him, and see her with him as he spoke the rebellious words. She wanted out of the conversation stat, but he kept talking.

"They give us everything we could ever want and then praise us like we're a bunch of heroes saving the world. But what if one day they decide to stop feeding us? I mean, why would Lilith feel the need to say that at every opening address? Every time: *Rebellious behavior of any kind will not be tolerated.* Why assume someone will rebel? It begs the question: against what? And the separation between the new apprentices from the elders, what's up with that? And now Dr. Buckley—"

"I'm not sure we should be talking about this," Tabitha cut in nervously.

Ambrose looked at her with curiosity, tainted with a hint of disappointment. "But it doesn't bother you at all?" he asked.

She looked out over the city in thought. "It's like you said, once you understand the system, you've already won, right?" she offered. "I don't need to know why, I just need to know how."

Ambrose stared at her, perplexed. Tabitha felt his eyes on

her face but continued to look straight ahead. Finally he stated, "And there's the strangest puzzle of all: people."

She met his stare but remained silent.

"No six color-coded sides, no mathematical equations… no. People are like knotted string, chaotic and unexpected. Just when you think you have them figured out, you find a new tie that's totally unique. Pull on a thread and you have as much of a chance of unraveling it all as you do of making it tighter. People… that's a puzzle that will always intrigue me."

His eyes bored into hers, glancing back and forth from one to the other, like looking for some missing piece that would put the whole picture together.

"So what's your puzzle, Tabitha Beckett?" Ambrose ventured softly, with an indication of her journal and the warehouse.

Tabitha felt an army of voices inside her demand that she stop the conversation at once, but her heart was prone to mutiny.

"My supervisor has me working on a case, some sort of security breach," she explained. "They've been stumped for months and now I am, too." She let herself look as anxious as she was.

"That's not homework stress," Ambrose pointed out, reading her expression. "Why does it matter to you so much?"

There were two answers to that question. Without her twin to confide in, telling Ambrose about her father and her revenge had a surprisingly strong appeal—but she knew better.

"I need the perks."

Ambrose took on a more serious air, picking up on hers.

"What for?" he asked.

Tabitha met his eyes, and reluctantly explained her mother's situation. Once she started talking about it, though, it wasn't hard to continue. She began to add little details, the ones that only mattered to her, the things people don't really care to know when they ask you a courteous question like 'How was your day?' But Ambrose listened to every word.

"I didn't even say goodbye," she continued, looking off regretfully. "It was stupid. But now the best option is to prove myself by catching this scumbag and earning her more antibiotics. If I turn him in, I save my mom."

Ambrose processed everything she'd said. After some time, he offered, "We can help, you know… Milo, Ella—all your friends. That case your supervisor has you working on, maybe we can—I don't know—set a trap or something. Milo could look for archaeological clues as to where he's hiding, I could use my music to control the environment—"

Tabitha had said too much. It was apparent that their pleasant conversation had given Ambrose a little too much traction, and the ease with which he'd managed to squeeze information from her was escalating. *This is weakness,* she told herself. *End it.*

"No, Ambrose, it's okay, I—I don't need your help."

There was an uncomfortable pause.

"Right," Ambrose remembered, "I forgot. Charity's not your thing." He smiled painfully. "Soup."

Tabitha confirmed with an apologetic nod, but inside she ached to take it back, to let herself lean on the people he'd called her friends.

The two returned their attention to the warehouse, watching as a man in a navy jumpsuit walked around the crates, jotting notes on a clipboard. Dominic. Tabitha skimmed through some pages in her journal again.

"You got any drawings of your mom in there?" Ambrose asked, glancing over her shoulder.

"Yup," she stated, but didn't leave her current page.

"What, you're not going to show me?" he prodded after her silence.

"Nope."

Ambrose tutted and folded his arms. "You know, I'm not convinced you even have a mother."

"Of course I have a mother."

"Really? How do I know you didn't make up this whole sap story to get attention?"

Tabitha turned to him with a exasperated expression. He raised an eyebrow playfully, demanding an explanation.

Huffing in defeat to her pride, Tabitha grumbled, "Fine," and flipped back in time.

Natalie looked rather sullen in her more recent drawings, which Tabitha didn't think did her mother justice; so she pushed the pages back to before the illness had gnawed away at the loveliness of her features.

"There, see?" Tabitha handed him the journal.

He examined the drawing, then snorted, "She looks nothing like you!"

"Oh, give me that!" she demanded, though she couldn't help but laugh a little with Ambrose. She snatched the journal away from him, but as she did so a page fell out. To her horror, the smiling face of Josiah Clay floated down to his feet. He picked it up, still snickering.

"Who's this?" Ambrose asked. Tabitha ripped the picture from his hands.

"No one important," she blurted, all sense of playfulness gone.

"*Clearly*," he commented, peering at it suspiciously.

Tabitha gave the sketched face a good long look, then crumpled the paper into a wad and tossed it in a nearby trashcan.

"Like I said: no one important." Tabitha closed her journal decidedly and tucked it away in her bag. "I should get going. I've got homework."

"All right," Ambrose accepted. "It was nice talking with you, Tabitha."

Tabitha mulled the sentiment over for a moment. "Yeah, you too," she replied, and was surprised when she realized it was true.

CHAPTER TWELVE

THE MAGICIAN'S BOX

"HE WAS A KIND MAN, THOUGH RATHER RESERVED. He didn't give you the impression that he wasn't listening, but there was always a sort of distance in his eyes when you talked to him, like he was off somewhere in his own mind."

Tabitha took down notes as the curly haired chef in front of her spoke, and tried her best to be unbiased in her interview questions. "This 'distance' in his eyes, did it ever make you uncomfortable? Make you think him... dangerous?"

"Dangerous? Oh, no," the woman replied fervently. "I never would have thought him capable of doing anyone unnecessary harm."

"As opposed to... necessary harm?" Tabitha asked.

The woman's eyebrows lifted. "I didn't mean—" she stuttered nervously.

Tabitha raised a hand to silence her, and was surprised when the motion worked. "So it surprised you, then, when he was accused of rape?" she pressed.

The lady nodded. "It surprised everyone. Whenever the

peacekeepers had a dinner party, he was the most courteous of everyone to my staff. Always remembered their names."

"Is there anyone on your staff who may have assisted him in his escape?" Tabitha questioned.

"No. Josiah was certainly likable, but no one would go against all of Security for him; that I can be sure of."

"And have any items from your stock been unaccounted for since his disappearance? Food supplies, uniforms, that sort of thing?"

"Last I checked, everything was in order. I can give you a copy of our inventories, if you'd like."

"Please do." Tabitha stood and extended her hand for a shake. "Thank you for your time."

• • •

"Clay was the best man I ever worked with," said a peacekeeper with a scratch of his head. "Hard-working, intelligent, and bloody principled. Hell, there was no messing around on his watch."

Tabitha scribbled down some notes in her journal, leaning over the edge of the outer wall on which they stood. The midday sun shone in the breezeway's arched openings, and through them Tabitha could see the cliff she'd once landed on by helicopter. Beyond it lay the vast, dry wilderness, scattered with brambles and cacti. Far away, an emerald river slithered through the earth like a slow and elderly serpent.

"Where were you on the day of his disappearance?" Tabitha asked.

"At a meeting in the Dining Hall. But all of our alibis have been recorded and sent to Chief Moore already, if you want a more detailed account."

The rank caught Tabitha by surprise. She knew that Rebecca worked for Security, but she'd never thought to ask about her specific position.

"Chief—that was Josiah's former title, wasn't it?"

"Yes ma'am. When there was a vacancy for Head of Security, the job went to Clay's next in command, Assistant Chief Beaux Fischer; but since that would put him in charge of Clay's case, Moore argued that it was a conflict of interest, and she got the spot. Off the record, though, I'd say she just wanted the position."

Tabitha took notes, wondering momentarily if this was why Rebecca was so determined to catch Josiah: to prove she could handle the responsibility of being Head of Security.

"From what I understand, your rank doesn't alter your uniform in any substantial way—how can you be sure Josiah's not hiding among you?" Tabitha asked.

"Everyone's on the lookout for him. There's not a man in Security who doesn't know that face. In my opinion, Clay's too smart to try and pull a move like that."

Tabitha tried a different angle, deviating from her script. "Did he ever talk about his family life?"

The peacekeeper cocked his head. "I'm not sure he had a family. He never mentioned any."

Tabitha made no response, but swallowed the lump in her throat. Of course he wouldn't have.

"Actually, now that you mention it," the peacekeeper added,

"he did wear a wedding band… inconsistently, though."

Two-timing bastard, Tabitha accused her father in her mind. "Can you elaborate?" she inquired.

"Had it on constantly toward the beginning of his time as Chief, then went without it for quite a few months. When he wore it again, it had been shined—looked brand new. I figured he'd sent it to the jeweler's. Long time to wait for a routine cleaning, though. And he wasn't wearing it the day before he disappeared."

Tabitha made a mental note to question the jeweler of Providence. Thanking the peacekeeper for answering her questions, she left the outer wall.

• • •

"Sure, I knew him," answered Dominic, the warehouse worker. He was less than pleased to see Tabitha again after Lilith had disregarded his accusations against her.

Tabitha, on the other hand, had high hopes for this interview. After discovering the mysterious crate, she theorized that there was an accomplice working at the warehouse. Someone could have easily provided Josiah with a uniform and let him walk straight through the outer wall. For all she knew, Josiah was halfway across Grexovium, hidden in a crate on a delivery helicopter.

"And what was your opinion of him?" Tabitha probed.

Dominic shifted in his seat before answering. "How can you have a good opinion of someone after they do what he did to Athaliah?"

"What about before then?" Tabitha clarified.

Dominic scrunched his brow, trying to recall. "I can't say. I didn't know him that well, before."

"And you know him better now?" she asked pointedly.

"Well yeah, everyone does!" Dominic replied. "His face was only plastered all over the city's walls for three weeks straight."

"So you agree he was nothing more than a criminal?"

To this, Dominic hesitated. "Well, no," he admitted. "I suppose, if Clay turned out to be innocent, I'd think very highly of him, actually."

"And why is that?"

Tabitha had begun to recognize the way people tiptoed around saying anything negative about Lilith or her administration, and Dominic's eyes showed signs of that now; but at length he shrugged, throwing caution to the wind.

"I just think it's funny to watch him outsmart you lot," he sneered.

Tabitha stifled the urge to punch his smug face.

• • •

Tabitha's head was swimming. The picture that her interviewees had painted of Josiah Clay was very different than she'd expected. He was… liked. Admired. Respected. And no one thought him capable of his crime.

But he'd done it. He must have, or else why would Lilith have it out for him? Athaliah's protruding belly was proof of that. His disappearance was proof.

Tabitha glanced again at her drawing of the mysterious crate in frustration. The interviews were getting her nowhere. Her opinion was biased, and she knew it. Her ears had filters on them, filters made by years of grudges, longing, fear, and hope. She couldn't trust them.

But she could trust her eyes, and her drawings. Tabitha decided she would investigate the crate again under cover of darkness. Something told her it was no oversight. That crate was there for a reason.

Apart from her new lead at the jeweler's, there was only one more interview to go: Popovic. She didn't want to pull him aside after class and interrogate him like some criminal's accomplice, and as far as she knew, there was no reason to interview him at all. He didn't wear a uniform. She assumed that Rebecca had a reason for the instruction, but after what Lilith had her do to Dr. Buckley, Tabitha was less inclined to follow blind orders against her teachers—disposable as they were.

Tabitha pushed through the door of Popovic's classroom, panting. It was ten minutes past the hour.

"Before you can master the art of disguise, you need to learn how to recognize one when you see it," Popovic stated as Tabitha burst into the room.

"Sorry I'm late!" she breathed.

"Not cool," he answered, keeping his disinterested attention on Maddie. Tabitha greeted her with a nod, dropped her bag on the desk, and pulled out a notebook.

"Anyhow, as I was telling the *class*," Popovic indicated his sole student, Maddie, "before you so rudely interrupted: you won't be able to convince an audience that you're the real deal—which you're not, by the way—until you can see right through another actor. To be in disguise, you need to first put yourself in the mind of the greatest skeptic. Master the ability to detect a deceiver, and only then can you become one.

"Now, the tricky thing with deception is that we often think that a lie is going to give off some sort of nasty scent that you'll be able to smell from a mile away. That's not always the case. Skillfully crafted lies are more like vegetables wrapped in bacon. You think your mother is giving you a treat, but really she intends to destroy your life."

Tabitha stifled a giggle. Popovic's monotone voice did not fluctuate, nor did his straight face waver.

"So, to start," Popovic continued, "we're going to play a stupid game: two truths and a lie."

The disapproving moans that Tabitha and Maddie let out would have sounded less rude if there'd been a class of a hundred other groaning students for them to hide behind. In this case it was just awkward.

"Shut up," Popovic demanded, which both frightened Tabitha into silence and again tickled her impulse to laugh. "We're playing the stupid game because, even though it's stupid, it'll give you practice in detecting a lie."

Popovic straightened his shoulders from his perch atop the desk, and Tabitha and Maddie gave him their full attention.

"As I gather from your obnoxious grousing, you already know how it works. I'll say three things, two of which are true, and you have to decide which one is the lie. Ready? One: I have a collection of rubber ducks."

Tabitha finally cracked. She snorted out loud and exchanged a look with Maddie, but Popovic's mouth stayed in a hard line.

"Two: I don't own a single article of non-black clothing."

That one's got to be true, Tabitha thought to herself, studying his current attire.

"Three: I'm deathly afraid of spiders."

This was ridiculous. The rubber ducks seemed the most likely option, but then again, Popovic didn't seem to have a large enough emotional range to experience a deathly fear. Even if he did, she thought he was too cool to admit it. Tabitha looked at Maddie, hoping she had some idea.

"I'd say the ducks," Maddie guessed. "Not that there'd be anything wrong with it if you did have a collection—" she started to defend.

"It'd be pretty weird though," Tabitha agreed, and the two looked at Popovic expectantly.

The corners of his mouth lifted, just barely. "Okay, next," he began. "One—"

"Wait, aren't you going to tell us the answer?" Tabitha asked.

"You got it wrong, so no. Try harder next time."

Disappointed, Tabitha sunk back into her chair, but then felt her spirits lifted when she realized that this meant Popovic did, in fact, have a collection of rubber ducks. She smirked.

"Now, don't focus so much on the content as on the delivery. No matter how absurd it seems, for all you know, it's 100% true; and no matter how logical it seems, it could very well be a complete lie. Focus on the subtleties in my expression, my voice, where my eyes turn when I speak. Ready? One: I care about you guys. Two: your supervisor will always have your back. Three: your friends are more important than your studies."

Tabitha's jaw dropped. This was a trap, some sort of test, she was sure of it. To deny the first would be insulting, the second would be seen as rebellious, and the third… well, the third was her only safe choice.

"Not cool," Tabitha shot at him, echoing his own words.

To her surprise, he grinned—a real, genuine grin. Tabitha didn't think that was physically possible for Popovic.

Maddie nudged Tabitha. "I went last time," she mumbled, "it's your turn."

Tabitha pursed her lips and gave it some more thought. Popovic hadn't shown any signs in his facial expression to give away the lie! She had to pick the third choice, she thought. It really was her only option to save face. Smiling wryly, she answered, "Well, of course you're more important than our friends."

Popovic's smile faded. "Wrong."

Tabitha's flattering attitude dwindled with his disappearing grin as she realized the implications of his statement. One was a lie… he really must not care about them. *That's not surprising*, she thought; but then she wondered—what if he did? And what did that tell her about Rebecca?

"It's critical that you get this, guys," Popovic asserted. "If you can't learn to detect a lie, the administration has you in the palm of their hands."

Maddie's face dropped at the brash statement.

"Are you saying they're lying to us?" Tabitha asked.

"Well, of course they are," Popovic confirmed. "And they want me to lie to you too, but I'm not going to do that—except within the context of this game."

"And how do we know you're not lying to us right now?" Tabitha posed.

"If I'm half as good a teacher as I think I am, by the end of this lesson, you'll be able to see that I'm telling the truth."

By the end of the lesson, Tabitha decided to postpone her interrogation of Professor Andy Popovic.

• • •

Tabitha didn't tell Rebecca that she was going to spy on Dominic. If she found anything substantial, she'd report it to earn perks; but after Popovic's subtle warning about her supervisor, Tabitha wasn't sure who to trust anymore.

She nuzzled deeper into her thick scarf with a shiver. The temperature had begun to drop for the night, but the heating panels had yet to be deployed. Above her, she could see the slightest remnant of sunlight, which cast a haze over the stars that peeked through the blue. Sheltered by the twilight, she snuck out of her apartment to revisit the mysterious crate.

Wearing a tight black dress and high heels to blend in with the night-life crowd, Tabitha navigated through the city toward its outskirts. She trailed behind packs of people so as to appear one of their party, just before slipping down a less-traveled alleyway.

When she was as close to the outer wall as she could get, Tabitha pulled off her heels and replaced them with quiet sneakers. She tugged on a pair of light-wash jeans and a large white sweater over her snug dress, and concealed her face with a scarf.

Tabitha oriented herself at an outdoor café table a few

blocks from the warehouse. From under a sun umbrella, which she turned to hide herself from open shops, she could see the restricted section through her high-tech binoculars.

The night vision setting turned everything green, bright, and clear. A few men passed in front of the open front doors. Tabitha could hear the distant clangs and clunks of machinery in the back, transporting goods into the building. At the center of it all was the inexplicable crate.

Dominic walked out. He looked around the front entrance. Then, to Tabitha's dismay, he yanked the massive sliding doors shut.

Tabitha immediately sought an alternative vantage point. To the left of the warehouse was a spa with a balcony, which might just give her a shot at seeing through the windows that still glowed in the dusk. Quickly but carefully, she crept to its entrance.

The woman at the main desk tried Tabitha's patience with eloquent praise of the spa's expansive selection of luxury massages, pools, and saunas. Eighteen listings in, Tabitha cut her off and requested a private jacuzzi on the balcony facing the wall.

"Right this way," she said flatly, and led Tabitha up a flight of stairs.

On the balcony, there were individual jacuzzis separated by sliding curtains, so that one could choose their level of privacy. *Perfect,* Tabitha thought, and dismissed the manager as quickly and unsuspiciously as she could. Pulling the curtain closed around every side but the one facing the warehouse,

Tabitha sat on the floor in front of the pool and whipped out her binoculars and journal.

She saw Dominic. Warehouse workers passed behind him as he stood facing a small desk by the window, checking his charts. Dominic glanced over his shoulder at them.

Once they had passed from view, Dominic slipped on his gloves, which he hadn't been using as he wrote. Then, with flawless stealth, he unlocked the crate in question and walked a few paces away from it, busying himself with some other task.

Tabitha gasped audibly, then quickly glanced over her own shoulder to make sure she was still concealed. With a bit more caution, she returned her eyes to the scene.

More men walked by. Dominic continued to work as though nothing had happened, until they were gone. Then he took a cardboard box out from under a stack of identical ones, carried it casually to the crate, and rolled up its door.

Tabitha leaned awkwardly sideways to keep him in view. It was difficult to see, but the crate appeared to be empty—that is, until Dominic threw the box inside. Closing the door once again, he walked out of sight, leaving the crate unlocked.

Tabitha waited. The box probably had provisions in it for Josiah to access, which meant Josiah might show up to claim them! Tabitha kept her eyes glued to her binoculars, afraid to blink lest she miss him.

But he didn't come.

Hours passed. Tabitha rubbed her eyes irritably. She had been too absorbed in the moment to sketch what she'd seen

Dominic do. Now she regretted it, having no proof to show for her efforts but her vague memory and rather untrustworthy word.

Then, from behind, Tabitha heard the spa manager's voice approaching someone a few jacuzzis down. "We're closing in fifteen minutes," she informed them. *Damn,* Tabitha thought, looking back through her binoculars.

"We're closing in fifteen minutes," she heard again—this time louder. The manager was opening each stall.

Tabitha looked around, realizing how very unusual she looked, completely dry next to a pool she'd been at for hours. Thinking fast, she stuffed her things in her bag, threw off her jeans and sweater and submerged herself—dress and all—into the water, turning on the jets as high as they'd go.

"We're closing in fifteen minutes," the woman stated, poking her head through the curtain. Just before pulling out, she hesitated, eyeing Tabitha's perfectly dry hair and the delicate straps of her dress. Tabitha smiled at her, striving her best to hide her heavy breathing. "That's an interesting swimsuit," the manager commented and, to Tabitha's relief, left it at that.

The curtain closed. Tabitha reemerged from the pool, wrapped herself in a towel, and returned to the scene.

Just ten more minutes, she instructed herself.

She only needed two. The lights at the warehouse had gone out, and just then, through her night vision optics, Tabitha saw movement. The crate door opened from the *inside*, and a man in uniform, carrying a cardboard box in front of his face, stepped out. His back was turned to her as he closed the door.

Tabitha held her breath.

I know those shoulders, she thought, feeling her hands begin to shake. *I know that hair.* He picked up the box again, and turned around. *I know that face.*

Josiah Clay set the box aside, turned the corner and disappeared from sight.

CHAPTER THIRTEEN

PUNISHABLE BY DEATH

TABITHA'S HANDS WERE NUMB. Her head was spinning, her heart pounding, and she wasn't sure whether to revel in her victory or cry out in emotional agony. There he was! She'd done it, she'd found him! One word from her and he'd be put behind bars. The thought sent a simultaneous warmth and chill through Tabitha's core.

"We're closing." The manager suddenly opened Tabitha's curtain again.

Tabitha jumped, fumbled an apology, and collected her things into her dripping hands. She looked awkwardly at her soaking dress and requested, "May I?"

The manager begrudgingly agreed to give Tabitha some privacy to change. Rather than pulling on her dry clothes, however, Tabitha darted back to look again at her father.

Josiah was outside the warehouse now, walking as casually as Tabitha had through the streets. She knew she had to draw him quickly, before the image faded from her mind, but she couldn't peel her eyes away. He hadn't changed a bit, except for the suspicious way in which he glanced over his shoulder now and again. His tall, slender frame was a bit more muscular than she remembered it, and maybe she could spot a hint of gray in his dark wavy hair; but for the most part, he was very much same man she'd once idolized.

But he wasn't the same man. Tabitha had to remind herself of this as a swelling urge to run into his arms fought its way up her throat. He was a criminal—a sick, cruel man who had turned on everyone he'd ever considered dear to him.

That was enough for her to snap back into spy mode. Tabitha pulled out her journal and made a note of which street he disappeared down. For a moment, she pondered whether to draw him in the warehouse or in the streets. She knew where he'd come out, but she wasn't sure yet if she should reveal that information to Rebecca. It could prove useful down the road if she failed to attain new information a week from then.

Pausing to recall the image, she sketched the memory, and lingered on his face. It had been so long since she'd seen that face.

Steps sounded on the marble stair leading up to the balcony. Tabitha threw off the towel and, with great difficulty, pulled her jeans and sweater over her soggy dress and burst out before the manager could burst in.

"Thank you, goodnight!" Tabitha said with a forced smile, and trotted off to her apartment.

• • •

The next morning, Tabitha wore a broad grin as she sprinted down the hall to the apartment's spiral staircase. She didn't have a session with Rebecca that day, but this couldn't wait. Breakfast, on the other hand, could. Tabitha decided to skip a meal and catch her supervisor before her *Survival of the Fittest* class, in which they'd be learning how to pin an opponent. That information might prove very useful in light of recent events, Tabitha mused.

Toby coincidentally stepped out of the hallway on the main floor of the complex at a most disagreeable time. Tabitha ran straight into him, knocking a bouquet of—flowers?—out of his hands. *He'll survive,* Tabitha told herself, and kept on moving, shouting over her shoulder, "Sorry, Toby, gotta run!"

"Hey, wait!" he yelled after her, but she was already gone. His brows knit together in thought as he bent over to salvage the dainty yellow orchids.

Tabitha rushed to Rebecca's office and gave a loud knock. No answer. After peering through the crack under the door, Tabitha saw that the room was dark and Rebecca was nowhere to be seen. Hoping Rebecca was somewhere outside the inner gates, Tabitha turned on her heel to search the grounds. Just then, Popovic emerged from his own office.

"Looking for someone?" he asked.

"Yeah," Tabitha replied, "my supervisor, Rebecca Moore. Have you seen her?"

"She's in a meeting. By the looks of it, they won't be done until this afternoon."

Tabitha hid her disappointment.

"Don't forget what I told you yesterday, Tabitha," Popovic mentioned.

Tabitha remembered the off-hand remark about Rebecca, and he gave her a look that encouraged her to take him seriously.

"Right, thanks," Tabitha brushed off, and Popovic left.

His warning did make her uneasy, but it wasn't enough to stop her from following through on this. She'd found her father—this meant steady perks for the rest of her apprenticeship. This meant her mother got to live.

The hours seemed to drag on. Even as Tabitha was applauded for pinning a fellow student exceptionally well in their practice fights for *Survival of the Fittest*, all she could think about was the sketch that lingered at the bottom of her satchel. Her awareness of it was so present that she was sure it would burn a hole through the bag and reveal itself to the whole classroom at any second.

Lunchtime came, and Tabitha approached the buffet tables on autopilot. Her mind was so preoccupied, she forgot that Provision food was much stronger in flavor than Privileged food, and only noticed the strange assortment she'd selected after she'd sat at a table by herself. She shoveled her teriyaki sauce-covered mashed potatoes into her mouth with a bite of salmon as she poured over her journal, and washed it all down with a spoonful of salted cherry jello.

"Hi," sounded a deep voice from above.

Tabitha looked up to see Toby, who sat down across from her. She bit the familiar taste of guilt as she noticed his flower-free hands, and dreaded an inevitable scolding.

"I'm sorry for running into you earlier," Tabitha began, sure he was there to reprimand her, "but I was on my way to something very important—"

"Oh, no—it's okay! Really!" Toby insisted. "Ella was able to rummage through the greenhouse and find a few more flowers to replace the broken ones… which weren't many, don't worry! She was the one who got them for me in the first place, for Maddie—" He blushed a little.

Tabitha's dread turned into shame. She hadn't considered who they had been from, or for.

"Which, by the way, is why I wanted to talk to you," Toby went on.

Uh oh… Tabitha braced herself. Playing match-maker was fun at first, but she really didn't have time for it now.

"I want to thank you," he started.

"I had nothing to do with setting you two up, that was all Ella—" Tabitha evaded.

"No, not for that," Toby interjected. "I'd be asking Maddie out tonight either way."

"Then what are you thanking me for?" Tabitha asked, still rudely shoveling her lunch into her mouth. She swallowed a thick bite of mint jelly-smothered cinnamon toast, stifled a gag, and placed it down. That wasn't the butter she'd meant to spread.

"For being there for her," Toby answered. "Maddie really looks up to you, you know. She doesn't have a lot of friends here and, well, I'm just glad she has you."

Tabitha choked on her food again, but this time from

Toby's statement. She wasn't sure how to respond.

Toby smiled and finished, "That's all. You don't have to say anything, I just wanted you to know." He quietly bent over his food and began to eat.

Tabitha looked down at her plate, no longer hungry. *That's all?* she thought, *That's it? No catch? No nonsensical request?* She watched him for a second and decided that if anyone in the world deserved the heart of Madeline Meyers, it was Toby Frankfort.

And Tabitha didn't deserve his friendship.

• • •

Tabitha rubbed her aching backside. She'd been sitting on the floor by Rebecca's office since lunch, waiting for her to return. More than once, the temptation to leave coaxed her into a standing position, but she forced herself back down. Finally, Rebecca's delicate figure appeared in the hall. Swiping aside her silky black hair, Rebecca spotted Tabitha and smiled.

"Have something for me?" Rebecca asked pleasantly.

Tabitha sprung to her feet and proudly replied, "Do I ever! Multiple things, in fact."

Opening her door with a key, Rebecca led Tabitha inside. Once their privacy was ensured, she beckoned her to speak again.

"I saw him. Rebecca, I saw him! Here in the city, last night. He's wearing a uniform, like we thought." Tabitha removed the page from her journal and presented it to Rebecca, who took it hungrily and walked past her, examining it. "Last I saw, he ducked down an alley by the library," Tabitha continued. "I thought about approaching him but, without backup, I figured that wasn't the best idea."

"Yes, that was wise of you," Rebecca commented, her eyes still glued to the paper. Tabitha was about to go on about the mystery crate and Dominic's involvement, but Rebecca spoke first. "This is wonderful. He's that much closer to the electric chair..." She said it more to herself than to Tabitha.

Tabitha's heart skipped a beat and the edge of her smile twitched. "What do you mean?"

Rebecca looked up, as if remembering that Tabitha was still there. "Oh. Sending him to his execution, of course," she explained indifferently, eyes returning to the drawing.

Tabitha's pulse quickened. "I thought the charge for rape was fifteen years in prison," she mentioned as nonchalantly as possible.

"Yes, well... not in Providence," Rebecca answered. "Besides, if you added up all the other crimes he's committed to hide this one, it'd probably amount to a death sentence anyway."

Tabitha didn't speak. She gripped her sketchbook tightly and thought. Was her mother's health and well-being worth her father's downfall? Maybe. But his death? Tabitha wasn't sure if she was ready to see that one through just yet.

Rebecca looked up, expectantly. "What else? You said you had more information—did you see where he got through? Or has he been inside the whole time?"

Tabitha tucked her journal in her bag and stuffed her increasingly sweaty hands into her pockets. "No," she lied, desperately seeking an alternative piece of information to offer. "I didn't see where he came from. Just happened upon him."

Rebecca pursed her lips in disappointment and rubbed her chin, thinking. She waited for what information Tabitha did have.

"The other thing—well, it's not as important as the fact that I saw Josiah; just a little observation, that's all," Tabitha stalled.

"Every little thing you find is helpful, Tabitha," Rebecca encouraged, her voice soft and kind.

Tabitha looked at her nervously. It was the only thing she had. She had to do it, there was no other way. "Remember Lilith's opening address, where she said, 'rebellious behavior of any kind will not be tolerated'?"

Rebecca nodded.

"Well, I've overheard a few things... from one of the apprentices. He's suspicious of Lilith's administration, really suspicious. But what's worse is he's been very open about it, talking to the other students, getting them to think the same. I can't be sure, but, it almost seems like he's trying to... start some kind of rebellion."

"Which apprentice?" Rebecca inquired.

"Ambrose Hurley."

Rebecca said nothing for some time. In the silence, Tabitha mulled over her own betrayal and hoped Ambrose would never find out who'd tipped Rebecca off.

He's disposable, a voice whispered in her conscience. *Your mother is not.*

The opposing side of her civil war spoke up: *But is your father?*

"I'll be sure to speak with him about it," Rebecca eventually responded.

At that moment, Rebecca's office door swung open and Lilith entered the room.

"Tabitha—I thought I might find you here!" Lilith announced.

Tabitha couldn't help but jump.

"What brings you here, Headmistress?" Rebecca asked politely. From what Popovic had taught her, however, Tabitha could tell that Rebecca was caught off guard by Lilith's abrupt entrance.

"I'd like for Tabitha to help with a little demonstration we'll be having for the fall recruits. We don't do it every year, but when we do, we try to have it either in the middle of winter or summer. I think the weather will be in our favor right about now."

"What's the demonstration for?" Tabitha asked.

"We do it to remind our newer students that we, Providence's elders and elites, are their life source—just as the Provision give life to the Privileged," Lilith explained. "With us, they will thrive in becoming the new face of Providence! Everything they've ever dreamed of can be attained, and they can live long, happy, and healthy lives. But without us… well, without us, let's just say that any attempts for success would be futile."

Tabitha heard Ambrose's words echo in her mind: *What if one day they decide to stop feeding us?*

Lilith went on. "When introduced to the world of ideas, many ex-Privileged have trouble adjusting, and don't yet know how to distinguish the good ideas from the bad. We do what we can in Detox, but it's not always enough. When this happens, and the apprentices in question step out of line, certain disciplinary measures must be enforced."

"Disciplinary measures?" Tabitha asked, her confidence wavering as she wondered if the demonstration involved herself, humiliated before all her colleagues.

"It's for their own good, of course. Some of our best elder apprentices were the ones who underwent this demonstration. If you asked them now about it, they would say it was… enlightening."

"If—if you don't mind me asking—which apprentices are going to be disciplined?" Tabitha inquired, a quiver of nervousness betraying her cool demeanor.

"Why, Ambrose Hurley, naturally," Lilith replied.

Tabitha's spirits sank as her betrayal sunk in. How had Lilith overheard?

"I think it would only be appropriate for you to be the one who saw to his reprimand. Oh, and there was one other boy I believe would benefit from the routine—Mr. Toby Frankfort."

Tabitha's heart shattered. *Deny the offer!* a voice inside her screamed, but just then, Lilith revealed another bottle of Rifampin. It glimmered with the hope of her mother's salvation, and the lure was too strong to resist.

This is what Tabitha had come to do. This was her mission. And it was for a good cause.

Tabitha straightened her shoulders and held her chin high. "What am I to do?"

CHAPTER FOURTEEN

DISCIPLINARY MEASURES

The next evening, Tabitha was brought before the great gate of the outer wall alongside Lilith, Rebecca, Cassady, and the peacekeepers. As the sun drooped ever lower in the sky, a bitter cold crept up from the shaded ground, nipping at her ears, nose, and fingertips. Presently, a pair of peacekeepers approached them, one on either side of Toby and Ambrose. Tabitha shifted uncomfortably.

Neither appeared worried, however, as they drew closer—just curious. Having finished their escort, the guards left to ascend to the top of the great wall, where—as Lilith had informed Tabitha—the other recent recruits had been brought.

"What's going on, Tabitha?" Ambrose asked trustingly. He seemed almost excited. The mystery of it all intrigued his puzzle-loving mind. His pleasant conduct only wavered when Tabitha did not respond, but instead averted her eyes.

Cassady approached her with a hefty ring of keys. Taking

them, Tabitha turned her back and approached the gate. Behind her, she heard Lilith speak.

"It has come to my attention that the two of you, whether in alliance with one another or otherwise, have been expressing explicit rebellious behavior, and as such are subject to punishment."

Tabitha's hands shook as she inserted each key into its lock and turned the vast cranks that appeared. She couldn't see, but she had a feeling that Ambrose's piercing eyes were glaring at her now. There was no hiding who had tipped Lilith off.

"You do, of course, have the option of admitting to your crime and imploring the clemency of your superiors, which may be granted depending on the level of your sincerity," Lilith said to the sentenced.

"Oh, I'm sure you'd like that, wouldn't you," Ambrose spat venomously. "You'd love to see us crawl at your feet, begging like dogs for mercy. Well, sorry to disappoint; you'll get no such apology from me!"

Tabitha looked this time. Ambrose leaned threateningly toward Lilith, and instantly two peacekeepers lunged forward to hold him back.

Lilith stood unwavering. "I had hoped better of you, Ambrose," she concluded. "And you, Toby?"

Tabitha hoped that Toby would refrain from following in Ambrose's footsteps, knowing what it meant for him if he did—but he simply shook his head.

"Very well," Lilith said, turning to Tabitha. "Open the gates."

Tabitha's face flushed red but she obeyed, turning the last of the cranks and stepping back as the massive doors creaked open. Peacekeepers forcibly led the two men through the opening and onto the stretch of flatland around it.

"Come back when you've had time to think about what you've done," Lilith instructed from the center of the open gates. "You need only knock, and we will gladly welcome you back home."

Ambrose glared at her. "That's never going to happen," he growled, and stomped off in the direction of the cliff.

The gates began to close behind Lilith as she walked back into Providence.

Tabitha strained to see where Ambrose and Toby had gone, but the doors shut, dividing them. She turned to Rebecca pleadingly for permission to ascend the outer wall and oversee the demonstration, as she'd been instructed. Rebecca nodded knowingly, and Tabitha sprinted up the stairs to the covered breezeway that spanned the entire wall.

When she arrived, Tabitha pulled her binoculars from her bag and leaned over the side to scan the stretch of land below. Farther down the tunnel, Ella, Milo, and Maddie stood watching the scene unfold. Maddie caught sight of Tabitha and rushed to her side.

"Tabitha! We have to do something!" she cried, gripping at her arm fiercely, "They've sent Toby out, they've sent him out to—"

Maddie stopped tugging at Tabitha's sleeve. Her eyes were fixed on the large key ring that was now looped over Tabitha's wrist.

Tabitha went to object, but felt a hand rest on her shoulder.

She wheeled around to see Lilith, smiling at her proudly. Looking again at Maddie, Tabitha was tempted to explain all that had happened, to say she didn't know that it would be this drastic, or that she had no other choice. In that moment, as Maddie backed away from her in denial, Tabitha was ready to make any excuse, true or otherwise, to take back what she'd done.

"I believe you'll have a better view from over there," Lilith told Tabitha, pointing past the other apprentices.

It was the last place Tabitha wanted to go—but when Lilith's gentle hand pressed lightly on the small of her back, she moved like a puppet to where she was instructed. Her head hung low as she passed under the disapproving glares of Ella, Milo, and Maddie.

When their backs were once again turned, Tabitha lifted the binoculars to her eyes. Toby stood still, looking about himself; while Ambrose walked frantically along the very edge of the cliff, peering over it. In her sights, Tabitha could see the deep wrinkles between Ambrose's eyebrows and veins bulging along his clenched hands. He paced back and forth like an animal in a cage.

Presently, Maddie removed the blue ribbon from her hair and released it over the edge of the wall. Toby spotted it as it fluttered to the ground. Picking it up, he gazed at its owner and kissed it, then tied it around his wrist.

Something caught Ambrose's attention. He stopped pacing and leaned forward, further examining his discovery. Turning around suddenly, he looked straight up at Tabitha. It took her by surprise, but she held contact, and his eyes—drenched in rage—drilled into hers. With one last accusatory scowl, he spun back around and disappeared over the cliff, climbing down its steep and perilous slope.

One of the nearby peacekeepers chuckled and pointed toward Ambrose.

"Hey!" Milo bellowed with a fury Tabitha had never heard from him before. Though a good six inches shorter than the man, Milo squared his shoulders in preparation to hurl him over the edge into the desert below.

Ella reached out a firm arm before his chest. Milo succumbed to the concern in her big brown eyes and pulled back reluctantly. The peacekeepers said nothing.

On the stretch of land beyond, Tabitha saw Toby begin to wander. Calmly, he observed the outer wall, pacing with unhurried strides toward where it met the ridge. She moved her binoculars back to Ambrose's general location. He reappeared far below, having successfully descended the cliff, and was now making his way around the clumps of cacti that scattered the rocky ground.

Unable to keep both in her field of view, Tabitha maintained her visual on Ambrose. Toby wasn't likely to go anywhere far, she figured. Ambrose moved away from Providence and toward a cluster of rifts, in which he took shelter. The sun had dissolved bloodily over the horizon, some of its peaks frosted lightly with snow, and the temperature continued to drop.

Dusk came and went. It was nearly eleven o'clock now. Toby had eventually followed Ambrose's trail down into the valley and entered a distant cave. Maddie, whose quivering breath could be seen in the dim twilight, pulled her jacket closely around herself.

Lilith broke the eerie silence. "Should you wish to leave now, you may. However, only do so if you fully comprehend the purpose of this demonstration. You are members of Providence, and should you disgrace so noble a title with such bad behavior, this will be your fate. Understood?"

No one talked back, but all stayed put.

The silence that followed left Tabitha's stomach feeling hollow—the uncomfortable ache one gets when waiting on the verge of something that never comes. The stars and moon were bright, casting a pale blue glow on everything beneath their kiss. Occasionally, a dark four-legged shape would dart across the valley below.

A howl pierced the night, sending a cold shiver down their spines. Maddie whimpered. Tabitha used her night vision to look for the source of the cry, but could see nothing. Her hands were burning and numb, tingling with pinpricks of icy fire. The temperature was now below freezing.

Ella shifted uncomfortably. No one spoke. Again, the howl shattered the quiet, this time answered by another. The two called back and forth to each other from either side of the gorge, followed by another, and another. They barked and yipped and wailed in a chaotic song of madness, a ballad of fretful, mournful hunger. The pack moved over the horizon, fading into the distant peaks, and was gone.

An hour passed. Ella was sitting now, cross-legged with her arms wrapped tightly around herself in an attempt to keep warm. She let out a massive yawn. Milo had gone to stand by himself farther down the tunnel. Sobbing quietly, Maddie kept her eyes glued to the valley, though there was little to see in the darkness. Lilith and Rebecca had left them in the care of the peacekeepers for the time being, with the assurance that they would return.

Another sound erupted in the black: a hoarse shriek that dissolved into a gurgling growl. It cried again and again until, with an echo of some dislodged rocks that clattered down the canyon wall, it ceased. Still, no sign of Ambrose or Toby at the opening of the caves in which they'd taken shelter.

Lilith returned and glanced at her watch. "Two-thirty… have they returned yet?"

"No," Tabitha breathed through numb lips, rubbing her tired eyes.

"Girls," Lilith addressed Ella and Maddie, "you know you are welcome to go to bed now. We'll make sure they get home safe; you can rest easy."

Maddie shook her head violently.

"Sorry, Headmistress," Ella croaked, "you're stuck with us. We ain't leavin' until our boys come back."

Lilith observed them without speaking for a moment, then said, "Very well. Rebecca will bring you some blankets, and I'll be back in another hour."

Rebecca came minutes later, a heavy stack of thick blankets folded in her arms. She took one and wrapped it comfortingly around Maddie. Maddie didn't peel her eyes off the vastness but gripped the edges of the blanket appreciatively.

Ella stood and received hers, managing to smile lightly in gratitude. Rebecca came to Tabitha's side.

"You okay?" Rebecca asked quietly, so the others couldn't hear. She draped the blanket over Tabitha's shoulders.

"Yeah," Tabitha whispered, "I think so… just tired, I guess." She didn't want to admit to the horrid way she felt whenever Ella, Maddie, or Milo looked at her.

Rebecca seemed to know, however, and rubbed Tabitha's back comfortingly. Then she strode gracefully to where Milo stood, hunched over in deep thought as he often was.

She couldn't hear them, but Tabitha saw Rebecca offer the blanket to Milo, who in turn jerked his bent head up to comprehend what she was asking. He stood a moment, staring at it, then waved his hand and turned away in rejection of the gift. Rebecca kept the blanket and left through a different exit farther down the corridor.

At 3:30 a.m., Lilith returned.

"I'm sorry to say it," she announced after coming to the conclusion that the disciplined were still at large, "but I do believe these boys will need a little extra incentive before they are willing to let go of their pride."

Lilith approached Maddie, placed a hand on her shoulder and spoke gently to her, "Madeline, you want them to come back, don't you?"

Maddie nodded, silent tears streaming down her face.

"I think you can help bring them back. Would you like to do that?"

She nodded with a glimmer of hope in her eyes.

"Good. Tabitha, come with us."

The two followed Lilith without question, though many plagued their minds. They arrived at the foot of the gate, and Lilith instructed Tabitha to open it once more. She did so, and Lilith stepped over the city limits, looking out into the gloom. Maddie and Tabitha curiously followed suit.

When Lilith didn't give an explanation, Maddie roamed freely onto the plain, inspecting her surroundings timidly. Tabitha stayed by Lilith's side, awaiting instructions; but Lilith merely stood, motionless, hands clasped behind her back, watching Maddie.

Maddie leaned over the edge, squinting at the tumbling stones that their friends had scampered down. Suddenly, Lilith turned on her heel and walked back through the gates, pulling the lever to initiate their closing.

Tabitha's breath caught in her throat. She looked frantically between Lilith and Maddie as the space between the doors shrunk. She couldn't leave Maddie—but what good would staying do?

"Come, Tabitha," Lilith calmly demanded.

Tabitha heeded swiftly.

From within Providence, Tabitha saw Maddie turn. A cry of horror escaped her lips as she realized what was happening and sprinted toward the gate. She was just inches away when the sliver sealed and the last lock fell into place with a clang. Throwing herself onto the wall in hysterical sobs, she pounded, slapped, and screamed in terrified pleas. Then all went silent.

• • •

Tabitha gawked at the gate, solidly shut with Maddie locked behind. Over her shoulder, Tabitha heard Lilith say, "It's for a good cause." Lilith returned to the lookout, leaving Tabitha with her shock.

Eyes wide and mouth dry, Tabitha rested her hands and forehead against the doors. *What have I done?*

Hands shaking, she made her way back up the stairs to where Ella and Milo were watching the canyon. They leaned over the side, Milo again next to Ella, staring speechlessly at their stranded friend. Ella gripped her face in her hands, peeking through her open fingers. Milo shook his head.

"Tabitha," he muttered, "Tabitha that's—that's wrong. That's very wrong."

Tabitha said nothing. Nor did she look at them. Unaware of her feet, they walked her to the balcony's edge and she peered over. Maddie stood motionless on the ground below, arms wrapped around herself, facing the great unknown. They could see her shivering—from fear, from the cold, from humiliation.

Then, Maddie steadied herself. Her shoulders raised and lowered as she took in a deep breath, and with sudden determination, she strode boldly to the edge of the cliff.

"Oh dear goodness, no—" Ella breathed.

Maddie began to climb down the steep and perilous slope, following Ambrose and Toby's path. Milo averted his eyes from the scene, pacing and ripping his rough hands through his manic hair. A minute or so later, they heard Maddie's voice echo against the canyon walls as it shouted for Toby and Ambrose.

Tabitha pressed her eyes to the holes in her binoculars.

Though Maddie carried herself bravely, Tabitha could tell she was terrified. The hoot of an owl made her jump, and she recoiled as she pricked herself on a cactus in the dark. Dodging the thorns as best she could, Maddie inched her way toward the cave where Toby had taken shelter.

"Toby!" she called again, her voice echoing back at her.

It wasn't the only thing that echoed back. The coyotes began to wail once more, and Maddie let out a little scream. Clapping her hands to her mouth, she forced herself to be silent and crouched down, listening. After holding her head between her knees to regain her courage, she stood and sprinted in the direction of the cave. Tabitha strained her eyes to see Maddie's form get smaller and smaller in her sights.

"She made it," Tabitha said when Maddie entered the cave at last.

The three let out a collective sigh of relief. They waited, relying on Tabitha's eyes and expecting Toby and Maddie to begin their return journey any minute.

But the minutes ticked on. Then the hours. Still, no sign of them.

Tabitha's head was throbbing. Her mind was past the point of being tired but her body ached and she longed to rest. She leaned against the stone banister and dug her fists into her sore eyes.

Suddenly, a muffled shriek erupted from the canyon. By the sound of it, Maddie was deep inside the cave. Toby should have been with her; why was she screaming? Tabitha desperately searched her mind for an answer. She'd kept a close eye on the cave, and Toby hadn't left. Unless there was another way out…

"Help!" Maddie cried. "Please, somebody!"

"Ella, get Lilith," Tabitha commanded, keeping her eyes glued to the canyon.

Ella immediately ran to one of the guards and spoke with him, and he in turn descended the stairwell to find the headmistress.

"Can you see her?" Ella asked once she'd returned.

"No," Tabitha replied. "I can't see any—wait, there's movement… it's Ambrose!"

Ambrose had appeared outside his shelter in the rifts. Through her optics, Tabitha could vaguely see his expression. He looked at his own cave, then back toward Toby's, as if waging an internal war with himself over whether or not he should abandon his original plan.

He gave in, and started sprinting in the direction of the cry. He must have stepped on something unpleasant, because he stopped midway and gripped his foot, and from that point on made his journey with a limp. By the time he reached the cave, Maddie's pleas for help had died out.

Over the horizon, the starlit sky began to grow a pale blue as the sun returned to their side of the earth, casting a faint gray glow upon the canyon floor.

"There they are!" shouted Milo.

Ambrose emerged from the cave with Maddie cradled in his arms, her head buried in his neck and her hands wrapped tightly around him. He walked very carefully, clearly in pain with each step but determined to get her safely to Providence.

As he neared the wall, the sun began to peek over the cliffs, painting the sky pink.

Tabitha, Milo, and Ella ran down the stairs to the front entrance, where they found Lilith waiting. She gave Tabitha permission to open the gates, and Tabitha did so eagerly.

Tabitha rushed forward to see if they were okay, but Ambrose pushed roughly past her. Gently setting Maddie on her feet, Ambrose grabbed a blanket from Rebecca and wrapped it around Maddie's shoulders. Both she and Ambrose were coated in red dust, leaning on each other for support. Maddie was sweating and shaking off violent shivers. Her pant leg had been folded up above the ankle, which was swollen and purple, held in place by a makeshift splint of sticks and torn t-shirt strips. A trickle of blood seeped out from two small puncture wounds below a tightly wrapped cloth.

"She got bit by a rattlesnake," Ambrose informed them. "Get her to the hospital. Now."

Ambrose passed Maddie off to Rebecca, who carefully escorted her into a white car that had just pulled up. Ella went with them, glancing over her shoulder at Tabitha as she left.

Ambrose remained where he was as the early-morning sun cast a copper glow on the edges of his features. Lilith looked at him with motherly concern. She approached, and slowly placed a hand on his shoulder.

"I'm sorry you had to go through that, Ambrose. I really am."

Ambrose pursed his lips and clenched his jaw, but said nothing. Breathing heavily, shoulders slumped and eyes drooping, he had all the likeness of a man defeated. Lilith gave him one last pat before walking away.

Tabitha took a step forward, nervously extending her hand. "Ambrose, I—"

He didn't let her finish. Shoving Tabitha aside, Ambrose walked unevenly into the city, Milo closely at his heel. Alone, Tabitha stood convicted. At the back of her eyes, she felt a prickling sting as long-subdued tears forced their way to the surface. They spilled over her cheeks and crept saltily into her mouth, and for the first time since she'd arrived in Providence, Tabitha had no mask to hide behind.

CHAPTER FIFTEEN

CIVIL WAR

REBECCA ENTERED HER OFFICE TO FIND Tabitha moodily slumped in the visitor's chair. Her hands hung limply at the end of the arm rests and she glared at herself in the long horizontal mirror that was suspended behind Rebecca's desk. They made eye contact through the reflection.

"Sometimes incentive isn't enough for people and they just… need to be put in their place," Rebecca explained cautiously.

"But Maddie!" Tabitha burst, spinning around to look Rebecca in the face. "Maddie's only crime was falling in love with a man who asked too many questions. If there was ever a person who didn't need to be put in their place, it was Madeline Meyers."

Rebecca fiddled with her hands and looked at the floor. "I don't like it either…" she confessed, her eyes still averted. There was a strain in her voice, a depth and honesty that caught Tabitha off guard. What else did Rebecca not like about the whole situation? What else was she keeping from her?

"But look around," Rebecca diverted. "There are no riots

in Providence, no complaints or division or chaos. Lilith told us from the start that there's a price to be paid if we're to be at peace."

"I'm not at peace," Tabitha countered, letting all pretense fall away. "Not with this, not with myself... sure, maybe now the rest of Providence can sleep better at night, but at the cost of someone who might never sleep again! You can't just sacrifice people like that in the name of a—"

"Good cause?" Rebecca finished her sentence. Tabitha cringed. "Isn't that what you're doing? For your mother?"

There was a pause as Tabitha thought long and hard about the statement. "But *he's* guilty," she weakly retorted.

Rebecca shrugged and Tabitha continued to think. Neither spoke for a time, though Rebecca looked as though she wished to say something. She watched Tabitha with inquisitiveness while Tabitha wrestled with her own contradicting thoughts.

Eventually, Rebecca let whatever words she wished to say recede to the back of her mind, gently placed her hand on Tabitha's shoulder, and said, "Tabitha, you need some rest. I know we were going to meet today, but it can wait. We'll resume our work on Thursday, as usual."

Tabitha nodded, and Rebecca walked her out. As the door shut behind her and Tabitha was again in solitude, her bloodshot eyes erupted once more. Her tears didn't stop when she arrived at her apartment, and the glorious sunrise through her window was no consolation.

As Tabitha let her bag slide off her shoulder and onto the floor, the thought crossed her mind to sketch the vague memory of how Ambrose had looked, standing there miserably with Maddie in his arms… but she immediately reprimanded herself for such an outrageous idea. She didn't want to remember this. Not one moment of it. She wished it would leave her forever and take all the painful regret with it.

A new bottle of Rifampin sat on her coffee table, presumably from Lilith. How it had gotten there, Tabitha didn't know. She didn't care. Snatching it up, she hurled it across the room with an anguished yell. It bounced against the wall and landed with a clang on the floor, and she sunk to the ground, burying her face in the cushions of her sofa. Muffled by the couch, she screamed out her fury and bawled angry sobs until exhaustion got the better of her.

Tabitha had seen this coming. She knew that growing attached to her friends would cause problems for her mission. What she hadn't foreseen was how they'd win her heart.

Ambrose, and the way he'd looked at her like she was the most interesting puzzle in the world. Maddie, whose love for Toby made her tough as nails. Ella, who was compassion itself. Milo, who would fight a man twice his size for insulting his best friend. And Toby—selfless, good-natured Toby. How could she not love them all?

When she stopped crying, Tabitha peeked up over the pillows at the jar on the floor. With a heavy sigh, she rose and walked to it, cursing at herself for being so careless. Picking it up, she checked it for damage, and found only a small hairline fracture near its base.

Setting it down once more, Tabitha sat in silence for a long while. Water poured steadily from her eyes as she wondered what Maddie must be going through at the hospital. Her wonder turned to resolve, and Tabitha grabbed her coat. Though fatigue hung like saddlebags on her limbs, she ran to the hospital.

Maddie's room was dim. Powder blue curtains shaded the sterile glow of the hall lights, and the sounds of busy medical staff members went silent as Tabitha closed the glass door behind her.

A tray of untouched food was perched atop the bedside table. Maddie lay silently beside it, her platinum blonde hair scattered in messy knots around her shoulders. Her face was pale, her lips dry, and her eyes red as they gazed sightlessly at the wall in front of her. She looked nothing like the sweet, trusting girl Tabitha had met at the Tolliver train station.

"Maddie?" Tabitha addressed timidly.

Maddie's expression changed to one of fear as she recognized the voice. She strained her eyes to confirm her suspicion that it was Tabitha, then rapidly sat up and began inching back into her pillows as if to escape an oncoming threat. Her quivering hand reached out for something beside her bed.

"Maddie, it's okay—it's me!"

Maddie pulled a red knob on a string and seconds later a nurse entered the room.

"Is everything all right, Miss Meyers?" the nurse asked.

Maddie shook her head to indicate that everything was *not* all right, and pointed a trembling finger at Tabitha.

The nurse turned apologetically to Tabitha. "I think you'd better leave," she said.

Tabitha glanced at Maddie, then back to the nurse in disbelief. "But—is she okay? Did the venom make her sick, is it life-threatening?" Tabitha stammered desperately while the nurse ushered her across the room and out the door.

"Don't worry, she'll be fine," she assured. "The anti-venom is taking effect and she should be better after a few days' rest."

Before Tabitha could say another word, the door was closed in her face and the curtains drawn before them. A fresh well of tears sprung up in her eyes, which she did her best to contain, but she didn't stand a chance when she caught sight of Ella standing in the hallway behind her.

Tabitha averted her eyes as a waterfall burst from them. Ella looked very serious at first, but upon witnessing Tabitha's sorry state, she was filled with compassion. Ella guided Tabitha to a sofa in the waiting area and they both sat down. Tabitha's bag landed upon the table and the jar of Rifampin rolled out. Ella caught it just before it fell, and placed it right side up.

"You have—every right—to hate me—" Tabitha choked through her rigid breaths.

"Hey now, it's all right," Ella comforted, rubbing her back. "It's not your fault, you were just doing what you were told."

"But it *is* my fault!" Tabitha sputtered. "They never would have had the demonstration if I hadn't ratted out Ambrose!"

Ella tilted her head. "You did what?"

"I told my supervisor that he was acting rebellious and turning people against the Institute. Lilith overheard me, somehow. I didn't want to, it just—it was the only—I had no—" Tabitha shook her head and buried her face in her hands again.

Ella stroked Tabitha's back once more, but her brows knitted together in thought as she studied her mysterious friend. She eyed the medication at the opening of Tabitha's bag, and gradually put two and two together.

"That for your mom?" she asked, pointing at the bottle.

Tabitha nodded feebly.

"They bribe you with more to do this discipline thing?"

Another nod.

"Doesn't make it okay, though," Tabitha sighed.

"Nope," Ella confirmed with a sad smile. They looked at one another.

"Oh Ella, how can you possibly forgive me? Maddie doesn't—she's positively terrified of me now," Tabitha moaned. "And Ambrose most certainly won't; he's furious. The way he looked at me... Then Milo does whatever Ambrose does, so he's bound to be all dramatic. They'll never speak to me again, I'm sure of it. Although Toby might. Besides you, I think he's the only one who will be willing to forgive me."

Ella grew very serious.

"What's wrong?" Tabitha asked, perceiving Ella's expression.

"Tabitha, Toby never came back," Ella replied somberly. "He's missing."

"*What?*" Tabitha sat up with eyes wide.

"Rebecca said the peacekeepers are doing everything they can to find him, but they haven't had any luck yet. Ambrose is convinced they aren't really looking."

Tabitha felt sick to her stomach. Her "extra credit" had gone too far. No good cause could justify this, not even her mother.

Her perks would have to come from Josiah's capture, nothing else. Tabitha would be Lilith's pet no longer.

"He wasn't in the cave?" Tabitha suggested.

"No, and they said there was no other way for him to get out besides the opening we saw. It doesn't make sense. It's like he vanished."

The magician's cave—it was just like her father in the mysterious crate. Had this somehow been Josiah's doing? Had he used his same method of disappearance to kidnap Toby as some sort of collateral?

Or was Rebecca just too concerned with the Clay case and her title as Head of Security to prioritize one lost boy? How else could Toby have disappeared under the peacekeepers' careful watch, unless they weren't permitted to waste their time watching?

Tabitha thought of Maddie, miserable in her hospital bed. "Does she know?" she asked Ella.

Ella shook her head. "Not yet. I was trying to figure out the best way to go about it," she replied.

Maybe there was still time to redeem herself. If Tabitha found Toby, maybe her friends could forgive her…

"Don't tell her yet; I have an idea."

• • •

Lilith was the last person Tabitha wanted to see after the demonstration—second only to Ambrose. Nonetheless, Her connection to Lilith was still Tabitha's strongest asset. Rebecca wasn't prioritizing Toby's rescue, and her ulterior motives to keep Josiah's former position as Head of Security continually put Tabitha on edge. Ever since Popovic's off-hand comment about her, Tabitha had grown suspicious of her supervisor. So she decided to take matters into her own hands—with a bit of help from the highest authority.

"Headmistress, thank you for seeing me!" Tabitha addressed politely on the following day.

"Anytime, Tabitha. My office is your home," Lilith replied. "What can I do for you?"

"I heard a rumor that one of the apprentices from the disciplinary demonstration, Toby Frankfort, has gone missing—I was wondering if I could organize a search team. I figured it would be good practice for me, if ever I am to be part of Security myself."

Lilith waited a beat before replying. "That's a wonderful idea, Tabitha, but—I'm afraid—your efforts would be wasted."

Tabitha's heart sank.

"Why's that?" she asked, hiding her anxiety.

Lilith spoke each word with care. "I'm afraid the poor boy is likely dead."

Tabitha's mouth went dry. The back of her eyes stung and suddenly all she could see in her mind was Maddie—alone, heartbroken, angry. The room seemed to swirl. Tabitha gripped the edges of the chair she stood behind as nonchalantly as possible, and managed to ask, "What makes you say that?"

"We found a body this morning. We haven't announced it yet because, well—the coyotes got to it before us and, quite frankly, it's difficult to identify."

Tabitha tasted bile.

"Can I—see?" She didn't want to, but Toby was her friend. She'd be able to identify him, surely.

"No, I wouldn't want to put you through that," Lilith said. "It's gruesome. And besides—who else could it be? I'm afraid the likely conclusion is that it was the Frankfort boy. Now—sit yourself down. I have something else I'd like to tell you."

Tabitha heeded willingly.

"When we found the body, we first assumed he was attacked by the beasts, and that's what killed him; but when we looked closer, we found a knife wound in his side. We think his death may have been at the hands of a man… your father."

Tabitha swallowed hard, but said nothing.

"You see, Rebecca has informed me that all the evidence suggests that Josiah is not hiding in Providence, but living in the wild, with the help of some accomplice to bring him provisions. If that's true, the Frankfort boy was likely a victim of being in the wrong place at the wrong time. He probably stumbled upon one of Josiah's hiding places, in which case Josiah would have found the need to silence him. And what better way to cover it up than by pinning the crime on the animals?"

Tabitha wasn't sure she could handle this information dump. Toby was dead. Her father might have murdered him. And Rebecca was a liar… she knew that Tabitha had seen Josiah within the walls; why would she tell Lilith the opposite?

"Are you all right, Tabitha?" Lilith asked.

"Yes, I'm fine," she lied. "It's just a lot to take in."

Lilith placed a hand on Tabitha's shoulder, and Tabitha did everything in her power not to shy away from it. She wanted it to be a lie—all of it: Toby's death, her father's murder, Rebecca's dishonesty. She didn't have the eyes to see like Popovic, to read people and tell when they were speaking the truth. Not with Lilith and Rebecca, anyway.

There was only one person in Providence Tabitha knew she could read, if she had the chance to confront him...

"Thank you for meeting with me," Tabitha said as pleasantly as possible, and left Lilith's office.

• • •

Tabitha spent the afternoon with Ella, the only person she seemed to have left in the world. Ella's big brown eyes welled up when Tabitha told her about Toby, but she only nodded in acceptance of what had happened. Ella was stronger than Tabitha had given her credit for.

Ella also agreed to break the news to Ambrose, Milo, and Maddie. Tabitha tried not to imagine their reactions, or how different things would be between her and them from now on. For all she knew, they would probably never speak with her again. She'd pushed them all away, considered them *disposable*, and only now that she was losing them did she realize how much she longed to have them in her life.

Tabitha wished Mayra Mae were there to tell her what to do, or that she'd write her a letter of sweet nothings for consolation, at least. It was immeasurably lonely in that moment to be Tabitha Clay.

Tabitha turned to Ella, who sat calmly on a floor rug with a clay pot nestled in between her crossed legs. From a smaller pot at her side, she carefully uprooted a spiky plant that looked nothing like the type of thing you'd want sitting on your windowsill. Placing it in its new home, she buried its roots with rich soil. Then she set it aside, revealed another one, and repeated the process.

Neither spoke. Neither had to. Their shared presence was enough to fill the silence.

Tabitha was so grateful for Ella. Though she knew she couldn't tell Ella all the things she might have told Mayra Mae, there Ella was, doing exactly what Tabitha's twin would have done: loving her at her worst.

A knock at the door splintered their tranquility.

"Come in," Ella called, and the door opened.

Ambrose limped hurriedly through. Upon seeing him, Tabitha stood and Ambrose stopped. His scowl resurfaced, and he turned back toward the door.

"Ambrose, wait!" she cried, "I'm sorry—please, don't—"

But Ambrose was gone.

Tabitha sunk to the floor opposite Ella in despair. "He doesn't even know about Toby yet… he'll be even more angry when he finds out."

"Don't give up," Ella affirmed. "Here—help me with this." She indicated the cactus in her lap.

Tabitha reached out to assist in the repotting, but pricked her finger on a thorn and flinched. "Ow!"

"Everyone's a little prickly right now," Ella explained. "You can't grab them head on, you've got to go for the roots."

Tabitha adjusted her grip on the plant and listened.

"When you replant something, it gives it more space to

grow—but it also makes a mess and can take a toll on the plant. You have to touch it gently, carefully—and let things sit for a while before handling it again. Wait for its roots to dig deep, and just keep showering it with water and sunshine from a distance. Then, when it's strong again, you can touch it once more."

Tabitha took a deep breath and felt her heart float up with it.

"I'll talk to them," Ella went on. "You just keep being the ray of sunshine that you are, give them space and time to heal a little, and I'm sure they'll come around."

Tabitha smiled. "Thanks, Ella."

CHAPTER SIXTEEN

THE RING

LATER THAT WEEK, TABITHA PAID A visit to Providence's jeweler. The peacekeeper Tabitha had interviewed said that her father wore his wedding band inconsistently. Tabitha knew what that meant. It meant that Josiah was cheating. Whether or not he killed Toby didn't change that likely fact. It was why she'd postponed this visit for so long—she didn't want the jeweler to confirm it.

But if Josiah had gotten his ring cleaned, the jeweler had made contact with him and might have useful information to share.

Tabitha closed the store's door behind her, and her jaw dropped instantly. She gaped around at the glass cases which displayed countless sparkling pieces of jewelry. As she caressed a gold necklace that hung delicately in the open, she wondered what it must be like to have nothing better to spend elite perks on than accessories like these.

"May I help you?" someone asked from behind.

Tabitha turned to see a man in his late sixties, polishing a watch in his hand.

"Yes," Tabitha replied. "I was wondering if you could verify something for me. Was Josiah Clay ever one of your customers?"

The man showed recognition at the name and nodded. "Sure, he came to me once or twice."

"What can you tell me about his visits?"

"Let me see," he mumbled, and rustled through some files from behind the counter. "He had a watch fixed about a year ago… bought a necklace a little while later… then a couple of rings about six months ago…"

"I'm sorry—can you elaborate on that last one? You said he *bought*—what kind of rings?"

"Two gold wedding bands."

Tabitha planted her hands on the counter to steady herself. She pulled her journal from her bag and checked her notes. What had the peacekeeper said? For a while, Josiah wore the ring all the time. Then, for a few months, it wasn't on his finger; and right toward the end, he wore it again, and it had been polished.

But it hadn't been polished. It was *new*.

Josiah had remarried.

His betrayal bit into Tabitha's insides. What more proof did she need? People could be sorry for rape; they weren't typically sorry for marrying someone they loved. What would Natalie think when she found out that her husband had left, not to save her, but for another woman? Would Mayra Mae still insist that Tabitha let it go? Could she?

"Are you all right, miss?" the jeweler asked. Tabitha came back to reality.

"Yes, sorry—that was just what I needed to know. Can I have a copy of those files?"

The man nodded, and handed over the papers.

"You can have the ring, too—if it's any help."

"What?"

"He sold one of the two back to me right before the warrant went out for his arrest. Here—" The jeweler hunched over and dug through another box in the desk, then returned with a small plastic bag in hand. Inside it was a man's wedding ring.

Tabitha took it gingerly. "What do I owe you?" she asked.

"Nothing. I'd rather not have it on my hands. I don't feel comfortable re-selling something once worn by a criminal."

Tabitha thanked him and left, the ring a heavy weight in her hand and on her heart.

Sitting on a patio bench, she toyed with the ring in her fingers. The sun reflected blindingly off the white cobblestone streets and cast halos of gold off the wedding band. Every time the metal brushed her skin, Tabitha felt the need to wash her hands of its contamination. She couldn't believe that her father would leave Natalie—the greatest woman on the face of Grexovium—for terrifying, wild-eyed, disheveled Athaliah.

Tabitha stopped fidgeting. A thought occurred to her—a terrible thought! Or was it wonderful? She couldn't decide which. Her head hurt and her heart felt constricted as she realized: if Josiah and Athaliah were married, her pregnancy wasn't the result of rape.

Josiah was innocent.

Hardly! a voice in Tabitha's head retorted. It was almost

worse, she thought, that he had married another. It wasn't just a moment of lust. It implied that he actually loved Athaliah.

Tabitha ripped at her hair. She couldn't stand it any more. She had too many questions, and no amount of interviews could give her the answers she sought. It was time to confront Josiah.

Tabitha looked at her watch. She had a meeting with Rebecca in just a few minutes. She'd need to provide new information if she wanted her supervisor to ship the bottle of Rifampin Lilith had left in her apartment. Tabitha considered the ring…

No; that information was too valuable. Plus, if Josiah was proven innocent, that would mean no more Clay case, and no more free passes into restricted sections to find him.

That gave Tabitha an idea. Standing from the patio bench in the sun-kissed square, she made her way to Rebecca's office.

"I heard you met with Lilith," Rebecca mentioned when Tabitha walked through the door. It sounded more like an accusation than a passing comment.

"I did," Tabitha admitted.

"I thought you said you weren't going to go looking for extra credit anymore."

"I'm not; it wasn't about that."

"What was it about?" Rebecca pushed.

How could she answer that? *It was about you not doing your job and finding my friend before he got stabbed by my father and eaten by coyotes…*

"Just a personal matter," Tabitha assured. "I'm still dedicated to the Clay case, no worries there. We'll catch Josiah, just you wait."

Rebecca looked at her feet. "I wanted to talk to you about that, actually." Rebecca closed the door to her office and sat down before continuing. "I've been giving your apprenticeship some thought, and I think now would be a good time to re-evaluate and revise our curriculum."

"I thought it was going rather well," Tabitha countered, suddenly worried that Rebecca might try to take her off the Clay case.

"Tabitha, you're a hard worker. You're determined and fearless—but at the disciplinary demonstration, I saw the toll this work has taken on you."

"I'm okay now, really. I just needed to get used to it, that's all," Tabitha insisted.

"But Josiah is your father," Rebecca urged. "It takes more than a tough cookie to do what I've had you do. I was wrong to put you in that position. We can find other ways to earn your perks—"

"Rebecca, you gave me an opportunity I've been seeking for a long time," Tabitha stressed. "I want to be the one to catch him."

"But you yourself said that you weren't at peace with sacrificing someone in the name of a good cause," Rebecca started. "Are you sure—"

"It's not just about the medicine," Tabitha interrupted. "I want to do this for… revenge."

The statement tasted bitter on Tabitha's tongue—mostly because she wasn't entirely sure it was false. She thought it would be what Rebecca wanted to hear, but her supervisor looked strangely disappointed. Whatever her reason for trying to get rid of Tabitha, Rebecca wouldn't shake her that easily.

Rebecca took a breath. "Well," she said, "then I suppose we should get back to work." Pulling an envelope from her jacket, she handed it to Tabitha. "This came from your sister yesterday. I hope it's good news."

Tabitha hungrily snatched it from Rebecca and ripped it open. It read:

Dear Tabitha,

We received the medicine you sent! Mom is doing so much better already—though I trust you'll be sending more. She still has a long way to go. Can you get more antibiotics? Providence sounds wonderful. They must be truly generous to help you like this.

Love,
Mayra Mae

Tabitha clenched her jaw. The letter was a heavy hand of reality slapped across her face. Her mother still needed her help…

Tabitha flipped it over, hoping for more details on the other side. *That's it?* she wondered. It gave her little indication of where Mayra Mae was at emotionally.

"Thank you," she told Rebecca, unable to express much enthusiasm.

"Is it not good news?" Rebecca asked in response.

"No—it is," she replied, "it's just… I have a lot of work to do, that's all."

"You're doing great, Tabitha," Rebecca reassured. "And I'm here to help, you know. Don't feel like you have to do this alone."

Yes, I do, Tabitha countered in her mind, but nodded with a weak smile.

"Will you send her my reply with this?" Tabitha requested, pulling from her purse a bottle of Rifampin and a new letter she'd written for Mayra Mae.

Rebecca took it with a nod. Then she winced, gripping her hand.

"Are you all right?" Tabitha asked.

Rebecca's finger appeared to have a small cut.

"Yes—I must have scratched myself on…" Rebecca paused, looking between the bottle and the letter. "Must be a paper cut." She placed the bottle and letter in a drawer, brushed herself off, and asked, "Were you able to find any more leads since last week?"

"Yes, actually," Tabitha replied. "I have reason to believe that one of the men I questioned has been helping hide Josiah: the provisions warehouse manager, Dominic Kaczynski."

"Good," Rebecca said. "Write up anything you have on him and leave it on my desk as soon as possible."

• • •

Tabitha felt no remorse for revealing Dominic's alliance with her father to Rebecca. Tabitha disliked him about as much as he disliked her, but that wasn't why she'd done it. If Josiah was guilty, she was right to turn Dominic in; and if he was innocent, Dominic would thank Tabitha in the long run for what she was about to do.

"What do you want?" Dominic barked as Tabitha approached the warehouse's front doors.

Tabitha held up a paper that Rebecca had given her, indicating her permission to enter restricted sections on account of her work in the Clay case. "I need to talk to you," she claimed.

Dominic's eyes glinted with both fear and malice. "What for?" he demanded.

Tabitha walked confidently through the doors and across the line that divided public space from restricted section. Dominic curled his lip in agitation.

"Arrogant brat," he started, but Tabitha waltzed right past him down an aisle of crates where she knew they would not be seen. Dominic followed after her. "Hey!" he called. "Just because you have access to be in here doesn't mean you can just—"

She stopped suddenly, slapping a hand on a particular crate—one that was out of place among the others: the Magician's Box. She turned, and Dominic swallowed hard.

"I know about Josiah, Dominic," Tabitha said coolly.

"I don't know what you're talking about," he claimed, but patches of red were forming on his neck, followed by a glaze of sweat across his forehead.

"No need for that," she said. "I came to warn you. Security knows, too." Tabitha conveniently left out what exactly it was that they knew, and that she had been their informant.

To her surprise, however, the flicker of fear in Dominic's eyes burned into something entirely different. "I'm sure they do, with you being on the Clay case," he sneered.

Tabitha stood her ground. "We need to do something about it, and quick, before—" she evaded.

But Dominic had something in his hands now. He took a step closer to her, wrapping his fists around the ends of a heavy metal chain. "We sure do," he growled menacingly.

As the chain inched closer to her neck, Tabitha's pulse quickened and her palms grew clammy. Her fate was starting to look a lot like Toby's. Thinking fast, she whipped a sheet of paper from her purse and slapped it against Dominic's chest.

Dominic lowered his weapon and took up the paper.

"What's this?" he snarled.

"Leverage. It's a list of people that Security suspects are helping Josiah," she replied.

Dominic scanned it, and the same hint of fear betrayed his eyes. Tabitha reached for it back, but he folded it to stow in his uniform pocket. "I'll be keeping that," he declared.

"Good—I trust you'll use it to warn them when Security is on their trail," she patronized. "But wait—you won't be able to do that, will you? How could you know when they're in danger, when you and Lilith are so very disagreeable to one another? She would never confide her plans to you… how could you possibly save your criminal friends?"

The ridges of Dominic's scowl dug deeper into his brow.

Tabitha took a step closer, her voice dripping with snide theatricals. "But I know someone Lilith *does* trust—someone she'd tell all about Security's plans to stop rebellions from rising in Providence. That would be helpful, wouldn't it? Now, who was that? …Oh!" She let out a mocking laugh. "Me!"

Tabitha's Cheshire grin turned upside down as she hissed, "Now trust me, or Josiah *will* be captured by the swarm of peacekeepers likely on route as we speak."

Dominic pursed his lips. "Why do you want to save him?"

"Because—I knew him," she replied. "I don't think it's right. No one should get the death penalty, even for rape."

"Rape? You think that's why they want him dead?" His voice was laced with painful cynicism.

Tabitha could feel the presence of the gold ring in her bag. She gave no response.

"How do you know him?" Dominic asked.

"I grew up in the same town as Josiah, in the Axelle Privileged sector," she replied.

Dominic leaned forward, glaring deep into her eyes, surveying her with the same skepticism Popovic would use to sniff out a lie during one of their exercises. "Anyone could figure out Josiah's home sector if they had access to what's left of his file, which—as I understand—you do."

"But there's nothing on file about his character," she refuted, "about how he traces a figure of eight on the table when he's nervous… or that his favorite color is that hideous shade of orange… or that when he laughs too hard, he gets the hiccups…" Tabitha eyes glazing over a bit as she recalled the memories. "Now you look me in the eye and tell me I don't know Josiah Clay."

Dominic remained silent for some time. Finally, after what

seemed ages to Tabitha, he succumbed. Ripping a key from a set on his uniform belt, he pushed past her and unlocked the mysterious crate.

Tabitha would have beamed a triumphant smile, but she knew better. Maintaining her serious demeanor, she looked over his shoulder into the Magician's Box. It was empty—but there was something odd about its floor. Tabitha raised her eyebrows in astonishment. It didn't have a floor! The bottom was the same concrete as the warehouse ground, and toward the back of the crate was a metal manhole cover.

That's how he's doing it! she thought to herself. Suddenly, it dawned on her that if Josiah was traveling underground, there was no reason to think he couldn't get outside the walls and into the canyon where Toby was murdered…

Dominic ripped a piece of paper off a notepad and scribbled something on it. Tabitha barely glimpsed what it said before he pulled open the manhole cover and left it inside: *Use library entrance.* Then he began to fill the crate with boxes.

"You gonna help me or what?" Dominic demanded from inside the crate.

Tabitha got to work immediately. She passed him scraps from a pile of discarded junk against the wall, and soon the crate was filled so that revealing the cover would be no easy task. If Security searched the warehouse, the crate would be disregarded.

Their task completed, Tabitha prepared to close the crate's sliding door. Dominic stood quite a few paces away, cleaning the mess they'd made.

Suddenly, Tabitha spotted peacekeepers at the warehouse entry. *Right on schedule,* she thought.

"Dominic!" she hissed. "Peacekeepers!"

He swung around in the direction she'd pointed, then started urgently toward her.

Wrenching the crate door shut, Tabitha opened her hands and ordered, "Key, now!"

Dominic hesitated, but the peacekeepers would be upon them at any second. He knew he couldn't trust her as far as he could throw her, but what choice did he have? Security would notice him rushing to the mysterious crate, but Tabitha was still concealed enough to escape their view.

Dominic tossed the key to Tabitha and she locked the crate. Then she smiled a deadly grin.

"I'll be keeping that," she taunted, and pocketed the key.

Rage swept over Dominic. He could have strangled her in that moment, but her voice bellowed out before he could silence her. "He's over here!" she called, and seconds later, Dominic was surrounded by navy-clad peacekeepers under Rebecca's command. He turned in all directions, searching madly for a way out.

"Dominic Kaczynski," Rebecca announced evenly as his hands were bound, "you are under arrest for assisting the criminal activity of Josiah Clay."

Dominic's eyes—seething with fury—pierced into Tabitha's. In the brief moment that their gaze met, Tabitha removed her mask for him. She tried to tell him, with her eyes, that the key to Josiah's crate was safe with her; that until she knew for certain that her father was guilty, it would never reach the hands of Dominic's captors. They had succeeded. Security would be distracted now with Dominic, and Tabitha would adopt his role as guardian over the Magician's Box.

But her efforts to communicate this were in vain. Were it not for his handcuffs, Tabitha knew that Dominic would have stopped her heart in a heartbeat. Now his jail cell would keep her safe from his grasp, and his secret would remain safe with her.

That evening, the peacekeepers searched every crate in the warehouse, and found nothing.

CHAPTER SEVENTEEN

CONFRONTATION

When blanketed in the safety of sacred darkness, Tabitha paid a visit to the library. If she'd understood Dominic's note correctly, there was another manhole somewhere inside through which Josiah could come and go at will. Five minutes with Josiah would be enough to tell if Lilith was lying about his many crimes, Tabitha thought.

A block or so away from the library, Tabitha watched through her night-vision binoculars as a motherly-looking older lady locked up. Once the woman was well on her way to the center of the city, Tabitha got to work.

There were three doors to the library: the main entrance, a side entrance, and an employee entrance. Taking the wire she'd discovered in her drawers of spy gear in her apartment, Tabitha wound it around the double handles of the front door until it could not budge if unlocked from the inside. Then she made her way to the side entrance and did the same, leaving only one way out.

The employee entrance faced an alley where no passersby

would see. A few feet from the door, Tabitha set her trap: a tripwire which would set off discreetly planted flares, and trigger spring-assisted cords to wrap around Josiah's ankles, should he get too close.

It was only a precaution. Tabitha planned to talk to him first; but if he didn't have a good explanation for his wrongs, if he turned out to be as dangerous as everyone said, she'd merely lure him across the line. Her flares would shoot into the night sky to signal the peacekeepers, who would put an end to him for good.

Her trap set, Tabitha waited. She waited and watched until her eyes stung and face went numb from the pinpricks of winter's breath. Finally, when all of Providence was sure to be fast asleep, a shadow stirred behind the library windows.

Tabitha remained motionless, but adrenaline surged through her veins as she prepared to spring upright. She faintly heard the sound of the lock sliding from its place, and the door opened slowly. Tabitha held her breath, and her insides squirmed like worms on a hook as she anticipated the sight of her father.

Naoko Araki emerged.

What? Tabitha wondered in shock, and stood involuntarily. The small, pale woman from the welcome dinner froze, grasping the handle of the door once more, ready to pounce back inside.

"Wait!" Tabitha called. "Is that you—Naoko?"

Naoko squinted in an attempt to identify Tabitha. "Come closer," she requested.

Tabitha heeded and walked as close as she could before

crossing her tripwire. "It's me—Tabitha Beckett. You were at my welcome dinner; remember?"

Naoko took a moment to respond. "How could I forget?"

"You disappeared after Bryce escorted you out. What happened?"

Naoko glanced about the darkness, pain written on her face. When her eyes finally returned to Tabitha, she reopened the library door and quietly invited, "Come inside."

It was a gamble on both ends. Tabitha knew the risk of leaving her trap behind and putting herself in Naoko's hands, but her curiosity was overwhelming. Tabitha carefully stepped over her tripwire and followed Naoko into the library.

As the door shut behind them, Tabitha strained her eyes to see their surroundings. She'd never been to the library. She was surprised they had one at all. Reading wasn't a common hobby for Privileged, thanks to the constant feed of entertainment projected on every screen.

Like everything else in Providence, the architecture was a masterpiece of beauty, though smaller than most structures in the city. There were two stories to the building, but the center of the second was cut out to feature a ground-level lounge that could be seen from the open railing of the top floor. A grand piano stood in the middle, surrounded by comfortable seating and study tables. The upper level was accessible by intricate spiral staircases, and every inch of the walls was lined with books.

Tabitha brushed her hand along the volumes and went to pull one out, only to find it stuck. Upon further investigation, she realized they weren't books at all—just the spines, glued to the inside of the shelves; no more than wallpaper to provide atmosphere.

Before she could decide what she thought about that, Naoko ushered her to sit.

"At your welcome dinner, I failed my duty as an elder apprentice," Naoko explained. "I was specially chosen, along with Mason, Leena, and Bryce, to be a big sibling to the new students. We were trained to speak and act a certain way to make sure you felt comfortable and only knew what you needed to know... I said too much."

Tabitha's brows contracted. "All you said was that we couldn't talk to the elders—"

"It was enough," Naoko insisted, "and I received the punishment I knew to expect for such a failure."

"Which was?"

"Exile. I was beaten and sent outside the walls."

Tabitha's jaw dropped. She thought of Ambrose, Maddie, and Toby, freezing in the desert. "How did you get back in?" she asked.

"There was a man... a man outside the walls. He saved me. I was too sore to walk, so he carried me over his shoulder through a cavern and showed me a place I could sleep. I have been hiding underground ever since."

"Who was he?" Tabitha asked.

Naoko looked intently into Tabitha's eyes and replied, "He never told me his name but, I knew his face. He was the felon—Josiah Clay."

Tabitha felt a flutter in her chest. Her father—the so-called rapist, the probable murderer—had saved this poor girl from Toby's fate...

"Where is he now?" Tabitha asked.

Naoko shook her head. "I never saw him again, though I have looked for him. I look for him every day."

"He never came back? How have you survived all this time?"

"A warehouse worker helped me. He said that Josiah told him to make sure I was brought food and water from their supply."

"Dominic," Tabitha realized.

"Yes—but today he left me a note that makes me think he's in trouble."

Tabitha fiddled with her thumbs. She'd cut this poor woman off from her life source, just to hash out her personal daddy-issues... "He was arrested by Security this morning." she informed, and found it difficult to keep eye contact.

Naoko paused in thought, but did not express any emotional reaction.

"What will you do now?" Tabitha asked, her voice filled with pity.

"There is another who will bring me rations," she said calmly. "He will come when he hears the news about Dominic."

Tabitha nodded, and wondered who this other mysterious hero might be.

Just then, Tabitha heard a hiss of air outside, and a streak of red shone in her peripheral. Naoko's white face went even paler.

"Flares!" she gasped. "We need to hide—they will find me!"

Someone had crossed Tabitha's tripwire. They had mere

seconds before peacekeepers came swarming through the door.

"Where's the entrance to the tunnels?" Tabitha asked.

Naoko hesitated. Tabitha knew how steep the request was, but they had no time. Suddenly, the employee entrance door opened and a figure filled the frame.

Tabitha and Naoko dropped to the floor and inched their way toward a reading nook in the back of the library. Tabitha glanced over her shoulder, but could not see who had entered.

When she turned back, she was shocked to find Naoko gone! She dared not whisper her name, but searched hopelessly in the dark for the little woman. Then, suddenly, Naoko's head popped out from behind a bookshelf and she signaled for Tabitha to join her.

It took Tabitha a moment to figure it out. It was an optical illusion: a section of the wall, nestled between the two shelves, stood farther from the rest with just a small gap on either side that led behind it. Creeping around the wall, Tabitha saw a stairwell made of cement, unadorned and wide.

Naoko and Tabitha sprinted down the stairs and around a corner, then through a closet door. Naoko shut it behind them and hauled a thick, musty rug from its place on the floor and dropped it aside with a flopping thud. Dust flew up from where it landed and coated Tabitha's tongue. Where the rug had been was a wooden door. Naoko twisted the latch and pulled it up, then urged Tabitha down a cold, metal ladder.

The air dropped in degrees. The longer they descended, the more Tabitha wondered how far the ground beneath them was. She gripped the rails tighter. Her hands were clammy, and she couldn't tell if it was her cold sweat or if the air was growing in moisture the farther into the earth they went.

Finally, her toes touched bottom. A rhythmic drip echoed vastly in the distance.

"Where are we?" Tabitha whispered.

Naoko shushed her and grabbed her wrist. Tabitha followed her lead through the pitch black darkness. She tried to remember which way they'd turned, but lost track after two lefts, one right, three lefts, two rights, and another left.

Eventually, Naoko crouched down and pulled Tabitha beside her. Their backs were against a jagged wall that felt like stone, cold and wet. Without her sight, Tabitha's sense of touch was heightened. She covered her mouth with one palm and and turned her focus to the loose dirt and rocks under her other, Naoko's thin hand still wrapped around her wrist. She listened for any sound besides her own muffled, heavy breathing, and cursed it for being so loud.

Silence ensued. After a time, Naoko let go of Tabitha's wrist and inched away. Tabitha suddenly felt very helpless and hoped Naoko wouldn't go far. She heard a faint scrape of metal against stone and suddenly there was a flicker of light.

The flame inside Naoko's lantern was no larger than a fingernail, but it made everything visible. Tabitha's eyes adjusted and she looked about. The room was not manmade, but a cave. Stalactites dripped from the ceiling and stalagmites climbed from the floor, all a muted rusty color. A ruddy wooden table was stationed in the middle of the cave and a shovel rested against the wall.

Naoko stood up. "The coast is clear," she said. But just then, footsteps sounded in the tunnel. Tabitha sprang to her feet and Naoko turned toward the hall. Setting the lamp down on the table, Naoko grabbed the shovel and planted herself against the cavern wall, ready to bash in any peacekeeper's head that showed itself around the corner. Her ferocity caught Tabitha off guard.

The footsteps broke into a run. Tabitha braced herself for the impact of metal against skull, when she heard a voice.

"Tabitha?"

Just as Naoko was about to swing, Tabitha shouted, "Stop!" and reached out to hold Naoko back. Ella emerged at the entrance of their cave.

Ella and Tabitha laughed as they embraced each other, but Naoko's eyes remained suspicious, darting back and forth between the two of them.

"What are you doing here?" Tabitha asked.

"I could ask you the same!" Ella replied. "We saw that you were out late and followed you to make sure you were all right."

"We?"

Then Ambrose appeared behind Ella, with Milo flung over his shoulder. His eyes flickered in meeting with Tabitha's, then averted to the ground. He was still mad.

Tabitha looked at Milo. His feet were bound by a rope— which she quickly realized was her own. She stifled a laugh.

"You set off my flares?" she asked.

"*Your* flares?" Naoko shot. Tabitha met her eyes and realized she had some explaining to do. Before she could, however,

Naoko added, "How did they find us?"

"I led them here," another voice from behind Ambrose sounded. Tabitha's eyes widened as she recognized it. Professor Andy Popovic came into view, a plate of food in his hands.

"There you are, dear," he said, and passed the plate to Naoko.

Popovic was the mystery hero.

"Sorry for the delay," he said after Naoko had taken the food. "I had to convince the peacekeepers that the flares were my fault—told them it was a practical joke. They didn't seem too surprised, coming from me."

"So there are no peacekeepers on our trail?" Tabitha confirmed.

"No—we're good," Popovic responded.

Tabitha heaved a sigh of relief and plopped herself down in one of the chairs around the wooden table.

Ambrose roughly dropped Milo into the chair opposite her, started to untie the ropes at his feet and said evenly, "Someone want to tell me what's going on?"

His tone wiped the smile off Tabitha's face. The others came around the table, each pointing their gaze at Tabitha, waiting for an explanation. Naoko looked especially perturbed.

"Right," Tabitha answered.

She hesitated. Tabitha was among rebels. Popovic had committed treason by helping Naoko, a woman who had been exiled for her fault. These—and Dominic, who risked everything, every day, to keep Josiah safe—were the people Rebecca had warned her of, warned her to stay away from… but they had done no wrong. Tabitha was not afraid of them anymore.

"When I heard that my friend, Toby, went missing, I went to Lilith to see if I could organize a search team," she started. At that, Ambrose looked up at her, his eyes softening slightly. Tabitha met his gaze. "But she told me he was dead."

Her voice cracked, and Tabitha took a moment to regain her composure. "She said that he'd been murdered by a felon I've been helping Security look for—Josiah Clay." Tabitha looked at Naoko now, whose black eyes looked suspicious. Ambrose furrowed his brow in thought as if recognizing the name.

"I didn't want to believe her," Tabitha went on. "I needed to know for sure, so I used what I'd found out about Josiah to track him here. I'd hoped to talk with him and get some answers, and set the flares in case I needed backup.

"I found Naoko instead. He'd *saved* her. Why would he have killed Toby? It doesn't make sense."

"That's because it's not what happened," Popovic stated. The party turned their attention to him. "Lilith is lying to you."

"But how can you be sure?" Tabitha asked.

"When people go missing in Providence, it's no accident," Popovic answered. "If Lilith wants somebody silenced, it's over. There's no keeping them safe. I don't know how, I don't know why, but I'm positive that Toby's disappearance was intentional."

"I knew it…" Ambrose muttered.

Ella and Milo exchanged wary looks.

"So you think Josiah didn't kill Toby?" Tabitha asked. She found herself hoping desperately for it to be true.

"More than that: I think Josiah's the key to proving that Toby was murdered by Lilith's administration, and for preventing further injustices at this Institute."

The others looked around at one another.

"How?" Ella asked.

"We need to get the New Order involved. Get Master Karl Thorne to issue a full inquiry of the Institute," explained Popovic. "If they did that, all of Lilith's secrets—including Toby, Naoko, Dr. Buckley, and countless others—would be unearthed; and Providence could be reformed."

"How would Josiah help us do that?" Milo asked.

"Josiah is the only man who's ever escaped Lilith's secret death sentence," Popovic said. "I like to think I had a part to play in that—he was my best student. At any rate, that's made Lilith desperate. So desperate that she's publicized her hatred of him to get the help of every pair of eyes in Providence.

"Because it's such a well-known case, both in- and outside the walls, if we can prove him innocent of the made-up sap story she's presented to the public—which I'm quite convinced is false—that'd be enough to get the New Order's attention.

"But, if that man dies according to her plan, Lilith will be without opposition. She'll have complete power over everyone, and people like Toby—anyone who so much as annoys her—is as good as dead."

There was a pause. Tabitha felt her heart beating in her temples with what she could only guess was resolve. She wanted it to be true…

"But," Milo said, "if we prove this Josiah guy innocent… won't that make us rebels?"

Popovic nodded. "Quite so. And if you want to live some

posh life in some Provision sector after graduating from the Institute, you absolutely cannot do what I just told you."

"I'm in," Ambrose said abruptly. He leaned back in his chair and folded his hands together in his lap. "Toby deserves justice." His eyes lingered on Tabitha with the same problem-solving look he'd had when the two of them talked puzzles, but she couldn't read its meaning.

"Me too," Ella resolved. "I couldn't live with myself knowing all this was going on here and I did nothing to stop it."

Milo nodded in agreement, and the three turned to Tabitha in expectation, waiting to hear her decision.

Her heart burned with the same fire that shone in Ambrose's eyes. This was Tabitha's chance to make things right, for Toby and for Dr. Buckley. And she already had everything they needed! The gold band that proved Josiah innocent of rape was sitting in her purse as they spoke…

Suddenly, Natalie Clay's sullen face came to mind. The bottle of Rifampin Tabitha had given to Rebecca that morning and Mayra Mae's letter resurfaced. It dawned on Tabitha that to join this rebellious cause would be to forfeit the cause for her mother.

Could she let her mother die to free her father, after all the suffering he'd caused them—innocent or not? The ring seemed to sink deeper into her bag. She couldn't tell them—not yet. But still, joining their cause would mean that all her friends were there to help her find her father faster—and turn him in if need be.

"I'm in," Tabitha decided.

Popovic allowed himself a small grin along with everyone else's whoops of agreement. Ambrose was the only one to refrain from smiling.

Milo stood suddenly and placed his hands flat on the table. Then, dramatically, he said, "We shall be the Fellowship of the Ring."

The room went silent. Tabitha's stomach sunk as she desperately thought of how Milo could have known about the ring, or what his cryptic statement meant. She wasn't the only one who looked confused.

When Milo gave no explanation, Ella cocked an eyebrow and asked, "I'm sorry—what?"

Milo looked at everyone with immense disappointment. "Oh come on, don't any of you read? It's a classic!"

Ambrose shook his head and laughed. "Only you, Milo. Only you."

"Normal people don't leisurely read random historical documents," Ella teased.

"It's not a—why, you—you don't know what you're missing!" he insisted.

Tabitha's gut returned to its appropriate arrangement and she let herself laugh with everyone else. Milo muttered something about a movie series as they stood to leave, looking thoroughly disgruntled. Tabitha glanced at Naoko, who had been silent for the majority of their meeting, and wondered what she might be thinking. Tabitha hoped she wasn't mad at her for compromising her hiding spot.

"I have two friends that I think will join our cause," Popovic said as they made their way back to the library entrance. "James and Gavin. I'll introduce you to them another time."

They said goodbye to Naoko and ascended the library ladder, then made their way discreetly back to the apartments.

As they walked, Tabitha slowed her pace so that she and Ella trailed out of earshot behind Ambrose and Milo. Then, she asked, "Ella, why did you follow me? What did you say to Ambrose and Milo to get them to come?"

Ella smiled gently—sadly. "I used to have a sister. She was always very melancholic, and I brushed it off as her being a dramatic teenager—but then one day we found her dead." Ella bit her lip and looked at her feet.

"She'd committed suicide," Ella continued, "and I should have seen it coming—but I didn't, and I didn't do anything to prevent it. That's when I started making my own drugs. I was trying to create something that would stifle depression—both in her honor, and for myself… but it's also when I resolved to always give people the benefit of the doubt; to assume the best, be quick to affirm people and build them up, because you never know what's going on inside their head.

"I knocked on your door tonight to see how you were doing, and when I saw you weren't home, I got worried. I knew you had a lot of things to feel guilty for, and was afraid you might do something reckless. That's all I needed to say to get them to come. They were upset with you, sure, but they still care."

Tabitha felt her eyes mist over. She smiled at Ella and squeezed her had.

"You're the best friend I've ever had," Tabitha said.

CHAPTER EIGHTEEN

THE WINTER SOIRÉE

A WEEK PASSED SINCE THE DAY OF THE DEMONSTRATION. Tabitha refrained from telling her new rebel circle about the ring that proved Josiah innocent, and instead racked her brain for a new way to find and confront him personally.

Since their secret meeting in the tunnels, Tabitha had seen nothing of Ambrose or Milo. There was no news of Toby. Like Naoko after the welcome dinner, he left no trace and was forgotten, unspoken of, and disregarded by most.

But not by all.

Tabitha stopped at the greenhouse where Ella was just finishing up her class, *Edible & Poisonous Plants*. When she saw Tabitha, Ella shook her head in disapproval, but beckoned her in.

"You know, they're going to start noticing that all the flowers are going missing. How is she even breathing with all that pollen in her room?" Ella peered around to make sure her teacher was out of sight. The two were huddled in a corner of the sunlit, glass-walled greenhouse, hidden from view by masses of hanging flower baskets.

"I have to keep trying. It's been a week," Tabitha said. "But get this: she spoke to me yesterday! I asked her if she wanted me to get the nurse, and she said *no!* If that's not progress, I don't know what is."

Ella gave Tabitha a sideways glance. It wasn't much to rejoice over.

"If you say so," she muttered, and snipped a handful of lilies at their base. She gave them to Tabitha, who wrapped them in string to hold the bouquet together.

"Thanks, Ella!" Tabitha said, and the two bid farewell.

Tabitha made her way through the streets of Providence and pushed through the doors of the hospital. The florescent hall lights illuminated a bustling medical staff pushing monitoring equipment and preparing IV bags. No one acknowledged her presence or took the time for pleasantries, except for Maddie's nurse, who had come to recognize her.

"She's asleep," the nurse informed with a kind smile when Tabitha reached Maddie's door.

"Thanks, Charlotte," Tabitha said, and slipped quietly into the dim room.

There, Tabitha saw Maddie bundled in her hospital gown and layers of blankets. Surrounding her bed, covering every bedside table and counter, were bouquets of flowers.

Tabitha crossed the floor and sat in a visitor's chair by the bed to observe the sleeping patient. Maddie's face had gained more color and she looked like herself again. According to Charlotte, the nurse, Maddie was physically well enough to return to her apartment now. Her emotional state was the only thing that kept her in the hospital.

Tabitha added her lilies to the collection of offerings around Maddie's bed. She expressed a faint smile at the thought that Maddie would soon be up and about as usual. Her smile faded, however, when she noticed what lay at the tips of Maddie's fingers on the side of her bed.

It was a small frame, in which she'd pressed a single yellow orchid—Toby's orchid. Amid all the vibrant colors of Tabitha's offerings, only one flower had Madeline Meyers fixated.

Tabitha hung her head and sighed.

Just then, Maddie stirred. "Tabitha?" she croaked.

Tabitha turned to Maddie, catching the frame with the orchid just before it slipped to the floor. She nestled it carefully in Maddie's hands and caressed them. "I'm here," she assured, "what is it?"

Maddie quickly but calmly pulled her hands from beneath Tabitha's. Tabitha did her best not to be hurt by this, and waited patiently for Maddie to speak again. Maddie held the frame close to her heart, looking distantly across the room.

"You don't have to do this, you know," she managed, looking around at the flowers. "They're sweet... but they can't bring him back."

Tabitha willed her tears to remain dormant.

"I know," she said, lowering her voice to a whisper. "But we can try to bring him justice."

Maddie's eyes were drained of hope, but they met Tabitha's with what little they had left.

"There's a ball tonight, the Winter Soirée. Come—if you're

well enough—and we'll tell you everything."

Maddie thought for a moment, then nodded.

"I'll see you tonight, then?" Tabitha confirmed.

"I'll be there," replied Maddie.

Tabitha smiled and left with her own hope expanded.

• • •

Tabitha's winter coat was removed from her shoulders and hung with her purse on a rack in the hall. With it gone and her Soirée attire exposed, she felt suddenly vulnerable, and suffered an odd case of the stomach butterflies. Why was she so nervous? She tried incessantly to convince herself it was because of the very serious business she was about to conduct with her new rebel band, but the fact that she needed the reminder gave her the impression that it wasn't quite true. She found herself scanning the room for a particular broad-shouldered, blue-eyed man…

Tabitha slipped away to check herself in the bathroom mirror. Her short, messy waves of hair had been curled elegantly, pinned back in the front with a delicate clip of cubic zirconium that matched her teardrop-shaped earrings. Her eyes were painted with long black liner and her freckles speckled her face like constellations in the night sky.

The midnight blue dress Tabitha wore shimmered slightly when she moved within its drapery. She craned her neck around to see its open back in the mirror and wondered if it was just a little *too* pretty. She'd never looked so elegant in her life.

The ballroom was on the top floor of the dining hall. Its long windows, adorned with luxurious curtains, displayed the star-filled winter sky and mirroring city lights, which twinkled far below. Candles lit round tabletops suspended on tall stands, scattered around an expansive dance floor. Tuxedo-clad elites weaved silently through the crowds, serving hors d'oeuvres; and in one dark side of the room, a band was playing soft music beneath the clinks of glasses and utensils.

Leena, Mason, and Bryce—the elders who had led the welcome dinner—stood chattering at the drink table. Tabitha wanted to punch them each square in the face for what they'd done to Naoko, but settled for slipping salt in Bryce's coffee instead. She glanced back from the other side of the room just in time to see him spew it all over Leena and Mason's fancy attire, and choked down a burst of laughter.

It helped ease her tension a little, but not enough. Eyes peeled for her friends, Tabitha wandered around a crowd of frilly girls admiring each other's garments. Their shrill voices put her on edge, and the noise of her heels clicking with each step added to her anxiety. Where *were* they?

At last, Ella entered with Maddie, followed by Milo. As Tabitha scanned the room for the last of her friends, she felt the same uncomfortable prickly butterflies again. It was more annoying than anything. She had every reason to be afraid of an encounter with Ambrose, knowing his temper and her crime which warranted it—but this was different. This was beyond her understanding.

A shadow moved from the band, and a tall, dark-haired man walked into the light. Then she understood the squirming in her stomach. Had Ambrose always been so handsome?

His jet black suit fit his frame perfectly, and the blue of his tie brought out the color of his sad, thoughtful eyes. They met hers, flickered down her dress, and then settled on the floor. He fiddled with his fingers for a fleeting moment before casually striding to the drink table.

Curse this dress, Tabitha thought. She felt her face with the back of her hand. Why were her cheeks burning? Firmly commanding herself to get a grip, she wandered as if aimlessly to Ambrose's side. Ella watched from the other side of the room where she appeared to be bickering with Milo over appetizers.

"So—tell me again why it's a good idea to plan our first move at the *Soirée*, where every blabbing apprentice we know is hovering within ear-shot?" Ambrose inquired under his breath with harsh skepticism, averting his eyes from Tabitha. His tone felt like a hot blade in her stomach.

"The best place to hide is in plain sight," Tabitha quoted, as if Popovic's words were her own.

"Right," Ambrose mumbled, giving his acute attention to the drink he was pouring. "And you've no problem being seen with a rebel?"

Tabitha couldn't tell if he was mocking her or being serious. "Seeing as I am one, people will have to get used to it," she declared.

Ambrose did not respond.

"Although," Tabitha added uncomfortably, "might still be best to keep contact to a minimum…"

"All right, then," he agreed, and turned briskly to leave.

"Wait—" Tabitha objected, but went silent when she caught

his eye. His expression no longer mocked her, but signaled her to look toward the door. She followed his glance and saw Rebecca approaching.

As Ambrose turned once more to walk away, Tabitha could read the *you're welcome* in his expression.

Tabitha posed a smile as Rebecca made eye contact. Her supervisor was dressed in a fitted gown that matched her silky black hair, which was pinned up in a bun. Rebecca smiled back and started toward her, but stopped as she noticed someone. Holding up a finger to tell Tabitha she'd be there in a moment, Rebecca turned to Maddie.

Tabitha just then realized how lovely Maddie looked with her loosely braided hair trickling over the neck of her floor-length, sunshine yellow dress. She showed no signs of fear when Rebecca approached her, and Tabitha could make out the words *thank you* on her lips. If only Maddie knew what Tabitha knew: that her double-crossing supervisor was a liar, who'd done absolutely nothing to help find Toby...

Just then, the song changed, and Tabitha saw Ambrose approach Maddie. He held out a hand with a charming smile and Maddie obliged, following his lead to the dance floor. Tabitha had to consciously stop herself from staring as they moved gracefully across the room. A twinge of unexpected discomfort bit at her insides.

"Hello, Tabitha." Rebecca's voice startled her. Tabitha hadn't even noticed her supervisor join her at the drink table. "Lovely evening, isn't it?" she added.

"Yes, quite lovely!" Tabitha replied, forcing a smile.

"Good to see Maddie is doing better," Rebecca commented.

"Mhm," was all Tabitha could think to reply.

Rebecca looked for a new subject. "How are *you* feeling? You've had a lot on your plate this week."

Tabitha hesitated. "I have…"

"You seem stressed—did you discover new information?"

Tabitha shook her head with an ironic smile. "You know, the Winter Soirée is only once a year—you can have tonight off," she said.

Rebecca humored her with a smile, and said, "I don't have to be on duty for you to come to me. It's my pleasure to work with you."

"But you want information."

"Well—if you have some," Rebecca said uneasily. "It'd be good to touch base; speed things up a bit."

"You're right—being on the same page *would* speed things up."

"What do you mean?" Rebecca asked, reading Tabitha's accusatory tone.

"I had Dominic at my mercy. He trusted me. I could have gotten a lot more information out of him had you not come and arrested him without consulting me first. I'm starting to think I shouldn't have told you about him at all."

Rebecca looked taken aback. Tabitha held her ground. She'd always known Rebecca would act immediately after she'd tipped her off about Dominic, but she needed an excuse to withhold new leads for a while.

"I'm sorry," Rebecca said. "I saw an opportunity and I took it.

Had I known your plan, I might have waited."

"I understand," Tabitha replied. "Just—give me some more time to work things out. I'll tell you what I have when I've made sense of it."

Rebecca bit the inside of her cheek, but nodded.

Tabitha hoped her fib would keep Rebecca off her back until she had some other piece of information to give her that wouldn't jeopardize her own plan.

"Well, you can have this anyway," Rebecca said flatly, and handed Tabitha a jar of Rifampin. "I would have sent it out already, but the headmistress likes for you to see it first. See you at our next meeting."

She walked away so briskly that the bottle slipped from Tabitha's fingers and fell heavily on the floor, leaving a crack at its glass base. Tabitha picked it up and brushed it off, fingering the damage. As Rebecca disappeared from view, Tabitha felt mildly guilty for blowing her off, but reminded herself that Rebecca's usual kindness was merely a mask to cover her ulterior motives.

Tucking the medicine in her purse on the coat rack in the hall, Tabitha made her way over to Ella and Milo.

"Why do they call it the *Winter* Soirée? It's Christmas. December twenty-fifth has always been Christmas," Milo argued. "There's nothing offensive about it. It's not like we celebrate any differently. We still put decorations on pine trees and eat sugar cookies shaped like reindeer and stuff presents into stockings. What's the difference if we call them *Christmas* trees instead of Winter trees, or *Christmas* cookies instead of

Winter cookies? What's the big flipping deal?"

"I agree," Ella responded back with a thoughtful nod.

Milo gawked at her. "I—I'm sorry, what did you say? It almost sounded like you said you agree."

"Don't make me take it back…"

Milo started to laugh, but reeled in his smile as he noticed Tabitha. Eyes narrowed and shoulders squared, he glared at her suspiciously. "Hello, Tabyrinth," he addressed in what seemed to be an attempted threat.

Tabitha stopped, perplexed. "What did you call me?"

"Tabyrinth. It's like labyrinth, because you're… puzzling… and puzzles are kind of like mazes, so—"

Ella put a palm to her forehead.

"Whatever. Listen," Tabitha cut him off. "We have to find a way to communicate more discreetly. My supervisor, Rebecca—she's here, and if she sees all five of us together she might get suspicious."

"Suspicious of what, that you don't hate us anymore?"

"Oh, get over yourself," Ella interjected.

"What happened to the whole, fellowship of the something-or-other?" Tabitha replied, getting rather annoyed.

"Fellowship of the *Ring*," Milo muttered.

"Yeah, that thing. We're a team, all right? I'm sorry for the disciplinary demonstration and I promise I'll never do anything like that again—you can trust me on that."

Milo folded his arms and replied something under his breath.

"*And* I'm sorry for the tripwire," she added.

Milo kept his arms crossed but she caught a satisfied grin on his face.

Tabitha couldn't blame him for suspecting her. She wasn't, after all, completely sold on the idea that her father deserved to be saved from Lilith's schemes.

Just then, Tabitha saw Maddie leave the dance floor. She made eye contact with Tabitha, then turned to walk away. As she did so, one of the pearls that adorned her braid somehow fell to the ground. Tabitha went to pick it up.

"Maddie, you dropped a hairpin," she called.

Maddie turned and placed a hand to her hair with an appearance of shock that wasn't entirely believable. They met in the middle for the exchange, and Maddie whispered, still smiling as if in gratitude, "Ambrose says there's a balcony on the other side of the hall where couples go to be alone. No one pays attention to them because the affection makes people uncomfortable, and the couples are too focused on each other to notice anyone else. We can trickle out at different times and talk there."

"You're welcome," Tabitha said, loud enough for a nearby crowd of apprentices to hear. Maddie registered the confirmation and the two separated, undetected.

Tabitha relocated Ella. Milo had left her side and was now sitting by himself in the lounge area, stuffing his face with finger-food.

"Maddie gave me information," Tabitha told Ella. "We're to go to the couples balcony individually, at different times. Once we're all there, we can talk. Can you tell Milo?"

Ella sighed dramatically, and waited an awkwardly long time to answer. "Fine," she agreed, and walked over to the seating area where Milo was. Tabitha stood within earshot of them.

"I suppose you can dance with me," Ella said loudly, as if the suggestion had been Milo's.

He gaped up at her, bemused.

"I don't—I don't d-dance," he refused, clearing his throat. He looked at her with as much determination as he could muster, but Ella wasn't phased. Forcibly grabbing his hand, she all but dragged him toward the dance floor. He fought back the whole way. Tabitha restrained a laugh, and watched as Ella tactfully relayed her message while pretending to teach Milo how to waltz.

Fingering her hors d'oeuvres, Tabitha surveyed the door to the hallway and waited. Maddie casually wandered out, followed a few minutes later by Milo, then Ella. Ambrose was nowhere to be seen. As a fast-paced and well-known song came on, Tabitha moved with the excited crowd heading for the dance floor and then slipped away to the couples balcony.

The cold December air blew in from the open lookout, but large outdoor heaters were stationed every few paces, under which pairs of lovers exchanged passionate kisses or gazed mushily at the glittering cityscape. Tabitha's nose wrinkled at the sight of them. No wonder this place was avoided.

Almost every heater was taken, so it didn't seem too odd that a group of four was sharing one toward the end of the row. Tabitha walked quietly over to them. On the right of the heater,

Milo and Ella stood side-by-side, awkwardly distant from each other and clearly not a couple. They bickered enough to be one, but weren't willing to play the part.

Maddie and Ambrose, on the other hand, donned the role quite nicely. Maddie leaned over the balcony under Ambrose's arm, which was perched protectively behind her on the heater's stand.

It was very convincing.

Tabitha felt a lump form in her throat, which she promptly reprimanded.

Easing in beside Ella, she whispered, "All right—we're all here."

"We just filled Maddie in on Popovic's plan to prove Josiah Clay innocent," Ella whispered back. "Now what's our first step?"

"I was thinking we could start by making a map of the underground tunnels," Tabitha said. "We know for sure that Josiah has been using them and that they lead outside the walls where Toby's body was found, because that's where Josiah saved Naoko. She can show us the areas she knows, and then we can explore the rest. I can draw everything so we don't get lost, and Milo can identify anything we find down there that might be significant."

"Seems like a good start," Milo affirmed.

"I'm going to touch base with Popovic and see if he can bring the two friends he mentioned," Tabitha added. "I'll also keep working the Clay case with my supervisor to get additional information."

"We're with you all the way, babe," Ella replied.

Milo and Maddie agreed. Ambrose said nothing.

The group settled on a date and time, then dispersed one by one in drawn-out intervals until the only ones left were Tabitha and Ambrose. Tabitha waited a while, wondering if he would leave first or if she should. The silence was painfully awkward, each standing on opposite sides of the heater.

"Well, I guess I'll be going now," she said to Ambrose, and reluctantly pulled away from the railing. To her surprise, however, he rounded the pole to her side and stepped in her way. He stared her down fiercely, startling her so that she leaned back against the rail.

"What are you doing?" he demanded.

"What? What do you mean?"

"What are you *really* doing?"

"I don't understand—"

"This has nothing to do with Toby, or us. You don't give a damn about what happens to us. Don't lie to me, Tabitha. I may be honest to a fault, but don't take that to mean I'm gullible."

Tabitha felt pain in her chest, in the area of her heart.

"That's not true," she claimed feebly.

"Oh, you think I'm a fool, then?"

"No, not that," she quickly corrected. "It's not true that— that I don't care."

There was hurt in her voice. Ambrose's glare softened. Heaving a sigh, he moved to the rail beside her and looked out over the city. Tabitha turned to face it too.

"If I'm ever going to believe that, I need some answers,"

he said after some time.

"Okay," she complied, swallowing down her fear. She was determined to be honest. She had to make it up to him for the disciplinary demonstration. Besides, what could he possibly ask that she couldn't answer?

"What's your last name?"

All of Tabitha's resolve to tell the truth was drained with the color of her face. She didn't answer.

"Well?" Ambrose urged, facing her.

"Beckett," Tabitha breathed, knowing it was far too late to convince him. But how had he known?

"I said don't lie."

She turned to him, pleadingly, without words to say. The determination in his eyes was so strong she thought it might push her physically to the ground. It was the dangerous side of Ambrose again. Many a man had succeeded in invoking Tabitha's anger. Few had instilled such fear.

Tabitha gave no defense. Ambrose shoved his hand into his suit pocket and revealed a crumpled piece of paper. On it, she saw her own drawing of her father, the one that had slipped from her journal the day she sat watching the warehouse with him.

"I thought I recognized him. I mean, he's obviously your father, but I didn't put a name to the face until you said it out loud the other night."

Tabitha's face fell.

"So what'll it be, Tabitha *Clay*," Ambrose demanded, "a rescue mission, or revenge?"

Very quietly, after a long time, she answered, "A rescue mission."

"Really? Because as I recall, last time you mentioned this case to me, you called him a scumbag," Ambrose stabbed. "You spoke of his imprisonment with *hope* in your eyes—a hope I made the mistake of associating with your mother's regained health. You haven't once mentioned that this man is your father, which leads me to wonder—what do you really plan on doing when we help you find him? As far as I can tell, you're just using us to get to him, and the moment you do, all this talk of rebellion and bringing Toby justice will be just that—*talk.*"

Tabitha could feel his eyes piercing into her, but she couldn't face him. She couldn't face the truth he'd uncovered, nor the question he'd asked. Was this really a rescue mission? Was this really about Toby? Had it really ever been about her mother? Or had her bitterness consumed her so completely that she'd claim vengeance at any cost? Was she any different from Lilith at this point, spouting off a good cause as cover for her own ulterior motives?

"I'm not one of your puzzles, Ambrose," Tabitha defended feebly.

"Ah, but the pieces fit," he harshly replied under his breath lest bystanders hear. "It wasn't that hard to figure out. Josiah's been at the Institute, what, three years now? You knew that by coming here you'd encounter him eventually, so it was never just about your mom. You changed your name, which means you probably already knew his reputation. I find it hard to believe you came for a little father-daughter team-up to save Mom."

"Wow, have you always been so—insensitive?" Tabitha remarked. "What makes you think you can just pick a person apart like they're your own personal play-thing?"

"Tell me I'm wrong and I'll stop. So what's in it for you? You can earn elite perks all sorts of ways; you didn't have to join the Clay case. But you did. Because you wanted revenge."

Tabitha turned away.

"Tell me I'm wrong!" Ambrose demanded.

"And what would you have done," Tabitha burst out, unable to contain herself, "if you'd finally found your father, only to discover him a convict, a rapist, a possible murderer, after he'd abandoned your mother to die, and left you to stand by and watch it happen? What did you expect?"

"Better, from you," Ambrose replied.

"Why?" Tabitha threw her arms up in exasperation.

"Because you're—" Ambrose stopped. His eyes softened. "Better than that," he finished.

"You certainly don't seem to think so." Tabitha strayed from the railing and folded her arms tightly. She squeezed hard, hoping it would somehow alleviate the immense pressure around her heart. Then her hands fell limply to her sides with her own crumbling resolve, and her tone changed as she said, "And you're right not to."

Tabitha had already felt despicable, but to be despicable in *his* eyes… the thought crippled her. He'd solved the puzzle that was Tabitha Beckett, and she was done pretending that she didn't care what he saw.

Ambrose said nothing. Tabitha didn't—couldn't—look at

him, but in her peripheral she saw him fidget and look away as her frosty green eyes blurred with tears.

"I did want revenge," she admitted. "Josiah left us the moment my mom got sick. He promised to send perks to save her, but he never so much as wrote to us to let us know he was even alive! So yeah, earning meds at his expense seemed like a dream come true…"

She looked at him.

"But, then I met you… and Ella, and Milo, and Toby, and Maddie." Tabitha's voice was strained now. "And to get to Josiah, I hurt you. I lied to you. I betrayed you and sent Toby to his death! And I had Dominic arrested, and I framed Dr. Buckley, and—"

"That was you?" Ambrose asked sadly.

Tabitha turned away again—her eyes squinted shut, her hand clasped over her mouth as if she longed to take back the words—but she nodded in confirmation. "I haven't done anything good since the moment I got here, and now… now I just want to make it right."

The silent stillness that followed left Tabitha wondering desperately what Ambrose was thinking, but she didn't dare look to see his expression. She didn't want to see his disdain and repulsion at the pitiful, vengeful creature she'd become.

After a long time, Tabitha heard Ambrose sigh. Then he said, "I'm sorry, Tabitha. I shouldn't have interrogated you like that. Please forgive me."

Tabitha whirled around. "What?"

Ambrose bit his lip, as if uncomfortable saying it again.

"Forgive me?"

"Forgive *you*?" Tabitha asked, her voice cracking with emotion, barely above a whisper. "There's nothing to forgive! I'm the one who should be begging *your* forgiveness—but I don't even want to ask for it because I don't deserve it—I deserve to rot out in the Tolliver canyon—I can't get Toby back and there's nothing I can do to undo what I did—"

Ambrose took her hands in his. "Hey, hey," he stopped her, a compassionate smile on his lips. "It's called for-*give*-ness for a reason."

Tabitha looked up at him questioningly.

"You're right: you don't deserve it," he said seriously. "What you did was wrong. You betrayed my trust, and it hurt me—a lot... but forgiveness is a gift, and I give it freely. I forgive you, Tabitha."

She looked into his eyes and waited. Where was the catch? He smiled. There was none.

Tabitha felt a warmth spread throughout her that she couldn't explain, but didn't care to. It was blissful. She'd confessed to everything ugly in her, everything she'd loathed herself for, and it didn't make him mad; quite the contrary, in fact.

"Thank you," she whispered.

Suddenly, Tabitha realized that her hands were still clasped in his. She bashfully broke free and leaned over the railing beside him once more. They stood there in silence for a while before Tabitha spoke again.

"If I go through with this plan of Popovic's, I could lose

everything. We get caught, and there goes my status, my perks, and my mom's life. I don't know if Josiah is worth that…"

There was a pause.

"You know, I never knew my father," Ambrose said softly. "Or my mother. I was raised by my aunt and uncle. They don't talk about my parents at all. I don't know a thing about them."

Tabitha listened curiously.

"I've always wanted to meet them—my dad, especially. I like to think he's someone important, doing some secret work that my foster parents aren't allowed to talk about. But if I'm honest, it's a lot more likely that he's a disappointment at best."

Ambrose turned to her. "But he's still my dad. I'd rather have a less-than-perfect father than no father at all. Wouldn't you?"

Tabitha took a deep breath. "I suppose."

"Besides—if Popovic is right, then your dad is innocent."

Tabitha shook her head sadly. "Even if we proved him innocent he'd never be innocent to me, Ambrose. He's brought me more pain than anyone else in the world."

Ambrose looked with compassion at her. "Maybe he doesn't deserve your help, but I doubt he deserves Lilith's condemnation, either. And most importantly, you don't deserve to live with another regret."

She met his gaze.

"We're going to figure this out, all right? Together."

Tabitha nodded hesitantly.

"Come on," Ambrose said with kindness in his voice, drawing her forward by the hand. "Let's have a dance."

Mildly astonished, Tabitha followed his stride, her hand tucked warmly in his. They didn't return to the dance floor, but stood a little ways from the heaters. The music from inside trickled out to the couple's balcony, playing a slow, smooth song. Placing his hand on the small of her back, Ambrose moved her seamlessly in steps of one-two-three, one-two-three, one-two-three.

Tabitha followed his lead like a ghost. How could he have just let her off the hook like that? How could any man be so… kind? For years, Tabitha had conditioned herself to be fervently frozen in the face of a man's pursuit… but Ambrose was the sun. Even the thickest wall of ice melted before his warmth.

Though everything inside her screamed that it was a trap, that somehow he would turn dangerous again and betray her, Tabitha paid no heed. Ambrose's chin rested softly at her temple as they spun, and she had no strength left for caution.

A minute into the song, Ambrose stumbled and winced.

"Are you okay?" Tabitha asked, pulling back to see what was wrong.

"Yeah, yeah—it's fine!" he brushed off.

"Oh my gosh, wait—you're still hurt. From the demonstration, you stepped on something," she realized.

Ambrose gave the kind of smile you see on a kid who's stolen from the cookie jar.

"Ambrose!" Tabitha scolded, suddenly laughing. "You can't be dancing with cactus spines in your foot!"

"Scorpion sting, actually," he corrected under his breath.

"*A scorpion?*" Tabitha shook her head. Ambrose laughed

as she playfully hit him in the shoulder. "Ambrose, what were you thinking?"

He met her gaze, and his smile softened. He didn't answer. Suddenly, his expression changed to something she couldn't quite make out. Was he mad at her again? No, it was the gentle Ambrose now… sad? His eyes flickered down for a moment and then returned. Pain, yes! That was it—but not physical pain, emotional. Why? It was almost as if he was arguing with himself in his mind. But then, quite unexpectedly, he raised the back of his hand to her cheek and brushed away a curl that had fallen out of place.

Tabitha breathed, suddenly realizing that she'd forgotten to do so for too long a time. Breaking eye contact, she pulled away from Ambrose's hand. "You should—get that looked at," she fumbled, pointing at his foot.

He chuckled quietly, his eyes on the floor. "Yeah, all right."

"Thank you for the dance," Tabitha said, and he looked up at her once more.

From the way he looked at her, Tabitha could tell Ambrose was thinking hard about something, but whatever it may have been, he didn't say. He forced a little smile, nodded, and hesitantly left for the main hall.

Tabitha waited until she was absolutely sure that Ambrose had gone before filling her lungs with a massive gust of air. Then she ran to the coat rack in the entryway of the ballroom. Trying not to appear desperate, she searched for her own jacket among the piles of fur and leather. When she located it, she reached into her purse.

Where is it? she begged, feeling around the bag for her journal in vain. She must have forgotten it while getting ready for the ball, she realized. It was gone, and so too would the memory be of the way Ambrose had looked at her.

Tabitha turned her back to the wall, sunk to the floor and closed her eyes. For the next five minutes while the image lasted, she watched it replay in her mind, over and over again, and smiled.

CHAPTER NINETEEN

FIGURE OF EIGHT

THE NEXT MORNING, TABITHA COULDN'T STOP SMILING. She looked at herself a bit longer in the mirror and toyed with her rust-colored curls more than usual. As she made her way to the dining hall for breakfast, she had to stop herself from skipping. Her cereal even seemed to taste better.

"What's gotten into you?" Ella asked when she joined Tabitha's table.

"What do you mean?" Tabitha diverted, but even as she said it, she felt the corners of her mouth lift up.

"You're acting really strange," Ella admitted.

"I'm just… glad the gang's all back together again, I guess," Tabitha said as she swirled her cereal a few more times than necessary.

Ella watched her from the corner of her eye. "A likely story," she hummed.

Tabitha's smile broadened.

Just then, Milo and Maddie sat across from them. Tabitha perked up noticeably and looked—not at, but past them—for Ambrose.

"Oooooh," Ella gasped. "I get it now. I know. Okay." Tabitha looked back at her. Ella pointed her spoon at Tabitha. "Have you been getting into my love potions?"

Tabitha opened her mouth to object, but then Ambrose sat beside her. She felt her face heat up. Ella turned back to her cereal and said nothing, but the smug smile stayed at the edges of her lips.

"Hey," Ambrose addressed everyone. Tabitha found it difficult to make eye contact, and froze when his arm settled against hers atop the table.

Ambrose looked around at them. "Did I miss something?" he asked, looking from Ella to Milo and Maddie.

"I was wondering the same thing, mate," Milo said.

Tabitha caught Maddie looking at her and Ambrose's touching arms. She quickly moved her hands to her lap.

"Sorry—Ella and I were just laughing about an inside joke, that's all," Tabitha dodged.

"Yeah, didn't want to make y'all feel left out, so we stopped talking about it when y'all showed up," Ella added. Before they could push the question, she asked, "So—you ready for *Survival of the Fittest*? We're kick boxing today!"

"I challenge you," Milo said.

"I accept," Ella replied. "But don't get too excited—I'm pretty sure the only thing we get to kick is the punching bag."

"Dang it…" Milo grumbled.

During their lesson, Tabitha found herself distracted from her assignment by the cries of, "Mine went farther!" and "Well,

I still hit mine harder!" from Milo and Ella. Tabitha and Ambrose exchanged a smile, and she tried not to think about how she looked as she hammered her own punching bag.

Then she glanced at Maddie and paused. Maddie wasn't part of Milo and Ella's competition, but if she were, there'd be no question as to who the winner was. Tabitha wondered if the punching bag would manage to stay connected to the chain. As the class ended, Maddie blasted the thing one last time with a high-pitched yell, glistening in sweat from head to toe.

Tabitha's heart sank. While she was giddy over one look from Ambrose, Maddie was still mourning the loss of Toby. She was changing—hardening. And even if Ambrose had forgiven Tabitha, she wasn't sure that Maddie ever would.

The men and women split to hit the showers, eager to freshen up. As the water washed over her, Tabitha wondered about Ambrose's statement: *Forgiveness is a gift…*

For so long, Tabitha had wondered if her father deserved her forgiveness. Maybe Ambrose was right. Maybe he didn't have to deserve it. Still, she wanted him to.

When she returned to her apartment, Tabitha sat at the edge of her loft and fiddled again with the wedding band. She would tell her friends about it. Ambrose was right, they were in this together; but first, she needed it for something. Before she committed treason and turned Providence on its head, Tabitha needed to get the story straight from Josiah himself.

Tabitha flipped through the pages of her journal. As far as she knew, Josiah was unaware of her presence at the Institute. If she could leave a message somehow, telling him that she was there and that she wanted to meet with him, maybe he would come.

Tabitha found her drawing of the smoky coffee shop that Rebecca had taken her to—where Josiah had left his fingerprints. She tore it out. Then she flipped back further, to when the Clay family was still intact. Finding a sketch of a fireworks display, which she'd drawn before the New Order deemed fireworks too dangerous for the Privileged, she tore that out too. Then she folded the papers and tucked them inside a plastic bag with the gold ring.

When she and the other nonconformists gathered the next day to inspect the tunnel system, Tabitha would look for signs of Josiah and leave the packet for him to find. He'd recognize the drawings as hers, and the ring as his; and if he was as clever as everyone said he was, he'd know to meet her at the café on New Year's Eve.

• • •

Unexpected jitters woke Tabitha before her alarm. Unable to fall back asleep, she got up, ate breakfast, and headed to the library early. She and her comrades would be mapping out the underground tunnels that day. The task hadn't seemed daunting to Tabitha until she'd added her own additional mission to the agenda. Now her sweat glands seemed to be working extra hard against her will. Tabitha rubbed her clammy hands on her jeans and tried not to think about the ring and drawings she'd be leaving somewhere for her father to find.

The librarian at the desk was older than most of the members of Providence, with a motherly face and silver hair. She had small eyes deeply set behind round glasses, which made them look larger than they were. Her name tag read *Amelia Barnes*. As Tabitha walked by, the woman watched her intensely, and Tabitha wondered if she knew about Naoko's secret hiding place under her library.

To pass the time, Tabitha sat down in the corner of a reading nook to write to Mayra Mae. As she unfolded a piece of parchment and prepared to write, she heard a sweet, soft piano melody tickle the quiet. It ebbed and flowed in volume and intensity, and was altogether pleasant. She was thankful to whoever was playing the grand piano in the lobby for brightening the atmosphere, and began to write. She didn't know how to contain everything she wanted to say in the limits of a letter, but did her best to summarize.

Dear Mayra Mae,

A lot has happened since I last wrote to you. In short, I've made a lot of mistakes, one of which resulted in the death of a good friend. I wish you were here to help me deal with it, but I'm doing the best I can to make things right. My progress in getting Mom her medicine might suffer a little from that, though. Hang tight.

I still haven't found Josiah, but if all goes according to plan, I'll see him before the New Year. And Mae, I've been thinking a lot about what you said... and I think you were right. I have become lonely and bitter in my search for him. I'm weary of caring—and *ready to settle things once and for all, however that might have to happen.*

I hope all is well with you. Write me again soon, please. Tell me the little details that don't matter. I miss you.

Always,
Tabitha

Tabitha's hand hovered over the page. Then she added:

P.S. — There's this boy...

Just then, Ambrose joined her at the table. Tabitha fumbled to scratch out the postscript and tucked the letter in an envelope before Ambrose could see it.

"Hey, Sweetheart!" he greeted her cheerfully.

"I told you not to call me that," Tabitha replied, but with a significant decrease in defensiveness. She made a conscious effort to stifle the burning sensation in her face.

"Right. Sorry, hun."

Tabitha shook her head and Ambrose sat down with a smirk.

"Wait a second," Tabitha realized. "Was that you playing piano downstairs?"

"Sure was!" Ambrose replied, showing off his laugher lines.

Tabitha grinned back. "You can play cello *and* piano?"

"And viola, and guitar, and harp, and double bass..." He bit his lip, holding back a chuckle. "You get the picture."

"You're a man of many talents," she affirmed.

He thanked her, and Tabitha thought she saw the slightest hint of red come into *his* cheeks. The butterflies tickled her insides.

"What's this?" he asked, pointing at the envelope in her hands.

"I'm writing to my sister," she replied, forgetting she had never told Ambrose about Mayra Mae.

"You have a sister?"

"Oh—right, yeah. A twin, actually."

"I don't believe you," he countered playfully.

"What, first I'm motherless, now I'm not allowed to have a sibling, either?"

"You never know; I heard some Privileged sectors bumped their child limit from two to one."

"I have a sister."

"Let's see a drawing, then," he prodded.

"We're identical. For all you know it could be a drawing of me," she teased. "Besides, last time I showed you my journal, you unearthed all my secrets, and I didn't appreciate that."

Ambrose chuckled and leaned back in his chair. "Not all of them, apparently."

He drummed his fingers happily on the table, moving with the music that occupied his mind—that beautiful, mysterious mind. He was right. Tabitha still had secrets to tell. Maybe one day she'd reveal them—but today?

Tabitha closed the seal of the envelope in her hands and kept her lips sealed with it.

Just then, the librarian came to their table in the reading nook.

"Tea?" she offered. Tabitha shook off her emotional state and accepted with a smile, cradling the teacup in her hands. The librarian did not offer any to Ambrose, who looked perplexedly between Tabitha and the woman.

"She's taken a liking to you," Popovic's voice sounded once the librarian had gone, "and Amelia doesn't generally like people. She only loves them."

Tabitha tilted her head and smiled. That was the closest Popovic would ever get to calling her special.

"Is she a rebel, too?" Tabitha whispered.

"In a way," Popovic replied. "She keeps her hands clean of most things, but leaves the door downstairs unlocked for us when we need it."

Tabitha nodded in understanding and watched the silver-haired lady return to her desk.

A moment later, Ambrose blurted, "Why don't I get tea?"

Tabitha laughed.

• • •

When the rebels convened in the tunnels beneath the library, Popovic's friends were waiting for them. Their names were James Quinn and Gavin Parker.

Mid- to late-twenties, lanky and brightly red-headed, James was an engineer who had just graduated his elder apprenticeship. After six years of studying at Providence, he eagerly awaited the choice Provision sector he'd been promised, only to find himself stationed at the Institute as a teacher instead. James had no intention of staying, but was too go-with-the-flow to pick a fight; so he joined their cause as a sort of pastime with the hope of ditching Tolliver down the road. He and Ambrose hit it off quick, which seemed to make Milo slightly jealous.

When James saw the red streaks in Tabitha's hair, he grinned and said, "My people!"

Tabitha smiled back in agreement and embraced their red-headed bond.

Gavin, on the other hand, had purposefully come to Providence in order to infiltrate it. He was altogether short, stout, and square in his features. Half his face had been badly burned, leaving one eye blind and milky-white. Within thirty seconds of conversation with him, Tabitha discovered that he was a borderline criminal mastermind, as each of his suggestions during their meeting consisted of using explosives and mass mayhem to achieve their goal. She also quickly learned that the general consensus of the group was to ignore everything he said.

"It's probably better if most of us stay behind," Popovic declared. Though it hadn't been decided out loud, everyone naturally looked to him as their leader. "It'll be harder to hide with such a big group. Milo and Tabitha, James will be going with you—he can tell you where *not* to go, since he's been given access to the tunnels before."

James, who was sitting in the corner fiddling with his thumbs, perked up at the sound of his name. His expression told them that this was the first time he was hearing the news that he'd volunteered, but he smiled willingly nonetheless.

"What do you mean, he's been given access?" Ella asked.

"Lilith's administration uses the caverns as well," Popovic explained. "She had James do some engineering work down here once."

Ambrose shifted in his seat and glanced at Tabitha.

"I want to come, too," Maddie said. Milo started to argue, but Maddie cut him off. "If there are clues to find about Toby, I'm the most likely to see them."

The rebels looked around at one another, and Popovic said, "All right—but that's it. Any more than four and you're bound to get caught. If Lilith's people find out we're using the tunnels, we'll have nowhere else to hide."

Tabitha glanced over at Naoko, who sat quietly, her porcelain face showing no reaction. If her underground home was compromised, she'd be as good as dead.

Popovic then revealed a large blank paper and smoothed it across the table. The others gathered around it as he drew a circle that filled most of the page.

"Here's Providence," Popovic said. "The library is roughly around here, and we know of two other entrances—one within the elder enclosure and the one at the warehouse." He drew three small squares, indicating each entrance, then began to attach them with squiggly lines.

"Looks like you've got some artistic competition, Tabby Cat," Milo muttered discreetly to Tabitha. She held back a giggle.

"Each opening is linked," Popovic went on, "but we never go from one to another underground unless absolutely necessary, because there are mirror rooms scattered in between."

"Mirror rooms?" Maddie asked. "What are they?"

"Ever wonder why it feels like you're constantly being watched in Providence?" Popovic asked. "It's because you are. Lilith's eyes are everywhere. She has mirror systems hooked up to all the main classrooms and a handful of other commonly used places."

"They basically act as security cameras and are watched 24/7 by a handful of nocturnal nut jobs who never blink," James added. "If you run into them, they'll notify Lilith so fast you won't be able to say *Privileged*."

Maddie swallowed audibly.

"Better to stay on this side of the elder gates in case you have to resurface," Popovic continued. "And the warehouse entrance is right by the extinguish room, so I don't think going near there would be worth the risk. Most of the tunnels seem vacant, but there's bound to be more traffic beneath the penitentiary. Just start with these ones near the library. As far as we know, there aren't any mirror rooms south of here, so you should be good moving out toward the wall."

Tabitha, Milo, and Maddie nodded. James stood to lead the way, taking a lamp, spare oil, and matches with him. Though it was broad daylight above ground, the caverns below existed in perpetual night. Tabitha was ready with her sketchbook, Milo with his notes.

"Please give me something to do," grumbled Gavin. His hands shook and he scratched at his dirty fingernails. "I'm going to explode down here."

"Don't joke like that—I mean it!" Popovic reprimanded.

Gavin smiled to reveal a gap between his front teeth.

Just before Tabitha left, Ambrose grabbed her arm gently and said in her ear, "Be safe."

"No promises," she said with a playful smile.

They kept eye contact a bit longer than Tabitha expected, and she found herself fighting again the voices that cautioned her. Despite her rebelliousness toward them, they reminded her that Ambrose had information she couldn't risk getting out.

"Ambrose, can you do something for me?" she asked.

"Of course," he replied, listening eagerly.

"Don't tell the others what you know about me—please."

Ambrose didn't answer right away. His jaw tightened, but eventually, he nodded. "I won't… but you should."

The intensity that shone in his eyes made her want to obey him, but before she could decide what she thought of his opinion, Milo called her name. Tabitha turned to join her party without making Ambrose any promises.

As they ventured into the deep abyss beneath the earth, Tabitha drew the things that stood out as unique landmarks to be used for navigation, being sure to mark if they'd gone left, right, or straight; and the approximate number of paces walked. Milo spoke to himself under his breath, occasionally stopping to examine a rock or touch a stalagmite.

"What is that?" Maddie asked, pointing at a wall of rock.

The others came around to look. Painted on the wall was some kind of cave drawing. James recoiled, and Tabitha covered her mouth. Depicted was a rectangular stone table, on which a baby lay in a pool of blood. Behind both was a black shadow with four arms, expansive wings and eight small, white eyes. A steam-like substance rose from the baby's body and entered the beast's nostrils, as though it was sucking out its soul.

"I've seen something like this before—" Milo said.

"Where on earth would you have seen this before?" Tabitha asked, disturbed.

"Archaeologist who reads obscure religious manuscripts in his spare time, remember?" Milo reminded her, pointing to himself. "It's some kind of demonic ritual."

"Demonic?" Maddie squeaked.

"Yes. Despite what they say on the screens to help you sleep at night, demons do exist."

Tabitha felt a shiver creep down her spine like the cold tips of spider legs.

"How old would you say it is?" James asked.

"Two—maybe three thousand years," Milo answered.

"Creepy."

"Agreed. Can we move on?" Tabitha said.

"Yes—but you should draw it first," Milo said, an unusual seriousness in his voice. Tabitha did so begrudgingly. "One thing's for certain," Milo added as she drew, "Lilith's administration wasn't the first to use these tunnels."

When Tabitha had finished, they continued on.

After half an hour or so, they stopped in a spacious cavern for a break, during which Tabitha drew an aerial map of where they'd gone so far, translating their number of paces into readable grid squares.

"We can't be very far from the wall now," she said. "Any signs of its foundation?"

"Nah," Milo answered, "but we gotta be getting close to an opening—look," he pointed up at a massive black stain on the cavern's ceiling. "That's from bats. Over time, the oil from their fur leaves that dark residue behind. They wouldn't have chosen this place unless it was near a cave that leads outside."

Maddie shivered. "But why aren't any up there now?"

"Dunno. Maybe they died out, or the cave was closed. Either way, we can't be far from the surface."

Just then, they heard voices echoing nearby. Tabitha felt a wave of prickles along the back of her neck and arms. James sprung to his feet and ushered the others up, putting a finger to his lips and pointing to a tunnel away from the sound. They padded across the smooth ground and climbed through the hole in the wall—which was a rather tight squeeze. James pushed Milo and Maddie forward, then whispered to Tabitha, "I'm counting on you to get us back."

Then he started to run.

Eyes wide, Tabitha jogged backwards and drew everything she could. James kept one hand on her back to keep her from running into anything, while his other held the light for Milo and Maddie to see.

Turning a corner, they paused to listen, struggling to keep their heavy breathing quiet. The voices were closer now—a male and a female. What they spoke was indistinct, but Tabitha felt reassured by their tone. It didn't sound like they'd just discovered an intruder in their caves. However, the female voice was vaguely familiar to Tabitha, who leaned out around the corner to get a better listen.

"Come on," James whispered, pulling her back, "we have to keep moving."

They crept along, quickly but carefully, being sure to give Tabitha enough time to plan their return journey. At length, they reached a fork in the tunnel and came to a halt. James held up his lamp to one entrance, then to the other, examining the flame. In one, it shrank slightly; while in the other, it remained constant and bright. He pointed in the direction of the latter, and they continued on.

"I think we lost them," James whispered, relieved.

"What was that?" the female voice sounded, from much closer than before. To Tabitha's complete horror, she recognized it as Athaliah's. James urgently extinguished the lamp and the four pressed themselves against the wall of the tunnel behind a cage of stalagmites. Footsteps echoed closer, bouncing off the walls so that it sounded as if they were coming from all sides. A faint light began to fill the corridor.

James pressed each of them down against the ground, then—leaving his lamp with them—crawled to a new hiding place a few yards away. *What is he doing?* Tabitha thought desperately, wondering if he was abandoning them or planning to act as a distraction to help them escape. Both possibilities terrified her.

Maddie lifted her head to protest, but Milo pushed it down just in time. Athaliah and her escort entered, their features glimmering from their lamp's golden light. As she held the lamp up higher, it illuminated her wild eyes, which darted around the room, obscured slightly by her disheveled black locks. She sniffed the air.

"It could have been a bat, miss," her escort suggested.

"Don't be an idiot," she retorted—then stopped to think about what she'd said. "Then again... I guess you can't really help that, can you?" She shrugged, and explained, "The bats don't fly this close to the furnace room anymore. They learned that lesson a long time ago." Athaliah let out a disturbing little chortle as if recalling a sick, twisted joke.

Tabitha scrunched her nose. This was a side of Athaliah she had not yet seen.

"Come along then, Dog," Athaliah ordered cheerfully to the man, and strode on—right past Tabitha and her friends.

Milo craned his head back to peer between the stalagmites that hid them, but as he did so his movements dislodged a pebble that rattled on its way to the cavern floor. The man Athaliah had called "Dog" turned around, squinting into the darkness.

He took a step toward them. James tensed up, as if ready to pounce. Tabitha felt as though her heart had stopped with the breath she held. Dog inched nearer, and opened his mouth to speak.

A sharp whistle broke the silence. Dog turned around to follow his master, whose back could be seen walking down the way Tabitha, James, Milo, and Maddie had come. The tunnel returned to darkness, and James scuttled over to the others.

Throwing care out the window, they sprinted without light

away from Athaliah and her pet. Tabitha jotted down Rs for when they veered right and Ls for when they veered left, but drew no more. She'd go back for the details if she ever made it out of the caverns alive.

Presently, they came upon another light. James instinctively put his hand out, ready to hide them again from the oncoming threat, but it was no lamp that cast the light. They felt a wave of heat blown toward them by a breeze. The light came from an opening on the side of the tunnel, one that was completely filled by its reddish glow.

Knowing they'd run into Athaliah again if they turned back, the four cautiously toed toward the light, James in front of the pack. He relit his own lamp, which seemed odd to Tabitha since it was bright enough to see without it. After examining its flame for a moment, however, James blew it out and whispered, "We're getting close to the outside."

Very carefully, they peeked down the fiery opening for signs of life. The tunnel curved so that they couldn't see inside the cavern from which the light came, but they could hear the roar of fire. Tabitha wondered if this was the furnace room Athaliah had mentioned.

"Let's keep moving," James instructed, and they started forward—but Maddie stood still. "Maddie—come on," he whispered.

"Can we go in there?" she asked. "I want to go in there."

Tabitha looked curiously at Maddie, frozen before the blazing orange opening.

James put a brotherly arm around her shoulders and turned

her away. "Not with Lilith's daughter so close by. We'll investigate that next time, all right?"

Maddie nodded and walked in the direction he moved her as if in a trance. As the furnace room shrunk behind them, Maddie looked back at it over her shoulder. Tabitha didn't understand, but she took Maddie's hand in hopes of comforting her. Maddie did not resist this time.

The farther they walked from the furnace room, the colder it grew. The air was fresher, and the breeze blew strong. Finally, they reached the end of the tunnel, which opened into a large cavern like the one they had rested in. From a small crack on the cave's far side, a silver beam of light penetrated the darkness.

"There it is!" Milo said. "We're outside the walls!"

They trotted across the cavern floor and began to climb the uneven walls to the source of the light. Though James was the first to begin the climb, Maddie quickly passed them all, squeezing through the crack with impeccable grace.

When they followed, they found her standing mournfully in the center of an open cave. Daylight streamed in from the cave's mouth, revealing a patch of ground that had been cleared of loose stones and sticks. Near it were strips of torn t-shirt and a dead, decaying snake. Its head had been crushed and its skin had shrunken against the length of its rounded ribs. Maddie sniffled.

"Is this—?" Tabitha began.

"Toby's cave," Maddie knowingly answered. "It's where I got bit by the rattlesnake, where Ambrose came to rescue me."

James strode around the site, then passed them to look outside. Tabitha gingerly approached Maddie, who was now crying silently, and put an arm around her. Maddie welcomed her comfort and embraced her, letting her tears wet Tabitha's shirt. Milo's brow was furrowed in weary thought. He shook his head as he surveyed the scene, muttering to himself.

"Wow," James sighed from the mouth of the cave.

The other three moved to his side, squinting as their eyes adjusted to the midday sun. The landscape looked vastly different at ground-level, compared to when Tabitha had seen it from the helicopter the day she arrived at Providence. The canyon floor was covered in gravel and bushy shrubs. High above them, cliffs loomed in tiers of striped brown, red, and orange. It was all dry, but Tabitha thought she caught a whiff of water nearby.

"It's a lot less scary during the day," Maddie commented. As the four of them stood there, Tabitha rummaged through her pack to find her binoculars, and scanned the top of Providence's wall. The peacekeepers paced back and forth monotonously, seemingly unaware that a new presence lingered in the canyon. James led them out of the cave and around its exterior so there was no chance of being spotted.

"We'll wait here for a few hours, then make the trip back," he informed them, and they set up camp under the shade of a protruding rock in the cliff. During that time, Tabitha updated the map with as much information as she could, drawing miniature copies of key landmarks along the map's paths.

• • •

As Tabitha, Milo, Maddie, and James sat in the shade of a rock, hidden from the peacekeepers' view, Tabitha noticed that the brambles near her were bent and broken in places, as if they'd been stepped on. She stood and walked closer to them.

"What's up?" James asked.

"Looks like some animals have been here," she said, pointing at the brambles.

Maddie shuddered.

Tabitha was reminded of the screeching mountain lion and yipping coyotes from the disciplinary measures that still haunted her dreams. Recognizing Maddie's fear, she assured, "They're probably long gone by now—I'll go check it out to be sure. You stay here."

Tabitha crept around the corner of their resting place. She kept her own nervousness hidden until there was no chance of Maddie seeing her, then promptly picked up a hefty rock to fend off any wild creatures.

Coming into a patch much like their own shaded area, Tabitha stopped and looked about. The dirt had certainly been tread over—more than once, by the looks of it. But the prints were sporadic, unlike any animal nesting pattern she'd seen before. As she inched closer, one patch of brambles looked particularly off.

Tabitha approached cautiously, in case it was some kind of nest for a desert creature she knew nothing about. She prodded the tangle of weeds with a stick, moving it from its place. To her surprise, it slid away to reveal a crawlspace dug out from beneath the cave's outer wall, about the size of a couch or bed.

It appeared to be manmade.

Tabitha knelt down next to it and peered inside. Had someone been sleeping there? Toby came to mind.

She crawled into the dugout. Her body heat seemed to get trapped inside and she instantly felt warm and safe. It was a good place to sleep, if one had to sleep out there.

Then, Tabitha noticed something on the dirt in front of her face: a figure of eight, drawn in the sand multiple times over. The marks were right where her hand would be, if she rested it outside the den.

A memory came to the surface of her mind: a pale green hospital waiting room. Cartoons shone on the wall-sized screens and magazines cluttered side tables. Mayra Mae sat beside Tabitha on a cushioned bench with an ugly pattern as they waited for news of their mother. Across from them, Josiah stared into space with a blank expression, and his index fingers moved across the arm rests in a figure of eight.

This wasn't Toby's Den. It was Josiah's.

If Josiah was living here, so near to the cave, Toby may very well have stumbled upon him, in which case, Lilith's story could be true…

Murderer.

The word echoed in Tabitha's mind from some unknown source, setting her hairs on end as goosebumps formed along her forearms and neck. Tabitha scrambled out from the crawlspace and backed away. She swung around, looking to see if he was there with her now.

He wasn't. She was alone. She was safe.

Telling herself to calm down, Tabitha remembered her drawings and the ring. It was a golden opportunity. He would find them. He would find *her*.

Suddenly, Tabitha wasn't sure she wanted that.

Still, her thirst for answers would not be stifled. Taking the ring and drawings from her bag, she tucked them in the crawl-space and covered them with the brambles. Then, collecting herself, she returned to the others.

"Anything?" Milo asked her when she returned.

"Nope, no monsters to be worried about," Tabitha said, smiling. *None except Josiah…*

To her relief, no one questioned her any more. Thirsty and tired, they rose to begin their return journey. All the while, the sides of Tabitha's civil war fought over what she'd say to her father if they met on New Year's Eve.

The initial portion of the trip was easy to navigate, but difficult to execute. The climb from Toby's cave was significantly harder on the way down than it had been on the way up. The furnace room lit the way for them until they reached where Athaliah had been, but after that they had nothing but blind notes of *right* and *left* to guide them.

Tabitha led the way this time, reversing her notes to take them back the way they'd come and drawing new sketches of their path. James kept a close eye on their surroundings, his lamp lit and a knife at the ready. Though they'd been there before, it all appeared new and frightening.

"We're almost there—" Tabitha started, but then knitted her brows in confusion. According to her notes, they were supposed to go straight for some time, but they'd come to an unexpected fork in the tunnel.

"Which way?" James asked her.

"I—I don't know," she admitted, glancing from her journal to the fork. Handing the journal to Milo, Tabitha reached into her bag and pulled out a small mirror she'd received at the start of her apprenticeship to be used for seeing around corners. "Wait here," she instructed, taking the lamp from James and venturing down the tunnel to their right.

Tabitha hadn't gone far when she noticed that her lamp wasn't the only source of light nearby. Placing it on the ground behind her and dimming it to almost nothing, she crept toward the new, white glow.

There were no voices to be heard, but Tabitha could feel a presence. Her back to the cavern wall, she stretched out her arm with the mirror to see beyond the curve of the tunnel. In the reflection, she saw a circular structure of panels that filled the height of the room—beyond it, in fact. The panels seemed to extend through the ceiling, and shone brightly.

Tabitha wondered if they were lights, but then she saw him: a man hunched over with eyelids peeled back so far she thought for sure his eyes would fall from their sockets. Unblinkingly, he surveyed what Tabitha now recognized to be mirrors—hundreds of mirrors carefully placed so he could see up the panels and into classrooms, streets, and corridors. Slowly, he turned, cross-legged on his swivel chair, scanning each panel for nonconformists.

Suddenly—so suddenly that Tabitha gasped and stumbled

back—he pulled a string and another man came running in.

"What is it, Krikor?" the newcomer asked.

"Student in Restricted Section 46-A," he muttered, keeping his eyes fixed on the mirrors surrounding his seat. Still, they didn't blink. Like an owl's, they stared searchingly from within his gaunt face, surrounded by dark bags that showed signs of sleeplessness. Perhaps they'd been surgically stitched open, Tabitha mused. When the man left to deliver Krikor's message, Tabitha used his footsteps to cover her own and rushed back to James and the others.

"A mirror room," she informed. "We must be back within the walls."

"So, I take it we go left, then?" James asked. Tabitha nodded, and they made their way back to the cavern where they had rested, on to their makeshift rebel conference room, and out through the library. Amelia wished them a good rest of their day, and they went straight to the dining hall to fill their grumbling stomachs.

CHAPTER TWENTY

THE NEW YEAR

THE NEXT FEW DAYS WENT BY faster than the silver bullets of the Axelle light rail, and New Year's Eve came. Tabitha nonchalantly stood outside the café where she hoped to meet her father, her anxiety skyrocketing with each minute that passed.

Though it was bitterly cold—which seemed odd to Tabitha, as there was no snow to justify it—a glaze of sweat had formed on her forehead and along the linings of her gloves. The inside of her scarf was wet from her breath, and her eyes dry from watching for signs of her father.

The massive gates of Providence were open and a group of elites stood out on the ledge preparing fireworks. Tabitha noticed that Gavin was with them, and somehow it didn't surprise her that he would risk capture for a bit of explosive fun.

In front of the gaping hole that now threatened to free the *enslaved*—as Popovic would call Lilith's students—was a full-fledged army of peacekeepers. Tabitha had not considered the possibility that so many guards would be on duty tonight on account of the open gates, but at least they were more likely to be watching the display, not the little coffee shop where she stood.

Eventually, Tabitha's anxiety was too much to bear. She needed a change of scenery. Leaving her post, she entered the shop and let the smell of vanilla cigar smoke engulf her. In a far corner past the bar was a narrow staircase that led to roof-top seating, where most of the shop's occupants had gone to watch the fireworks. It was empty save for the bartender and, to Tabitha's surprise, Ambrose.

"Well, hello!" he greeted her from a booth by the window. He was working on a puzzle she thought would take years to complete.

"Ambrose! What are you doing here?" she asked—too intensely.

Ambrose looked around. "Did you reserve the room or something? Should I not be here?"

Tabitha shook her head. "No—sorry. It's just…" She looked over her shoulder, then slid into the booth across from him. "I'm meeting someone," she explained.

Ambrose looked as though he didn't understand at first. "Oh," he said dryly, apparently coming to a conclusion. "Gotcha. I can leave, that's fine."

Tabitha hadn't meant to kick him out, but before she could decide if she should invite him to stay, he added: "Who is he?"

Now Tabitha was the one wearing a confused, blank stare. "What?"

"The guy you're meeting," Ambrose stated.

Suddenly it dawned on Tabitha that the expression on Ambrose's face was one of jealousy. She smiled. "Oh! No—it's not a guy—I mean, it is a guy, but he's not coming for—a date," she clarified.

Tabitha waited for his relief to show, but after a moment of contemplation, Ambrose merely shrugged. The motion sent a rock plummeting into Tabitha's stomach.

Of course he would be indifferent; why shouldn't he be? What did Tabitha have that every other pretty face in Providence didn't? How could she expect him to fancy her after how she'd treated him? Just because he had a heart twice the size of hers didn't mean he intended to give it to her…

Get a grip!

Tabitha placed her hands flat on the table and leaned forward. In a hushed voice, she informed, "Ambrose, I'm meeting with Josiah."

Ambrose straightened his shoulders and became very serious. "You found him? How?" he asked.

"When I learned that he'd married Athaliah, I had to—"

"They're *married?*" Ambrose asked in shock.

Tabitha bit her tongue. How did he always manage to weasel information out of her like that?

"What—in secret or something?" Ambrose questioned. "How do you know?"

"Providence's jeweler had sold him a set of wedding rings," Tabitha explained. "He gave me Josiah's. The timing of it lines up perfectly with everyone else's testimonies. They were married before she accused him of rape."

Ambrose's eyes widened. "Tabitha—this means we can make a case for his innocence! We have to tell the others—"

"No—Ambrose, stop! You're not telling anyone any of this."

"But—"

"Just drop it, okay?"

"I can't do that—"

"I need to talk to Josiah first, this is between him and me."

"No Tabitha, it's not," Ambrose said with so firm and stern a tone that Tabitha listened. He waited to make sure he had her attention. "You are not in this alone. This thing between you and your dad—it affects everyone. Not just Dr. Buckley, Toby, Naoko, or us rebels—but *everyone*. Teachers, apprentices, the New Order, future Provision elites, and the Privileged—we are part of a bigger picture here, whether we like it or not."

Tabitha looked away angrily. She didn't want to care about the conspiracy theories, overthrowing Lilith, and reforming Providence. It was too exhausting when she already cared so much about the potentially evil man that could walk through the café door at any moment.

"And even if we weren't," Ambrose said softly, "you still wouldn't be in this alone."

"Wouldn't I?" Tabitha said, frustrated.

"No. Because this whole thing would still affect you more than anyone." The softness in his voice caused her to look up, and she found the same softness in his eyes. "I know I've been a jerk about it, and I'm sorry," he continued. "I shouldn't have probed you like I did at the Soirée. You're not just a puzzle— but you are in one, and I want to help you figure it out."

"Why?" Tabitha breathed.

Ambrose seemed to think the answer was obvious, which

frustrated her even more. "Because I care about you."

"But *why?*" she said again. Ambrose smiled slightly, but furrowed his brow.

"You don't see it?"

She shook her head.

"Tabitha, you are one of the most strong, determined, courageous, and confident women I know. Yet, you think and care about everything with such… depth. Your passion is gasoline to a flame. You're adorably stubborn and handle my own brashness like a champ. You're willing to give up anything for the people you love, and I guess I don't express it well, but I admire and respect you for that. Please—let me help you through all this mess."

Tabitha sat in silence for a long time. She wasn't sure she believed him, but the walls around her heart were crumbling brick by brick. Eventually, she nodded.

"Good," he concluded, his tone a clear change of subject. "So where's this ring?"

The growing warmth in Tabitha's chest retreated back behind her heart's gate. "I don't have it," she admitted flatly. Had all that bolstering just been a way to get her to talk?

"What do you mean?"

"I left it in the Tolliver canyon," she said, as if she were proud of the fact.

Ambrose looked alarmed. Tabitha didn't offer any explanation. She decided she liked the bait-and-switch story. It was easier than believing he actually thought all those good things about her.

Ambrose started to form a question, but never finished. He glared at her as if she were a puzzle again, something to be solved. A problem.

Then the lights went out. Except for small, individual lamps on each table, the room was completely dark, and when Tabitha looked out the window, she realized the rest of the city lights had been dimmed for the fireworks display as well.

"They must be starting," she commented. Ambrose leaned to look out the window. All of Providence had come from their rooms to watch, from rooftops and balconies and down in the public places of the outskirts. The heating panels had been brought up, revealing the brilliant winter sky, riddled with stars.

The air outside was filled with a hum of chatter, until suddenly all voices ceased. A match had been lit. Anticipation hung in the air as the spark fizzled out. There was a pause of dead silence, and then the first rocket seared through the night sky, leaving a trail of red behind it. It exploded in a pattern of sparks and the crowd exploded with it, shouting cheers of delight and clapping their hands. Tabitha's spirits lifted timidly, and she let herself enjoy the fiery flowers.

Then the café door opened.

A man with a face wrinkled and obscured by a fur cap and thick beard walked inside. Tabitha watched as he shook out his coat casually and removed his gloves before looking around the shop as if deciding where to sit. He caught her eye.

Tabitha didn't recognize him—but then he pulled a gold wedding band from his finger and began playing with it, flipping it around in his hand. Then he slipped it on his right ring finger, turned away and sat in a far off booth.

"That's him," Tabitha whispered to Ambrose without turning to him. Though she could feel Ambrose's eyes on her, she couldn't peel her own from her father's frame—his edges painted red and gold from the lights that flashed through the windows. Tabitha stood.

She couldn't tell if her hands were shaking or if everything was trembling from the explosions of each firework outside. Shoving them in her pockets, Tabitha approached the bar and ordered tea with honey and lemon. When the barista handed her the mug, she took it to the bearded man.

"Tea?" she offered. As she met his emerald eyes, Tabitha recognized her own in them. Her heart did a backflip beneath her cool composure.

He nodded and held out a hand, inviting her to sit across from him. Tabitha moseyed into the booth and slid his drink across the table. He took a sip. Just like that. Tabitha could have poisoned him if she'd wanted to, and he would have drunk it without question.

"Just the way I like it," he said, his voice husky. When Tabitha looked up from her fidgeting fingers, she saw that his eyes were red at the edges. She averted her own, fighting to keep calm.

"Why are you here?" he breathed at length. It was strained with an undertone of agony.

Tabitha had many responses flying through her head. *Nice to see you, too. I could ask you the same. I'm here to save*

Mom—since you didn't. I came to get my revenge. You horrible,
evil, despicable excuse for a man—

But the only thing that seemed willing to come out was a bit
of salty water from her eyes, which she shoved back defiantly.
Tabitha was infinitely thankful in that moment for the dim
lighting and the distracting display of fireworks that sheltered
them from unwanted eyes. They filled the long, uncomfortable
pause with their continuous screeching and bursting. Tabitha
wanted to speak, but couldn't decide on one thing to say, where
to start, or what angle to approach the conversation from. Her
hatred and hope were so intertwined, she wasn't sure what
would come out if she opened her mouth. Finally, Josiah broke
the silence.

"I thought the ring was from Athaliah—some twisted hint
that they'd found me. But then I saw your drawings and knew
it was from you, somehow. When I realized my mistake—"

He stopped at Tabitha's sardonic snort.

"Did you? Did you realize your mistake?" she sneered,
her bitterness boiling to the surface and causing her voice to
shake. "I could turn you in, you know. I know someone who'd
be thrilled to find you're sitting here right now, defenseless,
with peacekeepers swarming the grounds just a few yards
away. She thinks you deserve the death penalty. Do you? Give
me one good reason why I shouldn't give her a holler."

From across the room, they heard the sound of a glass
shattering. The bartender left her idle state behind the island
and went to clean the spilled water beside Ambrose's booth.
She remembered then that he was there. She remembered

his question: *What'll it be, Tabitha Clay: a rescue mission, or revenge?*

Ambrose's eyes flickered up and met Tabitha's. She hoped he'd knocked the drink over intentionally to cause a diversion, that his glance was just a gentle reminder to maintain discretion. She couldn't bear to see his kindness wane again as the truth of her heart spilled off her tongue…

When Tabitha met Josiah's eyes again, she found them glistening. Beneath the thick beard he'd attached to his face, his lip quivered and nostrils flared as he struggled to swallow his own swelling emotion.

"I'm sorry…" he muttered, looking down at his hands. "I'm so sorry, Sweetheart…"

"So you admit it," she challenged, her jaw tight with anger. "You *are* a traitor, a rapist, a murderer!"

"What? No—I didn't, that was a setup—" He stopped, as if expecting her to protest, but she remained silent.

Please, Tabitha begged in her mind, *please prove me wrong.*

Carefully, he began again. "I found something while searching for breaches in Providence's security. I discovered the caves, which I guess you must know about. At the time I assumed they were unknown to anyone in Providence. I thought they were being used by someone outside our walls. There were signs of demonic rituals everywhere—fresh signs, but ancient rites."

"The painting?" Tabitha asked, remembering what she'd stumbled upon with Milo, Maddie, and James.

"So you've seen it, too. I found that, and manuscripts,

instruments, and more. It looked like someone was trying to gain unearthly power, perhaps to use against the Institute or the New Order. I told Athaliah this, and—well, she already knew. She and her witch of a mother were behind it all along. Security didn't know, and murdering me mysteriously would rouse too much suspicion, so they framed me."

"By saying you'd raped Athaliah?"

"Yes," Josiah affirmed.

Tabitha should have been happy. This news was good. It meant that their rebel friends had a fighting chance against Lilith's administration... but all she felt was spite. All she felt were three years of silence, and Josiah's terrible betrayal of a perfect woman named Natalie.

"How did that work," she said with heavy sarcasm, "considering she's your *wife*?"

The crackling fireworks outside echoed in the silence that followed. Josiah said nothing.

"How long did it take you to find yourself a shiny new working woman, huh? One that wasn't so frail, who could walk and change and feed herself? Off to save the wife—ha! What a story. You were off to find yourself a new one! Do you realize the hell you left us in?" Tabitha's voice was shaking, and the back of her eyes stung with fresh tears.

Josiah struggled to look at her directly, but managed a ginger reply. "When I left Axelle, I had every intention of helping your mother—I really did," he insisted. "I thought if I could just move high enough in the system, I could manage it... but the higher I went, the more I lusted for the power they offered me. I made a new life for myself, here, where I could escape the reality of your mother's decline…"

Tabitha looked away.

"We were pampered endlessly," he went on. "I just let myself go numb. When I did finally snap out of it, I appealed to be stationed in the Axelle Provision sector when I graduated, so I could see you again… but that's when they told me… and I just couldn't bring myself to go back. To see our old house, without her there—"

"Wait—what did they tell you?" Tabitha asked, her anger subsided by her confusion.

"Well—that she'd—that your mother had died, of course," he answered, perplexed. Tabitha's look of shock caught him off guard. "What is it?" he asked.

"But—Mom is *alive*," Tabitha breathed.

Josiah went white. "What?" he asked, his voice trembling, knuckles digging against his forehead as the reality sunk in.

Tabitha could no longer contain her emotion and let the tears pour down her face. "Mom is alive, and Mayra Mae and I have been slaving to keep her that way, day in and day out for *three* years without you! You never sent so much as a bottle of Tylenol or a letter to tell us you hadn't—I don't know, died or something. And you went and got married to a psychopath! How long did you mourn her fake death before doing that, huh? And now that you know your new wife is crazy, now that you have a way out of Providence and all the skills to stay off the radar, how come you haven't gone back? It's not like you didn't have two daughters who still loved and missed you.

What, were we not enough of a reason to come back? Mom was all that mattered to you? Why didn't you come back!"

Tabitha was standing now, flailing her arms hysterically and choking through her sobs. Through the blur of her tear-filled eyes, she saw Josiah stand and come around to her. He wrapped his arms around her trembling frame and held her close. At first, she fought it—but when she realized he was crying too, she let herself be nestled against him and welcomed the comforting stroke of his hand against her back.

After a while, their breathing slowed, and Tabitha pushed away from him. She remembered how much her fanatics put them both in danger, and looked around the café. From across the room, she saw that Ambrose had invited the bar tender to help him solve his puzzle, so that her back was turned from Tabitha and her father.

Tabitha sat back down, and Josiah followed suit. With her emotional hysteria under control, Tabitha found the strength to say, "Tell me what happened."

Josiah heaved a sigh. Wiping his eyes with the back of his hand, he told his tale.

"When your mother—when they told me she died, I was a mess… I was vulnerable. As Head of Security, I had gotten to know Athaliah fairly well. She's just as charming on the surface as Lilith, though less stable. In the midst of all the seemingly perfect people in Providence, we connected over our shared brokenness. She reached out to me in my grief, and I—well, I took comfort in her. She became my balm.

"Athaliah made life here seem livable. In time, I grew to

be content in this place with her by my side. I confided in her as I would have with Natalie. Eventually, we decided to get married…"

He trailed off regretfully, fiddling with the ring in his hands, his knuckles going white by his tight grip.

"We kept our marriage a secret to avoid any conflicts of interest, her being Lilith's daughter and I being Head of Security. It was her idea. When we wanted to go out, we would meet in public places like this and come at different times to make it look like we hadn't come together. This was her favorite place; so the week I discovered the caves under Providence, I told her to meet me here so I could tell her what I'd found.

"When I tried to warn her that someone was trying to unleash an evil power against them, she laughed… Just threw her head back and laughed—cold and manic. I'll never forget that sound. She said, *It's too late. The door's been opened—and you have yourself to blame!*

"I didn't know what she meant, but I knew it couldn't be good. I hadn't told her about the caves, so when the warrant went out for my arrest the next morning, they were the only place I could think of to hide. From what I gathered afterwards, Lilith was furious with Athaliah for revealing their involvement in whatever it is they're doing. I've been hiding ever since, trying to put the pieces together so I can stop them."

Tabitha thought of Toby. She thought of Naoko, and Dr. Buckley, and everyone else Lilith had hurt. That was why Josiah couldn't return to Axelle, to her and Mayra Mae. She already knew why stopping Lilith was worth any sacrifice, how it made you do crazy things like join rebel groups underground. They were all part of a bigger picture.

Josiah reached into his pocket to pull out a handkerchief. As he lifted it to wipe his eyes, the contents of his pockets came with it, and a blue ribbon fell on the table.

Tabitha's eyes grew wide.

"Where did you get this?" she asked urgently, picking up the ribbon.

"In the tunnels, not far from where you left your drawings," he replied. "Why?"

Tabitha eyed him suspiciously. She probed his expression for guilt, but found none, and decided to believe his innocence. She fingered the ribbon.

"It was my friend's… Maddie gave it to him, he had it tied around his wrist, when…" Tabitha trailed off. She pulled her journal from her bag and opened it to one of her maps of the caverns. "Show me *exactly* where you found it," she demanded, laying the book flat on the table.

Josiah looked over it carefully, then landed a finger down on the furnace room. "There—right outside the incinerator."

Tabitha smiled.

"Tabitha—if your friend was taken in there," Josiah said cautiously, "I wouldn't get your hopes up."

Tabitha's smile faded. "Why? What happens in there?"

Before he could answer, Ambrose came suddenly to their table. "Rebecca's coming," he said.

Tabitha stood, knocking over Josiah's tea. Then, she became acutely aware of a sound growing louder—the sound of voices and footsteps on the narrow stair. Spinning on her heel she gripped her father's jacket and pulled him out of the booth. "You need to leave!" she whispered, urgently.

"Tabitha—now!" Ambrose called as he peered through the front window.

People returning from the rooftop flooded the bar on their way to the front door, surrounding the pair and bumping against them. Amid the swarm, father and daughter locked eyes.

"Meet me next Friday at noon—where you left your drawings," Josiah said quietly. Then he disappeared into the crowd, walking straight past Rebecca as she entered the café.

Before Rebecca caught sight of her apprentice, Tabitha tossed her journal blindly over her shoulder in Ambrose's direction and hoped to God he caught it.

Rebecca's eyes met Tabitha's.

Tabitha forced a smile and threw her arms open. "Happy New Year!" she cried, going in for a hug.

Rebecca received it stiffly, clearly not expecting such informality. She tried to make conversation, but her eyes kept darting around the crowd of people, searchingly, and all she managed to say was, "Yes, you too."

"I'll be going, then," Tabitha said through a fake yawn, stretching. "Have a good—"

"Tabitha, I need to talk to you," Rebecca said with a sudden sternness.

"Now?"

"Yes, now. Come."

Rebecca turned toward the door, and Tabitha legitimately considered making a run for it, disappearing with the crowd like her father had done—but she dared not argue. Tabitha followed Rebecca into the night.

• • •

When supervisor and apprentice reached Rebecca's office, neither sat. Tabitha stood wordlessly opposite the desk. Rebecca's usual smooth and calming air was tainted with vexation. She picked up a bottle from her desk—Tabitha's next elite perk.

"I thought you wanted this," she said solemnly, examining the glass of Rifampin in her hand. "I thought you wanted your mother to survive, Tabitha. That's not going to happen like this." She leaned over the table and looked Tabitha hard in the eyes. "Why are you keeping things from me?"

This was it. She'd been caught. Next stop, death by rattlesnakes and coyotes.

"What do you mean?" Tabitha attempted.

"You know very well what I mean. You haven't been honest with me, Tabitha. I want to know why."

"All I've kept from you was to help the case in the long run," she tried.

"Oh really? Tabitha, you're not some kind of vigilante, you can't go picking and choosing how you're going to get your revenge."

"You think that's why I'm keeping secrets? After what happened with Dominic?" Tabitha shot back.

"Look, I get it, you want to earn the rebels' confidence—but we are running out of time here, a luxury we simply don't have anymore. I'm surprised Lilith hasn't taken me off the case yet, what with week after week of no new leads," Rebecca sputtered.

"I'm sorry if your job is at stake, but if we're ever going to get Josiah's accomplices to hand him over—"

"Tabitha, if my job were merely a matter of locating rebels and earning their trust, Josiah would have taken his seat in the electric chair ages ago."

"Then why did you bother to have me do it?"

"Are you really that thick? Why do you think we brought you onto the case—*you,* Tabitha? Josiah's beloved daughter, the one who knew his mind… Josiah probably never shows his face to those friends of his—but *you.* He'd throw caution to the wind for you."

Tabitha thought of how quickly Josiah had accepted the tea from her, and felt sick to her stomach. Now it was her turn to throw caution to the wind. She couldn't fake it anymore. She wanted answers just as well as Rebecca.

"So you're saying I was bait—nothing more than bait?" she accused.

"Call it what you like," Rebecca defiantly digressed. "Your purpose was to bring down a criminal."

"But Rebecca, he's *innocent*, Athaliah is lying—they're *married*—"

"Tell me something I don't know!" Rebecca burst, all pretense gone.

Tabitha stood stunned. "What?"

Rebecca appeared to be internally scolding herself for revealing this information. "Look," she went on, shaking her head as if doing so would brush away the words she'd just spoken, "now more than ever, it's imperative that you trust me—"

"Trust you?" Tabitha exclaimed, taking a few steps away from the desk. "All this time, you knew… you knew! And you fed me lie after lie that my father was… evil! You used me to get to him. You persuaded me to—to *murder* him! Trust you?"

Rebecca pursed her lips, her will no longer able to withstand the pressure of her frustration. "Tabitha Clay, there are things you don't understand! If you don't tell me where Josiah is *right now*—" She slammed the bottle of Rifampin on the desk and it split in half, spilling its contents in all directions.

The two halves of the jar tumbled to Tabitha's feet, and she picked them up. Holding them together along the crack, she saw its point of origin: a chip near the bottle's base—a familiar chip—the same chip—the same bottle.

Tabitha backed away toward the door, shaking her head. Her anger had swelled beyond reason. "No," she decided, disregarding all consequence. "I won't tell you where he is. Consider my apprenticeship completed. I've learned everything there is to learn from you."

With that, Tabitha strode swiftly out the door and straight to the library.

CHAPTER TWENTY-ONE

UNDERGROUND

AFTER SKIMMING HER MAPS FOR GUIDANCE, Tabitha descended the ladder into the caverns beneath the library and shut herself into darkness. The cold and clammy air caked the lining of her lungs, which seized as she fought off tears and fatigue. She told herself desperately to focus as her toes touched bottom. Her visual memory of the maps would only last seven minutes.

Groping along the sides of the tunnel, Tabitha felt for the landmarks in the drawings—an oddly shaped stalagmite, a smooth section that veered left, a series of three uneven steps. All the while, her mind raced with her feet.

Popovic had been right about her supervisor. Rebecca had been screening her mail—she must have been. How else would she have known to look for Tabitha with Josiah on New Years? Tabitha cursed and pounded her fist against the wet stone wall. How could she have been so stupid? Of course Rebecca would screen her mail. Maybe all those background checks required for shipment clearance were really lessons on how to re-seal an envelope seamlessly.

And she'd known. Rebecca had known about the marriage—and that Josiah was innocent. He really was innocent. That, at least, was one good thing that had come from all this. His only crime was breaking his daughter's heart. Except, now that Tabitha had taken a stand against Rebecca, there was no hope for Natalie's regained health.

Then Tabitha remembered the Rifampin. Had it been the same crack? The bottle she'd thrown across the room got a fracture… then the one Rebecca dropped at the Soirée had a crack… and now this one, split in half on the floor of her office along a break in the glass—all from a chip at the curve of its base. The same bottle.

Tabitha couldn't face the implications of that theory. She stumbled into the conference room table just as her memory map faded. Twisting her fingers through her hair, she buckled over and fought to catch her breath. Exhausted and miserable, she curled up in a corner of the cave and fell asleep.

• • •

When Tabitha awoke, she had no way of telling if it was morning or not, except that a lamp was now lit on the table. She started as she realized she was not alone. Naoko was standing across the room, staring at her. Tabitha fumbled to her feet.

"What are you doing here?" Naoko asked when Tabitha arose.

"I, um… I kind of quit my apprenticeship," Tabitha responded, realizing then how ridiculous and dangerous a thing that was to do. She looked around. "I had nowhere else to hide. What time is it?"

"Just dawn," Naoko replied. "You will need food, and a place to sleep?"

Tabitha nodded.

"Come."

Naoko led the way to a little cavern with a small entrance, like a bubble in the rock, private and hidden. Once they'd crawled inside, Naoko set the lantern down and its light filled the room.

"You can stay here," she said. "I will tell Amelia that you need provisions brought, and she will tell Popovic."

"Thank you," Tabitha replied.

Naoko bowed, and turned to leave.

"Wait—Naoko," Tabitha stopped her. She turned back. "I'm sorry that you have to live like this. I'm sorry for everything they've done to you. You deserve better."

Naoko looked at Tabitha for some time before responding, and Tabitha could not make out her expression. "It is not too late to regain my honor," she said simply, and with another bow, departed.

Tabitha fidgeted, wondering if that had been the right thing to say. With nothing to do but wait, she lay on her back with her eyes to the ceiling and made shapes with the swirls of stalactites.

A few hours later, Tabitha heard a commotion in the hall. She sat up just as Ella climbed through the opening in her cave, and before she could register what was happening, found herself strangled in a hug.

"I'm so glad you're safe," Ella said just before smacking a

kiss on her bushy head.

Tabitha pulled back and beamed a smile.

Moments later, a pile of blankets came tumbling through the hole in the wall, followed by Milo, who tripped. Rolling into a model pose as if the fall had been on purpose, he said, "Your bedding, madame."

"And your stuff," Ella added, heavily dropping her wicker basket onto Milo's stomach. "If you want anything else from your room, just let me know. I figured warm clothes and spy gadgets would be priority."

"How did you break in?" Tabitha asked, happily sifting through her things.

"Apparently, Gavin's expertise doesn't stop at explosives. He forged a key and picked the lock."

"If you had given me just a few more minutes, I would have had it—" Milo defensively claimed, brushing himself off.

"You were staring at it for forty minutes," Ella replied with a roll of her eyes. "You hadn't even touched it yet!"

"I was merely determining the make and model of the door's keyhole," Milo began to argue.

Tabitha felt her heart growing warmer with each passing second.

"I helped too!" peeped a high-pitched voice. Maddie entered the cave gracefully on her pointed toes. "I distracted all the apprentices heading toward the apartments by performing in public. It was really scary!" She looked at her feet with a little blush, but smiled proudly. "That was very brave of you to stand up to Rebecca," she praised with a more serious tone.

Tabitha felt as if her heart would burst with delight. Her little cave was completely cramped now, with all Tabitha's friends about her. Well, almost all of them. She watched the opening, expectantly. When no one came, her heart sank. "Where's Ambrose?" she asked.

Ella shrugged. "Haven't seen him since Popovic pulled him aside to talk him out of storming Rebecca's office. You gave us quite a scare, you know."

"Yeah," Milo added. "I've never seen Ambrose so worked up. Thought maybe Rebecca was torturing you or something."

"You looked for me?" Tabitha asked.

"Of course!" Ella scoffed.

"That's what friends do," Maddie agreed, sitting next to Tabitha. "They look out for one another."

Tabitha smiled. How she had ever once wanted to keep her friends at arm's length, Tabitha couldn't fathom.

Just then, Amelia stepped through the opening. Without a word, she placed a plate of cold breakfast food in Tabitha's hands, gave her arm a little squeeze, and left.

Tabitha gratefully shoveled the food into her mouth, and between bites asked, "Did Ambrose tell you what I found?" She thought of Toby's blue ribbon, nestled in her pocket.

The three exchanged wary looks before Ella spoke for them. "He told us you found your father," she said carefully.

Tabitha stopped chewing. "What?"

Ambrose had betrayed her. The one secret she'd trusted him to keep, and he went and told everyone. She should have known. All men were the same, nothing but talk until—

"Tabitha, it's okay," Ella assured, perceiving Tabitha's anger. "He wouldn't have told us except that we didn't understand what kind of danger you were in. You being Josiah's daughter meant that Rebecca might use you to lure him out, and the thought of that made him frantic."

Tabitha soaked it in. Ambrose was that worried about her? She couldn't decide if she wanted to punch him or kiss him.

"And you're not mad at me for lying to you?" Tabitha asked.

"Nah," Milo replied. "Anyone would've done the same in your shoes. We just wanna make sure you're safe."

"That's right," Ella agreed. "But no more lies, got it?"

Tabitha grinned and nodded. "All right."

"Promise," Maddie demanded.

Tabitha's smile faded at the earnestness in Maddie's big, round eyes. "I promise," she said firmly.

To keep her promise, Tabitha told them everything that had happened: how her father was innocent, married to Athaliah, and had been unaware that his first wife, Natalie, was still alive. She admitted to her previous desire for vengeance, then to her change of heart. She shared what Josiah had discovered in the caves, and the Damaras' involvement.

Then she reached into her pocket and pulled out Toby's blue ribbon. She handed it to Maddie. "Josiah found this outside the furnace room," Tabitha said. "It might help us discover what really happened to Toby."

"What should we do?" Maddie asked, holding the ribbon delicately.

"I say we go in there—all of us—and be prepared for

anything," Tabitha declared. "Ella—remember that plant you told me about, the one that can zombify people?"

"Angel Trumpet?" Ella clarified with a wide grin, "Girl, I got you covered. I worked up a memory serum the other day, too—should I bring that?"

"Absolutely, anything you can think of. We have no idea what we're up against down there. Maddie, you think you can use your silks on the stalagmites?"

"I can try," Maddie replied sheepishly.

"Great. You're the stealthiest of all of us, you'll be our eyes. And Milo, bring your… brain." They laughed. "Anything you can tell us about what we find in there will be helpful."

"Sure thing," Milo responded, happy to be appreciated.

"If someone could tell Ambrose the plan when you see him, then Operation Blue Ribbon is a go," Tabitha concluded.

The three agreed, and each promised Tabitha a bit of their dinner that night. They kept their promise, returning later with bits of news along with the bits of food they'd smuggled. Still, no Ambrose. Night came, and Tabitha slept.

Being in the caves felt like being in Detox, but from her friends' visits, Tabitha started to be able to tell when it was daytime and when it was night.

When Tabitha awoke the next morning, she found a package outside her cave's entrance. She picked it up curiously. Pulling the twine loose from the brown paper wrapping, she gasped with relief. It was her journal. Ambrose had caught it after all.

Beneath the journal was a 500-piece puzzle with a note

attached, which read: *Thought you might get bored.* Tabitha smiled, and this time did not curse the butterflies that fluttered through her stomach.

Venturing out from her cave to the conference room, Tabitha found breakfast left there for her by Amelia. She sat down and opened the puzzle box while eating the food. Gavin walked in.

"I heard Mad Moore's off her rocker," Gavin grunted when he saw her.

"Rebecca?" Tabitha asked.

"Uh huh. Lilith took her off the Clay case."

Tabitha felt mildly guilty despite her newfound hatred for her ex-supervisor. It was Tabitha's fault that Rebecca had lost her position as Head of Security—but there were more important matters now than status and posh perks.

"Serves her right, I guess," Tabitha mumbled.

"Want me to plant dynamite in her office?" Gavin suggested.

"What? No!" Tabitha replied with a chuckle.

"C'mon, you gotta give me something to do," he moaned, rocking back and forth in his chair while looking around at the walls, as if they'd soon close in on him. "I'm going crazy down here."

"You're telling me," Tabitha agreed, hugging her arms and glancing about the cave. Then Tabitha got an idea, and she no longer feared that it was dangerous. "I heard you can forge keys," she said.

"Sure, I could forge a key if I wanted to."

Tabitha took her journal and flipped back to a page from her first day in Providence. She tore out her drawings of the keys to Providence's outer wall and handed them to Gavin. "Have fun!" she said with a smile.

When Gavin registered the gold he held in his hands, he breamed a massive, gap-toothed smile and pulled Tabitha into an unexpected hug. "Thank you!" he growled in her ear, squeezing uncomfortably tight.

"You're—welcome," she managed, her voice muffled by his shoulder against her mouth.

He set her down and left, and she returned to her puzzle.

A couple of hours later, Milo and Ella stopped by to visit, having just returned from *Survival of the Fittest*. They sat across from Tabitha and helped with the puzzle while chatting.

"My memory serum is ready," Ella told Tabitha. "I just need to test it and we'll be good to—"

"Ella, how many times do I have to tell you? We already tested it," Milo corrected.

"What are you talking about?"

"You insisted on being the test subject," Milo said. "And it *worked*. Clearly."

"No I didn't," Ella insisted.

"Yes, you did. Three times. And three times, it erased a good twenty minutes of your memory."

Ella looked shocked for a moment, then smiled. "So it works!"

Milo grinned to himself.

• • •

It wasn't until late that evening that a long-awaited friend came to visit.

"Ambrose!" Tabitha greeted, leaping to her feet.

He smiled lightly in response.

She moved toward him as if to offer a hug, then retreated, remembering that they'd never actually done that before. "Thank you for the puzzle," she said, trying to cut through the awkward tension.

"No problem," he said simply.

There was a pause. Tabitha cast a nervous glance around the untidy piles of clothes on her floor and, feeling slightly warm in the face, kicked them behind her makeshift bed. "Care to sit down?" she offered, pointing at the floor as if it were the most luxurious chair.

Ambrose grinned a little and obliged—but something seemed off.

"So what have you been up to?" she asked, thinking it a stupid question but at a loss for a better alternative.

Ambrose scratched his ear and looked around the cave. "Oh, you know, the usual."

Another pause followed his vagueness.

"How was class today?" she tried.

"It was good. Dr. Buckley's back, I saw him on my way over. He asked about you. I told him you got sick from being out in the cold too long on New Year's. I'm surprised he believed me, I'm a horrible liar. Sounds like no one's spilled the beans about you being a runaway rebel; he just went on and on about the dangers of not using the heating panels and the psychology behind physical illnesses."

"That's good," Tabitha sighed. "I thought for sure my face

would be plastered all over town as the next most wanted criminal…"

Ambrose made no comment. Something was clearly on his mind.

Tabitha bit her lip, trying desperately to think of something else to say to fill the uncomfortable silence. She decided it was best to be up front. "Ambrose, what's wrong?"

He didn't look at her, but replied quietly, "There's something I need to ask you."

Tabitha felt her guard come up. "What is it?" she asked.

He looked her in the eyes sternly. "Tell me honestly—are you really out to save your dad?"

"I thought we'd been over this," she moaned.

"I know, but Tabitha—what I overheard between you and your father—you didn't sound like someone who's moved on."

Tabitha looked at the ground and fingered a loose stone. She couldn't really be upset with him for assuming the worst. She'd set herself up for it. Still, it didn't feel good; nor was this conversation going as she'd anticipated. He wasn't there to pay her a friendly visit. This was Ambrose the conspiracy theorist. It was in his nature to sniff out the rat. He needed to know if her own personal vendetta against her father jeopardized their mission. It was nothing personal.

"I assure you, I have no intention of betraying you guys," she said flatly. "I'm not going to turn him in."

"But revenge is out of the question, right?"

"Right," she replied.

"Promise me."

Tabitha sighed. She could promise him that. They would do what they had set out to do, and with no more crazy mysteries to solve or headmistresses to dethrone, he'd have no reason to look at her like the most interesting puzzle in the world.

"I promise."

"Then I believe you," he affirmed. She smiled, but only politely.

"Tabitha," he addressed, noting her forlorn expression, "I'm not looking to judge you. I know you've had some terrible things happen in your life that would leave even the strongest person scarred and angry. What I am looking for is reassurance that you won't let it destroy you."

That made her look up. Maybe this was a friendly visit, after all...

"You're starting to sound like my sister," she said with a slight grin.

"Well, I suppose now I can imagine what she feels like, a little bit."

Tabitha tilted her head, awaiting an explanation.

"I thought I'd lost you, Tabitha," Ambrose said, very quietly. "I thought you'd disappear like Toby had. And then I realized: you could be without so much as a scratch, but if you sent your dad to his death... Tabitha, you'd have to live with that regret for the rest of your life! You'd lose who you are, and—in a way—I'd still lose you... and Tabitha, I don't want to lose you."

He looked down, biting his lip at his loss for words. A queasy, uncomfortably excited sort of feeling erupted in Tabitha's gut and fluttered throughout the rest of her.

"Why?" she asked softly. The giddy sensation in her chest continued to rise.

Ambrose cast a funny little smile at the ground. "You're smart," he said with irony, little louder than a whisper. "Figure it out."

She had. Yet it all seemed too unreal, too wonderful and terrifying to be true. Terrifying, because to feed it was to pour gasoline on an open flame. Wonderful, because for the first time ever, she yearned to let it burn.

Tabitha timidly inched closer to Ambrose, whose downcast eyes perked up in hope.

What are you doing? an accusatory voice within her screamed.

Falling, she replied.

"But I thought it was never your intention to lure my heart to yours," Tabitha pointed out with a hint of playfulness, referencing his own words from the day they'd met.

"It wasn't then…" Ambrose admitted, "but now…"

His face was close to hers now. Lifting the back of his hand, Ambrose brushed her hair away from her face, then let his touch slide down her cheek and rest upon the base of her neck.

Tabitha did not pull away, but smiled up at him and leaned in closer. Though the snobbish voice inside her continued to shout obscenity-clad rebukes, Tabitha was sure in that moment that she'd been very wrong about a great many things, and one of particular significance. Love was, in fact, worth falling for.

Then, just as she closed her eyes and held her breath in the expectation of a kiss—

"Knock knock!"

James poked his fiery red head in, and Tabitha instinctively scooted a foot away from Ambrose. He let her go, but kept a hand gently on her arm.

"Ambrose, Popovic wants to talk with us about Operation Blue Ribbon," James informed. "He's waiting in the conference room."

James disappeared as abruptly as he'd interrupted. There was a little pause, in which both Ambrose and Tabitha expressed a reluctance to leave. In the end, it was Ambrose who stood.

"See you tomorrow, then," he said with a smile, and left Tabitha feeling like nothing in the world could ever go wrong.

CHAPTER TWENTY-TWO

OPERATION BLUE RIBBON

Operation Blue Ribbon began at daybreak the following Friday. Gavin had planted various explosives in select locations throughout Providence (which he reluctantly assured would not harm any of the city's occupants). These were set to detonate in a gradual sequence to keep Security busy for the next few hours as the others ventured into the "furnace room," as Athaliah had called it.

None knew entirely what to expect, but they were ready for anything. Ambrose had a viola, should musical manipulation be required, Maddie had her silks, Milo had everything he might need to collect and preserve archaeological evidence, and Tabitha had her journal.

Ella brought three vials of her newly-brewed serum that could be injected to wipe the short-term memories of her victims. One dose would give them about 20 minutes of erased memory.

Tabitha's fingertips tingled with expectation as she stood

alongside her fellow rebels in the caves under the library. While she and her friends scouted for clues about Toby's mysterious death, Popovic would be above ground searching for documentation of Josiah's marriage to Athaliah to use in the case against Lilith's administration. But, thrilling as that all was, Tabitha was most excited for what came after their excursion: a visit with her father.

She hadn't told anyone except Ambrose about it. Not for any particular reason—it had simply slipped her mind until it was uncomfortably late to bring it up. Besides, they had so much else to think about right now. They wouldn't even notice her slip out for half an hour or so while they were collecting evidence in the furnace room, and she'd be back before the journey home.

The rebels stood with bated breath, listening for the rumble of Gavin's first explosive above ground. When it sounded, they began their trek through the tunnels. Their party consisted of Tabitha, Ambrose, Ella, Maddie, Milo, and James. Naoko opted to stay behind. Traveling the road to the furnace room would take a good hour or so, judging by their last venture. They moved quickly, but carefully.

About halfway in, Ambrose came alongside Tabitha.

"You know what doesn't quite click?" he whispered.

"What?"

"Why Rebecca doesn't know about these caves."

"You don't think she does?"

"No. You'd think that, with a convict on the loose who has access to a massive underground tunnel system, the Head of

Security would take some precautions, send a few extra troops around the tunnel openings, you know? Plus, she was so desperate to use you to get to Josiah, I feel like she would have brought you down here by now if she could have."

"Well, Josiah said he found the caverns when looking for breaches, so none of Security knows. Why would Rebecca?"

"See—that's what's interesting," Ambrose insisted. "If Lilith wouldn't tell Rebecca about the caves, why would she tell her about your dad's innocence? Rebecca wouldn't need to know that in order to get the job done. No one else in Security seems to know; they all believe the rape story."

"True… Rebecca and Lilith must be pretty close, then," Tabitha shrugged off.

"I highly doubt that. You should have seen Rebecca's face this past week at Lilith's welcome address: stone cold! She is not happy about losing her job as Head of Security. You know what I think?"

"What?"

"I think Rebecca figured it out on her own, while tracking down your dad."

Tabitha considered the possibility. "Didn't seem to change much, though," she sadly pointed out. "It made no difference to Rebecca so long as she got her dream job."

"Yeah, that's a shame… At any rate, Lilith must not completely trust her."

Tabitha thought about that for a minute, then concluded, "I don't blame her."

They eventually came to the edge of the warm, glowing

tunnel where Maddie's blue ribbon had been found. Very faintly, a rumble reverberated through the ground above, announcing another one of Gavin's blasts. The rebels silently extinguished their lanterns.

Ambrose gave Maddie a little nod, and she threw the coils of her longest silk up around the thickest stalactite in reach. She twisted it around the hanging structure, then tightly tied one end to a stalagmite on the ground. With the other loose end, she pulled herself up into the spiky ceiling.

The others peered around the corner to see her scamper onto a nearby ledge of rock that had the appearance of a mushroom's underside. She kept her silk with her, occasionally tying it to a column to prevent it from falling. From there, she could look down into the cave without being easily noticed.

It was a long time before she sent the all clear signal: a series of vibrations through her silk. Milo counted them, then whispered, "We're good to go." Together, they crept soundlessly along the cavern floor, taking care not to slip on occasional patches of water.

The air grew progressively hotter as they approached the burning light, so that some of them shed a layer or two of outer clothing. They heard the sound of a fire roaring, like waves of melting wind. Something moved. Tabitha's eyes darted to the motion, only to find it was merely the flickering light playing tricks on her.

When they came into the clearing, Tabitha surveyed the scene. Maddie's silk hung limply, its owner nowhere to be found. Before them was a massive, cylindrical furnace in the center of the room. Flames licked the edges of its four openings and slithered through the grate that encased it. Along the walls of the cave they could see equipment, desks, and other objects used by Lilith's administration.

Ella gave the silk a tug. "Maddie?" she hissed. She and Milo went to look for her, while James and Ambrose stood guard. Tabitha sketched the room and began to examine the various artifacts in it. She toyed with some metal tongs and aimlessly tried on a welding glove. As she moved through the evidence, a pile of sacks on the ground caught her eye.

There had to be a hundred of them. They were roughly three feet long each, made of thick tarp, tied with twine, and covered in blotches of dust from their handlers. Tabitha knelt down beside one and untied it. Stretching it open, piles of white ash poured out, covering her hands.

Tabitha glanced over her shoulder at the fire. They must have been for collecting the ashes from under the furnace after things were burned, she figured. Standing, she clapped her hands together to get some of the dust off, then leaned over to re-tie the bag. When she pulled it upright, however, she stopped, noticing a lump in the smooth ash. Something else was in the bag, something hard and white.

Curiously, Tabitha reached inside, letting her hand disappear in the ash. The hard thing was smooth and rounded, like a stick that had been stripped of its bark. She thought it odd that it hadn't burned in the fire like the rest of the bag's contents. Wrenching it from its burial place, she brought it into view—and knew immediately what it was.

A human bone.

Letting out a scream against her will, Tabitha leapt away from the bag and dropped the bone, which clattered on the ground. The bag toppled over when she let it go, and spilled more of its contents on the cavern floor. A skull rolled to her feet.

Tabitha's breaths came in short bursts. Her hands trembled inches from her mouth—which she would have clapped shut were it not for the ash. She stumbled backwards, desperately wiping her hands clean of the victims' remains.

"Ambrose!" she called with a shaky voice. He came running to her side. "I—I think I found... Toby."

"No," Ella said quietly from behind them, "you didn't." Her face was more somber than Tabitha had ever seen. Ambrose cast Tabitha a wary look. "C'mon," Ella said, "this way."

They circled the furnace and rounded a corner into an adjacent cave. James had his arm around Maddie, who was fighting back tears. Milo shook his head, muttering with his hand over his brow. What were they looking at? Tabitha came around the corner, afraid of what she might find.

Then she saw it: an adjustable sawhorse of metal and wood, upon which was Toby. He was arched backwards over the thing, limbs sprawled out, bound by iron chains pegged to the cavern floor. His abdomen was bloated, and his head hung limply, eyes blankly staring into nothingness.

"No!" whispered Tabitha, feeling sick. She couldn't look. She went to avert her eyes when suddenly Toby's body lurched. Tabitha stared, unable to comprehend what had happened.

"He's still alive," Maddie explained in a strained voice. She left James's side and knelt by Toby's head, cradling his face in her hands. "My Toby," she whispered through shuddering breaths. "My poor, poor Toby…"

"What did they do to him?" Ambrose asked Milo.

Milo glanced uncomfortably between Ambrose, Maddie, and the contraptions in the room that he seemed to recognize. Maddie did not turn her gaze from Toby, but said, "Tell us, Milo."

"Looks like water cure," Milo hesitantly answered. He fidgeted incessantly, casting wary glances at Maddie as he explained. "It's a kind of torture that dates back to the fifteenth century, I wanna say. They would, er, force the victim to ingest too much liquid, resulting in water intoxication, which in turn would cause death or—in this case—severe psychological damage. He's alive, but he's… gone."

This had been no accident. For Toby to have died in the canyon now seemed a preferable alternative.

Milo returned to examining the torture tools, mostly to break visual from the horrific image of Toby—whose fingers were now pointlessly groping the air around his chains. Tabitha felt the need to vomit. Turning away, she found a nearby desk chair and leaned over it to steady herself.

"We need to get him down," she heard Ambrose say from behind her.

"I saw some welding tools we could use to break his chains," James suggested.

"How do we take him with us without revealing our activity in the caves, though?" Ella asked.

"Maybe we can make it look like he broke free. It would

seem at least plausible; everyone knows he was strong as an ox," Ambrose suggested.

"Sounds good enough for me," James replied. "We'll pull the pegs from the ground, then take the chains with us so they won't see where we cut them."

"How will we carry him?" asked Ella.

"We can use one of my silks to make a hammock and cradle him in it," Maddie answered.

James and Ambrose left to find the supplies, and Ella knelt beside Maddie to comfort her. Milo jotted down some notes in his book for future examination.

Tabitha buried her face in her arms, taking care not to touch herself with her soiled hands. She tried to calm her racing heart by slowly breathing in and out, but with little success. She waited for her dizziness to wane.

Then she noticed something. On the desk before her were piles of letters, different kinds of pens and papers, and a half-written draft in the works.

Tabitha came around the chair to sit in it and look through them. The draft read:

Hi Sweet Pea,

I'm so glad to hear that your classes are going well! Aunt Ava and Uncle Ethan stopped by today. They went on and on about how proud they are that their own niece was selected for the Institute. We all know how much of a sacrifice it was for you to leave home—but you're making the world a better place—

Under the unfinished letter was another, signed off with *Your Sweet Pea, Emma.* Tabitha examined the note and its reply. Surely, Emma's mother wasn't writing from an underground cave. This letter was forged.

To Tabitha's horror, she realized that the piles of letters stacked against the wall on the desk were all from students within Providence. There were boxes on the floor labeled with the sender's name, and a crate for the ones doomed to burn in the furnace. Some dated back as far as the year before—all screened and never sent.

Tabitha rummaged through the boxes in search of her own name. When she found it, it came as no surprise that all her letters to Mayra Mae were there. She landed her fist on the desk in anger. Rebecca hadn't just been screening Tabitha's mail, she'd never sent it! Her twin's reply had been forged; she hadn't been writing at all!

But Mayra Mae *had* been writing. Just then, Tabitha noticed a file divider in the box labeled *Received.* Flipping her own letters forward, she saw a small stack of envelopes addressed to *Tabitha Clay, c/o Providence Institute for Higher Education, Tolliver.* With trembling hands, she lifted the flap of the first envelope, which had already been opened.

Dear Tabitha,

Thanks for the sunflowers—but you should have said goodbye, you jerk. I miss you already... I hope it's worth it, though. I still think you ought to have stayed, but I hope it works out and you do find Dad. If you see him,

tell him I send my love—and that's an order. I don't care
how mad you are at him, savvy? You tell him that Mom
and I send our love. And Tabitha—take care of yourself.

Love you,
M.M.

Tabitha clutched the paper to her heart, a steady flow of
tears now moving silently down her face and neck. She opened
the next one.

Dear Tabitha,

Are you in Providence yet? Let me know that you made
it there safely. Mom says hi. Lucy from the bakery won't
stop asking about you, like you're some sort of celebrity
(as if). My shift requirement did go down, like you said,
but not by much. I've been managing well enough, though.
What's Providence like? The advertisements make it look
like the most beautiful place on earth—but you can never
trust the screens. Anyway, write to me—okay? It's not
right, being separated. I feel like my soul was split in
half. Jerk. I love you.

Always,
M.M.

Tabitha shook her head, furiously realizing that Mayra Mae
would have never heard from her that she'd made it safely to
Providence—or that she missed her, or that their father was

innocent, or that the Institute's administration was full of monsters. The next one she read was proof of this, and the one after that. Mayra Mae grew increasingly impatient and colder with each note. Despairing with every word, Tabitha tore into one from the day after the disciplinary demonstration in December.

Tabitha,

I got a bad feeling when I woke up this morning. Is everything okay? I wish you'd write to me already! Mom's not doing too good... Tabitha, I don't think she has long. Forget the medicine, all right? If you ever do manage to make your way up and get it, by the time you send it to us, we won't need it. Just come home. Come be with us before it's too late.

Mayra Mae

Tabitha's fury at Lilith turned into fear. Her heart pounded as she read the last note. It was tearstained and the ink was smudged.

Why did you have to leave? Why couldn't you have stayed with us just a few more months? I'm trying so hard to wish the best for you—but you need to know how badly your decision has impacted me. I am broken, Tabitha—utterly broken. I don't know where to go or what to do. I've never been so alone.
Mom died this morning—

Tabitha dropped the letter with a gasp. The clangs produced by James and Ambrose's attempts to uproot Toby's chains hid the sound of Tabitha's choking sobs. Her throat grew tight and her head spun as the reality sunk in. Natalie was dead. Tabitha had been lied to all this time.

Timidly, Tabitha retrieved the letter she'd dropped with shaky hands and read the remaining lines.

—*She went in her sleep, peacefully. The Casketeers came and took her before I had a chance to properly mourn. I have nothing now. Nothing and no one. I suppose it makes no difference to you.*

Goodbye, sister. I won't be writing you again.

Tabitha hurt all over. The pain in her heart felt physical, as if someone were actually breaking it in two. The searing sting spread to her neck and shoulders, and up into her head, which spun and pounded with grief, rage, and everything in between. Her hands were balled tightly into fists, so hard that her nails cut into her palms. She slammed them against her forehead, hiding her scrunched eyes.

Tabitha heaved a few irregular breaths, trying desperately to contain her anguish. She glanced at the others, helping Toby from his torture chamber. Now was not the time to grieve in their arms. They, too, were grieving.

Tabitha stood and started toward the tunnels. Ambrose caught her eye.

"I have to go," she whispered, trying to keep her torment in. She hoped he'd assume her sadness was due to Toby, and that she was on her way to see her father.

He did. Nodding without question, Ambrose let her leave.

Tabitha did not go to Josiah's dugout. She didn't care where she went, so long as she went somewhere she could let her waterfall of tears flow freely. Sprinting down the dark corridors, Tabitha let her feet fall loudly on the cavern floor and her heavy breathing echo against its lofty ceilings.

Natalie was dead. Mayra Mae was broken. Toby was… gone.

And it was all her fault.

Tabitha clutched her hand to her chest, pressing it with the vain hope that it would relieve the pressure around her heart. Never had she felt such remorse—not after leaving home, not after framing Dr. Buckley, not after sending her friends into the Tolliver desert. How could she undo this? She couldn't. She would never again feel her mother's sweet, frail hands lovingly frame her face. She would never have a conversation with Toby again—though he was alive—and Maddie would never be the same. Tabitha might never see Mayra Mae again, either. And even if she did, what would her twin think of her? It was too painful to consider.

Suddenly, Tabitha slipped on a wet patch of rock that sent her flying forward. Her lantern crashed on the ground and was extinguished, leaving her in total darkness. Wincing, she grabbed the wrist she'd landed on and groped in the dark for the broken lamp; though she knew it would be useless now. Unable to see the map in her journal, she'd have to try to remember the way back by touch, or else be lost for Toby's torturers to find her. Starvation might actually get to her first, she thought. That might not be so bad. That might not be a bad thing at all.

Tabitha curled up against a stone wall, pulling her knees to her chest. As she buried her face in them, she sobbed. Saltwater seeped through her clothes to the skin. Could this day, this situation, this life get any worse?

Then she heard the sound of softly padding footsteps nearby.

Yes, this situation could get worse. Now was not the time to mourn; she could mourn when she made it back to the rebels' hideout. Tabitha rolled into a crawling position and quietly made her way across the cold, hard ground. Rather than use her faulty visual memory, she tried to re-live the terrifying moments when she had run from Athaliah and Dog when James's lamp had gone out. What had she felt along the way? Did the air change temperature? Did the ground sound different beneath her feet?

A tiny flame emerged around the corner. Whipping behind a thick stalagmite, Tabitha pressed her back against it and held her breath. She did not stop to examine the cave dweller that passed her by. He or she would soon find her broken lamp and know they were not alone. Tabitha crept to her feet once more and toed her way around the corner, her hands outstretched blindly in front of her.

Once some distance had been established between her and the threat, she continued at a slow jog. A couple of times she thought herself lost, but after a few circles around a stalagmite (and a panic attack or two) she discovered something familiar to set her back on track. It seemed ages before she finally reached her underground home.

There, Tabitha collapsed on the floor. Wrapping her arms around her face, she sobbed as she'd longed to for the past hour. Her rib cage ached from heaving, her eyes swelled and stung; but none of it felt as bad as the incessant pressure, banging from within her to get out, to do something about everything—to fix it! She couldn't. She could do nothing. Nothing but sob and pound and shout.

Then, Tabitha felt a small, soft hand on her shoulder.

Tabitha stopped crying. Suddenly self-conscious, she wiped the wetness from her face onto her sleeve, and cautiously turned around to see who was with her.

Naoko looked back at her with concern.

The frail little woman hadn't known Toby. She was not in grieving. She could withstand the weight of Tabitha's sorrow. A great joy swept over Tabitha—the joy of not being alone. Wrapping her arms around Naoko's feet, she let her tears soak the ground once more.

"What is wrong?" Naoko asked, sitting beside Tabitha.

"My mother is dead," Tabitha replied. Saying out loud made it real again, and she felt the choking sobs erupt from her throat again. "My sister wants nothing to do with me now. And we found Toby. He was tortured to the point of madness. He's lost his mind. Naoko, I don't know what to do!"

Naoko sat comfortingly beside her, but did not touch her or say anything. Tabitha didn't mind.

"And I'm supposed to meet with Josiah in—goodness, just

over an hour now. What will I say to him? I just told him that his wife was alive! Now I have to bring him the bad news that she's dead, all over again?"

"You're meeting your father?" Naoko asked. Tabitha nodded. "Where?"

Helpless and defeated, Tabitha opened her journal to the map and pointed at Josiah's dugout beyond Toby's cave. "There," she replied sadly. She sat in silent thought for some time, fingering the page. "Do you think—" she began, but when she looked to her side, Naoko was no longer there.

Tabitha stood and turned around. The last thing she saw before all went black was the cold metal head of a shovel flying toward her skull.

CHAPTER TWENTY-THREE

CAPTURE

Tabitha woke up to a blazing headache. Feeling her forehead, she found it caked in dry blood. It took her a moment to remember how she'd gotten there, sprawled across the floor of the rebels' cave under the library.

Then she saw her journal. It was open, and a page had been torn out: the page with the map.

It started coming back to her. The reality of her mother's death and Toby's discovery hit her like a… like a shovel…

Naoko.

Naoko had betrayed her. Naoko had the map. Naoko knew where to find Josiah!

It is not too late to regain my honor, Tabitha remembered Naoko saying. She was going to turn him in—to earn Lilith's respect once more and get her life back in Providence.

Tabitha could not lose her father again—not after she'd just lost her mother! She stood up quickly—too quickly, and collapsed back on the floor as her head spun sickly in circles.

"Woah, there!" she heard a gruff male voice say. Tabitha

looked up to see Gavin standing in the hall. "What happened to you?" he remarked with no attempt to hide how horrible he thought she looked.

"I—Naoko—she… Gavin, what time is it?"

"Eleven forty-five; why?"

Tabitha gasped. She'd been out cold for forty five minutes. That meant she was supposed to meet Josiah in fifteen! There was no way for her to get there in time through the tunnels. She had to warn him! He'd think it had been she who'd set him up; he'd go to the electric chair!

"Gavin!" Tabitha cried, grasping him by his square shoulders. "Gavin, did you forge those keys to the outer wall? Did you manage it?"

Though mildly shocked, he replied, "Yeah—but I haven't tested them out yet. Why?"

"Give them to me," she demanded.

He pulled a jumble of iron keys from his pocket and placed them in her outstretched hands.

"Thank you!" she cried and hugged him. "Oh—and I need you to set off a smoke bomb or something in the surveillance tunnel on top of the tower so the peacekeepers can't snipe me."

"Sounds delightful," he said with a smile that wrinkled the burn scars around his milky eye; and despite the fact that he had no idea what she was up to, Gavin followed her orders with eagerness. Tabitha was grateful for that; she had no time to explain. Her father was in danger… and she was going to save him.

On her way out of the library, Tabitha passed Amelia.

Suddenly it crossed her mind that she might never see her again if she did what she was about to do. She might never see Ambrose, or Ella, or Maddie, or Milo. She might suffer Toby's fate and lose everything she'd worked for.

But it would be worth it. Yes, Josiah was worth it. Lilith would not have the satisfaction of taking yet another one of Tabitha's loved ones from her.

When Tabitha emerged into daylight, she saw Rebecca walking just as briskly across the courtyard. They met eyes for a brief moment. *Not now!* Tabitha thought. *I don't have time to deal with you!*

However, Rebecca did not pursue her. She did a double-take, but moments later continued on her path. Tabitha didn't give herself time to wonder why Rebecca wouldn't alert the peacekeepers of her presence. Gavin had appeared from within the library and was hurrying toward the wall.

"It's now or never," Gavin muttered as he passed. He went straight up the stairwell to the outer wall's observatory, and Tabitha sprinted to the gate.

With shaking hands, she followed the directions in her drawing and turned each key in the proper order. Some jammed, causing her to curse out loud and look frantically over her shoulder to see if she was being watched. Fortunately, most everyone was busy cleaning up after the explosives Gavin had set earlier. She wiped the sweat from her forehead and attempted to jimmy the lock. Finally, the last bolt clicked, and the massive door swung open.

The sound of peacekeepers shouting above her drew Tabitha's

attention to the top of the wall, where black smoke was now billowing out. Gavin had succeeded! Stepping into the wild, she sprinted down the cliff of loose stone and into the canyon.

Brambles and cacti clung to Tabitha as she passed, scraping where her skin was bare. She ignored them. She knew how to get there, having watched Toby's trek to his cave. Her lungs ached as she ran and the sound of her heavy breathing filled her ears.

Tabitha pelted around the cave and into Josiah's meeting spot. It was empty. She spun around herself, searching the clearing for signs of her father or the peacekeepers.

"Hello?" she panted.

"Hey there, Sweetheart," she heard Josiah's voice reply.

Rounding toward the sound, Tabitha saw a man climb out from a crevasse in the canyon wall. He had a bald head and short red facial hair. In his left ear was a gold earring, which matched one of his teeth. If it weren't for his glasses and dining hall uniform, Tabitha would have thought him a pirate. His disguise was even more convincing than the one Tabitha had seen him wear on New Year's—but she could tell that it was him.

Tabitha had done it. She'd made it before Naoko; they were safe! She opened her mouth to warn Josiah that they had to leave immediately—but then a cold, cackling laugh erupted from behind her. Josiah's eyes left Tabitha and looked past her. His face went white, and Tabitha's stomach churned.

She knew that voice.

Josiah donned a poker face. Tabitha turned around to see Athaliah standing in the clearing. Then Lilith, six peacekeepers, and Naoko emerged from different hiding places around them. Two of the peacekeepers grabbed hold of Josiah. He didn't fight them.

"Tabitha!" Lilith said in a frighteningly sweet manner, "I didn't expect to see you here! How did you get outside the gates?"

"I brought her," another voice sounded. Tabitha turned around to see Rebecca, climbing into the clearing from the direction of Providence. "We were just on our way to capture Josiah Clay."

Tabitha looked at her supervisor in confusion. Why was she covering for her now?

"Good—I had hoped you two would come around to our side," Lilith commented.

"But—*I* brought you here—*I* found him!" Naoko hissed in Lilith's ear.

"Yes, you did," Lilith replied coldly. "But can you identify him? Can you confirm that this truly is Josiah Clay?"

Tabitha felt a strong urge to scrape Naoko's eyes out. The traitor inched closer to Josiah, staring hard, trying to identify some semblance of the man they sought; but—as Tabitha knew—she had only ever seen Josiah once before, after she'd been badly beaten.

"Sorry—might I ask who it is you think I am?" said Josiah, with a higher voice and different dialect than his usual. Lilith ignored him.

"I'm—not sure," Naoko admitted.

"I thought as much," Lilith concluded. She turned to Tabitha. Pulling her aside for a bit of privacy, she said, "It seemed you'd abandoned the mission we had entrusted you with, but perhaps we were wrong? Come. Tell us if this is really your father, and everything can go back to the way things were."

The way things were? When had reality ever been the lie that Tabitha had been coerced into believing?

Lilith ushered Tabitha toward Josiah. Taking advantage of Lilith's trust, she looked at her father as if in genuine search of recognition. After a moment or two, she shook her head. "I don't recognize him," Tabitha lied, still staring at her father. "We may have been mistaken—"

"Ah, but he'll recognize you," Lilith said from behind, and suddenly there was a cold, sharp piece of metal at Tabitha's neck. She winced as her hands were grasped behind her back and the knife pressed against her skin.

Before Tabitha could stop him, Josiah stepped forward. "No!" he cried. "Let her be—I am Josiah. Do with me as you will, but please—let her be!"

Tabitha felt the blood drain from her face as she was released and the peacekeepers closed in around her father.

"I see you've proven yourself useful, after all," Lilith said in Tabitha's ear before walking away.

Tabitha said nothing, but stood stunned as her father was bound and dragged toward the city. Her mouth dry, her limbs limp, she stared, helplessly.

"Didn't I tell you she was the key to our success?" Tabitha heard Rebecca chime at Lilith as they walked toward the great white wall.

The words bit into Tabitha's gut. She wished she could

deny it, but Rebecca was right: if it hadn't been for Tabitha, her father wouldn't be here right now. Unsure of how her feet managed to move themselves, she followed at the tail of the group. Time seemed to stand still.

"Rebecca," Lilith remarked, "I distinctly recall decommissioning you when you failed to catch Josiah on New Year's after I told you about Tabitha's letter. What makes you think you have a right to put yourself back on the case?"

"Well, aren't you glad I did?" Rebecca responded confidently, despite her lack of authority. "Look—we've finally done it. Thanks to Tabitha, we've caught the notorious Josiah Clay!"

"Thanks to *me*, you mean!" Naoko protested. She was ignored.

"I suppose you'll be wanting your job back," Lilith said to Rebecca.

"That is up to you, Headmistress," Rebecca replied.

"Yes—rewards will be given according to their merit," she commented.

Naoko lit up. Scurrying up to Lilith's side, she asked, "When, then, might I retrieve the key to my apartment again?"

"Oh, you won't be returning to your apartment."

"What do you mean?" Naoko questioned nervously.

"I'm afraid our venture here has made it clear that you simply know too much." Lilith held up a folded piece of paper, which Tabitha recognized as the map torn from her own journal.

Naoko must have taken all the credit for it; Lilith didn't know there was anyone else using the tunnels. Tabitha felt a flicker of hope in the midst of her dismay. She had to keep up this facade to protect her friends and keep Toby safely hidden underground.

Naoko opened her mouth to speak, but Lilith spoke first. "You're headed to the same place as Josiah, my dear."

Tabitha tripped on her own feet. Naoko was going to be executed, too?

Naoko's jaw dropped and she stopped dead in her tracks. The others continued walking around her. "But—" she stuttered. "But I—they—!" She pointed back toward Toby's cave, but before she could say any more, a peacekeeper came and bound her. She fell silent, resolved to walk to her death with dignity.

With every step, they drew closer to the electric chair. Tabitha searched her mind for a solution, but she could think of none. She and her father were outnumbered and unarmed. Her friends were underground, unaware of her situation. Helplessly, she trailed behind Josiah, surrounded by peacekeepers, to their defeat.

The great white gates opened. Lilith was the first to walk through, followed by Athaliah, who walked with an odd sort of skip to her step, while twirling her unruly hair in her long-nailed fingers. The prisoners followed, Josiah surrounded by four of the peacekeepers, and Naoko between the other two.

"Tabitha, we'll take it from here," Lilith announced when everyone was within the city limits. "Thank you for your assistance in bringing this criminal to justice! You will be rewarded."

Naoko looked acidly from Lilith to Tabitha. "And what about me? Is this my just reward?"

Again, Lilith didn't answer.

Just as the gates closed behind Tabitha and Rebecca, Tabitha saw a group of apprentices emerge from the library: Milo, Ella, and Ambrose. A look of shock and confusion spread across their faces as they saw two of their rebel team being led away by peacekeepers in the direction of the penitentiary. Ambrose looked especially disheartened.

"You coming, Rebecca?" Lilith called over her shoulder.

"Of course! I'd just like to have a quick word with my apprentice. You go on ahead," Rebecca answered with a smile. Her grin disappeared as she turned suddenly to Tabitha and whispered urgently, "Josiah *must* survive."

"What?"

"I kept too many secrets from you. I realize now that was a mistake, and I'm sorry; but we don't have time to dwell on it. Listen—I rigged the electric chair."

"I don't understand—"

"I intended to fake his death but everything's gone wrong now. They've probably fixed it since I was decommissioned. Even if they haven't, though, they'll figure it out once they use it on Naoko. She'll come to and blow everything."

Tabitha's head was swimming. Rebecca was a rebel?

Rebecca took Tabitha by the shoulders and looked deep into her eyes. "Josiah *must* live. I don't care how you do it, but find a way. I'll try to stall them as best I can."

Rebecca left without giving Tabitha a chance to respond. She stood flustered and frantic, wanting to collapse from the weight of it all. Milo's voice broke through her shock.

"I can't believe you," he accused. She turned, her eyes wide with denial.

"No, I—!"

"You turned him in!" Ella added. "You said you'd changed… how are we supposed to justify Toby now?" Tears were forming in her eyes, and for the first time, Ella's compassion seemed to be spent.

"It's not—" Tabitha tried, but found no words.

Maddie emerged from the library. "What's going on?" she asked, gently taking Tabitha's hands in hers.

"Tabitha turned Josiah in," Milo said.

Maddie let go of Tabitha's hands. "What?"

"We saw them come back," Ella confirmed. "They're on their way to the extinguish room now."

"How could you do that?"

The three began to talk over one another, asking questions, spouting accusations, and filling the air with chaos. Tabitha fell to her knees in despair, bent her head low and shut her eyes. What could she say to make them trust her now? She didn't bother to try. She stayed in the blackness behind her eyes where she couldn't see the disapproval written on their faces. She'd lost… everyone.

"No."

Tabitha opened her eyes to see Ambrose, looking fiercely down at her. "I refuse to believe it," he concluded.

This man, the man who had always suspected her, accused her, threatened to expose her—could he believe her now when all the evidence pointed against her?

Ambrose came down to Tabitha's level. With strength and gentleness, he gripped her arms and brought her to her feet. "Tell us what really happened, Tabitha," he requested softly.

Tabitha began to cry. She let herself fall against his chest and heave wet sobs into his shirt, and welcomed the comfort of his arms as they closed around her. With great difficulty, muffled by Ambrose and her uneven breaths, Tabitha explained what had happened.

"I was going to meet Josiah during Operation Blue Ribbon. I didn't tell you; I'm so sorry. But then—then I found letters from my sister in the furnace room that said—my mom had died. So I left. I was too overwhelmed; I needed to get away. I found Naoko and told her what had happened and that I was supposed to meet Josiah. She asked me where—then knocked me out and stole my map. I tried to get to him in time—Gavin gave me the keys he'd forged to open the gate, and I ran. I ran all the way to the spot—but they were already there! The Damaras, Naoko, and the peacekeepers were there; they caught him, and now there's nothing I can do! And Rebecca said she'd been trying to save him all along by tampering with the electric chair. She demanded I keep him alive like the world depended on it—but I can't!"

Her friends went silent. Tabitha pulled cautiously away from Ambrose and turned to see them. Milo and Ella looked dreadfully ashamed.

"Tabitha, I'm so sorry," Ella whispered. "I shouldn't have—"

"It doesn't matter now," Tabitha replied. "It's—too late…"

"No—it's not too late!" Ambrose said, turning her toward

himself. "Rebecca gave you one last order—to save Josiah, right? Then by God, we're going to do it!"

His charisma electrified her waning hope, and as the others nodded, she thought it might be possible. "But how?" she choked. "We can't get into the extinguish room."

Milo's eyes enlarged. "Yes… we can!"

Everyone looked to him.

Suddenly self-conscious, Milo took a moment to collect his thoughts into cohesive words, scratching his five o'clock shadow. "Remember when we made a map of the caves, and Popovic told us not to use the tunnels under the warehouse that Dominic had used?"

"Yeah?" Tabitha replied.

"Well, it was because they were *right by the extinguish room!*"

Tabitha gasped. "Milo, that's it! We can use Dominic's entrance!" She dug into her purse and revealed the small silver key that she'd stolen from Dominic, which would unlock the mysterious crate.

Ambrose smiled broadly at her. "C'mon, Sweetheart," he said. "Let's go save your dad."

With that, the five of them sprinted toward the warehouse.

CHAPTER TWENTY-FOUR

A RESCUE MISSION

Tabitha and the others still had everything they'd brought for Operation Blue Ribbon with them. Ambrose had his viola, Maddie had her silks, Milo had his equipment, and Ella had her memory serum and zombie powder. They were ready for anything.

As they approached the warehouse, Tabitha heard the workers shouting at one another about Gavin's bombings. It sounded as though they were temporarily shutting the place down. *Perfect*, Tabitha thought. By the time the doors were closed, she and her friends would be inside, and no one would be around to stop them from unloading Josiah's crate to enter the tunnels.

Sneaking into the restricted section, Tabitha wondered if Krikor, the owl-like man in the mirror room, could see them now. There was no time to wonder—and Lilith would be too busy with Josiah to bother with some reckless kids. It was a risk worth taking.

Grabbing some work gloves from a cabinet, Tabitha handed

them out. "Here," she said, "put these on."

They did so, and the five of them made their way through the labyrinth of crates to the Magician's Box. They hid in a corner until the long, florescent lights flickered out above them and the great doors were secured. Tabitha unlocked and opened the crate. The clutter that she and Dominic had piled over the manhole into the tunnels was as tall as Ambrose. The rebels looked at one another.

"This will take ages!" Milo moaned.

"Then let's get to it," Ella said, and determinedly clutched the first large metal object on the pile.

Milo joined her, but the crate was so narrow that the two of them blocked its entrance, rendering the others useless. They tugged on a frame of iron but it was stuck, wedged between other fragments of rubble. Rummaging was getting them nowhere; Dominic had done his job well of hiding Josiah's entrance. The pile was like a knotted necklace, each piece's release dependent on another's.

"We need to move faster," Tabitha stressed.

"This isn't going to work if we're all scraping away at it in a free-for-all frenzy," Ambrose concurred. "We have to work together."

"Okay," Milo obeyed, stepping back from the jumble.

"Ambrose, you're good with puzzles—what can you see?" Tabitha asked, touching his arm. "Is there a way to take it apart?"

Ambrose studied the mess, breaking it into sections within his mind. "I think so," he answered. "Maddie, get your strongest and widest silk. Milo, find me some sort of screw eye or ring that we can attach to the crate's ceiling."

They did as they were told, and the others awaited orders.

"Now," Ambrose continued, "Maddie, help me wrap the silk around this piece here." They climbed into the crate, securing the silk around the scrap. "No, not that one—right here—perfect!"

Ambrose took the two loose ends of the silk and looped them through the ring they'd screwed into the crate. Then, drawing it out, he instructed everyone to grab hold.

"Someone needs to be inside the crate to push the pieces out once we've lifted the bundle," Ambrose said.

"I'll do it," Maddie volunteered. She was the most nimble, and easily made her way over the junk to the back of the crate.

"On my mark, we'll pull and Maddie will push," Ambrose said. "Maddie, once it gives way, give us a shout so we can move. I don't want anyone getting pelted by that stuff! Ready? Pull!"

They all tugged as hard as they could, moving together as one. When the bundle was dislodged from the pile, Maddie lifted the bottom of the silk to empty its contents.

"Now!" she shouted, just when the heavy pieces of metal and wood tumbled out, scattering on the warehouse floor. The others jumped out of the way just in time, then returned to move the scraps away for another go. They did this six more times before they could reach the crate's floor.

Milo lifted the manhole cover and it hit the cement with a loud clang. "Anyone have a lantern?" he asked. Ambrose found one, lit it and handed it to Milo, who peered into the hole. "Damn. There's no ladder!"

"It's okay," Tabitha said, "we can use Maddie's silks to get down—look!" She pointed to the hook they'd added to the ceiling. It was directly above the manhole. Ambrose and Milo volunteered to grip one end of the silk while the other would be used to lower each of the girls into the cavern. Ambrose wrapped the silk around his waist, planting himself steadily, while Milo held it from a few paces in front of the manhole.

"I'll go first," said Tabitha.

"Shouldn't I—?" Maddie offered.

"No, you guys wait until I give you the all-clear," Tabitha protested. "If I get caught, don't come after me. Someone will need to carry the mission through to the end and take care of Toby."

Ella smiled proudly at Tabitha and gave her a nod of approval. Maddie tied a loop at the bottom of the silk for Tabitha to set her foot inside. She gripped it tightly, and was slowly lowered into the pit by Milo and Ambrose.

In moments, Tabitha was engulfed in darkness. She groped to find a cavern wall to rest her hands on and listened intently. Distantly, she could hear the echo of voices, muffled as if through a thick wall. They were close, but not in the caves. Tabitha gave the silk a tug, and one by one the others—save Ambrose—were lowered into the tunnel with her. Milo came through last, and they all held their end of the silk so Ambrose could lower himself down as well.

They crept toward the voices, and before long were beneath the penitentiary. There was only a thin layer between them, and everything that was said could be heard clearly now.

"What matters is that Athaliah will have her justice!"

Rebecca's voice could be heard through the cavern's ceiling. "A rapist is no longer at large. You've made Providence safe again, Lilith. Come on—let's celebrate!"

"Josiah is still alive, Rebecca," Lilith could be heard saying, "and until his heart has stopped beating, we need to be on guard."

Tabitha and the others heard footsteps walk away from the conversation, followed by a second pair.

"You think he can escape?" Rebecca asked.

"He escaped Providence, didn't he? We can continue our discussion after the execution—"

"You're right. Would you like me to supervise the process to make sure everything goes smoothly?"

"No, I'd like to see it through myself."

"Don't worry about it, I can—"

"Rebecca, I appreciate your eagerness to prove yourself, but I've made my decision. I—"

Just then, a loud rumble shook the ceiling above them, sending loose stones tumbling down throughout the cavern. Instinctively, Tabitha and her friends put their arms above their heads for protection.

The sound of a door opening in the room above them caught their attention once more.

"Headmistress," a male voice beckoned, "you *must* make a statement to the public. The people are going frantic. We'll have an uprising on our hands if we don't do something now!"

There was a pause that seemed to last forever.

"All right. Rebecca, see to it that Josiah is extinguished and disposed of properly. I'll meet with you later to discuss the nature of your position. Until then, remember: you're still on probation."

Two pairs of feet left, closing the door behind them. A moment or so later, the third pair sprinted in the opposite direction, fading out of earshot. The rebels looked at one another, then ran in pursuit of the steps. Rebecca was most likely on her way to the extinguish room, so following her was the surest way to find it.

"Stop!" hissed Milo suddenly.

Tabitha didn't react fast enough and slammed into Ella, who fell onto Ambrose, who barely caught the lantern that slipped out of his hands from the impact. There was a large clearing in front of them. The ground was smooth and there appeared to be no danger.

"What is it?" Ambrose whispered.

"Isn't it obvious?" Milo replied.

"Nope," Ella curtly responded.

Tabitha couldn't see but she sensed that Milo rolled his eyes.

"They excavated down here, but stopped midway," Milo explained. "They must have found something… We can't go through. We have to find a way around."

"Around where? We'll get lost," Tabitha moaned. "And we're running out of time…"

"No—he's right," Ella added, ashamed to admit it. "Can't you smell it? There's some sort of gas in the air."

As she said it, Maddie wobbled slightly and Tabitha caught her. "I'm sorry!" she muttered. "I just got a little lightheaded."

"Can we use this?" Tabitha asked, revealing the compact gas mask she'd found in her apartment drawers for use in the Clay case.

"We'd have to share," Ella pointed out. "Switching back and forth the whole way… I don't think it's worth the exposure. It could be poisonous."

"Come on," Ambrose agreed. "We'll find another way."

The only alternate route they could find was a cramped tunnel near the base of the cavern wall, barely tall enough for them to crouch in with their bags. It'd be a squeeze. Milo examined the hole and decided it seemed safe. By the draft, he figured it led to another opening on the other side, in which the air was well circulated.

Taking a deep breath, they began the crawl, at times lying flat on their stomachs to fit through. Tabitha felt claustrophobic, but her father needed her. She would persist through any fear or pain.

You needed him, too, a nagging voice inside her pestered. *He wasn't there for you when you needed a father; why should you come to his aid now?*

Because it's the right thing to do, she retorted back, mildly surprised at her own answer, but convinced now that it was true.

There was a crumbling sound of rock against rock.

"Ow!" Tabitha heard Milo say from directly behind her at the back of the line.

She craned her head to try and see him, but the tunnel was too narrow and dark. "Everything all right?" she asked quietly.

"Yeah, yeah—fine," Milo replied.

Tabitha kept moving forward toward a faint light, now visible ahead.

"I can see the exit," Ambrose whispered from the front. "We're almost there!"

"Don't go through right away; we need to be sure it's safe," Ella instructed.

Tabitha heard a scuffle behind her. "What's going on?" she asked.

"Nothing—it's fine—" Milo responded.

Tabitha snaked on, but the sound continued—and grew farther away as she moved. Milo let out a painful grunt.

"Milo, what's wrong?" she insisted, loud enough for the group to hear. There was a pause as everyone stopped moving.

At length, Milo huffed defeat. "I'm stuck," he admitted. "A rock dislodged and landed on my backpack... which is stuck to my back..."

Tabitha sighed, closing her eyes in frustration. Josiah could be minutes away from death; they couldn't delay... but Milo was in danger, too. Scurrying forward, she found a spot in the crawlspace that was wide enough to turn around in and did so. Facing Milo, she began to pull at the rock.

"Be careful!" Milo said urgently. "I don't know how stable the ceiling is; it could collapse on us."

Tabitha cautiously heeded his order, trying instead to pry the rock upwards so he could slide his pack out without altering the rock's position too much.

"Shh!" Ella hushed. "I think I hear someone in the clearing!"

Tabitha went still as stone. They waited, holding their breath.

In silence, Milo fought against the rock that held him captive. As he finally wriggled free, he beamed a victorious smile.

Crack.

The stone above them groaned like a waking giant. With a terrified gasp, Milo loudly demanded, "Go!"

"Quiet, they'll hear—" Ella argued.

But Milo shouted again, "*Go!*"

The creaking was replaced with the sound of smashing stone as sections of the tunnel began to cave in behind them. They slithered toward the light as fast as they could, Tabitha crawling backwards with eyes wide at the terrifying thought that she might have to witness Milo's death inches from her face. He appeared equally terrified.

Just as a massive hunk of ceiling collapsed where Milo had been only moments before, Tabitha fell out of the hole in the wall and onto the floor, followed by Milo—who landed roughly on top of her. The momentum pelted all five of them against a small cellar door, which reverberated loudly. A pair of footsteps passing beyond it stopped walking.

They quickly bounced back up, ready to fight whoever was on the other side. Milo automatically put his hands up like a cartoon ninja.

The cellar door opened.

To their surprise, it was Rebecca's face that bent down to peer at them through the door. "You did it!" she cried with relief when she saw them.

The rebels didn't share her feelings of reassurance. They looked warily at Rebecca and scanned to see if there were others with her. She was standing alone in a manmade hallway, crisp and white as the rest of Providence.

Rebecca looked around at the red stone inside the cellar. The tunnel through which Tabitha and her friends had crawled was not the only opening in it; there were at least three others leading to unknown caverns beneath Providence. Perplexed, Rebecca asked, "What is all this? Is that how he was—?" Before the apprentices could answer, Rebecca shook her head. "Never mind, you can tell me later." She squeezed herself through the tiny cellar door and climbed down. "We need to get to the extinguish room—"

"And why should we trust you?" Ella asked—not so much as a challenge, but in genuine curiosity.

"Look, you have every reason to doubt me," Rebecca answered. "And I promise I will explain—but right now, you'll have to take my word for it that I have every intention of saving Josiah. Every minute we waste could be his last."

The rebels looked—not to Rebecca—but to Tabitha.

"Your call," Ambrose said quietly.

Tabitha took a deep breath and nodded. "What's the plan?" she asked.

"I'm not sure," Rebecca admitted. "I can tell the guards I'm escorting you to visit a prisoner; that'll get us as far as the prison ward, at least. Whoever we go to see will give us away if they don't recognize you, though…"

"We can visit Dominic—he'll recognize me," Tabitha suggested. "Maybe we can find a way to free him in the process!"

"We can try," Rebecca said. "After that, though, we'll have to get into the extinguish room. Peacekeepers will be patrolling the corridor. I have access, but I can't imagine they'd let you all in, and they certainly won't let Josiah out. Did you bring anything—any sort of weapons?"

"I have a thing or two we could use," Ella suggested with a malevolent grin. "Tabitha, remember when I told you I'd show you what my little green babies could do? Well, it's show-and-tell time. Ambrose, know any lullabies?"

"Sure do," replied Ambrose, who still had his viola case slung over his shoulder.

"We're gonna put these suckers to sleep. They'll doze off so fast, they won't remember a thing."

"But what about the mirror rooms?" Tabitha interjected. "There's bound to be one surveying the extinguish room."

"What are the mirror rooms?" Rebecca asked.

"It's how Lilith sees everything," Milo explained. "Someone's always watching the mirrors for her."

Tabitha shuddered at the remembrance of the sallow-skinned, unblinking man, endlessly rotating among the sparkling reflections beneath the red earth.

"We could break them," Maddie suggested.

"He'll sound the alarm if we do that," Ambrose countered.

"Not if he's zombified."

The group turned to Ella. She was grinning again, like she had when she first told Tabitha about the Angel's Trumpet plant she'd learned of on their first day of classes. She revealed a vial of white powder and toyed with it, waiting for the green light.

"What will that do?" Rebecca asked.

"It's a deliriant. This dose should make him submit to do whatever we tell him, and hinder any memory of it from being formed. It might also leave him with a hallucination or two… but it should be fine. It's odorless and tasteless. He won't notice he's breathed it in until it's too late. We can even write a message on a piece of paper and hold it up to the mirror to make him tell Lilith that Josiah was successfully executed."

"How are we going to use it on the guy from inside the extinguish room?" Milo asked.

"The mirrors are lined up along a chute that leads to the room they're observing," Tabitha explained.

"Yeah," Ella agreed. "There will have to be some sort of hole we can slip the drug down."

"Brilliant!" Ambrose said.

"It won't kill him though, will it?" Maddie asked.

"It better not. That would be a hard one to cover up," Rebecca added.

"No, I'll be sure to limit the dose," Ella answered.

They agreed on their rough plan and got to it. Led by Rebecca, the team crept down the hallway to the prison ward. Peeking around the corner, they could see a long line of cells, where criminals sat behind a thick layer of one-way glass, like zoo animals on display. The extinguish room was at the other end of the hall behind a heavy metal door. Pacing back and forth along the stretch were four peacekeepers.

"All right," Rebecca whispered. "You guys follow my lead. Once we're in with Dominic, Ella can release the sedative and Ambrose can play his instrument to put the guards to sleep."

With that, the rebels stood and walked casually into the corridor.

A peacekeeper approached Rebecca. She held up a badge to indicate her authority. "These apprentices are here to visit one of the prisoners, Dominic Kaczynski. They were hoping to brighten his day with a little music, if that's all right. Part of this young man's class assignment." She indicated Ambrose, who held up his viola.

"Right this way, Chief," the peacekeeper replied.

They approached Dominic's cell, where they could see him slumped on a chair in the middle of the room, shoulders drooping but eyes fierce. Tabitha could feel her excitement rising. Finally, she could make one of her wrongs right!

The one-way glass opened, and Dominic looked up. The rebels stepped inside, and the peacekeeper closed the door behind them. Tabitha met the prisoner's gaze and smiled.

Suddenly, Dominic leapt from his chair and closed his rough hands around Tabitha's throat. "Traitor!" he cried.

Tabitha couldn't breathe. She started to see dark and light patches in her vision as she lost control of her limbs, which thrashed at his grip around her neck. Through the blur, she saw more hands come into view, pulling at Dominic in an attempt to get him off her, but Dominic was too strong.

Through the ringing in her ears, Tabitha faintly heard the cell door opening and peacekeepers shouting. Her throat felt raw and her head spun. In the tiny hint of air she managed to breathe, she thought she smelled a strange sweetness.

A viola began to play *Wily Winter's War*. The room started to go black, and the sweet smell grew stronger. Was Tabitha dying? Was she reliving moments with her mother, singing the cherished lullaby one last time before she left this earth to join her?

Tabitha was seconds from losing consciousness when Dominic's grip loosened. She fell to the floor. The strange odor wafted into her lungs as she sputtered and choked for air.

Something rubber pressed against her face. Her coughing slowed as the air became clean and oxygen found its way to her head. The voices around her grew more distinct, and she recognized Ambrose's.

"Tabitha—Tabitha, are you all right?"

She opened her eyes. He was crouched above her, one hand resting on her forehead and the other holding her compact gas mask to her face. Ella signaled to him to let go of the mask, took a puff of the purified air herself, then pressed it against Ambrose's face. He took a deep breath, then returned it to Tabitha.

Tabitha used the little strength she had to give him a nod of confirmation that she was all right. Looking around, she saw Dominic and all of the peacekeepers that had rushed to their aid fast asleep on the floor. Ella's bottle of sleeping potion was lying with them, and from its spilled contents rose a faint, purple mist.

Tabitha made an attempt to stand, and Ambrose smiled as he helped her up. As he stood, however, he swayed and nearly toppled over, himself.

"Ambrose!" Tabitha croaked, and reached out for him.

Ella held him up. "He's all right, just *reeeeally* drowsy. Give him this—and take one yourself," she ordered, tossing Tabitha a couple of pills and a water bottle.

Ambrose groaned as he attempted to stay awake. Drawing his head up carefully, Tabitha slipped the pill into his mouth and helped him swallow it down. She took hers, and within a minute was feeling alert again.

"What was that?" Tabitha asked.

"A heck of a lot of caffeine," Ella replied. Milo was bouncing up and down on his heels and snapping his fingers annoyingly. "Probably a little too much…"

"Come on, this way!" said Rebecca.

As they ran toward the extinguish room, Maddie nearly slipped on some of Ella's concoction. It had spread farther than they'd thought. To prevent further effect, they took turns covering their mouths with the gas mask Tabitha had brought.

When they reached the barricade, Tabitha held her breath—not for fear of inhaling more gas, but with the painful anticipation of whatever awaited them in the next room.

CHAPTER TWENTY-FIVE

SACRIFICE

"My key isn't working," Rebecca said, frantically jiggling her key in the lock. "They've changed it since I was put on probation!"

"What about the guards?" Maddie suggested. "Would they have a key?"

"No," Rebecca replied. "They don't have access to the extinguish room."

"Let me see," Milo offered, and crouched by the keyhole. Ella looked away to hide her doubtfulness. Tabitha watched as Milo examined the lock, then the doorframe. He opened a book from his backpack and flipped through the pages. When he'd found what he was looking for, he landed a finger on the page and said, "There!"

"What did you find?" Maddie asked.

"It's a variation of the Bramah lock, originally patented in 1784. It took Alfred Hobbs fifty-one hours to crack it."

"We don't have fifty-one hours," Ella pointed out.

"Right." Milo slapped his book closed and pulled a flathead

screwdriver from his bag. Walking to the opposite side of the door, he pried open the steel covering around the hinges. "Ambrose, go grab a rock from the rubble in the cellar—something heavy," he requested.

"On it," Ambrose replied.

Then, to everyone's surprise, Milo pulled a pickax-like contraption from his backpack.

"What is that?" Maddie asked.

"A mattock."

"You've been carrying that around this whole time?" Ella asked.

"What, don't think these guns could manage it?" Milo flexed his bicep.

Ella smiled and rolled her eyes.

Just then, Ambrose returned with a hefty red rock in his hands. "Now what?" he asked.

Milo wedged the ax against the top hinge at a forty degree angle and answered, "Hit it—hard."

He did, and the mattock penetrated the screws that held the hinge in place. Adjusting the mattock's position, Milo had Ambrose hit it again, then again, until the tool was wedged deep between the door and its frame. They did the same thing to the middle hinge, then the bottom.

Once all the hinge screws had been sheared, Milo had Ambrose hit the door to pop it off the hinges, and together they used the mattock to pry it open. The metal gave way and the door was dislodged from the frame.

"How'd you learn to do that?" Tabitha asked.

Milo shrugged. "Firefighters did it for centuries. I read about it once."

The team peered inside the extinguish room and were surprised to find its occupants fast asleep. Ella's potion must have seeped in under the door and gradually knocked them out. Naoko lay in a dark corner, face down, and Josiah was crumpled by the wall nearest them.

Tabitha rushed to check his pulse. He was out cold, but his face was warm and his blood pumped strongly through his veins. Tabitha breathed a sigh of relief and rested her forehead on the wall.

Meanwhile, Milo located the mirror surveillance, and Ella slipped her zombie powder down it, covering the hole with her hand while she waited for it to take effect.

A snore disturbed the quiet, startling Tabitha. She looked up to see its source. The sleeping extinguisher was sprawled out on the floor, gun still in hand, beside a large white chair.

The chair was smooth and rounded, almost like the inside of a broken egg shell. Though it was hard and undoubtedly cold to the touch, Tabitha thought it must be rather comfortable, actually. From the back, thick wires attached it to a glittering machine covered in buttons.

"How long until they come to?" Ambrose asked Ella, who was now crouched over Naoko.

"For the extinguisher and Josiah: twenty minutes to an hour. For Naoko…" Ella sighed, then finished, "never."

"What?" Maddie gasped.

Rebecca examined the status of the machine. "She was

already executed," she said after reading the screens. "We made it just in time."

"You mean we were a touch too late," Ambrose corrected sternly. "Naoko's dead—"

"Yes, but Josiah is alive," Rebecca stressed painfully. "Let's keep it that way."

Ambrose didn't pick a fight, but looked mournfully at the small, pale woman on the floor. Tabitha felt pity for her as well. Though she had betrayed them, she was still a person who was now no more.

"Okay, let's get to it, then," Tabitha commanded. "Ella, write a message to the eyes downstairs to tell Lilith's informers that Josiah and Naoko are dead, and that Rebecca had them sent to be incinerated."

Ella nodded and began the task.

"We'll have to carry them both…" Tabitha said. "Rebecca, what's the best way out of here? Rebecca?"

Rebecca was silently examining the readings on the machine. She had an odd look on her face, and when she spoke, her voice was strained. "Looks like they had it pre-set for both executions."

"Is that a problem?" Ambrose asked.

"Everything the machine does is automatically documented. If it doesn't go off a second time, it'll be obvious that one of the executions wasn't conducted."

"You said you'd tampered with this thing before," Ella pointed out. "Can't you cancel one of the executions and modify the settings so it won't record it?"

"Since I was put on probation, I can't access the settings, only the on switch. And even if I could—" Rebecca's voice broke off, and Tabitha got the feeling that they were about to reach a checkmate.

Rebecca finally turned to look at them. Her brows were knitted together and her eyes were wide with worry. "Lilith is monitoring the machine," she said at last, pointing to a screen that listed remotely-linked devices. "She's watching the readouts now. If no one sits in that chair within the next ten minutes, she'll know... she'll come."

The room went silent. Tabitha glanced back at her father.

"Well, what about Naoko?" Milo asked. "What if we put her body in the chair and turn it on; would it document a second execution?"

"No," Rebecca replied. "The chair won't go off unless it registers vital signs."

"What if we just run and hide in the caves?" Maddie suggested.

"There's nowhere we can go where she won't find us; not unless she isn't looking," Tabitha said.

If Lilith saw that a second body didn't sit in the electric chair, she'd know they had escaped, and she would never stop hunting them. It wouldn't take long for her to deduct that they were hiding in the tunnels. She'd find them—and kill them. Then, without the rebels, there would be no one to stop Lilith from doing what she'd done to Toby and countless others a thousand times over.

Someone needed to sit in the chair.

Ambrose opened his mouth to speak, but Tabitha knew what he was going to say before the words came out. If she waited any longer, she wouldn't be able to stop him. She couldn't talk him out of being the man he was: the selfless man, the good man, the hero—the man she would have liked to look up to, maybe even fall in love with, had there been more time.

Steadying her shaking hands, Tabitha strode to the electric chair and sat down.

"What are you doing?" Ella cried.

"Stop!" Maddie joined.

"What? Wait! Why—?" Milo stuttered.

Ambrose lurched forward. "Tabitha—no! Let me do it, please, don't—"

He was inches away from ripping her out of the chair when Tabitha ordered, "Flip the switch."

With a solemn nod, Rebecca heeded. The chair came to life. It strapped her in with more of its hard white substance that sprung from nowhere. Immediately, a buzzing sound erupted from within the chair as it began to charge.

Tabitha's heartbeat quickened as the reality of her impending death dawned upon her. She struggled to calm her breathing and looked to her father's motionless body. *He's worth it. They all are.*

Ambrose reached the chair and gripped madly at her bonds in an attempt to break them. His hands slipped on their smooth surface and he faltered as a static shock stung him. He kept fighting, despite the pain.

Tabitha, however, sat still as Ambrose struggled. She gazed at him, sad that they would never get to talk puzzles again, tease one another, dance together, or sing in perfect harmony. What a life that might have been.

Ambrose gave up on removing the straps and feebly took her face in his hands. "Tabitha, please," he begged, his voice barely a whisper. "You don't have to do this."

They locked eyes. "I know," she breathed.

Click.

The charge was complete. The chair began to vibrate and the air was thick with static electricity. Ambrose stepped back helplessly. Tabitha's hairs stood on end and she looked to her father for the courage to face death.

Just then, he stirred. His eyes opened.

"Tabitha?" Josiah croaked.

A searing pain as Tabitha had never known sent fire through her bones. She felt her back and neck arch against her will. The sharp shock bit at her toes and fingertips, vibrating her violently from the inside out. Her heart felt as if it was being slammed with a massive hammer.

"Daddy!" Tabitha cried feebly with everything she had left. Then all went back, and Tabitha was gone.

• • •

In the depths of the earth, a hunched man with bulging eyes peered upon a series of mirrors. He sat perched on a swivel chair on all fours like a frog and spun slowly around, and around, and around. Like an owl, his head stayed stationary and his eyes never blinked.

One of his dark lower lids twitched as he caught sight of something. Men were falling asleep on duty, falling over as if under a trance. Krikor climbed down from his chair on his long, skinny limbs and leaned in close to the mirror, but waited to sound an alarm.

A group of six young men and women ran past the sleeping bodies and broke into the extinguish room. Krikor turned from one mirror to the next. In moments, one of the men—a short fellow with wild hair—pointed directly at the mirror. Krikor blinked.

Suddenly, the entirety of his view was filled with one large, brown eye, which disappeared momentarily, followed by a cloud of white dust. The mirror went black and Krikor stumbled backwards, coughing as the powder reached his nostrils. Regaining his composure, he returned to the mirror and peered into it. All was dark.

He went to pull the string that would summon his messenger, but stopped. A bubble-gum pink squirrel, bearing a set of tiny, silver vampire fangs, was chasing its tail on the ground in front of him.

Krikor shook his head and blinked again. The squirrel was gone. Where it stood was no longer stone but grass, which vibrated like the wings of an insect and produced a sound like a hundred pairs of scissors. He leapt back onto his chair in confusion, peering at the shaking floor around him.

Where the mirror had gone dark there was light. Krikor's head jerked up. Reflected before him was a hand-written note, which read:

'SUP, CREEP. IN EXACTLY TEN MINUTES, TELL YOUR GOONS TO TELL LILITH THAT NAOKO ARAKI AND JOSIAH CLAY HAVE BEEN EXTINGUISHED. EVERYTHING WENT SMOOTHLY AND REBECCA MOORE HAD THEM TAKEN TO BE INCINERATED. DO NOT MENTION YOUR HALLUCINATIONS. THANK YOU, AND HAVE A NICE LIFE.

The grass was gone, and all seemed normal once more—except for the fact that Krikor did not question why he stood obediently ten minutes later and pulled the string. Or why, when his messenger came, he relayed the information word-for-word, calmly, and even courteously—which he never did on a normal day. Or why, when his task was complete, he went back to his spinning observatory routine and never again mentioned the living snowmen that were now building themselves in every room in Providence.

• • •

Tabitha opened her eyes, but closed them quickly after. The room was spinning and she felt sick. *Where am I?* she wondered, putting a hand to her head. Every part of her felt numb and tingly.

Suddenly, she felt herself being moved by a pair of strong arms. There was noise—was it a voice? Someone was shouting, but it was muffled as if under water. She might have groaned, but she didn't hear it—she only felt the rumbling of the noise in her throat. Her head was throbbing with pain, and her chest felt constricted.

Tabitha tried to open her eyes again. The swirl of the spinning room was brighter now, and the light hurt her pupils. Her eye sockets were sore, too, and she had no strength to fight the hands that were now shaking her, slapping her, gripping her tightly.

Tabitha felt the need to vomit, and suddenly it dawned on her that if she did, whoever was holding her would get the worst of it. Maybe that'd be a good thing. Maybe the people pushing and pulling at her uncomfortably had put her in this state to begin with.

Nothing came from her stomach, but air filled her lungs. She gasped loudly and tried to lift her mind to reality. Nothing made sense—where was she? What had happened?

Dad… Tabitha thought. *We need to save him…*

Little by little and piece by piece, the puzzle began to come together. She'd been with her friends: Ella, Maddie, Milo, and Ambrose. They had dug through the crate and rode Maddie's silk into the tunnels… There was gas in the air and they had to crawl through a tiny crack, which caved in and almost killed Milo… Rebecca brought them to the prison ward and Dominic tried to strangle her. Ambrose put him and the guards to sleep with the help of Ella's potion, and Milo helped them break into the extinguish room. Naoko was dead, and then…

Tabitha tried to sit up. How was she alive? Had it all been a dream? Or maybe she wasn't alive. Maybe this was all that awaited after death. Maybe, if she could just stop the throbbing in her brain, she wouldn't mind being dead.

But Ambrose wouldn't allow that. The moment Tabitha stirred, he pulled her from the chair and shortly after, transferred her into the arms of Josiah, who was now awake. She dozed off again, but Ella and Maddie slapped and shook her to keep her with them. Milo paced the floor, and Rebecca watched from beside the machine.

"Tabitha!" Ambrose shouted, and finally, she heard.

Sitting upright and staring about herself, Tabitha groped the air in confusion. The blurs became shapes, and the shapes became the faces of her loved ones. Turning around to see who held her, Tabitha went still. "Dad?" she croaked.

Josiah held her tight to his chest, breathing a heavy sigh of relief. She wrapped her arms around him in return and caught Ambrose's eye from over Josiah's shoulder. Through his tears, Ambrose beamed a huge smile. Ella and Maddie were hugging one another and giggling with joy; Milo threw his fists in the air as if a goal had been scored at a football game. Rebecca, however, looked concerned.

"I thought you were dead! I woke up and there you were, motionless in the chair. I thought you were dead!" Josiah cried. "Why did you—you never should have—I didn't deserve—"

"I know you didn't," Tabitha said quietly.

He kissed her hard on the cheek and helped her stand up. She wobbled a little, but held onto his hand for support. The girls quickly descended upon her, hugging her mercilessly.

"Tabitha, you did it!" Ella burst.

"It worked," Maddie concurred. "The chair registered a second execution, and Lilith saw it!"

"No one's sounded an alarm," Milo added, "so bug-eyes downstairs must have delivered our message!"

"We're safe—we're all safe now!" cheered Ella.

Ambrose just beamed down at Tabitha without a word.

Tabitha grinned, but then remembered the question that had come to her mind when she'd woken up. "But—how am I alive?" she asked.

Rebecca seemed to be wondering the same thing. "They must have never reset the chair. My hack worked," she replied. "But that would mean…"

"You!" a voice cried viciously from a forgotten corner of the room.

Everyone turned to see Naoko's once limp body spring up from the ground, very much alive. Her eyes burned with fury, fists clenched and teeth bared.

"You robbed me of my honor!" She cried, "I'll rob you of your life!"

Tabitha gasped. Naoko snatched the sleeping extinguisher's gun and aimed it at her. Time seemed to stand still. A bullet left the chamber as Naoko pulled the trigger.

Tabitha looked to Ambrose, knowing what he would do. "No!" she cried, holding her hand out to stop him—but Ambrose flung himself around her, bracing his soul for death.

Nothing happened.

From within Ambrose's protective arms, Tabitha opened her eyes. They darted to the corner where Naoko had been, which was now a dog pile of Ella, Milo, and Maddie, struggling to hold the traitor down. Tabitha pushed Ambrose away from herself and scanned him for bullet holes. She turned him around, then back again. It was a miracle—Naoko had missed!

But Naoko hadn't missed.

Crumpled on the floor between them and Naoko was Josiah Clay.

"Dad!" Tabitha cried, flinging herself upon the ground beside him.

He choked and sputtered, blood dripping from his mouth. Kneeling beside him, she placed her hands on his wound, which drenched his clothes in crimson red.

"I need a tourniquet, anything—!" Tabitha screamed.

"Tabitha," Josiah wheezed.

She looked to his face, which was growing rapidly pale. "Ella—you must have something, some sort of medicine—"

"Sweetheart—listen," Josiah croaked.

Tears streaming down her face, Tabitha heeded, and cradled his hands in hers. "I'm here," she whispered.

"I'm—sorry—" he breathed. "For—everything."

Tabitha choked a sob and looked up at the ceiling through bleary eyes; wishing, hoping beyond hope, that she could escape this reality, that she'd wake up and find it all a dream.

"Tabitha—look—at me—"

She did. His face was contorted in pain—but more than the pain, his eyes held sorrow and remorse for his abandonment, his cowardice, his pride.

"I'm—sorry," he repeated with the last bit of strength he had left.

His time had come. In that moment, Tabitha knew there was only one thing left she could do for him.

"I forgive you, Dad," she managed through the strain of her tears.

At these words, the muscles in Josiah's face relaxed. His eyes became bright as though washed with purifying water. A gentle smile spread at the corners of his mouth, and he let out a sigh. As the air which he exhaled left his lungs, three years of shame and self-hatred left his heart. In Tabitha's mercy, Josiah found the strength to forgive himself, and left the world in peace.

• • •

Tabitha could not clearly remember the hours that followed. As her father passed from this world into the next, she could do nothing but mourn. Yet, strangely enough, though the pain in her heart was astounding, there was an odd sort of weight lifted from it. She felt at peace knowing that, before the end, they had finally made amends.

When Tabitha sought to recall the events that passed on the day her father died, there were things she knew for a fact had happened—but she was at a loss for how they happened or in what order.

Ella had injected Naoko with her memory serum, but unfortunately had given her a stronger dose than intended in an attempt to overpower and disarm her. The result was that Naoko no longer knew who she was. She remembered nothing of her betrayal, or her murder of the man called Josiah Clay. It was a clean slate for Naoko. She had a chance at regaining her honor, after all.

Ambrose carried Josiah's lifeless body from the extinguish room. Ella and Maddie led the child-like Naoko out after him. Popovic met them on their way through the caves and helped them close up the crate in the warehouse. Amelia took Naoko away to help her cope with her complete loss of memory, and Gavin saw to it that the havoc he'd wreaked throughout Providence would not leave a trail for Lilith to find them.

Milo stayed behind to help Rebecca reset the extinguish room and hide what had really happened there. They collected Dominic from the pile of sleeping peacekeepers and Milo took him through the cellar tunnels back to the library. Rebecca later went on to explain to the confused peacekeepers that Dominic had escaped when they'd dozed off on their watch, but that she'd taken care of him—permanently.

She told the extinguisher separately that he had passed out part-way through the execution, but that she'd finished the job for him, and promised never to tell a soul about his little mishap. As an extra precaution, she would be having a couple of repair men come to reinforce the door to the extinguish room. They came later that day and fixed the sheared screws on the door's hinges. One was short and gruff with a dark five o'clock shadow, and the other was a tall, lanky fellow with bright red hair. No one asked any questions.

When Milo, James, and Rebecca caught up with the others beneath the library, they all trekked through the tunnels to Toby's cave and beyond, where they buried the body of Josiah Clay beneath the Tolliver earth. Like the coyotes and cougars that howled to the wind, they wailed in songs of lamentation, unheard except by the ears of the wild and free. The winter stars gazed down upon them, and Josiah's soul joined their twinkling light to watch for all eternity over his daughter who forgave him.

CHAPTER TWENTY-SIX

A CROSSROADS

"How are you feeling, Tabitha?"

Lilith's voice was smooth and motherly as ever. The former Tabitha might have tackled Lilith to the ground and pummeled her out of existence in that moment, but the Tabitha that stood before the headmistress in her office was calm and collected.

To answer Lilith's question, Tabitha was feeling many things—none of which were pleasant—but nowhere in her emotional stirrings was a craving for revenge. The day her father died, Tabitha saw a mirror of herself in Naoko—a picture of who she would have become had she given in to her desire for vengeance. Naoko destroyed herself from the inside out, and took Josiah with her. If the only control Tabitha had at the Providence Institute was over herself, she'd use it to be better than Naoko, better than Athaliah, better than Lilith. She'd use it for good.

No, Tabitha would not get revenge on the Damara family. She would, however, stop them. Now that she knew the depths of their evil intent and just how far they would go in their thirst for power, control, and order, she knew that every human being in Providence was at risk. If she didn't take a stand—she who had seen what she'd seen and endured what she'd endured—who would?

"I'm a little overwhelmed, to be honest, but thank you for asking," Tabitha replied politely.

Lilith offered her a seat, and sat across the desk from her. "That's understandable. You've been through a lot these past few months, which is why I wanted to talk with you. Do you think yourself quite well enough to continue with your apprenticeship? Because if not, we might find some other career path for you—perhaps in entertainment?"

Tabitha smiled gently. "No, thank you. I should be all right."

"You're sure? Security is a stressful field."

"I understand that. I may not have performed to the best of my abilities during this past case, but I can assure you that I've learned from the experience and will do better next time. My place is with the defenders of Providence."

"Very well, if you're absolutely sure. And do you think Rebecca Moore is a good fit for you? I know you had some issues with her during this last case. We try to match each apprentice with the perfect supervisor, but every now and then there's a pair that needs revision," Lilith offered.

"No—Rebecca has been a fine supervisor. No need to change anything."

"All right. Then I suppose I'll leave it to her to decide your next course of action. I would advise you not to bite off more than you can chew, however. The Clay case was an unusual situation; you really shouldn't have to deal with such a high level of security until you're initiated into the elder class. Take a break! You deserve it."

Tabitha nodded.

"As for your elite perks, we'll find another way to earn you those rewards. Your mother will be needing—"

"Oh, that won't be necessary," Tabitha interjected.

The corner of Lilith's mouth twitched. "I'm sorry?"

"I—I no longer wish to aid in my mother's recovery. I'm afraid—I'm afraid it really is a lost cause."

Lilith nodded solemnly, fictitious concern shining in her eyes. The look of it made Tabitha sick, but she smiled in false gratitude nonetheless. Their meeting at an end, Tabitha left to resume her classes.

Dr. Hugh Buckley, who had been given his teaching license back, taught psychology with his usual mirth. During class, Tabitha felt as though she and her friends were on a new plane of knowledge. The other apprentices talked and laughed in blissful ignorance of the horrors that took place at their pretty school. Dr. Buckley was as sweet as ever, joyfully instructing his students in his high-pitched, raspy voice. Did he know? Did Dr. Buckley fully comprehend who it was he worked for, or the warning she'd given him by having Tabitha plant drugs in his home? Did he know what the price of "peace" was? Or was he as ignorant as the doe-eyed apprentices surrounding him?

The question made it difficult for Tabitha to respond agreeably to him at the end of class when he pulled her aside to congratulate her on catching the criminal mastermind, Josiah Clay.

"I knew you'd be a good one! *Providence's pride and joy*—yes, it's no understatement! I'll be sorry to see you off; I'm sure you'll join the elder class in no time. Or perhaps you'll take one of my upper-level classes? Do consider it; I'd love to have you again!"

Tabitha smiled and nodded courteously, then turned her back to the innocent oaf who knew not the danger he was in. Part of her hoped he would remain happily in his ignorance.

Mysteriously, the professor known as Popovic decided to give his *Disguises for Stealth & Stage* students the day off. Though he gave no explanation as to why, Tabitha and Maddie knew, and were grateful for the extra time to recover from recent events.

When Tabitha's supervision meeting came around later that week, Rebecca knew they wouldn't be talking business. Rather than meeting in her office, the pair decided to take a walk in the winter air. Sunshine peeked through the heating panels above them, casting sparkles on the white cobblestone streets. It warmed their skin but left the air cold in their lungs.

"Where would you like me to begin?" Rebecca asked when they were sure to be out of earshot.

"At the beginning," Tabitha replied simply.

Rebecca nodded with a sigh, and told her tale.

"Since my installment on the Security team last year, after I graduated from the elder class, I started to see a side of Lilith that disturbed me. Our headmistress, as you well know, has an insatiable lust for control and power. I grew to fear her for it, and gradually that fear turned into hate.

"Then, a friend of mine by the name of Beau Fischer told me about a case he was working on—the Clay case. He told me that he'd never seen Lilith scared before, but that she was terrified of this guy. I didn't know what Josiah had done to instill that fear in Lilith, but any power over her was power worth harnessing.

"By then, I had decided that Lilith's administration needed to end. Since she would stop at nothing to destroy Josiah, I was determined to stop at nothing to keep him safe. I convinced Beau to let me take over the case, and devised a plan to fake Josiah's death.

"By rigging the electric chair, I made it so that it would knock the person out for a good long time, even slow their heartbeat to the point of fooling someone into thinking they had no pulse. Then, I'd offer to take Josiah to be incinerated, but in reality, I'd take him into my own care.

"All the details were in place; the only thing I had left to do was catch him. But that was the problem—I couldn't do it! Josiah dodged me at every turn. I never even had an opportunity to tell him I was on his side.

"Then, Officer Logan Malloy told me about how you blackmailed him to get into Providence. You came here, and I thought you were my big break—that I'd finally gotten the upper hand! I was convinced you hated him, so I intended to use your hate to propel you to find him for me. I even encouraged you to hate him. That's where it all went wrong."

They were sitting now on a bench in the square. Rebecca leaned her elbows on her knees and stared into space.

"I should have told you… I'm so sorry, Tabitha. I never got shipment clearance to send your letters or medicine, because the screening process would have required a more thorough examination of my work. I couldn't risk them finding out what I was doing.

"I thought about coming clean to you, but I knew that the administration had no intention of saving your mother anyway. Lilith told me to just keep giving you the same bottle of medicine and say it was new. When she informed me that your mother had died, I was scared you'd give up on your search after that. I was afraid I'd lose my shot at seeing my plan through to the end. Josiah was my only hope. I didn't know anyone else in Providence who had gotten on Lilith's bad side and gotten away with it. So I played along with Lilith's lie.

"After a while, though, she started to grow impatient with me. I was taking too long to locate Josiah, and she threatened to take me off the case. So I pushed you. In my desperation, I pushed you further and further into what you were naturally repelled from and, in the end, ruined everything."

Rebecca hung her head, her silky black hair falling over her face. Tabitha studied her curiously. If both of them had been honest with one another—truly honest—maybe they could have prevented the whole thing.

Tabitha ran her fingers through her auburn waves and huffed a heavy sigh.

"It was all for nothing," Rebecca breathed, her eyes now misty with regret.

Tabitha looked intently at her and shook her head. "No—it

wasn't. Not in the slightest. Rebecca, Lilith thinks she won a victory the other day. I say *we* won. My dad wasn't executed, he gave his life freely for the people he loved. And when he did that, he gave us an example to follow. No worthy cause is without self-sacrifice. She has no idea there's a team of rebels who are now enraged by her actions, who bonded together more strongly over his death. And we'll keep growing stronger because of him. His legacy will live on through us, and even without him, we'll see this thing through to the end. I promise."

Apprentice and supervisor locked eyes, and in their gaze, a pact was formed. Later that day, Rebecca was officially welcomed by the rebels as one of their own.

When Tabitha entered her apartment, she thought it funny that nothing had been searched. None of the authorities had looked for her when she'd gone missing. It was almost symbolic of how very insignificant she was to the administration of Providence.

Tabitha returned the things she'd had while in hiding to their proper places. When she'd finished, she sat on her couch and looked out over the sparkling city. Her fingers toyed with her journal as her father's voice echoed in her mind. *I found something while searching for breaches in Providence's security…It looked like someone was trying to gain unearthly power…*

What was it that he'd found? What were Lilith and Athaliah trying so desperately to hide, and what could be done to prevent it?

It's too late. The door's been opened—and you have yourself to blame! The words Athaliah had spoken to Josiah sent a shiver down Tabitha's spine. She placed her journal on the coffee table and looked around at her luscious abode. As much as she loved her wall-sized window and cozy bedroom balcony, the barren cave beneath the earth was starting to feel more and more like her home.

Toby occupied that space now. He was homeless—but far from friendless. There wasn't a day in which Maddie didn't come to ensure he was cared for. He never spoke, and needed assistance doing even the littlest of things. Maddie would feed him like a mother feeds a child, unfazed by the mess he'd make or when he'd lose the will to swallow. It broke Tabitha's heart to see him like this—but every once in a while, Toby would make eye contact with them, and in that fleeting moment when they locked eyes she could see that he was still in there, somewhere. He wasn't completely lost.

Tabitha sat next to Toby and stroked his arm. His head rolled awkwardly in her direction but he didn't look directly at her. All his movements were jagged, as if his limbs were prosthetics. He bared his teeth in what might have been an attempted smile, and emitted a low grumbling sound.

Maddie grinned affectionately at him.

"He responds when you speak to him," she said. "I didn't notice at first, but I've started to recognize patterns in what he does."

"Do you think he'll ever recover?" Tabitha asked quietly. She wasn't sure what level of sensitivity she should apply to their conversation. Toby didn't seem to register what she said, but maybe his comprehension was merely masked by his limited bodily control.

Maddie sighed. "I don't know. But whether or not he does won't change the fact that he's still Toby—my Toby."

"But where will he go, if we ever leave Providence?"

"He'll stay with me. I know that people with certain—well, people like *him*—aren't given any place in the New Order's system, but I'll find a way. They won't take him from me—not without a fight."

They sat in silence for a while, watching Toby as he toyed with a pebble on the ground.

"I'm sorry about your parents," Maddie said at length. "It was hard enough to lose my mom, I can't imagine losing both parents."

Tabitha looked at Maddie in painful surprise.

"Oh, I suppose I never told you," Maddie said. "She died in childbirth when I was twelve. Lost the baby, too."

Tabitha didn't know what to say. She stared at Maddie, blown away by the incredible tower of strength that hid behind the face of a seemingly simple girl.

"How did you manage to cope?" Tabitha asked.

Maddie gave it some thought. "With gratitude, I suppose," she replied with a shrug. "I figured: at least she had been a wonderful mother for the short time I had her. And I tended to my daddy's broken heart. It's what my mom would have done, and it gave me something to do."

There was another pause as Tabitha soaked it in. A short time later, James poked his flaming red head through the cave's entrance.

"Hello!" he announced cheerfully. "I brought you some warmth."

Stepping inside, he handed a mug of tea to each of the girls. Slung around his neck were three blankets, which he passed out, draping the third over Toby's hunched shoulders.

"How's he doing?" James asked.

"He's very well, today," Maddie replied with a smile.

"Wonderful. Let me know if you need me to fetch anything else," James offered. "Also, Popovic wants to meet with everyone in the conference room, just to touch base. Join us when you have a minute." With another freckle-wrapped smile, James eased his lanky frame through the hole in the wall and left.

"He'll be all right without us?" Tabitha asked Maddie, indicating Toby.

"Yeah, he'll be fine," Maddie replied with a smile. She stood and kissed Toby on the forehead. "I'll be back soon," she promised him, and left with Tabitha.

"Ambrose said you have a twin sister," Maddie mentioned on their way through the tunnels. "What will she do now that she's alone?"

Tabitha had been wondering the same thing ever since she'd read Mayra Mae's letters in the furnace room. Mayra Mae might have been content once to work at the bakery for the rest of her life, but with no one to come home to at the end of the day, Tabitha was sure she'd be miserable.

"There's no way of knowing," Tabitha answered. "I can't reach her, and she said herself that she wouldn't be writing to me again. Maybe if we ever get out of this place, I'll find her and take her with me wherever this mission leads. She won't like being a rebel, but we have to stick together. She and I— we're all we've got left."

"Hey now, you've got us, too," a gruff, stuttering voice sounded behind them. Milo's short and stocky silhouette appeared in the tunnel, followed by Ella and Ambrose. Ambrose caught up with Tabitha and slipped his hand tenderly around the small of her back without a word.

"Yeah missy," Ella added, "you need to get over yourself and accept the fact that we're your adopted family now, and you ain't gettin' rid of us anytime soon."

Tabitha smiled broadly, accepting Ella's side hug. The five of them emerged into the cavernous conference room to find Popovic, James, Dominic, Gavin, Amelia, and Rebecca chatting around the table, which held on its center a framed picture of a familiar face: Tabitha's drawing of Josiah.

Tabitha's eyes misted over, and she looked at Ambrose. "Thank you," she whispered, knowing he must have salvaged the crumpled drawing.

"Sure thing, Sweetheart," Ambrose responded.

As the rebels talked and laughed, Popovic cast sideways glances around the room and allowed himself a grin. Dominic seemed to have loosened up a bit, and babbled freely without his usual suspicious air. Amelia cast disapproving glances at James, who was lazily leaning back in his chair with his feet propped up on the table. Rebecca remained fairly quiet, but beamed timidly at her new comrades. All the while, Gavin's knee bounced violently up and down with the surges of his pent up energy, and he watched for breaks in the conversation where he might insert an absurdly explosive suggestion.

As Tabitha looked at all of them and the friends on either side of her, she knew Ella was right. This was her family now.

"About time!" Popovic announced upon their arrival. "Sit."

The apprentices did so and gave the professor their attention. There was a little silence before he began, in which Popovic collected his thoughts.

"We suffered a terrible loss the other day," he said solemnly. "Josiah was a great man. Before him, there had never been hope for opposition against the Damara administration. Each of us were in some way impacted by his life—some more than others—but all, just the same. We are indebted to him for paving our way, and he'll never be forgotten."

Dominic closed his eyes in respectful grief, and many nodded somberly in agreement. Amelia seemed to have something in her eye, and turned away to tend to it.

"But now we've come to a crossroads," Popovic continued. "Josiah was essentially the glue that held together our team of rebels. With him gone, our mission has changed and our pact is voided. We're free to go our separate ways, if we wish."

Some of the rebels cast looks at one another, but no one gave any indication that they planned on leaving. Everyone sat firmly in their seats.

"Nonetheless—though Josiah told us little of the darkness he'd discovered, and we are drastically ignorant of his previous plans—our fellowship need not be broken. We are and will always be joined by the bonds of friendship, and our sense of duty won't easily be smothered. Should we remain, however, my question for you is this: what do we do now?"

The rebels pondered the possibilities. Tabitha looked at the man in the frame, and saw herself in his likeness. The sketch of her father's eyes seemed to bestow upon her a responsibility. She stood slowly, her hands placed sturdily on the table and her face set with determination. Ambrose looked curiously up at her from his neighboring seat, and all awaited her answer. With a confident and oddly mischievous grin, she gave it.

"We finish what he started."

A WHITEWASHED TOMB
WILL BE CONTINUED.

ABOUT THE AUTHOR

Rebecca Loomis is a photographer and graphic designer from the New York Hudson Valley. During college, she studied under screenwriter Christopher Riley, who is considered "The most authoritative figure for the official screenplay format of Hollywood," according to IMDb. Switching gears from entertainment media to mass communications, Rebecca graduated summa cum laude from Benedictine College. She then spent three years doing stateside missionary work, counseling college students for the nonprofit Saint Paul's Outreach, after which she dabbled in marketing at BBG&G Advertising. Rebecca has won multiple awards for her poetry, published articles in various media outlets, and teaches online classes through Skillshare.com.

WWW.REBECCALOOMIS.COM

Made in the USA
Columbia, SC
22 December 2017